A Funeral for an Owl

JANE DAVIS

IN MEMORY OF SARA

Too little, too late.

"Kwakiutl Indians were convinced that owls were the souls of people and should not be harmed for, when an owl was killed, the person to whom the soul belonged would also die."
The Owl Pages

"We can't establish for certain how many children are missing. You'd have more chance of finding a stray dog."
Lady Catherine Meye

CHAPTER 1:

AYISHA - JULY 2010 -
ASHFIELD COMPREHENSIVE

Her hand sliding smoothly down the gun-grey stair rail, Ayisha was cursing her choice of footwear when the thunder of surging feet drowned their staccato clipping.

"Slow down, Nathan!" She raised her voice, naming the first face that span into view. Referred to in the staffroom as 'But Nathan', this boy came equipped with an unusually comprehensive range of excuses. "There's no need to cause a stampede. And before you ask: No, I don't care if it *is* the last day of term."

Neck twisting self-righteously, he didn't disappoint. "But Miss, there's a fight -"

Why now? was Ayisha's first reaction; now, when the day was winding down nicely and all she had left to do was set her Out of Office Assistant? Glancing through the picture window, she identified the back of a male colleague cutting diagonally across the quad: Jim Stevens. Hand taxi-hailing, he was heading towards a boxing ring formation. Moments behind, her moral support was all that would be required.

Reassured, she said, "Slow down! Whatever's happening outside doesn't concern you!"

"Why are you always pickin' on me, Miss?"

"I don't know, Nathan." She countered aggression with sarcasm, a tactic she had developed for the classroom but found overspilling into personal conversations. "Maybe it's because you make yourself an easy target."

"But that's, like, discrimination -"

Side-stepping Nathan's protests, Ayisha tightened her mouth - "I'm sure you'll get over it" - and elbowed her way down, reaching the halfway landing between the second and first floors. Another glance outside: Jim had been absorbed within the outer ring. Through the bottleneck outside the boys' toilets (where she instinctively held her breath), Ayisha used the side door, which was already hooked open, and briskly crossed the quad, shouting, "Alright! Break it up." At the same time, she delved into her over-sized shoulder bag, needing the feeling of security that having a mobile phone in her hand provided. The fading of the chanting (*Fight! Fight! Fight!*) and the slow disintegration of the ring gave the impression that Jim was already busy refereeing proceedings. But the witnesses who staggered backwards, the eerie hush, a single high-pitched scream, suggested the need for a different drill.

Fighting her instinct for flight, chest tightening, Ayisha wove through a maze of kids who no longer seemed sure why their hands were clutching carrier bags containing ingredients for flour bombs and bottles of Coke spiked with vodka. "OK, stand aside." Confronted by the harrowed face of a girl, she paused. "What happened? Are you hurt?" *One question at a time*, Ayisha cautioned herself, heart thumping so wildly it shook her slender frame.

The girl shrank into the maternal embrace of a friend. "Not me, Miss."

She followed the girl's unswerving gaze, expecting to see Jim towering over the heads of teenagers.

A slump - barely a shadow - in the periphery of her vision: between the grey-trousered legs of boys, she saw her colleague sprawling on the tarmac. His face a perfect illustration of surprise, he was struggling to breathe. He reached one hand out to a boy - the only one to run forwards - who came to a halt as if colliding with an invisible barrier.

"Shit!" Ayisha said audibly. Bag avalanched from shoulder and she made no attempt to catch it in the hook of her elbow. As it collapsed by her feet, she had already dialled 999. "Come on, come on!"

"What service do you require?"

Jim was clutching his chest, an irregular red shape he could no longer disguise growing in circumference, spreading unevenly over the white breast-pocket of his linen shirt. A love of horror films (something her friends thought uncharacteristic of her) hadn't prepared Ayisha for her first sight of blood - real blood - in these proportions. Her lungs inflated in stages, so that she was aware of an expansive void in her chest.

"I'm sorry. What service?"

She wasn't prepared for this. "One of my colleagues... he's been stabbed." It was as if her body was slow to catch up with this news. Only a couple of weeks ago, a staff meeting had been held to discuss the possibility of weapons being brought into school; just a *possibility*, or so Ayisha had believed, recoiling from the statistics that had been bandied about.

"Where?"

The calm voice of the telephonist couldn't hold her attention. Her mind was galloping furiously: should she line the witnesses up against the wall? But, scanning faces and hands, there was no obviously guilty party.

"Where?"

"I'm sorry. In the playground. Ashfield Comp."

"And the wound? Where's that?"

"His chest. The left side." Ayisha said this, knowing all it implied.

Address confirmed, she thumbed the red exit button. By now, she had reined in her coltish thoughts but felt no less panic. Several pairs of eyes raked the tarmac; some glancing sideways, open wide. With the worry that she might be dismissing the boy responsible or - just as important - those who had egged him on, Ayisha identified two faces from the few who had yet to fall under her radar. "Max! Otis! Stand by the gates and show the ambulance crew the way! No one goes out, do you understand?" Silent on the question of police, her head dipped repeatedly as she conducted a rough headcount - five, ten, fifteen. When she reached twenty, she realised that, having stepped apart, the boys were still standing there. "Well? Do you understand?"

One eyed the other, suspicious at their pairing. "Why us, Miss?"

"This is an emergency! *MOVE IT!*" Incredulous as her voice sounded, it wasn't a job she would have relished. "Everyone else: stay where you are!" Knowing they would mill about, Ayisha tried to memorise the groupings - the twos and the threes.

"Aw, Miss!" The speaker's shirt was unbuttoned, revealing crescents of pink nipple and a white band of underpants. His tie was loosened; his cheekbones smeared with a war paint of glittery blue eyeshadow. Pinched between his fingers was the neck of a sagging balloon, stretched to capacity like a bloated udder, ripe for milking. Not him.

Protest was their default reaction. Murmurs of discontent, even among the shocked, brought an illusion of normality. Next to him, a girl's blouse knotted in Daisy Duke style revealed an expanse of midriff. Not gym-toned or beautiful, her trophy stomach was defiantly displayed, its cavernous bellybutton pierced. "It's not like we asked for this, did we?" Definitely not her.

With one hand pointing, Ayisha retraced the same 180 degrees, repeating, "I said, STAY WHERE YOU ARE!" then turned to cover her back. Experiencing a sense of how ridiculous she must have appeared, she dropped the smoking gun.

For many of the kids present, these were to have been the final moments of their final day of school. Exams over, some had attended just so they could leave again. One last assembly, the Head's message about "sending our fine boys and girls out into the world" was delivered to the half-delirious crush pressing against the double doors at the back of the hall. No shouts of 'Three cheers'; no rendition of 'For He's a Jolly Good Fellow': this generation doesn't do pretence. Well, this is it, boys and girls: the 'life' you were so impatient for. Sucks, doesn't it?

Conspicuous among those holding uncapped lipsticks and laundry-markers, ready for the autographing of cheap polyester, stood a girl with covered head and limbs. Neither envious nor condemning, her religion freed her from the gaudier obligations of ritual. Earlier, Ayisha would have recognised her look of quiet bemusement. Their eyes met briefly before she tore herself away, confused by the apparent knowing she found in the girl's expression.

All this in the space of a couple of seconds.

She swallowed. "And I want complete silence!"

The boy had positioned himself behind Jim, kneeling awkwardly on the tarmac: "Like this, Sir?"

"Hands under my arms. I need to lean against you."

This was not the time for Ayisha to remember how she had failed her St John Ambulance practical. She, Little Miss Perfect, without a filling to blot her dental record. And Jim, one of three First Aiders on the staff, had witnessed her disgrace.

The examiner had jovially referred to the pensioner playing the injured party as her 'victim'. His dimensions had proved challenging when Ayisha tried to secure a broad bandage, not assisted by bouts of theatrical hyperventilation...

"Miss, I think you should be doing mouth to mouth."

Faces leaned inwards with expressions of fear and fascination, while Ayisha felt as if she were paralysed.

"Not for a stabbing, you eejit! Don't listen to him, Miss."

"I saw it on telly last week, man!"

"That was *Holby City*."

"No way! I thought it was one of them documentaries."

Nerves quadrupled Ayisha's irritation. "I said SILENCE!"

Since qualifying on the retake, she had distributed plasters, refused to administer painkillers, and once ran cold water over a burn for twenty minutes, never dreaming that a colleague would be her next victim. To do nothing - now - with everyone watching. She must give the appearance of control.

"Kris! Run to the nurse's office for help. And fetch the first aid box." Remembering the textbook instruction she twisted her head, seeing a tangled blur of uniform-grey. "Bring it back here!"

Then she knelt, recoiling as pain fuelled by a single stone - the princess's pea - rocketed into her bones: "Argh!"

"You," Jim rasped.

Colour draining but conscious: no need to check his airway just yet. "Florence Nightingale," she concurred, scraping the toes of her shoes on the tarmac, kicking them aside.

He graced her with a one-sided blue-tinged smile, despite his obvious pain. "I was banking on Abby Lockhart."

Ayisha wasn't yet thinking *a minute earlier, and it could be me lying there;* the shakes had yet to set in: those things would come. "You'll have to make do," she said. How unconvincing her attempt to instill confidence sounded! "What happened?"

Looking down towards his chest, Jim lifted his hand, mourning, "My best shirt!"

She caught sight of the entry wound beneath the slashed linen. "They *attacked* you?"

Ayisha pulled back her sleeves, sensing from the shifting of feet behind her that this lumping together of pupils was considered an effrontery. 'You were attacked?' would have been a better choice, but her intended emphasis had been on the 'you'. Jim: perhaps the one teacher students related to. Something about his insistence that, just because some kids don't have the vocabulary to express themselves, doesn't mean their arguments aren't valid. (Ayisha detected no disadvantage on their part: at the same age she wouldn't have had the confidence to confront an adult.)

Jim's eyelids began to flutter. "They were going for each other."

His speech increasingly slurred, Ayisha prioritised keeping him talking. "So you thought you'd be the big hero?"

"I thought I wa-schblocking a punch!" he spluttered.

She closed her eyes momentarily. *Focus!* "Shamayal," Ayisha addressed the boy who was supporting Jim, speaking slowly: "Very gently, lie Mr Stevens down."

"Don't move, Shamayal!" Jim said, weakly but firmly. "She's trying to kill me."

The boy looked from one of them to the other. "Which one of yous knows what they're talkin' bout?"

Jim locked eyes with Ayisha, lucid. Momentarily, she was back in her first aid practical, humiliated, with the examiner announcing that her actions would have killed a stab-wound victim. Fountainous movements of the pensioner's hands described spouting blood: a loud groan, his final demise. Just by sitting him in the wrong position. A surge of adrenalin rocked through her: "Mr Stevens is right," she gasped.

"Should of guessed as much."

"Let's not panic." Jim's voice calm, he was trying to reassure her! "Pressure on the wound."

She nodded, her training coming back to her: *stop the bleeding.*

"If you hear a sucking sound, or if the blood starts bubbling, I'm in bad shape. Anything in that suitcase of yours we can use for padding?"

"Tissues." She reached for her discarded bag, casting aside the copy of *The Wasted Vigil* she was halfway through.

"Let's hope they're man-sized." While Ayisha plucked at a couple, as she would when dispensing to persistent sniffers, Jim's attempt at laughter morphed into an ugly grimace. "The whole box, for God's sake!"

Feeling heat rise to her face, she cautioned herself: *just do what you have to do.*

Ripping through an oval of perforations, her increasingly uncooperative fingers freed a wad several inches thick. Pressing it in place, Ayisha leaned closer. "So, who was it?" But, finding his hands limp, one glance at Jim's face confirmed that priorities had changed.

"Miss?" Shamayal reacted to her eyes, whites now making up the greater proportion of his own.

Was it time to move Jim into the recovery position? *Think!* ABC: airway, breathing, circulation. Ayisha felt his breath against her cheek: weak, but still there. "It's alright."

The boy exhaled noisily, shaking his head. Ayisha detected doubt rather than relief.

Hearing the scrape of approaching footsteps, she raised one hand, shouting, "Over here!"

"All of you: move!" the Head's voice was uncharacteristically decisive. "Against the wall of the chemistry lab. NOW."

Her hard work: undone in an instant.

He bent down, hands on knees, framing Jim in a triangle. "Is an ambulance on its way, Miss Emmanuel?"

"Yes, I…" As if in affirmation, she heard the waver of a siren. Her part over, there was nothing more she could do.

"We'll take it from here. Shamayal, you're OK staying put for now?"

"I guess."

"Good lad."

Relief flooded through her in waves, bringing with it an urge to cry. Here was the nurse, ripping the green and white hygienically-sealed packaging with her teeth; ably folding her triangular bandage, using her thighs as a tabletop. The discarded mass of sodden and desiccated tissues lay oozing on the tarmac, like a steak on a butcher's slab. Except that this was no horror movie: this was Jim's blood. So real, Ayisha imagined she could taste iron. The enormity of what had happened hit home. Someone else had stabbed Jim but, had he not known what he was talking about, she might have been the one to kill him! As she backed away - one hand clamped over her mouth - as the look the boy cast her said, 'I got you sussed,' the Head was reassuring an unconscious Jim that everything was going to be fine.

Since they had gone for a drink a few weeks ago, Ayisha had begun to look forward to their exchanges. Earlier she had passed Jim in the corridor and had said, "One more lesson. I can't wait!"

"Six weeks of thinking time isn't good for me. I've never liked the big holidays."

She had laughed at that: "Where are you? At primary school?" And, rather than ask why, she'd quipped, "You can help me decorate if you're not doing anything."

Now, in the space of an hour, everything had changed.

Removing her hand from her mouth, she realised it was sticky with blood: the taste of iron wasn't imagined. She balked as she licked her lips unthinkingly in an attempt to rid them of their unwanted coating. And again, Shamayal's eyes bored into her. No, Ayisha acknowledged, shoeless, tights laddered, shivering in the bright July sunlight: she hadn't been in control of the situation. Not for an instant.

CHAPTER 2:

SHAMAYAL - APRIL 2010 - SUTTON HIGH STREET

It began in March. March, April. Late at night, anyhow. Making himself scarce had been fine by Shamayal before it started chucking it down. Sheltering under the awnings of KFC - the only shop without its metal grille lowered - he heard the sound of tyre treads making spray out of standing water. Turning in time to see a driver's window slide down he clocked the make of car as it drew alongside the kerb, deciding it posed no threat.

"Shamayal!"

At the sound of his name hurled unexpectedly into the dark, the boy's shoulders froze.

"What are you doing out so late on your own?"

Recognising his history teacher, he breathed out; swaggered over, jeans low on his hips, eyes blinking, beanie dripping. Slapping one hand on the roof of Mr Stevens's car, he threw back his head. "I'm walkin', innit? What you doin'?"

"Offering you a lift. Get in before I change my mind."

Shamayal didn't appreciate the presumption that teachers' authority extended beyond the wire-fenced perimeter of the school. "Nu-uh. I ain't getting in no Corsa, see?"

Mr Stevens's friendliness turned to exasperation. "Only you can worry how you look in the dead of night!"

"Do I have to, Sir?" But, seeing he had reached Situation Unavoidable, Shamayal loped around the bonnet, the slant of driving rain picked out in the headlights, wipers cranking back and forth. The passenger door dropped inexpensively as he opened it. *Two Door Cinema Club* was playing on the stereo, not his scene but definitely not the Dad-rock he had expected. A bag of chocolate limes lay open on the dash. Shamayal got in. He felt every inch of wet denim where it adhered mercilessly to his skin.

"Help yourself." His teacher nodded to the overspill of sweets, then, just as the boy took the cellophane wrapper in his teeth, he turned. "Do your parents know where you are?"

Look busy: use your shivering as an excuse. "Know something, Sir? It was w-warmer outside."

"You need to get out of those wet clothes." Mr Stevens twisted the control of the heater to red, the second dial to four. Waiting for the blast of Arctic air to turn tepid Shamayal rubbed his hands together then held them in front of a round vent.

His teacher looked in the rear-view mirror before pulling away from the kerb. "You'd better tell me where you live."

"You won't know it." The rain changed direction, drops forcing themselves in the spaces between each other, aiming for a setting beyond torrential. "Ralegh Grove."

Shamayal didn't expect an explosion of laughter as a response. Boiled sweet clashed with teeth as he moved it to his other cheek, chocolate cutting through the sharpness of the lime. "You got somethink against Council?"

"God, no! I know it well."

"How come, Sir? You get dragged out to see some pupil?"

"I grew up there."

Now it was the boy's turn to hoot. "For *REAL?*"

"I haven't been back in a long, long time." Taking one hand from the steering wheel, Mr Stevens scratched the side of his nose. "Not since my mother died."

"That's harsh, man."

The word, "Yup," was virtually inhaled.

Counting a moment's silence out of respect, timing himself with the windscreen wipers, Shamayal got to forty-nine. "Then how come you're always actin' like you're some big teacher-guy?"

"Haven't you noticed? I *am* a big teacher-guy."

"Nah! I meant you talk all posh, Sir."

"I had to adapt. You will, too, once you have a job."

The boy's eyes flashed. These teachers, they think nothing of disrespectin' you. "This here's my *voice*, man."

"There's nothing wrong with your voice: I'm talking about your language."

"You think this is how I talk all the time? I'm adaptin' right now, as it happens." In protest, Shamayal cleared a porthole so that he could stare into the night-time gloom. The boy had to admit that Jim's knowledge of the back streets was a match for his father's. He had ridden up front in the minicab many a night before he was old enough to be left alone. Opening a heavy eyelid, half asleep, he might register a signpost for Gatwick's North Terminal or the upside down table legs of Battersea Power Station, all floodlit. He always preferred the night.

The front wheels skimmed the edges of a speed bump; the car barely rocked. He had almost forgotten he was supposed to be sulking when his teacher said, "We're not so different."

This definitely called for an answer. Shamayal regretted folding his arms as cold wet t-shirt pressed into his chest. "Oh, we're different, Sir, if there's one thing I can assure you of, it's that."

Jim - teachers' names were the worst kept secrets - upped the speed of the windscreen wipers from loud screech to manic. "Let's change the subject, then. How's life on the estate these days?"

"If you grew up there you'd know how it is, wouldn't you?"

"Fair enough."

Each fresh semicircle etched onto the windscreen was violently erased in a smattering of rain.

Shamayal thought that maybe he'd been too quick to jump down Jim's throat. The guy was only trying to do him a favour. "I remember once," he conceded, "we was aksed to draw pictures of our homes in Art. Most people drew square boxes with triangles for roofs and smoke coming out of chimneys, even though most houses wouldn't have had real fires, yeah? Outside, they drew two big stick people and two likkle stick people. Some drew cats or dogs. I drew this rectangle." He pronounced the word with a harsh 'k' he thought suited the ninety-degree angle of the shape. "With rows of square windows and satellite dishes - actually the satellite dishes looked more like them old metal dustbin lids you used to have - and the head of a stick person in each. Apart from my own flat, where I drew two faces, givin' them each eyes and a mouth. I left the others blank because I'm no good at drawin', not faces anyway. Then I drew a cross on each window to show that the people was on the inside. Some smart arse aks if I live in a prison, but my teacher says, 'That's very emotive,' noddin' her head, all serious. 'And what does this represent?' 'It represents where I live,' I says. 'Hundreds of people stacked on top of each other -'"

Jim nodded. "Like Lego bricks."

Shamayal's mouth fell open: he had bin goin' to say that.

"Whose was the other face at the window?"

"That'll be my dad, innit?"

"Just the two of you?"

The headlights of an oncoming car blinded, prisms of light reflected through each coursing raindrop. Shamayal shielded

13

his eyes. This was close to being none of his teacher's business, but you have to let some things pass. "Since my mamma left, yeah."

Jim swung the car into the entrance of the estate, past the scattering of For Sale signs. "It looks different," he mused.

"That's the Residents' Association. They got security buzzers, working lifts the high-rises would have wet dreams about, even double glazing. Under the second arch, turn left, yeah? You can -"

A dark shadow shot in front of the car.

"Shit, man!" The boy's arms reacted automatically as Jim stamped on the brakes. Lurching forwards, his head came close to hitting the dashboard. They were both jolted back, seatbelts tightening across their chests. Challenging, the whites of eyes glared through the windscreen: a cyclist - bike unlit, dressed in black. "Don't think he likes you, Sir."

Shamayal was relieved to hear the locking mechanism click all about him. His heart pounded slightly less wildly now that he knew his teacher wasn't up for some big confrontation.

A fist slammed down on the bonnet of the car. Shamayal saw Jim reach for the door handle. "Ain't no point tryin' to lay down no law," he warned. "Round here, the Ralegh Boyz *are* the law."

Beside him, Jim rocked back in his seat, mouth tight. Crisis averted. There were shadows on both sides now; guys in hoodies and cycle masks standing up on the pedals of too-small bikes and circling, or huddled about, round-shouldered. The paranoid view was that they were surrounded. Shamayal chose to believe that the gatekeepers were simply making their presence known. They protected their own - that's what they'd told him; what they'd offered him, too. But, from the hints they've dropped, their protection comes at too high a price, so, while he can, he'll stick to his promise to make his mamma proud.

"Think they own the bloody place." Dispatching gritted words, Jim cranked the gears.

Go slow, *slow*, Shamayal willed his teacher, sensing he might still drop them both in it. "They got competition from the Waddon Warriors, as it happens."

"Which side are you on?"

The speed of the car was controlled. No one was made to lose face by having to back off. And although the Ralegh Boyz peered through the glass - although one of them pointed straight at Shamayal and then at his own chest - You: Me - they were allowed to pass.

"I don't roll with nobody. You don't make no trouble, but you don't wanna get too pally either, f'you know what I mean." His mouth was running away with him like it did when he was nervous. "Course, both sides tryin' to talk me round, upping their offers, like phone companies with their tariffs." Moments later, he pointed out a marked space under a streetlight. "You can drop me here."

"I'll see you to your door."

"Oh, Si-ir!" This wasn't how he'd planned it.

"I didn't realise things would be so lively at this time of night."

Second thoughts, might be just as well. Who knows what You:Me boy had in mind?

"I should have guessed!" Jim said, cranking on the hand-brake; looking up at the flickering electric lights. "What number are you?"

"Sixty-eight."

"No kidding? We lived next door."

"You never!"

"I bet yours is the small bedroom."

"Yeah, man. That's my hang-out."

"Mine was on the other side of your wall."

"That's the thing, yeah? You can be sleepin' inches away

from someone you'd go out your way to avoid, only this thin w-" Shamayal checked himself. "You know? I'll just stop talkin."

They threw the car doors open, and Jim unfolded himself, narrowing his eyes against the lashing rain to inspect the fist-shaped dent in the bonnet. Shamayal felt guilty even though it din't have nuffin to do with him. "Is it bad, Sir?"

Jim let out an exasperated sigh. "I hate them thinking they can get away with it! Anyway…" The boy thought his teacher was looking for distraction as he glanced up in the direction of Shamayal's front door, raising his collar. "Mr Anscombe: he used to be the other side of the wall from me."

"Never heard of 'im."

"Perhaps they gave him the ground floor flat he applied for." Jim shoved his hands deep in his pockets and started across the car park, the purposeful walk of after-dark. His head shrank inside his jacket, tortoise-like. "Perhaps he's dead. Good riddance!"

Shamayal, who had never heard his teacher speak carelessly about anyone, jogged a few paces, kicking up spray. Each step squeezed water out of his socks, soaking the insoles of his trainers. "Who was this guy, anyhow?"

"An ex-boxer who took too many punches." A crisp packet flapped like the tail of a dying fish in an overflow from a drain. "The last one broke his neck, leaving his legs useless, but my other neighbour said not to feel any sympathy: he was a bastard before he ended up in the chair. She wasn't wrong either." This wasn't no classroom lecture. Shamayal, whose trainers had developed a squelch, detected anger doing the talking. "There was this time when I was… I don't know: about eight, I suppose. I heard banging coming from the other side of my bedroom wall."

As they reached the refuge of the porch, it was as if someone flicked an off-switch. Jim immediately lowered his collar. The reek of ammonia and Dettol was inescapable, but Shamayal's teacher was either immune or too polite to mention it.

"Turned out Mr Anscombe had fallen out of his wheel-chair and was wedged across the hall." Their ascent was accompanied by the slap-slap of hands and the scrape of trainers. "I yelled through the letterbox not to worry; I'd fetch my brother."

Shamayal frowned. "What's your bruvver's name?"

"Nick." Jim laughed. A single syllable: reluctant. "The lock expert. Once we had Mr Anscombe back in his chair, I thought I'd do the neighbourly thing. Stick around, make a cup of coffee! The layout of the flat - your flat -" breaking off, Jim snorted air through his nostrils. "I've just realised this isn't exactly the most appropriate story to be telling a pupil."

"Is it rated 18 or somethink?"

An electric light buzzed with the fury of a trapped blue-bottle.

"Or something."

"If you don't finish it, Sir, I'll only dream up an endin' that's far worser." The slip was deliberate.

"Be my guest!" Jim shot the grinning boy a sideways glance.

"What I think happened was -"

"If you must know, the old man made a pass at me. But that's all you're getting."

"Shit, man!"

Pausing at the top of the stairs, Shamayal could hear Jim's laboured breathing.

"Look: your lights are still on. Someone's waited up."

A fresh wave of apprehension. "That'll be my Dad and his drinking buddies. This is his first night back."

"Works away, does he?"

"Sometimes, yeah."

Jim sniffed. "Who looks after you?"

Shamayal licked his lips. Stupid, stupid, he'd said too much.

"Christ, Shamayal. You're - what - fourteen? Couldn't you stay with your mother?"

You have so many secrets floating round, one's bound to slip out occasionally. "She din't exactly leave no forwardin' address, f'you know what I mean."

"I should have a word -"

"I thought you was off-duty, Sir!"

"Teachers are never off-duty."

Can't take nobody's word for nothing. Minute you trust them, they betray you. One thing was guaranteed: his dad was going to kill him.

Rounding the corner, Shamayal recognised the man who was hanging onto the doorframe, holding his mouth. "Seamus," he nodded.

"Alright, boy!" Staggering forwards, Seamus raised his hand to high five him, displaying a bloodied lip. "Word of advice: watch your mouth." As Seamus tapped the side of his broken-veined nose, a bottle came flying out into the darkness and over the top of the clothes line that was strung between the pillars of the balcony. "Your father's on form tonight."

"And don't come back, you Irish bastard!"

Seamus leaned out over the railings. "Hah! Missed, you black bastard!"

The boy executed a handbrake turn. No way was he walkin' into that!

"Wait a minute!"

Defensive, Shamayal shrugged the hand that gripped his shoulder aside. "Hey! Don't touch me, man!"

"Alright, alright! I was only going to ask who that was."

The person he should be angry with was himself. He should have refused to get in the car. Now, in the space of ten minutes, he had gone and ruined everything. One call to Social Services was all it would take. Damage limitation.

Shamayal had to contain this and that meant his temper had to stay under control. "Seamus? That's my dad's boss, innit?"

"And what is it your father does?"

Somewhere close by there were raised voices, followed by distorted echoes: a door slamming, footsteps running. Shamayal waited until he was sure it was nothing to worry about. "Driving, mostly."

"Not in that state, I hope!"

With a new rage he barely understood, Shamayal pointed an index finger at his history teacher's face. "Back off! You shouldn't go turnin' round and sayin' things you don't know nuffin about."

"You're right." Jim's hands were up at shoulder level, fingers splayed.

"It's not like he's a complete idiot, is it?" Fury subsiding, Shamayal performed small shoulder rolls and realigned his head.

Jim glanced at his watch, his expression reluctant. "Where are you planning on sleeping?"

Good question. "The stairwell, the arches, the bin sheds... they all lookin' like good options."

"You'll catch pneumonia!"

"If the Ralegh Boyz don't get me first."

His teacher seemed to be weighing possibilities, none of which he liked the sound of.

Shamayal was able to laugh at the situation. They were both in what you might call a predicament. "You regret offerin' me that lift, Sir?"

His teacher covered the face of his watch with one hand. When he made his mind up, he made it up fast. "What about my sofa?"

"I din't think that was allowed, Sir."

"One thing at a time. Right now, you need a change of clothes." Jim's damp hair was skewiff from where he'd been rubbing his brow. He seemed angry to be put out. "How long has this been going on?"

There wasn't a fat lot of point in holding back. "My mamma said he never touched a drop before he came to this country. Trus' me: he's been makin' up for it since."

Few words accompanied their rectangular descent. Shamayal was shocked to feel the heat of his teacher's rage and to realise it wasn't aimed at him. Outside, the rain seemed to be letting up, or had at least reduced to a heavy downpour. Shamayal eased himself onto the uninviting dark patch of the Corsa's passenger seat.

Driving back towards the arch, Jim jammed on the brakes a second time. Having kept a keen eye out and seen nothing to concern him, Shamayal's forehead grazed the dash before the belt jerked him backwards. "Man, what's with all the emergency stops? You tryin' to kill me?"

Jim flung the driver's door wide. "It can't be!" His voice was pure disbelief.

"*Now* you forget about the fact I'm soakin' wet!" Shamayal lectured the dashboard. "Sayin' nuffin of who might be lurkin' in them shadows."

As Jim jogged over to an old man who was loitering by the bin sheds, Shamayal unwrapped another chocolate lime, confused to see his teacher greeting the estate's resident Johnny-no-stars like a long-lost uncle, shaping his hands into spy holes and raising them to his eyes, then clasping the old geezer's elbows. *This I got to hear.* The boy got out of the car and moved closer, in time to catch Jim asking, "Still fishing?"

"The council took away my license, didn't they?" the old man lisped.

"I'm sorry to hear that. Really."

"What can you do?" The tramp hooked his thumbs under the piece of string that was strung through the belt loops of a once-beige raincoat. "I'm into recycling these days." Like an estate agent, he gave Jim the grand tour of the bin shed: its flat roof pooling with rain; one door hanging from its hinges to reveal metal drums overflowing with plastic bags and takeaway cartons. "The electric's out, see?"

Shamayal shied away from the ripe, damp-enhanced stench of disposable nappies and decomposing vegetables.

"You've no idea how happy I am to see you."

"Remember your little friend?" Reflected in the light of a lamp, the old man's watery eyes were bright. He blinked frequently, as if it was part of the process of dispensing words. "She was a sweet little thing. All that bushy hair."

"I still miss her." Jim appeared to consult the moon. "Summer holidays, especially."

Thinking himself undetected, Shamayal had been edging forwards when the old man turned to nod. "This your son, is he?"

Jim did a double take and then said, "One of my pupils, Shamayal."

"Shamayal. What does that stand for?"

Shamayal stepped into a circle of reflected light, blurred at the edges. "Hey! It stands for no crap, old man."

As Jim stabbed him with a look, the tramp tipped onto the toes of his worn shoes, paying no notice to the puddles. "Ah, very good! They all know how to stick up for themselves these days, don't they? I suppose you teach them that. Life skills they call it, don't they? I didn't b-bother with school. My dear old mum taught me everything I needed to know."

"Is this still a good place for you, Bins?"

"Where else would I go?"

"Well." Jim squeezed the old guy's arm. "I need to get this young man home."

Shamayal could barely wait until they were back in the car to air his disgust: "He stinks, man!"

"Bins didn't seem to know you. How is that? He knows everyone."

"Like I told you, I keep myself to myself. I don't like no busy-bodies."

"Bins? He wouldn't hurt a fly."

"Whatever!" As they pulled away, Shamayal detected sock among the damp smells circulating in the warm air from the heater. "He's rank, man. You know he goes through people's rubbish?"

"How do you think he got his name?" Shamayal heard his teacher sigh. "Bins is one of life's special souls."

"You can say that again! He's scope."

"That's not a very kind term."

"Better than spazzo. That's what you used to call people who ain't right in the head, innit?"

A moment passed. The rubber of the wiper blades screeched as it skimmed the curve of glass. The night had almost cried itself to sleep.

"I always thought it must be nice, being in a world of your own."

"You sayin' he's fakin' it?"

"Nothing's as simple as that."

"Then what?"

"They wanted to send him to a day centre to sew mailbags, but Bins was always clear what his role in life was. Every day, from early morning until the light faded, he would sit in the same place in the middle of the estate, dressed in galoshes, fishing rod in hand."

"You're kiddin' me!"

"'Catch anything today?' I'd ask. 'Alright, Jim Stevens,' he'd smile. You've heard how he talks?"

"Yeah! Like his tongue's too big for his mouth!"

The way that his teacher ignored his tone made Shamayal feel shamed. "'They're not biting,' he'd say, blaming it on his latest batch of maggots, or the footie being a bit on the noisy side. Never that he was more than two miles from water and that the nearest fish was keeping warm under a light at the chippy." Jim sighed loudly, shaking his head. "And now they've taken his license away, poor bugger."

Shamayal scoffed, "There wasn't no license!" *Was his teacher that gullible?*

"Perhaps someone upset him. Perhaps they moved him on. I don't know." Jim nudged the windscreen wipers off. "You really don't know him?"

The boy pulled a face. "He's just some old man, innit? Don't see what he's got to do with me."

Turning onto the main drag, they drove over the road that bridged the railway; a divide as clear as barbed-wire fencing, separating the concrete of the estate from the neat grid of bay-windowed houses it overlooked.

Shamayal adopted a game show host's voice to read the floodlit signs. "DANGER. Private Property. KEEP OUT, Entry only with permit to work." He turned to Jim. "I must be breakin' some law or other."

"I grew up listening to talk about the day we'd leave for a house on the other side of the tracks." Turning into a narrow side road Jim swore loudly. "Someone's in my parking space. Permits don't guarantee you anything round here."

"This is you? No shit? You could of got further away from the trains."

"You'd think so."

Jim drove a couple of lampposts down and then, throwing his elbow over the back of his seat, reversed into a space, a practised manoeuvre.

Outside the car, Shamayal said, "Nice," nodding to the beat in his head at all the little front gardens and picket fences, their tidy tiled paths. It lived up to the tree-lined road of semi-detached houses he'd imagined teachers living in. "What's that?" He pointed to a long-legged tree clipped into a neat round while Jim grappled with his keys.

"It's a herb called a bay."

"For cookin' an' that?" He rubbed a leaf between his fingers and sniffed. "Don't smell of much. What's it taste of?"

"I don't know. Bay, I suppose." Jim yawned, the door sticking slightly. "Home! I'm knackered."

Where Shamayal expected to see a wide hallway and a staircase, there was a small lobby and two more front doors. Jim flipped a few keys over, selecting another.

Shamayal stood shipwrecked, dripping self-consciously, awaiting rescue. Inside, the downstairs flat was smaller than his own place. Corsa; half a house: teachers' salaries don't buy that much.

Ahead of him, Jim was pointing to the first door on the left. "The sofa's in there. Take your shoes off. I'll find you a sleeping bag and something dry to put on."

The boy peeled off his socks, hoping the smell would be mistaken for damp. Left them tucked inside his shoes on the mat.

Jim thrust a bundle into his hands, the towel on top smelling of fabric softener. "Bathroom's up the hall. Sling your wet stuff over the radiator."

He hesitated outside the living room, taking in the haven of gadgetry, the piles of video games. "Wicked!" Shamayal felt wired. "Mind if I play *Medal of Honour?*"

"Yes, I do! Three o'clock is time for bed."

"What's this, Sir?" Stepping forwards the boy balanced the bundle on the arm of the sofa and picked up a pair of binoculars from the coffee table. Holding their lenses to his eyes, he spun around playfully, his vision blurred. "You from MI5 or somethink?"

Jim's bristle was unmistakable. "Would you mind putting them in their case?"

Shamayal turned them over. "These are proper battered."

"They might look old, but they're very precious. My

mother gave them to me."

The boy hung them around his teacher's neck solemnly. "Then you shouldn't leave them lyin' around."

Half an hour later Shamayal was jolted awake by the sound of glass shattering.

"Who's there?" Finding he was unable to move, the boy panicked - the Ralegh Boyz must have tied his legs together - before he remembered he was in a sleeping bag on Teacher-Jim's sofa. He had thought he was beyond sleep but it seemed he had drifted off. "You broken somethink, Sir?" he called out.

"I thought it was you," came an alien voice from the dark.

They appeared at their respective doors. Jim, bleary-eyed, was stuffing his arms into the sleeves of a dressing gown. The fact that his teacher seemed on edge unnerved Shamayal. Looking towards the front door, he saw that the security chain was still in place. "Is there some other way in?"

"Go back to bed," Jim instructed, reaching for the kitchen light switch. "I'll see to this."

Bright shards lay scattered on the white tile.

"You must have one of them polterghosts. Hey, you don't wanna go in there with no shoes -"

Jim stooped, picking up two of the largest fragments by their edges. He examined them closely in the palm of his hand. "Damn!" Straightening up, Jim stood one foot on top of the other, wobbling.

Shamayal saw the bloody trail: too late. "You got a pair of tweezers? I'll sort that, no worries."

"*I'll* sort it, alright!"

Jesus! "Hey!" He backed off. "Forget I'm even here.

CHAPTER 3:

JIM - SUMMER 1990 -
WANDSWORTH PRISON

There had been no false illusions: from as early as Jim could recall his father Frank had been a temporary presence. His second home - as he called it - was Wandsworth, a credential he shared with one of the Great Train Robbers. Jim's brother Nick - older by six years - had been shoe-horned into the role of the man of the house. Both boys were monitored for signs that they were taking after their dad, as vigorously as their scalps had once been checked for head lice. Shortly after Nick reached the age of sixteen, Jean ironed and folded his clothes for the last time.

"As long as you're here, you'll be a bad influence on Jim. Your brother's smart. He's still got a chance."

Named as the reason for Nick's ex-communication, a stunned Jim was the recipient of his brother's venom. Nick spat on the doormat before he slung his bag over one shoulder and loped away. Agape, Jim had begged, "Mum, tell him you didn't mean it! You've got to stop him!"

"No, Jim. This is the way it's got to be." Jean herded him away from the door and closed it firmly. The patch of white-yolked spit would stay there, stepped over, until the rain swept in diagonally to wash its imprint away. "If the neighbours ask, you're to tell them your brother's left home."

"If Nick goes, I go!" Jim protested, knowing his threat improbable - if not downright impossible - to carry out.

He packed a bag, used it as a punchbag and stuffed its contents back into a drawer before hunger lured him towards the smell of bangers and mash.

"I can't watch over you all hours. I've got to earn a living. But, make no mistake: if you choose to be like him..." Jim wrapped his foot around the closest leg of the chair that had been his brother's. Mid-sentence, his mother seemed to relent, placing her knife and fork among the debris of her meal and reaching out to ruffle his hair. "You're my last chance."

Although Jim didn't know it, the decision that had seemed spontaneous was brutal, causing Jean no end of heartache as she lay in her bed alone at night listening to her ten-year-old son vent his anger. And no end of earache when they next visited his dad to break the news.

"What chance does Nick stand now?" The boy tensed as his father exploded; face crimson, brow veined, missiles of spit landing on the table. "He's got no choice but to go robbing."

"Listen here, Frank." Jean Stevens jabbed her finger, as only a woman can when she is surrounded by CCTV and prison guards. "Do you think it was easy for me? Nick had a choice, same as you, and I've given him dozens of last chances. Don't try telling me he has to steal while I'm working all hours. If you were at home you'd have been entitled to your say, but I'm not budging - and there isn't a damned thing you can do about it!"

As she steered Jim towards the exit, he felt her entire body trembling. For the first time since she'd shown his brother the door, Jim experienced something close to pride for the way his mother had stood up to his father, but the only words he could summon were, "Alright, Mum?"

Shock erupted, expelled under the guise of a laugh. "Christ Almighty, that was some speech!" She clutched her handbag to her stomach and fumbled with the clasp. "Look at me, rubber-fingers. Light us a ciggie, will you, love?"

"I don't smoke, Mum." Jim popped the fastening open, unsure if she was testing him.

"Course you don't, love. You're so grown up, I forget who I'm talking to."

Cigarette placed between quivering lips, the contents of the matchbox rattled as Jean nudged its cardboard drawer open. Just as she produced a flame the head broke away, fizzling out like a miniature rocket.

"Give it here!" Jim scraped a match the full length of the box several times, inhaling the gunpowder smell. He cupped the flame and Jean bent her knees, pulling back her hair as he offered it to the end of her cigarette.

"Get yourself a hobby," she said, calmed after an extended drag. "Something to keep you out of trouble."

With that advice echoing, a strap looped around the metal railings caught Jim's eye. "What's this?" He reached up to unhook whatever it happened to be. The gadget's twin barrels felt perfectly balanced as his hands curved to their shape. Raising the lenses to his eyes, Jim's vision blurred.

Jean blew a nicotine plume. "Binoculars. Nice ones by the look of it - although someone's had good use out of them. No, *not* at the prison windows, Jim! You'll have us arrested. Try up there instead."

"Where?"

She spun him round by the shoulders then pointed to the branches of a tree. "A pair of doves."

"They're not doves: they're pigeons!"

"Same difference," Jean shrugged, doing the twist to crush the stub of her cigarette.

"Doves don't lie in wait under the railway bridge and crap

on your school blazer."

"Don't use that word!" Her voice suggested she was trying not to crack up.

"What word, Mum?" All innocence.

"I'll *what word?* you." She set a brisk pace down Heathfield Road in the direction of the common without a glance over her shoulder. "Hang those things up where you found them, love. Someone will be back for them later."

Finders keepers, was Jim's motto. Testing his jacket pocket for size, he found it lacking.

"Course, it was pigeons that almost drove your granddad insane."

"How come?" The boy dawdled two steps behind, eyes trained on the back of his mum's head.

"There was this one pigeon sat on the roof of his house who'd start his noise the minute the sun was up. If you ever wondered what time sunrise was, your granddad would be the one to ask. 'It was four o'clock this morning! Four-oh-clock. I'm going to get a gun and shoot the little bugger!' he'd say..."

Come on, Granddad, help me out. Jim's only other option was to slip the binoculars inside his jacket.

"...You see, the chimney acted as a loudspeaker. There was a fireplace in every room, so there was no escaping the noise. Your granddad would leap out of bed and shout up the chimney, 'If you don't stop that racket by the count of three, I'm going to light a fire and burn your sorry arse!'" By then, Jim's mum, vibrating like a leaf, had to lean against the railings to compose herself. Jim was conscious of the bulge in his jacket. With one arm bent, the binoculars nestled in the crook of his elbow. Still wiping the tears from her eyes, Jean demanded, "Why are you holding yourself funny?"

He licked his lips. "I'm not -"

"Your shoulders are all stiff. Look."

"I was only laughing at your story." Stealthily, Jim lowered his arm, trapping the binoculars against his body, and stuck his hand into his pocket as far as it would reach.

"You miss Granddad, don't you?"

Jim felt that the old man was winking at him. "S'pose." He winked back.

A week later, left to his own devices much of the time, Jim had mastered the binoculars.

"For Pete's sake!" Jean barked from the kitchen. "JIM!"

"What?" he yelled non-committally from his kneeling position on the sofa.

"Not *what?* 'Yes, Mum!'"

"Yes, Mum."

"I don't expect to come home after I've been out working all day and find the breakfast dishes in the sink! Was what you were doing so important that you couldn't spare two minutes?" He heard the sound of running water. "The cornflakes have set like concrete. I'll have to let them soak. *JIM!*"

Her voice right behind him now, Jim secreted the binoculars on the windowsill behind the curtains before turning to face her. She was standing there, her folded arms pushing her bosom directly into his eyeline.

"Who are you spying on?"

"No one." Standard-issue reflex-reaction.

As she held out one hand, palm up, one breast sagged. "Let's have them."

The idea of the binoculars being taken away was unbearable. In truth, his main interest up until then wasn't birds of the feathered variety. Ever since he'd seen his first episode of *Baywatch* and watched C J Parker run in slow motion - boobs swaying as her elbows pumped, her beach-damp pony-tail streaming, mouth pouting - his dreams had been invaded by her, diving into the shallows, coming to his rescue. That had been the beginning of his fascination with women. Because they didn't know they were being observed, Jim saw them in their natural environment, marvelling how much work went into looking that natural. Rollers, razors, wax and other instruments of torture procured from Superdrug. Miracle bras that shored everything up and squeezed it all together. There were no Pamela Andersons in Ralegh Grove - wrong climate for red swimsuits - but what Jim saw terrified him.

Through the lenses, he witnessed comings and goings previously concealed. Men who visited women who weren't their wives in the middle of the day. Money exchanging hands on doorsteps. Packages exchanging hands in bathrooms. Items secreted on windowsills where people thought they were hidden from view. Private Gardens of Eden: tomatoes growing side by side with cannabis; coloured underpants strung across balconies like bunting; daydreamers gazing towards a horizon of rooftops, the homes they'd been brought up in, kidding themselves, 'Once Labour's back in charge...' Mothers bouncing babies on their hips, pointing out clown-shaped clouds and lingering vapour trails and small yappy tail-chasing dogs. Parents scattering cigarette ash as they kept an eye on children below. People making patterns on the ground like lines of ants. This was Jim's view of what life had to offer.

"Honest, I'm not spying." He sulked in the way of those caught red-handed, looping the strap of the binoculars over his mother's proffered wrist.

"What would *you* call it then?" They dangled hypnotically. "I thought I told you to leave these where they were! Keeping something you find is only one step short of stealing!"

Mrs Stevens's disappointment was enough to make any boy hang his head. "What am I going to do with you?" Her sigh signalling a weakening, Jim grabbed the opportunity to look dog-eyed. "Find something useful to do with them, or I'll put them back where we found them!"

Hopping back onto the sofa with a silent celebratory *Yes!* Jim moved his line of vision towards the railway. Something hovering eerily white made him gasp, "It's a ghost!"

"Don't talk daft. Give them here." Jean pulled at the binoculars until he loosened his grip. *Now, you're interested,* he might have said. "Nothing there. Can't see a thing." As Jim twisted the dials, she breathed, "My word," a near whisper. "I haven't seen one of them in years - and they were a rare sight then!"

"One of what?" The boy danced impatiently.

"That's no ghost, love." Her unmoving eyes were disbelieving. "It's an owl."

"Give us a look, Mum," Jim whined.

She batted his hand away. "Just look at it!" Jim squinted, but could see little. "Ah, that's our lot for tonight," she said at last, glancing at her watch. "Your granddad told me that owls usually come back to the same place. If we're lucky, our friend might be a regular. Get yourself a book on birds from the library and we'll figure out which type he is."

Jim spent the following evening training the binoculars on the railway cuttings, while his mother trawled through the borrowed book. She was concentrating so hard that, for once, she barely seemed to notice the trains rumbling past below. After a while her voice became animated. "This is the one! Listen: '*Barn Owl, Recognised by its distinctive white, heart-shaped face.*' Isn't that a great description? '*Golden buff upperparts with pale grey and black mottling. The female is larger with more streaking and spotting. Couples pair for life*' - ah, that's nice. '*Eats small mammals, frogs, birds and insects.*' That must be why they like it down by the tracks! The place is swarming. You see! It says here that they hover. And listen to this! Lots of people make the mistake of thinking they're seeing ghosts at first." She carried on, not expecting any response, while her son focused on the spot where he had last seen the owl.

Sunday: "I'd like you to keep me company this afternoon." Jim's mother trapped him in the frame of the living room door. She had worked six days on and, contrary to instructions from on high, had spent the morning cleaning their own home.

"But I'm playing footie down the park." It was a lie, of course, but there was always a game to be found. A man down, it didn't matter how weird the lads thought you were. And what did Jim care if he didn't get to be Lineker or Gazza?

"They've had you all week." She zombie-walked him into the living room. "I'm not asking, I'm telling. And don't *Oh Mum* me! There's a film just starting I want you to see."

"What's it called?" He glared dubiously at the opening credits. There wasn't even any music.

"*Kes*." Having walked backwards, Mum levered herself onto the sofa with a groan. "It's about a boy who keeps this hawk as a pet."

"What sort of a name's Kes?" he scoffed.

"Kes is the bird. The boy's name is Billy." She extended one hand towards the screen. "Look at him: he breaks my heart."

Jim clocked a boy, eyes set too far apart in a pinched face. A concave-chested boy, too skinny for his school uniform. "He talks funny," he sneered, flopping down heavily.

"He'd probably think *you* talk funny." She slapped his knee, playfulness barely disguising her serious intent. "Shut up and watch."

Jim crushed a cushion against his chest, preparing to sulk. For the next ninety minutes he was riveted, watching this boy - the runt of a family that was like theirs in many

33

ways. Ridiculed. Picked on. Using goalposts as a climbing frame when he should have been defending. Caned for being caught sleeping during assembly. Asked to explain himself, shrugging: 'Dunno, Sir.'

"Don't know when to keep your mouth shut, that's your problem," Jim muttered, then caught his mother's bemused expression. "What?"

She held her palms up, stifling a laugh. "Did you hear me say anything?"

But it was in protest that Jim turned to his mother when Billy's brother killed the bird: "Ah! You can't *do* that! All because he didn't put the bet on for him?"

Jean had clamped one hand over her mouth. She was crying. His mother only ever cried when she watched the television.

"You upset about the bird, Mum?" he asked.

Then the scene cut and the credits started to roll. Feeling as if he'd taken a punch in the guts, Jim protested, "That can't be it, can it? There's got to be a part two." There had been no attempt to make anything come right. Billy's dad didn't turn up and give his bastard brother the kicking he deserved, and his mother sure as hell wasn't going to do anything about it. She was only interested in her boyfriend.

Mum swiped at the corners of her eyes, attempting to smile. "I didn't remember it ending like that."

It was brutal, brutal enough to make Jim want to stay curled on the sofa, thoughts of football forgotten. Knees up, he put a cushion on top of his head and pulled two corners down around his ears.

Jean's hands were busy gathering up the foil from their Viscount biscuits. "I wanted to show you that you can rise above your background, not that it just -" She cut off, just like the film.

Numb, Jim stared at the place on the mantelpiece where the photograph of the four of them, all laughing, used to live. Perhaps the 'happy ending' was only ever a Polaroid. Perhaps all stories should cut to the credits like *Kes*.

"You be my exception, love," his mother was saying.

It hit him, then. He'd always thought Mum was trying to make things alright for him, but that wasn't it. All along, she'd been asking him to make everything alright for *her*. And it was too tall an order for a small boy.

CHAPTER 4:

AYISHA - JULY 2010 -
ASHFIELD COMPREHENSIVE

Stage 1 - Deal with the disclosure as it happens; ensuring that the child's immediate needs are met and that they feel supported.

Accompanied by an ear-piercing wail, the ambulance left. Ayisha watched its yellow regalia disappear from view. Several blades had been discovered, secreted in socks and waistbands.

Latex gloves held knives by the ends of their handles and dropped them into clear polythene bags, but not one had any obvious signs of blood on it. Chances were, as a police officer had speculated, the boy/s they were looking for had disappeared before Ayisha arrived on the scene. After closing ranks, eight students had been taken to the police station for questioning, their parents informed.

"No! Not my Otis."

"Not my Will. You don't understand. He's a good boy."

What parent would want to believe that their son had come to school armed? But Ayisha recalled the heated discussion at the recent staff meeting. It had centred around teachers' increased powers of search which would take effect in the autumn term. And this, the last day of the summer term!

"One of the little buggers in every class!" Mr Baker - English Department and resident voice of doom - had railed, quoting the latest statistics about the numbers of knife-carrying children.

"That's the national average," Mrs Walker, Home Economics, contributed. "In London, we can expect double. And I hardly need remind you: they have access to knives in my class -"

The room had erupted, words flying, colliding mid-air.

"You should count the sharps out and count them back in again!"

"What a farce! I haven't even got any facilities to lock them away!"

"Another Risk Assessment." As eyes flashed judiciously towards Mr Peel, the Head scribbled furiously. "Something else to look into."

Now, Ayisha wondered briefly if she should mention to the police the possibility that the knives might have come from within the school. No, if that was the case, it would be obvious. A set of six identical paring knives: that would be a scandal.

Counselling was offered to those who remained, but all the kids wanted to do was filter away, arms draped heavily around one another's shoulders. Tonight's celebrations would be subdued. Bodies clinging to each other, offering what comfort they could. But first, they had to be prised away from friends. Reluctant voices, uncertain of allegiances, gave names and addresses, details of where they could be contacted over the next couple of weeks. As she supplied her mother's address, it struck Ayisha that she had a legitimate excuse to postpone her visit. Almost immediately she felt sickened. Was she really contemplating how she might use this appalling situation to her *advantage*? A new measure of how infuriating her mother was.

Now the grounds were virtually clear, an unsettling hush had descended. It wouldn't have surprised Ayisha to see tumbleweed rolling across the quad, accompanied by the hollow breath of dry wind, the speciality of the Westerns her father used to fall asleep in front of on Sunday afternoons. Kneeling on the tarmac opposite Shamayal, Ayisha saw his hands on the ground, as if he needed something to hold on to. Angling her head, she lifted her eyes to his face. "You did really well back there. Are you OK?"

Shamayal was only fourteen. How he came to be in the quad with the older boys was a mystery, but not one the police felt deserved their overstretched resources. He sniffed, sitting back on the heels of his trainers. The look he threw her suggested that she, with her flawed knowledge of first aid, was hardly the best of judges.

"Din't have a fat lot of choice, did I?"

Whatever his vocabulary lacked, Shamayal's tone compensated for. He could clothe a word in sarcasm. Disguise disdain with respect. Ignoring his tone, Ayisha conceded that the boy had a valid point: told to kneel, he had knelt. "But you didn't panic - which is more than I can say for myself!"

"S'pose." He pulled the end of his nose twice, moved his mouth in a circle. "So, what happens now, Miss?"

"Now? Once the boys' parents have arrived, the police will question them. Hopefully, they'll make an arrest."

"That's not what I meant, is it? I want to know what happens to Jim."

Immediately, Ayisha felt her shoulders tense, aware of her duty to act on any suggestion that the boundaries of the teacher/pupil relationship had been breached. "If you mean *Mr Stevens*, he'll be rushed into surgery."

"I meant exactly what I said. Jim's my friend."

Not now: please don't make a disclosure to me while Jim is fighting for his life. Her next choice of words must be measured. Her role was to listen, not to lead. "Has Mr Stevens been assigned as your mentor?" Ayisha asked, hoping for an easy explanation.

"Din't you hear me?"

We're both in shock, she told herself. It would be a turn of phrase, no more. "Shamayal," Ayisha was firm. "Mr Stevens is *my* friend. I know he's a very helpful person to talk to but he's your teacher -"

"You don't know nuffin about it! We do stuff together." This description, combined with the boy's indignation, implied significance. "We go places together, yeah? If you really was his friend, he'd of told you. What *you* are is his colleague!"

Ayisha crushed her urge to hiss *Think what you're saying!* Surely the boy wasn't so naïve that he would be open about a friendship? Not unless there was an innocent explanation. Jim would know the boy's family, that was it! Perhaps they attended the same church.

Footsteps: a male police officer was approaching. Grabbing the opportunity for time out, Ayisha retrieved her ruined shoes, her paperback, and brushed her trousers to rid them of several clinging tarmac nuggets. She walked to meet him halfway.

"How's the boy?" he asked.

"Shaken." Ayisha's smile was a wince. "He's had a lot to take in."

The policeman glanced over her shoulder towards Shamayal. "I should give him a lift home. Explain the state he's got himself into, if nothing else!" He scanned the playground. "We're just about done here. If you want to be on your way, we'll seal the scene."

Ayisha lowered her voice. "Did the kids have much to say?"

"No one saw a thing, would you believe? To be honest, we expected as much. It'll be easier to convince them to talk in their own homes. Your Head thought you might know if Jim Stevens has any family we can contact." Ayisha's eyes followed the police officer's nod in Mr Peel's direction. He looked up from his clipboard, meeting her gaze apologetically. "The number down for next-of-kin turned out to be an ex-girl-friend's."

Ayisha looked away. What did she really know about her colleague? "And there are no contacts in his mobile?"

"Nothing obvious. We don't want to start calling people at random, not if we can help it."

Her mind strayed back to that drunken Friday evening in the *Windsor Castle*. She'd barely let Jim get a word in, too busy complaining about her mother.

"According to her, my trouble is that I cut myself off."

"Is that true?" He'd asked, as if on cue.

"If you must know, I want to decorate my living room. Until she mentioned it, I wasn't aware that there was any trouble with me at all!"

"I -"

"You want to know what her answer was?" Ayisha was aware that she had interrupted, but wanted to finish her story. "*'Internet dating? My friend tells me there's a very good website. I wrote it down for you: Asiandating - all one word - dot com. Have you got that?'* It's as if everything I've achieved counts for nothing because I don't have a husband." She had nudged the leg of his stool with the toe of one shoe. "Don't tell me *your* mother isn't demanding grandchildren?"

"I'm sure she would be." Jim absent-mindedly picked up a beer mat and ran it through his hand, rotating it onto each of its four sides on the tabletop.

Now, she winced at the memory. His conversation killer. "All I know is that his mother died some years ago," she told the police officer.

"He's got a father and an older bruvver."

At the sound of Shamayal's voice, they both pivoted. He was standing right behind them, looping the strap of an Adidas bag over his head. The square of purple sat awkwardly to one side, the strap a little too short; his blood-stained shirt untucked on one side. The boy's feet were planted wide and his hands were folded over his chest. "Can't stand to be within a mile of 'em. Least, that's what he said."

Ayisha's throat tightening, she waited for the police officer's reaction.

"Shamayal, isn't it?" he asked.

"Yeah," the boy elongated the simple word, nodding.

"You've earned yourself a lift."

Feet shuffling uncomfortably, Shamayal's trainers raked the tarmac. "No, you're alright."

"Come on. You're going to stick out like a sore thumb wandering the streets looking like that."

Shamayal glanced down at his shirt, surprised but apparently not shocked to find it blood-stained. "S'pose," he said. "Don't want to get myself arrested."

"You go," Ayisha told them both. "I'll let Mr Peel know."

As Shamayal dragged his feet away, Ayisha returned her attention to Mr Peel, the school's Designated Person for child protection. She knew the protocol: she must report her exchange with Shamayal, using his precise words.

At her approach, Mr Peel broke off from his conversation with the school manager to defer to her. "Everything under control?"

"The police are taking Shamayal Thomas home. I need -" Her mouth had dried up. Already, after the interruption from the police officer, the boy's words seemed less distinct. And Shamayal was in no immediate danger.

"You were about to say?" Mr Peel prompted, his voice weary but not unkind.

She recalled Jim's crooked, pained smile. *You.* Imagine

he didn't make it. What kind of headlines would the papers print?

"Nothing." And with a self-deprecating smile, her decision seemed to have been made. "I mean, it's just it's all been…"

Mr Peel studied her face paternally. "You look pale. Did you get yourself checked over?"

"I'm fine. Honestly."

"Why don't you get off home? We can finish up here."

"If you don't need me, perhaps…" Ayisha had the strange impression of being outside herself, of watching herself go through the motions. How surprisingly easy it was to put one foot in front of the other and walk away.

"Ayisha!"

Heat rushed to her face. Was she really so transparent? She turned, asking, "Yes?" Her voice sounded unnatural.

"I'll need your report, I'm afraid." Mr Peel's expression was apologetic. It took Ayisha a moment to realise that it was only her first aid role he was referring to.

"Of course."

"I'd love to say there's no rush, but it's best to write it while everything's still fresh. Why don't I give you my home number? Here."

How simple it was, the lie of omission. But with each moment's delay, how difficult it would be to unravel.

She took the triangular scrap of paper he offered and waved it. "I'll be in touch."

CHAPTER 5:

JIM - JULY 2010 -
ST HELIER HOSPITAL

Jim's body anaesthetised, his mind was free to wander. And, in the manner of dreams, it wandered all the way back to 1992 where it lingered on a face: the golden face of Aimee White. Lying back in the grass, his stomach muscles tightened as he lifted his head a couple of inches, squinting up at her through narrowed slits. "What kept you?"

Hands behind her back, she swung. "I've been busy, haven't I?"

At the time, as she positioned herself in the grass, unnerving him with her electrical proximity, he remembered observing that she wasn't pretty and she wasn't ugly, but somewhere in between. Just as well: if she'd been a Pamela Anderson - or even a Winona Ryder - she'd have frightened the crap out of him. But Aimee was still a girl, an older one at that, whose limbs exuded the scent of digestive biscuits and White Musk - from the Body Shop, so she told him. Now he contemplated that he found that face beautiful: its wide-spaced eyes, its constellation of freckles, its gap-toothed smile. Perhaps it was her youth that was attractive. She was still thirteen years old, but, from the way he was dressed in his favourite Ted Baker shirt and his size twelve Converse trainers, he appeared to be thirty.

"What's our robin been up to?"

"*Our* robin?"

"What? Just say if you mind me being here." She leant over him - so close he had no option but to breathe the scent of her hair - reaching across an eighteen-year divide, as vivid to him as any recent memory. "It was your place first."

They appeared to be replaying the scene: he, the thirty-year-old, she the thirteen-year-old - the child - and still, it seemed, she had the upper hand. Conscious that he was dreaming, Jim was happy to play along, reciting words he had rehearsed many times over since that six-week awakening.

His 'place' was down by the side of the railway lines. A scrubland refuge set in a backdrop of brambles and ivy; somewhere Jim had discovered when home no longer provided privacy, where his thoughts flowed uninterrupted. He was used to the silence - or *his* version of silence, comprised of train and bird and the telltale rustling of leaves.

"I don't mind," he shrugged. Better to be polite. He still wasn't sure who he was dealing with.

Obviously unconvinced, she badgered him. And, in the end, just as before, there was no choice but to play her at her own game.

"Do you mind *me* being here?" Jim shot back. "I mean, I'm not getting in your way, am I?"

"No," she replied, a small shift of her head rearranging a section of unruly curls.

He ruled the conversation surplus to requirements. "Well, then."

But she couldn't leave it alone. "I like coming here," she shrugged, toying with the seed-heads in the long grass. "With you."

A yellow and black missile zapped angrily past his face. "Is that what you're trying to get me to say?"

"What makes you think I'm trying to get you to say any-thing?" And from this Jim knew that, no matter how much she protested that she was different, he was dealing with a girl.

"You want me to say that I like you being here."

"Well, do you?" she challenged, pouting.

Jim pretended to consider her question. "Most people would hack me off by the end of the day -"

"Oh, so I don't *hack you off*?" Rolling onto her back, the girl acted as though she had the right to be offended.

"Like you said." Jim elbowed her in the ribs. "It's my spot."

They both lay back, ignoring the unfamiliar proximity of their hands; pretending to enjoy the warmth of the sun on their faces, the questioning bursts of birdsong, the low hum of winged insects.

"You see!" He pushed himself up and started stuffing things into his rucksack, one by one. His mouth twitched as he recognised his bird book, his notebooks, his chewed pencils.

"Doctor, he's getting restless."

"Keep an eye on him. We might need to top him up."

Aimee assumed an expression of surprise. "What?"

"A bloke would just take it as read that if you choose to spend time together, it must be because you like each other."

As he heaved himself to his feet, the ground vibrated. A flurry of wings, camouflaged birds broke cover. He first sensed and then heard the rush of electricity, and backed away from the railway line.

"Sit down." She patted the rough ground. Having procured an admission that he liked her, an infuriating smile rounded her face. "Why are you so upset?"

She was inviting him to stay, as though the place were hers! "I'm not upset, alr-"

A train thundered past, the force of the pressure-wave

hitting him smack in the face, tugging his hair by the roots, rocking him back on his heels, and Jim - thirty years old and a gangling six foot four - dropped to his haunches with the shock of it, the violence of it.

"*Doctor -*"

"*Alright, let's top him up.*"

He hugged his knees hard, pretending the disappearing view of the Sutton to Victoria fascinated him. This was how he imagined he would feel if a ghost had actually passed through him: not a shiver, but something that solidified on impact, a ten-tonne wall of power.

"'*The pair of legs that carried him were rickety, and there was a bias in his gait which inclined him somewhat to the left of a straight line.*' Do you like the way Hardy puts that?" She acted as if it were perfectly normal to read out loud after what was practically an argument. Still reeling from the aftershock, he wondered what new rules she had switched to. "'*Somewhat to the left of a straight line.*' Don't you think that's genius?"

Jim pictured his father, eight o'clock in the morning, staggering into the kitchen, a can of Guinness in one hand: "*Cheers, Jimbo! Breakfast.*" "Pissed," he said.

"Your trouble is you've got no poetry in your soul!"

"What's a soul?" Blood still channelling fiercely through Jim's veins, his heartbeat slowed to the speed of a car running over a pothole: bo-boom, bo-boom. "Look! The only book I've ever read that I wasn't forced to is my bird book. Other than that, it's just comics."

His awareness that this scene was not being played out in real-time allowed him to reflect that this statement was no longer true: because of her, it was no longer true.

"You don't have to read to like the way words sound," Aimee insisted, refusing to succumb to his confrontational tone.

Seeing where this was going, he shook his head and

half-laughed. "Lay off, will you!"

"It could be a song lyric, or a line from a film. Just one teeny thing." Head cocked to one side like a robin, she waited.

Jim's mouth twitched again with the memory of the lines that he recited, completing his sense of disloyalty: "There are holes in the sky..."

"...*where the rain...*" And again, he remembered being gobsmacked when she stole the line straight from his mouth. "What? You're not the only one who knows Spike Milligan! I've got a book of his poems."

Something sank. His grandfather - perhaps the person he'd trusted the most - had betrayed him. "That's a poem?" he asked.

She laughed, a sound as glorious and carefree as sunshine. "You're funny, Cheese-and-pickle Jim, you know that?"

He took the same decision now as then. There had to be rules if they were going to be friends. "Look, the thing is, my mum was never big on bedtime stories. We don't even own a bookcase."

"I get it," Aimee said, beetroot tinged. "You don't have to go on."

"No, you don't get it! Look, I'm sorry I tricked you into thinking I'm a boffin by throwing in a few Latin names -"

"Aren't you?"

"God, no! I just find remembering stuff easy."

"The way you're acting, you'd think I'd accused you of stealing or something! Remembering takes work."

"Not if you have a system, it doesn't." He registered a rustling to his left, a bird or a small rodent. "I make up stories, that's all."

A blackcap emerged, tail feathers twitching.

"Have you got one for him?"

"No brainer." He lowered his voice. "But it's a her."

"*Her*, then."

47

"Shhhh! You'll scare her off. She's a blackcap. I call them mop tops because they've got Stone Roses haircuts."

"Not the Beatles, then?"

He pulled back his head, frowning. "They were just a bunch of hippies weren't they?"

"Ha!" She fired the first syllable of an astonished laugh.

"It's *my* way of remembering, not yours!"

"Tell me, then. How come it's called a blackcap when it's brown?"

"Only the males have black tops. The females' caps are brown, but the shape's the same." She was interested. Actually interested. "I call them 'Sylvias' because that's the Latin: *Sylvia atricapilla*. It's easy to remember: Sylvia was my gran's name. Then the 'atri' bit's dead easy: I just picture the bird sitting in…?"

On cue, Sylvia retreated to a nearby branch to observe them observing her.

"A tree." Aimee's mock-bored voice said she knew she was stating the obvious.

"Next comes the 'cap'. Nothing needed for that. And for the 'illa', think of Godzilla."

Her mouth was gaping.

"What now?"

"You've made up word connections like that for every single bird?"

"Aren't you missing the point? You're the only person I know who reads because they like the sound of words!"

"That's a character flaw, is it?"

"See? You're at it again!" She was sitting on her hands, her face so close that it confused him. "*And* you keep wanting to know what I'm thinking." He ripped long strands of grass from the matted ground. "Listen, this won't come out right, but you and me," - he looked away - "We're different. Don't you get that?" And again, Jim didn't feel he should have to apologise for being who he was. He wasn't asking her to.

Having been facing in opposite directions, they turned to each other and both started speaking.

"You first," he volunteered, this tea-party politeness feeling fake. *After you. No, I insist.*

"I was just wondering if you want to borrow my Spike Milligan book." Aimee flicked her hair back off her face, a good impression of someone who didn't care either way.

"No!" He couldn't have been more appalled. "I want to go back to thinking my granddad made that poem up for me!"

"Fair enough!" Her biting tone relented. "Anyway, what were you going to say?"

"I don't *mind* that we're different. It's not like it's" - Jim paused, wincing - "bad or anything." Realising that, in her roundabout way, Aimee had tricked him into saying what she wanted to hear all along, he added, "I was only going to ask if we're still going to be friends."

But that wasn't enough: Aimee had to have the last word. "Jim," she turned on him. "Just because you *haven't* done something before doesn't mean you *can't*. Look what you've learned all on your own." She pointed to his book. "I bet you could do most things if you want to badly enough."

CHAPTER 6:

AYISHA - JULY 2010 - AT HOME

Not knowing whether the incident would make the national news, Ayisha decided she must warn her mother. It wouldn't be fair to let her see footage of Ashfield Comprehensive and leave her wondering. She was frustrated to hear the ansaphone kick in:

"We're not home at the moment, but leave your name and number and we'll get back to you."

This wasn't the sort of thing you could leave a message about. "Oh, hi Mum. It's me." She addressed a small sandstone figurine on the bookcase in her living room. A figure that might have been a souvenir from an exotic country, but came from her local Oxfam shop. It was difficult to know what to say next. "Do you think you could -?"

"Hello, darling. Listen to me, all out of breath!"

"You're there -"

"You caught me doing a spot of spring cleaning - or should that be *summer* cleaning? I don't know. And your father is waging chemical warfare on the dandelions. We're both really excited about seeing you."

So sweetly sing-song. Ayisha squeezed her eyes shut, preparing for the inevitable onslaught. "About that, Mum. I'm afraid I won't be able to visit this week. Everything's on hold."

"Are you ill?" The voice - noticeably chillier - suggested that this would be the only acceptable explanation.

"No, nothing like that. In fact, it's not the sort of thing I'd usually worry you with over the phone -"

"Oh?"

"Promise me you won't overreact?"

Her mother's voice was clipped, preparing to be judgmental. "I promise to react appropriately, as I always do."

Appropriately? Having been a witness - to the aftermath, at least - Ayisha still wasn't sure what the appropriate response was. "There was an incident - on the last day of term, would you believe? One of the teachers was hurt when he stepped in to break up a fight."

"Hurt? But he's OK?"

She tried to pitch her reply midway between reassurance and making her mother understand that she couldn't just drop everything. "He's hardly OK, but he's made it through the night. The knife -"

"A *knife?*" Ayisha imagined her mother sinking into her favourite green armchair, the one by the 'real flame' gas fire. "What kind of animals carry *knives* to school?"

"Thankfully, only a small -"

"So he's not hurt: he's seriously injured!"

"They missed his heart, but yes, they've done a serious amount of damage. And as I was the first teacher to arrive on the scene -"

"You were there? Ayisha! My God!"

"No, Mum. I arrived *after* it happened. But I need to write a report for the Head, and the police want to speak to me." Every time she opened her mouth, Ayisha's collection of lies grew. She felt obliged to stay, that was true, but her report was already written. Posted through Mr Peel's front door with a note, for fear that something in her manner might have given her away, a fear equalled only by the possibility that guilt might cause her to blurt something out to her mother. The minute she set foot in her parents' house, Mum would detect that something was wrong and she'd chip away until she wore Ayisha down. "To be honest, I don't want to go anywhere until I know Jim's out of danger." That, at least, was the truth.

"Not your friend, Jim? The history teacher you've told us so much about?"

Ayisha only remembered mentioning that they'd gone for a drink. Perhaps it was her mother's implied suggestion that she was sad and friendless that had made her invite Jim to the pub in the first place, just so that she could report: *I am not a failure; I managed to bribe a man to spend a couple of hours with me with the offer of free beer.*

"And now I suppose you'll have to spend your summer looking for another job -"

"Who said anything about another job?" Again, Ayisha felt as if her thoughts were being tapped, although her reason was very different from the one her mother would be thinking of. She knew she wouldn't be able to sleep for fear of discovery.

"Well, you can't possibly be thinking of going back? Not now you know it isn't safe!"

"This sort of thing could happen anywh-"

"Not here, Ayisha. Think about it: if you were nearer to us, we wouldn't have to worry about you walking home on your own at night."

"I don't go walking about on my own at night!"

"But that's just the point. You're entitled to live and work somewhere you feel safe."

At this juncture, Ayisha became surplus to requirements. "Mum! I. Feel. Safe -"

"It's so very sad. What makes children want to kill each other?"

"This is an isolated incident."

"Don't patronise me, Ayisha. I watch the news. This sort of thing is on the increase. You know better than I do that the worst of it takes place in London."

"The school is taking precautions to make sure it doesn't happen again." Ayisha recited lines, lines she wondered if she actually believed. She saw birthday cards that needed taking down from the mantelpiece. Two weeks was more than enough. "And anyway, I have no intention of leaving! I refuse to live my life as if something bad's going to happen. It's that attitude that has kids carrying knives in the first place."

"So you admit they're all at it."

"That's not what I meant, Mum!"

"What I've never understood is why? It isn't your background. There are plenty of schools in Wiltshire in need of teachers. Good schools."

Wiltshire: a million miles away. For a millisecond it sounded tempting, but no. All the time that her parents insisted her bedroom was waiting - *just as you left it* - it felt more like a threat than an offer. *This is my home*, she staked her claim. *Even if it might not look like much.* When her parents visited for the first time, they seemed to fill her living room, turning around and looking as if there was nowhere for them to sit. But here Ayisha's identity was not just that of someone's daughter. She was judged as herself, not the wink and the, 'I know your father.' To go back to Wiltshire would be...

"It's all very worthy, this wanting to make a 'difference'. But what about us? You know how we worry."

"Please!" Ayisha picked up the card from her mother, opened it. *May God soften the pillow you rest your head on at night; may he smooth the path you walk by day.* She sighed. "Why do we have to argue?"

"Oh, I suppose you'd prefer it if I hid my feelings!"

"This was supposed to be a quick call to say that I can't make any plans yet."

"No! To *break* your plans. You always come for the first week of the holidays." Her mother's voice was choked. "I was so looking forward -"

Knowing that her mother would have said '*looking after my little girl*' irritated. She was a grown woman. And there was little point protesting that, just because she'd gone home for the first week of the holidays for the past two years, doesn't mean she always will.

"I didn't want this to happen!" Recognising in her protest something one of the kids had said to her, she relented. "And I *will* come. In a couple of weeks' time."

Ayisha found herself trying to pacify a dead line. Letting out a frustrated cry, she hurled the handset across the living room, paced the Turkish rug furiously and then threw herself down on the sofa, finding her mother's card crumpled in her fist. If she was the one to phone back, Ayisha would find herself agreeing to something she didn't feel she should have to do. But if she didn't? Well, she would have committed the ultimate sin: upsetting her mother. Even smoothed out, the card refused to stand. It was a lose-lose situation. Her mother wouldn't call. And Ayisha would have to tolerate her father's lecture on how disappointed in her he was.

Shamayal was right, damn it! Jim Stevens was a colleague. She remembered the boy's pronunciation: the hardness of the 'k'. A suitable match for his assessment of her! And now, because of Jim, she had broken the rules, rules necessary not only to protect pupils but teachers too. The sad fact was that innocent friendships - supportive friendships - had become taboo. The teacher who used to invite Ayisha and her sixth form friends home for coffee, offering a safe refuge where smoking wasn't frowned upon and there was always a shoulder to cry on, would probably lose her job these days. Having put her career on the line for Jim, Ayisha must wait to see if he comes round before hearing what he has to say for himself. And waiting is something Ayisha has never been terribly good at.

CHAPTER 7:

JIM - JULY 2010 -
H.D.U., ST HELIER HOSPITAL

Jim was aware of voices floating in and out, some near, some further away. Of busy hands. The blue-orange hue inside his eyelids. The assault of familiar and unfamiliar smells: sweat, disinfectant and something that he couldn't - or perhaps didn't want to - identify. And of pain. Excruciating pain, spreading like the warm glow of whisky.

Trying to lift a heavy eyelid, it took Jim a moment to identify the flickering dark feathers as his eyelashes.

"Nurse! Nurse! I saw him move. I think he's back with us!" That unmistakable tone: the last he expected to hear.

Assaulted by bright light, Jim's head swam. *If this is what it feels like to be awake,* he thought, *I would rather sleep.* Instinctively, he shrank away from a touch of his shoulder.

"Don't shake him, Mr Stevens. If you dislodge his chest tube we'll be back to square one." A no-nonsense voice. "Wait for him to come round. And don't expect too much. He'll be very confused."

"I always said you were a fighter, son!"

These words distracted Jim from the mystery of how his father came to be in the same room as him. All of his energy was diverted to the impossible reconciliation of his father's statement and his memory of what was actually said: *"It wouldn't be much of a fight. You're not worth the energy."*

Frank Stevens had been the sort of father who expected to be stood up to. The thought of having weaklings for sons would have embarrassed him no end. Tall for his age, never one to walk away from a fight, Nick enjoyed the sport of egging him on. They called it playing, but both father and son had competitive streaks; neither would back down. With Jim's mother out of the way, they practised wrestling moves on each other, a rug in the living room their ring. Until he turned fourteen, Nick's speed was no match for his father's bulk, and Frank wasn't one to go easy on an opponent, even if it was his teenage son.

"Stop!" Jim would yell from the safety of the doorway. "You're hurting him!"

"Best way for him to learn," Frank would growl.

If Nick was injured, he never bore a grudge. That he could stand up to a grown man was proof he was tough enough. He'd seen Barry McGuigan beat far heavier men.

Once Nick turned fourteen, it was payback time. Jim bounced on the sofa, punching the air and shouting, "Yes! Come on!" as his brother won his first fight. Frank was pinned down with one arm twisted behind his back. He looked up, a vein standing proud on his forehead, a snarl curling his top lip: "Don't know why you're laughing. You're next, sunshine."

Now, compelled to protest, Jim found he could only produce a dry rasp. "When?"

"What's that, son?" Frank's voice was animated.

He opened his eyes a second time. The light was violent, everything brilliant white, apart from two faces, one pale, one dark, beyond the blur of his vision.

"I think he asked you 'when?'" the second voice chortled, a riotous duck-like noise.

"Hear that, eh? He hasn't seen his old man in years and now he wants to pick a fight!"

Jim had never been his brother, that much was painfully clear. With Nick out of the way, Frank missed his sparring partner. He would clench his fists at shoulder-height when he cornered Jim in the narrow hall - "Put 'em up" - punching the air on either side of his son's face in time to *The Eye of the Tiger*. But, with Jim still flinching, Frank would blow on his knuckles, the tails of his dressing gown trailing: "Nah! You're not worth the energy."

"Jim," a deep, rich voice was saying, pulling him back to the present. "I'm Ella. I've been looking after you for the last couple of days. Do you know where you are?"

"Am-I-in-hell?" he groaned.

She beamed a tooth-filled smile. "No, darlin'. This here's St Helier. You're in Recovery."

Close, he thought.

"And she's your guardian angel," his father interrupted.

Attempting to raise his head, Jim experienced a new level of pain ripping through his left-hand side.

"Don't try to move," Ella purred. "You've had a serious accident. Your lung's been punctured. We've put a tube in your chest to inflate it. The doctor will be along shortly to explain everything."

"An accident?" his father protested loudly. "I wouldn't have got a special permit for an accident!"

So nothing had changed. Even as a child, Jim had recognised the pattern. His father would spend a couple of weeks hanging round the flat before he got bored and ventured out to the betting shops, gambling money he fooled himself he would have when his horse came in. Faced with the prospect of admitting to his wife that debt had caught up with him, an old associate would tempt him with a 'business proposition'. It was then that the arguments escalated. When Frank got caught, as he invariably did, it ended the weeks of tension. Watching him being led away, Jean always cried. As an adult, Jim understood that his mother felt so guilty for expecting him to let them down, she convinced herself she was to blame. And now here he was, taking the credit!

"My son's a bleedin' hero. That's what they said on the radio."

Jim didn't know how much more of this he could take: a hero? "What-are-you-talking-about?"

"If it wasn't for my boy, there'd be one more dead teenager! They should give you a medal. Hey, Jim! There's a man outside wants to take your picture for the papers."

Ella sighed, saying, "He'll have to wait. The police will want to speak to you before the reporters get a look in."

A foggy memory tried to make itself known: of running, of raising one hand. More afraid of not remembering than remembering, Jim followed the thread: stepping between two boys, then staggering, clutching his chest. He heard himself groan: he was lying on the ground, looking up at faces: Shamayal and Ayisha...

Blinking, he saw that it was Ella who was bending over his hospital bed, eyes full of concern. "First things first: I'll give you something for the pain, Jim. Give your son some space, Mr Stevens. We haven't saved his life so that you can suffocate him."

Jim's stomach lurched like a belly-dancer's. "I'm-gonnur-be-sick," he slurred, managing to turn his head sideways. Even this small movement pulled on the tube, causing a jabbing in his chest. Effort disproportionate, he dry-retched, producing a thin trail of foul-tasting saliva.

"I got you," Ella said, and he felt something that turned out to be the cardboard edge of a kidney-shaped dish graze his chin. "That's the anaesthetic wearing off." His mouth was wiped for him as if he was a small child, but the miserable green taste of bile remained.

"Dance with me, nurse. I feel like dancing."

Letting out a small shriek, Ella turned to a figure beyond Jim's range of vision. "Can't you control your father?"

"Never have been able to. No point trying." Another ancient echo: another image of happy families. His teenage brother, Nick, straddling his father's prostrate form, twisting his arm tighter: *"Leave Jim alone, you hear?"*

"I'm trying to give your son some morphine, Mr Stevens, and you're not helping."

Jim felt hands alight on his arm, pressure and then the pain subsiding, replaced by a paralysing sensation he hadn't the strength to fight.

"Better?" Ella turned away from him. "If you want to say hello to your brother, do it now." She beckoned. "I'm going to run some tests in a minute, and then he'll need his rest before those vultures get their hands on him."

"Jim." The face hovering over him was fuller than when he last saw it. The hair was thinning. He hadn't been surprised to see his dad looking old - his friends' fathers were all in their sixties. But it was shocking that Nick was no longer eighteen, as he was when Jim last saw him. "Can he hear me?"

"He can hear you." The nurse drew the curtains around the bed with sharp little movements.

"Jim, it's Nick." The face moved out of range. "Are you sure? He's not saying anything."

"You wouldn't be saying a lot for yourself if you'd had your lung punctured for you."

"Mate!" Back in view, he grinned sheepishly. "We thought we'd lost you."

There was only one thing Jim wanted to say. With difficulty, he moved his lips. "Where-were-you-at-Mum's-funeral?"

"Don't wear yourself out," the nurse fussed. "You're going to need your strength."

"I'll shift out your way." Nick's Adam's apple moved. "I'll be back to see how you're doing later."

Jim closed his eyes. He thought he had said, "Don't bother," but, sinking, he realised that he may have just thought it.

"Son!" Jim jolted as his hair was ruffled. "How you doing?"

"Let's be having you, Frank," a voice called out from the direction of the door.

"My chariot awaits. Any chance of a swift half on the way back, boys?" The request was good-natured.

"'Fraid not. They'd never forgive us if we didn't get you back in time for your dinner."

He shrugged. "Can't blame a man for trying." Turning back to Jim, his tone was confidential. "I don't know when I'll be able to get out again, but I was glad I was here when you came round." Sniffing loudly, his father cleared his throat. "Like seeing you being born all over again. Good on you, son. Your mother would have been proud. Very proud."

Jim closed his eyes, felt tears overflow as his father walked away, confused as to who they were for.

"Just the two of us now," Ella was clucking. "I'm going to do your bloods. See how it's settling down. We had to lend you a pint or two of someone else's. There now. Your daddy's quite the handful, isn't he?"

Jim's mother used to tell him he got his cheek from his father. It wasn't much of a legacy. He recalled the last conversation they shared.

"Was Dad like that when you met him?" he'd asked, old enough to deserve an honest reply. The almost skeletal hand that Jim held so gently was marked with the points of numerous needles.

"It was at a school disco. I'd had my eye on him for weeks." Conversation paused while her body was racked by coughing. He didn't tell her not to talk, not when he had good reason to think it might be their last opportunity. "He was fifteen, and as cheeky as you like. A real character, and I fell for him. I thought he'd come round when he had family. As it was, I ended up worrying enough for the both of us. Your father missed out on so much of your childhood. Either he wasn't there or he… well, he never felt the connection with you that he did with your brother."

"I wasn't Nick, that was for sure."

"But you must remember how he taught you to do up your school tie?"

He had shaken his head.

"Honestly? Your dad hadn't been around to teach you how to ride a bike. He never really forgave me for letting your granddad do something he saw as his right. So when he said that next time there was something you needed to be shown, he wanted to do it, I said, 'I'll hold you to that.'"

"Red, white and blue. Diagonal stripes."

"You *do* remember!"

Jim winced: his memory had been of the tie, no more.

She'd smiled. "Your dad was so proud to see you looking so grown up."

And that was when it had come back to Jim. They had been in the governor's office.

"Right, you want to start with the wide part on your right-hand-side. Your right-hand-side, son. That's your left. That's better! Now you bring the wide side over the top of the narrow side like so. That's it. Bring the wide part under the narrow part, like this. It's always the wide part that moves…"

"…God only knows how many times he had you practise, but you never forgot. And when he was happy, he crouched down and whispered -"

But it was his father's voice Jim heard: *"Now you're a real man, Jim. A real man."*

And Jim had found that his mother was comforting him. "I've never seen him so proud of you as he was that day," she patted his hand, misinterpreting the reason for his tears. "Do you think your brother will visit?"

"I'm sure he will, Mum."

Touring the local pubs, Jim had finally managed to locate someone who promised to get a message to Nick - but there was no reply. And very soon afterwards it was too late.

CHAPTER 8:

JIM - APRIL 2010 - AT HOME

"No child or young person should be invited into the home of an adult who works with them, unless the reason has been firmly established and agreed with parents or carers and a senior manager or Head teacher."

Shuffling into the kitchen, Jim bristled. The sight of anyone seated in his chair - the one with the best view of the small garden - would have discomforted him. He protected his privacy fiercely. The fact was, Shamayal was also a pupil. And rules were rules.

"Mornin', Sir," the boy said brightly, looking up from the book he had been thumbing through. Jim recognised the small volume of British birds he kept handy for reference. "You overslept?"

Jim located the blackbird that was trilling outside, conversational and enquiring. Suddenly conscious that his dressing gown was hanging open, he saw how easily the situation might be misconstrued. "I thought you might have gone," he said, hoping the hint would be taken.

"Din't want to leave without sayin' goodbye, did I?" *Leave* was pronounced as 'leaf', crisp and autumnal. "How rude would that be?"

"I thought you'd have somewhere you needed to be."

"No place specific. Saturday, innit?"

Jim smiled wryly at the *specifiK*. "I'll just grab some clothes. Did yours dry?"

"I've got to be honest, they could be drier."

"That wasn't exactly your typical April shower."

"How's that foot of yours?" the boy asked Jim as he returned, dressed in Levis and a t-shirt.

"Fine." He extracted two cartons from inside the fridge door - one of milk, another of Tropicana - and placed them in the middle of the table. In fact, his foot wasn't fine: since he had removed a glass splinter with tweezers it had been throbbing.

After filling the kettle, Jim reached for the bread bag.

"You're down to the crusts." The boy examined the pictures in the book studiously. "Hope you don't mind. I made toast."

"No problem." Grinding his teeth, Jim opened an upper cupboard. A cafetiere and mugs presented themselves. "Will you have coffee if I make a pot?"

"That stuff rots your stomach somethink chronic."

"You're probably right." He took a seat opposite the boy. "I drink too much caffeine, that's for sure."

Shamayal eyed him intently. "No disrespec', Sir, but I ain't all that surprised you got no girlfriend."

Jim was taken aback. It was true: girlfriends had been few and far between. A girl would have to show a great deal of interest before he'd issue a cautious, 'If you're not doing anything…' His mind settled on Lisa Flannigan, a college girl Jim had admired from behind a weighty Tudor history long before she noticed him. A natural brunette. Confident enough not to plaster herself in make-up. Often found in the library after everyone else had relocated to the bar.

"We seem to be the only two left," Lisa had said as the

lights in the corridor were switched off one by one.

"Hm?" He'd looked up, pretending not to have noticed.

"Fancy a drink?"

Convinced that the only reason for her offer was that any company was preferable to nursing a half of lager alone, Jim's reaction was that of someone caught misbehaving. "I - I have to get this essay in tomorrow."

"I'll give you one more chance," she said, bending so close to his ear that he could hear her tongue click against the roof of her mouth. "I don't like being turned down twice."

The next day she had scraped back the chair opposite his. Distracted by the way one of her feet gave chase to its lost shoe, each new paragraph appeared to be exactly the same as the last. He spent much of the day re-reading Mark Smeaton's confession to his affair with Anne Boleyn, the image of Smeaton creeping into the Queen's bedchamber supple-mented by the dark outline of Lisa's thighs. Knowing the man's grisly fate lent a sense of inevitability to the afternoon, but it was only when Jim showed signs of packing up that she'd acknowledged him, saying, "Last chance. How about it?"

Jim had thought the evening a disaster but, when he clammed up, Lisa said she found it 'sweet'. He'd suggested a follow-up date because it seemed rude not to. The same etiquette demanded he slept with her. Everybody wants to believe they're irresistible. Why should he be the one to disillusion her? And it had been glorious for two sleepless nights, two lazy days, but when it fizzled out Jim experienced the same relief he felt when his father was led away: a return to normality.

Shamayal's presence, here in his kitchen - a boy who had been mistaken for his son - gave Jim a heightened sense that time was passing him by; that perhaps he should take tonight's date seriously. "How do you know I don't have a girlfriend?"

There was a knowing sigh from Shamayal. "I see what I

see, don't I?" The shake of his head suggested it was a hopeless case he saw. For his part, Jim saw that the boy needed to start shaving. However close to home he hit, much of the swagger was pretence.

"For one thing, I don't think a woman's set foot in this place for a long time."

"Is that right?"

Clearly, Shamayal interpreted Jim's folded arms as a challenge. "That's right. You see, women, they like to leave their little reminders." Except that he pronounced it 'likkle'. "You find their pink toothbrush and their *Impulse* in your bathroom cabinet. They plant their *Pussycat Dolls* and their *Take That* bang in the middle of your CD collection. They leave their DVDs of *Love, Actually* and *PS I Love You* on the coffee table to hint at what they want to watch. They put their bottle of white wine in the fridge, next to the milk."

"*I* like white wine!"

"Whatever." His laugh was deep like Frank Bruno's, a 'hee, hee, hee', that he seemed to be trying on for size. "They pin photographs of themselves in bikinis on your noticeboard. It's territorial, innit? Spells out that any other woman who invites herself back for coffee is treadin' on someone else's turf. I don't see nothin' like that."

"Well, Sherlock, it sounds as if you have more experience in this sort of thing than I do."

"Are you surprised, man? The binoculars? All these bird books? Makes you look creepy!"

"I'm not going to apologise for my hobby." The boy needed to know the alternatives to playing the tough guy. "Anyway, we 'creeps' are called *twitchers.* "

"See! Even that name freaks me out." Shamayal's elbows pressed further forwards. "Are you gay or somethink?"

Although Jim shook his head with disbelief, the leap from hobby to bold assumption wasn't new to him. Still, he would never have asked that of a teacher. He replied with a rebellious, "Would it bother you if I was?" And again, he saw how something said in jest might easily be misconstrued.

"ME?" It was as if Jim had accused the boy of an outrage. "No, I'm cool with all that. You express yourself whatever way you want."

"I'm not."

"So, sort your act out, man! You're not that bad lookin'. You got a good job. A nice enough pad. You could get Mr Stevens some action. Hee, hee, hee." Shamayal's eyes settled critically on the Smeg Union Flag fridge - an extravagant buy - its proportions swamping the room. "Except that's got to go. Girls don't like that sort of shit."

Up until then, Jim had thought his purchase - admittedly made while the European Cup was on - rather cool.

"Kettle's boiled," the boy said, matter of factly.

Welcoming the opportunity for a breather, Jim added two generous scoops to the pot, inhaling the rich roasted aroma. Shamayal's eyes lit up as Jim returned with his plate of toasted crusts and the cafetiere.

"Hey, can I do the plunger?"

Jim surrendered, saying, "I thought you didn't like coffee."

"I don't." The boy grinned, claiming the cafetiere as if it were an exam paper he wanted to protect. "So, who's the man and the woman in the picture?"

Ambushed by another subject-change, Jim turned to the cork noticeboard. "That's my mum and my granddad: her father."

"Thought it must be," Shamayal nodded. "Shame you don't take after her. Hey, Sir, I din't mean to -"

"No, no." Jim checked his expression. "I'm more than happy to talk about Mum." So many people avoided the subject. "It's just... well, you know what it's like... you can't help thinking, can you?"

The boy bunched up his mouth and nodded seriously. "What if she was still here."

Jim recognised that his own situation was not dissimilar to the boy's. It might be the best opportunity he would get to ask about Shamayal's family. "Exactly. That's my favourite picture of the two of them. My grandfather was around more than my dad." Looking at his grandfather's face, Jim ventured, "I think my dad was probably a lot like yours."

Shamayal put both hands on the plunger, one on top of the other. "Hee, hee, hee. Man United supporter?"

"Away a lot. Drunk." Seeing the boy's eyes flash darkly, Jim judged it was too early to say, *Handy with his fists*. "But Granddad - he was a gentleman."

Shamayal's recovery swift, the mocking manner returned with a vengeance. "Posh?"

"God, no! He had a face full of stubble and tattoos up to his armpits. I meant in the old-fashioned sense. He was born at a time when showing manners and respecting his elders weren't seen as weaknesses."

Shamayal looked doubtful. This definition implied a loss of face.

"Granddad understood me better than anyone else." Jim found himself smiling. "He was just old enough to remember what it was like to be really young."

"That don't make no sense, Sir."

The ice-cream van's *Greensleeves* filtered in through the kitchen window, providing a soundtrack for a string of welcome memories: tadpoles in a jam jar; the new season's shiniest conkers skewered and knotted on strings; the telling of ghost stories as he sat in the tatty green armchair in his granddad's shed on the allotment, the nub of a candle welded onto an old lid from a paint can; sledging on tea-trays down uneven tracts of snow; the old man's wink; jumpers that smelled of bonfires; Saturday morning trips to the sweet shop for supplies of Space Dust. But Shamayal wouldn't even have heard of Space Dust. How could he draw him in?

"He built me my first bike with parts rescued from the dump, put back together again in his shed and sprayed red."

"You must of been seriously strapped."

"Compared to what kids have now, maybe." Try telling a teenager who thinks he can't live without the latest trainers and gadgets, when he has already seen Jim's cache, that it was never *things* that were important. When did that change?

"*Let's go down the Co-op. They've got a new chest freezer and I've asked Stan to put the box by for us.*"

"*It's the biggest one I've ever seen! How are we going to get it home?*"

"*We'll turn it upside down, see, and carry it on our heads, like a canoe; me at the front; you at the back.*"

"Where d'you go?" The boy was snapping his fingers directly in front of Jim's face. "I lost you for a moment."

"Dreaming." He poured himself a large coffee, but the truth was Jim was never anchored securely in the present. Often, he would look in the shaving mirror, surprised to see an adult staring back.

"I was aksin' if you see much of your granddaddy these days."

Finding himself with a view of his folded arms and the table top, Jim felt as if the stuffing had been knocked out of him. But how could he expect the boy to give a little if he clammed up every time Shamayal asked a question? "He died."

Embarrassed, the boy shuffled in his seat.

"It happened in his garden. A neighbour found a robin standing guard on his fork handle. I can't imagine any other bird doing that." Jim was touched to see Shamayal reach for the milk carton and angle it above his mug with an enquiring look. He seemed to have acquired a robin of his own. "Thanks."

"That sucks, man." Shamayal said, as Jim drank deeply. "How old was you?"

"Ten." He sheltered the mug in both hands. "It was the year Palace beat Liverpool in the semis. One for the underdogs. My granddad was a huge Eagles' fan and he had taken me to my first game. We won 4-3. Super Alan Pardew scored the final goal. One of the Palace fans had a banner saying, 'Thank you, God. Now I can die in peace.' Granddad must have taken it literally."

In the pause that followed, Jim remembered how he had saved his tears until after the finals, which he watched on his own, sinking into a bean bag, convinced that his granddad would send him a sign. When Palace lost to Man U in the replay, Jim knew that the extra star his mother had pointed out in the night sky was just a satellite.

"I never met my grandparents." This was what Jim had wanted and yet now Shamayal's words were a distraction. "Fact, the only family I know is my parents."

Sipping his coffee, he forced himself to focus. "Don't they stay in touch with relatives?"

"Mum used to send Christmas cards. My dad don't bother. Says he left all that behind for a reason."

"And where is home?"

Fuelled by anger, Shamayal's accent was exaggerated. "You know where I live! You turnin' round an' sayin' I don't belong?"

"I didn't mean it like that. I just thought you might have connections you'd like to explore."

"They'd be strangers, wouldn't they? That's if they're still around." Shamayal's hands, flat on the surface of the table, flickered. "You can't get time back, can you?"

"No." Jim was happy to let silence take root.

"Wanna do somethink?" The boy knocked against the

table leg as he sat up.

Unaccustomed to dramatic mood changes, Jim cringed. "I've got boring stuff to do today. Housework, mainly."

Rejected, Shamayal scraped his chair back. "You should jus' say if you don't want to."

He hated to have to spell it out, but it needed to be done: "Shamayal, you must realise that we can't hang out like friends."

"Don't see why not. You said it yourself. We're not so different."

"Listen to me: I'm your teacher. Even you being here?" Jim looked about the room, shaking his head. "If anyone at school were to find out, I could lose my job." *And I worked too hard to throw it all away*, he reflected.

"Who's going to tell? I'm not, if that's what you're bovvered about."

"That's not *all* I'm worried about," Jim ventured. "The things you told me last night. What I saw? You know I have a duty to report them."

"You don't need to do that, Sir." The boy's voice was stubborn. "I'm fine."

Deliberately softening his own, Jim persevered: "You were planning to sleep rough. That's not exactly fine."

"From what you was sayin' earlier, sounds like you din't always get along with your old man."

"We're not talking about me."

"I can take care of myself. What's more, I keep clear of trouble and my grades - well they're not brilliant, OK, but they could be a whole lot worse."

Jim had a pretty good idea what would happen if he informed the school's Designated Person. Shamayal's home-life would be investigated. Either the boy and his father would be subjected to ongoing monitoring, or Shamayal would be taken into care.

"I say we both keep quiet," the boy said.

Jim knew that he couldn't promise - or expect - confidentiality. He opened his mouth to speak but the boy cut in.

"See, you don't know me. I'm good at coverin' my tracks. I got your back. Let me tell you what I'm willin' to do for you. We start a new gang. Very exclusive. You and me."

Jim sat forwards, elbows on knees, hands clasped in the space in between, laughing in a way that was painful to him. Why must he distance himself when he was most needed? It was wrong, so wrong. "I don't make the rules."

"You don't have to make up your mind right now. I'm goin' to leave you on your own, that's what I'm goin' to do. But promise you'll do one thing for me, Sir." Jim looked up to see the boy pacing from side to side. "If you decide you gotta pick up that phone, you tell me first so that I can disappear myself. Because I ain't havin' none of that. No way."

Seeing the boy's tortured expression, Jim knew he had to take him at his word. And if he was to take him at his word, he couldn't make the call. "OK. But you've got to promise you'll ask me for help if you're in trouble."

"Fair deal. Do we spit or just shake?"

"Actually," Jim took the dry hand the boy offered, "I've got to get a move on. You may not believe this but I've got someone coming to dinner tonight."

"Not a date?"

"Maybe."

"My man!" Shamayal nodded approvingly. "I take it back. You eatin' in here? Because we've got to pack away them books."

Under no circumstances should pupils assist with chores or tasks in the home of an adult who works with them. "You don't need to do that -"

But the boy had already picked the small pile up and was

taking it through to the living room, still fragrant with damp sock and the musty smell of sleep. The empty sleeping bag lay discarded like a snakeskin. "Here, right?" Shamayal pointed to the empty shelf space, then paused in front of the large framed photograph over the fireplace. "I bin meanin' to aks about that. When I woke up it was starin' right at me. It's some kinda owl, right?"

"A barn owl." Aimee's owl, to be specific, because that is how Jim thought of it. Looking at the photograph afresh, he was still struck by the image: the bird's talons extended, its whole body taut as it landed on a slim post.

"Right, right. The wings, all spread out and that?" The boy mused. "They're kind of like an angel's."

Funny kind of angel. If that's what she was. "In some cultures, people think they become owls after they die. That would make them ghosts."

"Ghosts? Yeah, I get that."

Standing looking at the owl, Jim lost a moment - just as he sometimes did when driving long-distance. His trance was broken by Shamayal clapping him on the back. The boy's jacket was slung over one shoulder. "And while I think of it, don't get started on your stories."

He followed the boy down the hall. Although Shamayal thrust his hands deep into the pockets of his jeans, the seat remained baggy and low on his hips. From the thighs downwards they were tightly fitted. Jim looked down at his comfortable 501s with renewed affection. "No?"

Reaching the door Shamayal turned, shook his head. "Girls? They like to do the talkin'. 'Bout themselves, mostly." He prodded Jim's chest playfully, then slapped him lightly under his chin. *Made you look.* "Just nod every now and then, pretend like you're listenin', know what I mean?"

As the boy shuffled into the lobby, Jim said, "Lucky for me

you happened to be here."

Without turning, the boy casually raised one hand, then opened the front door. "Laters."

Watching Shamayal walk away, Jim worried what the boy would face when he went home - *if* he went home. It seemed more than likely that he would wander the streets. Challenging a sense of growing unease, he tried to reassure himself: *you did the right thing. What else* could *you have done?*

CHAPTER 9:

JIM - APRIL 2010

But Jim was restless after Shamayal left. Having had his possessions analysed, as he nosed the humming Dyson into corners and under chairs, Jim couldn't help questioning what they said about him: the floorboards he had sanded; his experimentation with olive in the bedroom; the brilliant white of the living room as a backdrop for Aimee's owl; especially the Union Flag of the fridge door. To be honest, it was so rare for Jim to find himself firmly focused on the present that he felt in need of distraction. After throwing on an old t-shirt and some shorts, he perched on his bed and doubled over to check the plaster on the sole of his foot and tie the laces of his new Adidas Supernovas. Ghosts confronted Jim at every turn, not just in his kitchen, where the occasional glass got broken (although, some might have blamed the trains). There was little point in hiding. Better to meet them head on.

Ordinarily, pounding the pavements would have been a good way to stop thinking. His foot appeared to be bearing up. Jim concentrated on his breathing, the length of his stride, the pumping of his arms. But soon these things took care of themselves, and his mind strayed to the boy. Just fourteen, and the only relative whose whereabouts he knew was his father: often absent; otherwise drunk. It was something Jim wished he didn't know so much about.

Rounding two corners brought him within view of the ponds. A row of Mediterranean gulls balanced on the metal chain overhanging the water's edge. Others bobbed about, tail feathers like the black sails of pirate ships. The honking of Canada geese competed with Saturday afternoon traffic. Occasionally straining their necks to filter the water, the fleet swam in choreographed synchrony trailed by V-shaped wakes. Smaller birds that hadn't learned how to surf were projected off course. One rebel goose spread its dirty brown wings, generating enough momentum to launch itself onto dry land. It shook its tail feathers free of water, a quiver coursing through its body like an unscratched itch. Approaching menacingly, closing the gap, the goose held its head low, neck snaking, bulk swaying from side to side with each black scaled step. It snatched at the grass, blinking; white eyelids standing out - a coalminer's face.

It was as if nothing had changed over the past nineteen years. And yet everything had changed - as the shapes of cars queuing on the road built for nothing wider than a horse and cart testified. He sniffed the air, hayfeverish with pollen. Soon enough it would be summer; a string of anniversaries.

This is where Aimee White had asked him, "Know much about water birds?"

Outside his comfort zone, Jim fell back on humour. "My granddad used to tell this joke. 'What's the difference between a duck?'"

"I don't know. What *is* the difference between a duck?" she droned, feigning boredom.

"One of its legs is both the same."

Her nose wrinkled. "I don't get it."

As he ran on, leaving the echo of their childish laughter

behind, a pair of swans sailed serenely from the far side of the small island, their necks arched elegantly, their heart-shaped wings displaying the delicacy of their feathers. And again, Aimee's voice insisted on haunting him. "Now that's what I call a proper bird."

"They can fly as high as Mount Everest." He awarded himself another point.

"How can they measure that sort of thing?"

"Pilots reported it."

"What? *We're cruising at an altitude of 29,000 feet.*" Spoken through a clenched fist, her voice was distorted. *"And... just one moment... I don't believe it! Isn't that a swan?"*

Jogging on the spot, Jim waited for a break in the traffic to cross the road dissecting the two ponds. Turning right at an iron-gated entrance in a red-brick wall, he ran over a stone bridge. Here, coots swam among mallards and gulls, their nests small islands of sticks. Batches of chicks, small balls of squeaking black fluff with red faces, struggled to keep up with Brylcreemed parents. Jim's footfalls displaced the inevitable pigeons. They lifted and settled to purr and coo elsewhere, heads bobbing up and down to a strange rhythm.

A grey heron stood in the shallows at the top of a small waterfall. Whilst mallards darted about, scooping up crusts thrown inaccurately overarm by an anorak-trussed toddler, he alone was watchful, knowing he only had to extend his neck and the food was his. No doubt it was a different heron, but this had been Aimee's offering. She'd grabbed his arm, whispering, "He's here!" Grinning, the gap in her front teeth was displayed. "You're impressed, admit it."

They were close enough to see individual feathers, his grey crown topped with white, and the black on white of his mottled neck, the dark plumes of his chest spiky in the flow of water. Impressive but ugly, a misfit in the world of Sunday picnics and after-school trips to the swings. He was a loner: Jim's kind of bird.

"Swapsies." She'd hugged herself. "My heron for your owl." At the time, he hadn't been aware that she considered a bargain had been struck. They never even shook on it.

Jim now ran towards the small wooden bridge at the foot of the waterfall where he made his first stop, arms out straight, hands grasping the wooden rail. Looking down towards his trainers, he bent one knee and then the other, flexing his calf muscles. Aware of the throbbing of his cut foot, he tried to recall if his tetanus jab was up to date. Then, using the rail for support, Jim grabbed one foot behind him, stretching his quads. Sunlight bounced off the water, very much like that other day when they'd stood here, hands close together; Aimee's small and white, a splash of pink at the centre of each chewed nail, the warmth of her skin radiating outwards. Embarrassed, he had walked his hands away from hers. As still as the heron and as watchful, she gave no hint of having noticed.

"Alright, Jim." Hearing a voice, threatening in its insincerity, he had turned his head, instantly on the defensive. "Is this your girlfriend?" Andy Naylor: an older boy from school. A swirl, elbows on the rail, Aimee had presented herself for inspection. A strand of her hair had attached itself to her cherry lip gloss.

"Aren't you going to introduce us?" Andy stood, hands in pockets, flanked by two foot soldiers.

Jim assessed their choices: pushing past - which might have wound them up - or admitting defeat. "Come on." He grabbed Aimee by the elbow, intending to lead her back the way they had come, but she shrugged him off, giving him a look that demanded, *Are you embarrassed to be seen with me?*

He could only watch as she took the cigarette from Andy's mouth, blew a ribbon of smoke and grazed his lips with her two fingers as she returned what she had borrowed. "Aimee White," she said and walked on accompanied by a low whistle, swinging her hips, the slap-slapping of her yellow flip-flops - those same yellow flip-flops - like a lazy tide against a rock. She wasn't exactly beautiful, but, beyond all that hair, you couldn't ignore the intensity of her cat's eyes, her limbs, lazy and yet graceful. It was then - only then - that Jim realised he had a chameleon on his hands.

"Fuck awf!" She responded to the whistlers in BBC English.

"Mate!" Andy recovered his voice. "That girlfriend of yours has bigger balls than you. You're going to have to watch her."

Jim kept a steady pace, silently fuming. "What did I tell you?" he demanded when he caught up with Aimee by the children's playground, where she was swinging on the squeaking gate. She had pulled her short cardigan tightly around her and, having subdued her vibrant colours, appeared newly fragile.

"You don't get to tell me!" He was close enough to smell the smoke on her breath. "I deal with worse than that every day of the week. Try being a girl for a change. You might start to think you don't have so many problems after all!"

At the time, of course, he'd thought she was being over-dramatic.

Of their own accord, Jim's Adidas running shoes seemed to have decided on an unscheduled detour. Sprinting, ignoring any protest from his foot, they re-traced their steps: beyond the ponds; past his own front door; to the bridge. His legs a dynamo, they powered the film as it rewound, taking him all the way back to 1992: the beginning of the summer holidays. He ran down the concrete steps used by the men who worked on the railway lines, breathless, re-claiming the place where it had all begun. The place he had made his own - before Aimee White interrupted his peace with her constant questions and her quotation marks.

CHAPTER 10:

JIM - JULY 1992

"How do I look?" Jean Stevens turned sideways in front of the mirror in the hall, frowning as if someone else's reflection was staring back at her. Her nerves were contagious. "Nice," he'd said, swallowing. "Sure?"

The sight of her bare calves and ankles was so unusual to Jim that she'd looked as undressed as the women he watched through his lenses. "*Sure* sure."

"Your dad'll be here soon. I'd better make a start on dinner. Now, remember what I said, love. It'll take a while for us all to adjust."

From the moment his father declared, "You don't know how good it is to be home!" squeezing a handful of Jean's bottom, it took Frank an hour and ten minutes to ruin everything. Jim was surprised. He'd bet on half an hour

"Honestly, the faces on the pair of you!" his father said, elbows on the table. He had failed to compliment his wife on the effort she had gone to, making his favourite toad-in-the-hole with onion gravy. "That story had them doubled over last week!"

"Change the subject, Frank," Jim's mother said, her yellow card.

If Frank Stevens hadn't been his dad, or if he thought it wouldn't upset his mother, Jim might have been tempted to laugh. But these weren't the sort of things you should tell a young son.

"Eh, Jim!" his father continued, barely pausing for breath. "Fergie's got herself splashed all over the front page again. Apparently that American bloke of hers has this foot fetish."

"That's enough, Frank!" Scraping back her chair, Jean whisked Jim's plate away. Turning to protest, he saw his mother staring out of the window to the place where Richard Gere would come trotting along on his white charger to carry her off to the life she deserved. *Dad's in for it*, he thought, quietly pleased.

Reduced to eavesdropping, travelling between bedroom and bathroom, Jim paused at the sound of hushed voices.

"I don't know how much more of this I can take, Frank. I promised to stand by you for better or for worse. It's just… well, I imagined them evening out."

"I've said I'll try, Jean. What more can I say?"

"I don't want you to *say* anything: I want you to understand what it's like for us. It's like living in a… a game of snakes and ladders! Just when we're getting somewhere, you land us on the long snake that takes us right back to the beginning."

It wasn't the first time Jim had heard this comparison. The board lying on the table in front of them, his mother had been steaming ahead, making it all the way to eighty-six before she threw a one, landing on the blue snake. "Story of my life!" Jean had dissolved into her father's shoulder. "It's alright for you. You always land on the ladders."

Jim knew his mother wasn't a bad loser. He was shocked to see her crying.

"Go and find me another beer, will you, sunshine?" Grand-dad had said, a sure sign that something worth listening to was about to be said. "There's no such thing as luck, Princess.

It took hard graft to start our carpentry business, but we stuck with it. Then just when the books started to balance, your poor mother passed away. All I could think was how to make things alright for you. That's what keeps you going." Jim had spied on them through the door, watching his granddad kiss the top of his mother's head. "Though why you had to marry that lugget, I'll never understand."

Standing there, a beer in one hand, a Coke in the other, Jim had understood then that his father was the blue snake.

Well, the snake was back, taking up Jim's place on the sofa - the best place to watch owls - laughing like an idiot at the rubbish on telly. Even first thing the next morning he was there, trainers planted on the coffee table.

"What?" His father's index finger paused in the ring-pull of a can. "Haven't you seen the ads? Guinness is good for you." Sssssssss.

Jim had as good as heard his mother tell Dad she didn't feel that she should have to adjust. It was evident his father had no intention of changing. So that left Jim, and he sure as hell wasn't going to be the only one making an effort. There was a place he'd been meaning to explore, ever since he had started watching the owls: the sides of the railway lines. Deserted by day, somewhere a boy could find a little privacy.

"I'm off out," he said, packed lunch in his bag.

"Out where?" His father didn't lift his eyes from the television screen.

"*Out* out."

"Suit yourself."

And so they found ways to avoid each other, an adjustment of sorts.

From his seated position, Jim saw a girl come running down the concrete steps. He felt immediately defensive. What business did she have being there? Wild-haired, she looked as if she might be a gypsy. She hesitated at the second set of warning signs, glancing back up to the bridge: an adrenaline junkie, gulping back breaths that told Jim her heart was thumping, each beat a blow that threatened to knock her off-balance. Feet restless, she twisted the cotton of her loose-fitting top into a ball as though she were wringing it out after the wash. There was an area of flatter ground near the steps before the banks became steeper; more comfortable for sitting on, but you ran the risk of being spotted from the bridge. Completing her calculation, she stomped through the tall grass and sharp machine-cut twigs, ignoring the small red flecks that appeared on the white skin of her feet and ankles.

Her top still lifted, Jim's attention was diverted to the smooth skin above her waist, the outline of her ribcage. She was tall for a girl - by that he meant taller than him, which not everyone would have considered an appropriate measure. Her leggings sagged at the knees, the way they get when they've been worn twice between washes. As she came nearer, Jim wondered if he shouldn't speak up, but something made him hesitate.

"Bastard!" the girl cried out, grabbing a fistful of hair near her scalp. Then she released a wail that Jim would have preferred not to have heard. The disturbance cleared the area of birdlife, then there were just the two of them and the constant hum of bushes alive with insects.

Having thrown herself down on the bank, she made herself small, hugging her knees to her body. Her hair covered her face as she shuddered, rocking backwards and forwards, muttering something halfway between a mantra and a curse. To Jim, who knew next to nothing about girls, his second impression was that she seemed like a wounded animal. It's not just cats who go and find a safe place to die: he had seen an old fox who had given up the fight and wanted to be alone, curled in on itself. Watched as the shakes set in.

He did the only thing he knew how: reached for his

notebook and sketched, starting with her neck, the lines of her pale limbs. His tongue traced the openings to previously unidentified caverns and grooves on the roof of his mouth. *The shape of her small breasts.* His pencil was in motion for over an hour while she cast her spell. His eyes lifted and fell. *The curve of her behind.* He smudged hard lines, softening edges; blew away the rubbings from his eraser. *The narrowness of her almost-bare feet.* Eventually, she stood. Eyes fixed on the tracks, her feet edged forwards, one small step at a time, a bather about to dip her toes.

"I'd stop there if I were you!" he called out.

She gave a start, her eyes darting, locating the place he was sitting, bag and books strewn about him. Directing all her fury at him, she railed, "How long have you been spying on me?"

He still couldn't get a good look at her face, partly covered by her frizzy hair. But her voice gave her away: no gypsy, she was from the other side of the tracks - the side with the big houses.

"Well? I asked -"

"Jesus, let us get a word in! I've been here since early morning, like I always am. I come to watch the birds." He held his binoculars up by way of proof. She was hugging herself, shivering in the shadow cast by the banks. "Here, have a loan."

As he held up his faded denim jacket she frowned slightly, as if the idea of being cold hadn't crossed her mind, and he saw that her eyes were pale amber, a colour you'd expect to see on a cat. There was a gap in her front teeth. When he knew her better, she would tell him that pushing her tongue into the gap helped her concentrate. He approached slowly, no sudden moves; draping the jacket around her shoulders; avoiding any contact with her skin. Then he retreated, going about his business as usual. When he dared to look at her again, she was sitting cross-legged and had slipped her arms into the sleeves. That was the last he'd see of that: there'd be explaining to do. Stomach rumbling, he waited for the girl to leave before opening his lunchbox. Half an hour passed. An hour. There was nothing else for it.

"You hungry?" he called over.

She shrugged, but it was more of a yes than a no, so he breached the few metres separating them, holding the box at arm's length. "Cheese and pickle. It's Jim, by the way."

She accepted his offering wordlessly, so he retreated to his original position. "You want to eat that before the B.F.Ps pick up the scent."

Jim did rifle impressions to shoo away the scattering of hopeful pigeons that descended, right on cue. She took a couple of timid bites from the edge and then larger and larger mouthfuls. Jim wondered if this was what it was like to be a creature awakening from hibernation.

"What's a B.F.P?" she asked unexpectedly.

"Big Fat Pigeon. The only birds I've got no time for."

"That one there." She nodded at a particularly obese spec-imen. "He must be a F.B.F.P."

Jim snorted air through his nose. It was a revelation that posh girls swore.

"How old are you, Cheese-and-Pickle Jim?"

"Twelve." As lies go, it wasn't a big one. He was trying the number on for size.

"You're the year below me. What school are you at?"

"Stanley Park."

"My dad's just announced I have to go to Wimbledon High."

"Right," he said, wondering how this news concerned him.

"It's all girls, that's his thinking. Boys are evil, don't you know!" She hugged her knees, rocking back.

"That's us. Evil."

"I don't belong anywhere at the moment. I don't suppose you know how that feels?"

"I do, as it happens." Jim was an expert at not belonging. To fit in he would have had to be someone he didn't want to be, so you could say he chose not to fit in. There was always a choice. Just didn't feel like it half of the time.

"You don't say much, do you?" she asked after a while, swinging her feet around in his direction and crossing them at the ankles. With her hair tucked behind her ears, she displayed her face properly for the first time. Hers was the sort of skin with freckles that multiply and fill in the gaps, rather than tans.

"I only talk when I've got something to say," Jim shrugged. "No point otherwise."

"People spout far too many words," she said. "It makes me feel like I want to... *arrghh!*... EXPLODE."

"Is that what you were doing earlier?" Jim asked, thinking it might explain her behaviour.

The way she hung her head made him regret asking. "If you like," she said, looking at her feet.

They were silent for a while until Jim became aware that she was observing him from behind a curtain of hair. "What are *you* hiding from?" she asked, cradling her knees.

He looked through the binoculars. "Like I said, I'm here to watch the birds."

"There's *got* to be better places than this."

"For your information, railway sidings are some of the best places to see wildlife, now there's so few hedgerows. They call this a 'biological corridor'. It's protected."

"No need to be sarcastic. Anyway," she looked around at the litter that was so ordinary Jim could ignore it, "Whoever's supposed to be protecting it isn't doing a very good job. How do you know about this place?"

"I live on the estate off Carshalton Road." He pointed uphill. "We've got a great view. At night, I watch the owls out of the living room window. There's a pair who nest here."

"I've never seen an owl." She looked around her anew as if to say, *Here?* "That would really be something."

"I'm hiding from my dad," he admitted.

"What's he done?"

Tell a girl one thing and they want to know another. He should have known. Mum was the same.

"Must be something," she fished.

"He's not around much." Jim winced. "But when he's home, he wants to act like…"

"Don't tell me. Like everything's normal." There was no question mark. "I hate the bloody holidays."

Jim couldn't help himself. He laughed.

"What's so funny?"

"You. Swearing: 'I *hate* the bloody *holidays*.'"

"I don't sound like that!" she squeaked.

"If you say so."

"Do not!"

Distracted by the call of a bullfinch, Jim raised his binoculars. "Hang about."

"Can I have a look?" she asked, thrusting out an expectant hand.

Reluctantly, he passed her the binoculars. "Over there." She followed the diagonal of his arm. "It's a male bullfinch."

"How can you tell?"

"The male has a bluey-grey back and rosy cheeks and belly, while the female is dark brown and pinky beige."

"Like that one?" she asked, handing back the binoculars and pointing.

"Snap!" He reached for his notebook.

"Is that unusual?"

"There's less of them than there used to be. Only used to be seen in the countryside, but they like it down here. They make neat work of the blackberries." As she hadn't hogged the binoculars he felt charitable. "Want another look?"

While she was distracted, Jim watched the girl's face relax as her shoulders lost the weight they had been carrying.

"So, you really are a bird-watcher!"

"Thought I was trying to impress you by pretending to have a cool hobby, did you?"

She closed the gap between them, walking on her knees. "What's that you're writing?"

"I note down all my spots. If everyone does it, it helps build up a picture of which birds are in trouble."

"Can I see?" Without waiting for permission, she took the notebook and flicked backwards through it. Powerless to prevent the girl from finding his sketches of her, Jim felt his body temperature rise. "Are these supposed to be of me?"

Gas mark seven. Caught red-handed, there wasn't much point making excuses. She studied the rough sketches, saw the lines his pencil had made.

"Is that what I look like?"

"I'm not really any good."

"You are." She compared his sketch of a greenfinch with the photograph in the library book. "This is obviously a greenfinch. So I'm asking: is this what I look like to you?"

He swallowed. "Not now…" It was easy for Jim to pretend his embarrassment was because he had captured her at her most vulnerable, but it wasn't, of course. He could hardly pretend he hadn't noticed all of her glorious detail because it was there, recorded in pencil. He waited for angry accusations, but she closed the notebook.

"Mind if I come back tomorrow?" she asked.

Taken aback, Jim shrugged. "If you want."

"I'd like that."

"Hang about! What's your name?"

"Aimee!" she shouted back. "Aimee White."

Aimee White, he repeated to himself, narrowing his eyes. *Take Aim.* He shot an imaginary arrow after her. *Me:* he touched his chest. *White:* the colour of her feet.

She was already halfway towards the steps when he remembered: "Hey! Can I have my jacket back? My mum will go -"

She smiled, looked down at it and skipped away.

"- mental," he sighed. "Shit."

Jim got up earlier than usual and made an extra roll for his lunchbox in case he had to share again. His mother watched the food supplies like a hawk, but he knew she'd blame it on his dad, who wouldn't understand what the fuss was about. "It's a roll, for goodness sake!" he'd roar if challenged. "A bloody roll!"

Yesterday, when they had run out of something, his father had said, "What's the problem? I'll buy some more when I go out."

Mouth shut was Jim's policy when his mother put her hands on her hips and squared up to Frank. "With what?"

"The change tin on the fridge. I'll take it out of that." He rustled his copy of *The Sun.*

"That's not change. It's for bills and emergencies." Looking up from his breakfast cereal, Jim had seen the colour of his mother's neck rising. She had reached for the tin and, expecting something heavier, rattled it. A frown distorted Jean's brow as she opened the hinged lid. "You've only been home a couple of days and you've already spent most of what I'd saved!"

"It was just a few quid. Fat lot of good that would've been in a crisis." He winked at Jim, thinking he was being smart.

"In case you hadn't noticed, Frank, there's a recession on! Not many people can afford a cleaner." She stormed out of the room, returning briefly to point a finger. "And don't you *dare* joke about how little I earn when it's me who's putting food on your table."

Expecting company, down by the side of the tracks, Jim couldn't settle. His eyes drifted from the lenses of his binoculars to his watch, to the railway bridge. He found that he was rocking back and forth. Even recording his first entry of the day led him back to his sketches of Aimee. They weren't too bad, he decided. In answer to her question, they were exactly what she had looked like.

A crow alighted close by and rearranged wing-feathers so black they contained hues of green and purple. Jim rehearsed what he would tell Aimee about crows. "My granddad used to tell me this story. There was a thirsty crow who found a pitcher that was only half full. As hard as he tried, he couldn't reach the water. But instead of giving up, he collected a pile of stones and dropped them in, one by one. With each stone, the water rose up and up until, before long, it was in his reach."

As if on cue, the bird hopped lop-sidedly to a discarded Coke can and upended it.

"Think you're so clever?" He was addressing the bird now. A black eye regarded him sceptically; a black tongue probed the sickly-sweet spillage. "There's this one crow - I expect you know him. He used to hammer nuts against stones to crack them open, but that was before he worked out how to get someone else to do the job for him. By accident, he dropped a nut at a road junction and found that the shell cracked when a car ran over it. So he started dropping nuts in front of cars whenever they stopped at the traffic lights. Soon, the drivers went out of their way to run over them for him, job done. Don't go giving me all that 'Necessity is the Mother of Invention'. Laziness: that's the mother-fucker."

"Oh, yeah," he said, turning back to where Aimee White would be sitting. "I've worked out a system to share the binoculars. One with the binoculars, one with the book."

Damn her!

By three o'clock restlessness had sucked the enjoyment out

of the day. Feeling the need to kick something, Jim decided to search out a game of footie. "She's just someone else who's going to let you down," he told himself. "You're better off without her."

As he walked the curve of the sloped path leading to the playing field, a squirrel, fat on a diet of monkey nuts, risked scampering between Jim's feet and sat on his haunches making eye contact.

"What do you want, stupid?" he demanded.

It turned with the twitch of its tail, retreating to the safety of the trees in a series of liquid jumps, claw-deep in pine needles. Jim's eyes followed in the direction of the children's playground. Shrill shrieks drew his attention to a wooden frame under a wide slide, which formed a wigwam. In that compact triangle sat a cross-legged figure, her face half-hidden by frizzy hair. She was hugging her knees and rocking, thinking that she couldn't be seen. This was a girl who was hiding. His usual view of the world a figure-of-eight knocked over on its side, Jim crouched, training his binoculars on Aimee White.

In the part of her face that wasn't concealed, Jim detected loneliness, but it was the signs of fresh bruising that were unmistakable. Remembering her asking, "Are you spying on me?" he swivelled around and sat. For the first time in his spying career, Jim felt ashamed.

Of course she hadn't been able to come today.

You wouldn't.

CHAPTER 11:

AYISHA - JULY 2010 -
ST HELIER HOSPITAL

Afraid she might be turned away without the answers she sorely needed, Ayisha had rehearsed her explanation of how she knew Jim as she walked up the three flights to the High Dependency Unit.

"I'm here to see Jim Stevens." To her own ears, her sentence sounded like a question.

"You're not another reporter are you?" The receptionist looked up with a weary shift-work smile.

"No, I'm one of his colleagues. Actually -"

"Sorry, but we've had to turn a few journalists away. And you haven't had any signs of infection?"

"No." Ayisha had worried unnecessarily. The woman had no real interest in who she was. She just wanted to put ticks in boxes. What Ayisha should have rehearsed were the questions she needed to put to Jim.

"No diarrhoea, vomiting, fever, a cold, rash on your skin?"

"No."

"And you've used the alcohol rub?"

"At reception -"

"Have another go." The nurse pointed out a green

wall-mounted siphon, then lowered her voice. "Can I ask? You're not the Aimee he's been talking about in his sleep, are you?"

Ayisha imagined the ex-girlfriend whose number was listed in Jim's mobile. While rubbing the cold gel into her hands, she began her short speech. "No, I was the first teacher on the scene -"

"I can only discuss medical details with family, but you'll see for yourself that he's on organ support."

Ayisha experienced a quickening of her heartbeat: a memory of her own panic: the moment of realisation that she would have to act; that there was no one else; the wad of tissues oozing blood.

"Are you alright?" The receptionist was asking.

"Fine." Realising she wasn't prepared mentally for what she might see, Ayisha struggled to keep her fear in check.

"This isn't for everyone. You needn't be embarrassed."

"No. I need to see him."

"You want to reassure yourself." The nurse smiled kindly - although Ayisha doubted she could possibly understand.

"How is he?" she asked cautiously.

"It's early days. All I can say is that the surgery went as well as could be expected."

She buzzed Ayisha in. "Try not to wake him if he's sleeping. The police have already been today."

Entering the ward Ayisha passed a silent crepe-soled nurse dressed in a white tunic. Acknowledged, perhaps as an inconvenience, Ayisha wished her heels wouldn't click quite so loudly on the sealed and polished floor. There were four beds, arranged for privacy, two on each side of the ward with curtains in between. If they were drawn back, if the inhabitants were capable of raising their heads - which Ayisha doubted - they would only be able to see their opposites.

An elderly female visitor glanced up from behind a

newspaper - perhaps offering empathy, perhaps hoping to be relieved from her sentry duty - then returned to her crossword puzzle, murmuring a commentary to the figure in the bed whose face was covered by an opaque mask.

Seeing Jim lying there, the little girl who had tried on her mother's high heels and subjected her teddy bears to tea parties reasserted herself. Ayisha recalled an accusation her father made during an argument: "You've swapped your school uniform for the garb of a teacher, but I wonder, did you choose teaching as a profession so that you could avoid growing up?" She remembered feeling incensed, storming out, then her father's humbling apology: "Actually, there's a lot to be said for it. Adults forget most of what they knew was important as children. Friendship. Truth. Justice. Happiness..." It was hard to reconcile her father's idea of what goes on in the classroom with her experience of being a child - and now of being a teacher. What would he say if he were here?

The top half of Jim's bed was elevated. Even with his eyes closed, he wore that look of exhaustion she'd seen in newborn babies. A faded blue pyjama top, together with the length of his eyelashes, gave an impression of boyish vulnerability despite several days' worth of stubble. The youngest resident of the H.D.U., he looked strangely out of place, as if there had been some sort of mix-up. Ayisha was relieved his face wasn't masked - that conversation would be possible. But small plastic tubes emerged from his nostrils. She noticed the line that had been left in the top of one hand; the bulge under one arm that suggested more tubing. Her eyes passed quickly over a half-full plastic pouch suspended from the side of his bed.

As she sat, the scraping of the chair legs seemed disproportionately loud.

Jim opened one yellowed and bloodshot eye. "You again?" he asked, breaking off painfully in a dry, hacking cough.

"Anything to get out of helping me decorate." Mid-sentence, the last couple of days took their toll. Ayisha rummaged in her handbag for a tissue, before remembering how she had disposed of the entire box.

"Mine," Jim rasped. She followed the direction of his eyes to a bedside cabinet.

While she rounded the foot of the bed and plucked two tissues, Ayisha thought she could feel his eyes following her, imagined his quiet bemusement, almost sorry that she would be forced to change the mood. But by the time she began to say, "Listen, I'm sorry to do this but," his eyes had closed over.

She took a seat, at first waiting for him to wake, then unsure how long she should watch her colleague sleep open-mouthed. What felt like silence was actually the whir of the air conditioning. When it cut periodically, Ayisha became aware of other sounds. Hearts being monitored, bleep by bleep. Underwater noises of life continuing elsewhere. Repeated bomb-like screeches of self-closing doors, their dull-thudding impact. She had the sensation of being cut off. Rather than being an unpleasant experience, sitting perfectly still, Ayisha became aware of the rise and fall of her chest, the regular rhythm of her breathing. It was strangely like being at prayer. The urgency accompanying every waking moment since she'd walked away from the quad had no place here. Words, if they were spoken, were whispers. She made a fragile peace with her decision: in good faith, she had done the only thing she could have done. As if registering her thoughts, one of Jim's fingers twitched, the slightest flicker. "Me," he murmured pleadingly.

"You," Ayisha responded automatically, before considering that this might have been the last syllable of the name she had heard several times recently. Aimee.

The elderly visitor was now separating the delicate strands of her husband's hair with a comb. Her calm the calm of acceptance, it appeared important that she ensured everything was as her husband would like it. Watching this tender interaction made Ayisha wonder if there was something she should be doing. *I can be Aimee if Aimee is the person Jim needs*, she thought. Pulling a brush from her handbag, Ayisha found herself under the approving gaze of the elderly crossword woman who, accustomed to solving puzzles, thought she had the answer to five down.

When a kindly white-tunicked nurse who came to fiddle with the plastic tubes said, "You must be very proud of your husband. We hear he was very brave," Ayisha didn't have the heart to contradict her. Although her initial reaction was to scoff, *Stupid, more like!* when the suggestion was repeated with a shoulder-squeeze, she found herself agreeing: "Yes, we're all very proud."

Over the next few days, whenever this trusting nurse was on duty, Ayisha became known as Mrs Stevens and it felt no more like acting than playing the part of a grown-up.

Sometimes Jim would mumble a few words, but mainly he slept, barely capable of acknowledging her presence, let alone correcting the nurse's misunderstanding - Ayisha's second lie of omission. As Mrs Stevens, she learned that Jim had been given a blood transfusion. In this comforting, alien environment, she gained an understanding of how important it was to ensure that just the right amount of oxygen was in the air that ventilated Jim's lungs, "In order to prevent further injury." She learned the fluids in the IV line were not just drugs, as she'd assumed, but a balance of nutrition designed to prevent dehydration and improve blood flow, ensuring his lungs didn't fill with fluid, delivering oxygen to the body's organs. She became familiar with Jim's drug regime: preventative antibiotics, anti-inflammatories and diuretics, inhaled bronchodilators to open his air passages. She learned that Jim could expect to suffer short-term problems such as shortness of breath, fatigue, muscle weakness, and problems with thinking, or depression. All the time pondering: *if I had been the one to arrive first, that could have been me.*

The nurse caught Ayisha looking at elderly crossword woman and whispered, "Childhood sweethearts, married sixty-five years."

"Incredible," she said.

The occupants of the beds around Jim's changed regularly. Then, one day, the bed that had housed elderly crossword woman's husband was stripped bare, the walls disinfected, every trace of him removed, insensitively, brutally. Grief hit Ayisha like a blow. Grief at his passing, yes, but the fact was they hadn't even spoken. Her knowledge of him had been purely vicarious, evidenced by the liver-spotted hands that smoothed his downy hair with such tenderness. No, the main part of Ayisha's grief was personal - the unpalatable knowledge that she would never know what it was like to look back on a lifetime of love.

CHAPTER 12:

JIM - APRIL 2010 - AT HOME

As Jim answered his front door, Shamayal edged past into the shadows. "So? Did little Mr Stevens get some action? Hee, hee, hee."

The boy hesitated outside the living room door.

He sighed, "To be honest, it wasn't the best of first dates. Look, what -?"

"You told her you's a twitcher." The boy's voice sounded deliberately cheerful. "Man, I tried to warn you!"

Jim noticed that Shamayal was wearing the same clothes as before. "And how was your night?"

Having reached the kitchen, Shamayal still hadn't turned around. "I bumped into the old geezer, din't I? You was right. He's cool, man."

"You slept rough?"

"No! He has a flat, like you said. It needed a tidy up, din't it?"

The boy was hiding something. "Look at me, Shamayal."

"What? You want to see this?" He pivoted, holding up his face for inspection.

Jim's mouth fell open at the sight of the swelling. Filling up with hate, he struggled to control his voice. "Who did that to you?"

"This?" The boy put one hand up to touch his face and pulled it away, wincing. "I think it was someone sent by them Ralegh Boyz, if you aks me. When they get bored of tryin' to persuade you to help them out with their likkle jobs, they send someone over to rough you up, so they can say, 'You need our protection, Bruv.' Anyway, they had me up against a wall, when who should walk over but Bins. 'Excuse me, boys, if you don't mind I need to borrow Shamayal for a moment.' They was so surprised, they let me go."

Jim found that it was possible to smile. "Think he's just an old man now, do you?"

"I dunno who he is! He's too stinky to be a guardian angel."

That was the second time Shamayal had mentioned angels: there might be hope.

"He can definitely handle hisself. You can be so weird that people give you respect. I kinda got what you said about him being happy." Shamayal shook his head. "Fact, I'm not sure I've ever met anyone so happy! He aksed *a lot* of questions. I thought he was being disrespectful at first, but I think he was just…" The boy shrugged, as if what he was about to propose was inconceivable. "I dunno. *Interested* or somethink."

"Tell him something and he'll never forget it." As he spoke, it struck Jim that Bins constructed his world from facts the way he constructed his world from possessions. They made him feel secure.

"Right, right. I might go back. Check up on him, you know?" The boy nodded. "You should come with me. He thinks very highly of you. That's what he said, anyhow."

Jim wondered what other facts Bins had told him. "I don't go back."

"'Cept that's not strictly true, is it, Sir? What about the night before last?"

"That was an exception."

"You're within shootin' distance."

Jim recalled he used to say 'spitting distance'. But the boy still hadn't explained why he was there. "Have you been home yet, Shamayal?"

"Nah. My dad would kill me if I turned up looking like this." He was doing a very good job of trying to look casual. "Thought I'd keep my head down, you know."

Jim didn't need to ask what that meant. "Won't he worry?"

"Doubt it. My dad only cares about one person, f' you know what I mean."

"But he must have tried to call?"

"Every time he buys me a new mobile, I tell him the Ralegh Boyz jacked it, dun I?" Shamayal looked pleased with himself. "He don't really bovver me no more."

Jim had read *A Kestrel for a Knave* many times over since he first watched *Kes* with his mother, and the fact that people could have children and then neglect them never became easier to stomach. Finding he was welling up, he turned towards the fridge, asking, "Have you eaten?"

But Shamayal had seen him. "You act like it's bad, Sir. But I can't tell you if it's good or bad. It's jus' my life, right? Right?"

"Right." His face fixed, Jim managed a smile.

"I'm only here because I thought we had a deal. But if it's too awkward -"

"No. I'm glad you thought of me. We should get something on that eye." He wrapped a bag of frozen peas in a clean tea towel, and had Shamayal hold it to his face. "So, what would you like to do?"

"If you don't mind, Sir, I'd like to see what you get up to."

Jim followed the boy the short distance to the living room. "X-Box," he nodded, referring to the boy's previous visit.

"No! I fought you could show me what that twitchin' is all about."

It dawned on Jim: Bins must have told him.

As if reading his mind the boy said, "Bins mentioned some

stuff. But I fought it would be easier if you just showed me."

"Showed you what?"

"Kay, straight up." He nodded at the photograph on the wall. "I want to hear the story 'bout that owl."

CHAPTER 13:

AYISHA - 2010 -
ST HELIER HOSPITAL

The receptionist behind the monitor at the H.D.U. was new; young enough for Ayisha to think of her as a girl. "I'm sorry, but Jim Stevens doesn't appear to be with us anymore."

Feeling her legs threaten to give way, breath coming fast, Ayisha managed to ask, "What do you mean, *not with you?*"

The girl glanced up, clearly unnerved.

Ayisha gripped the counter. "Is he... you mean...?" But she couldn't bring herself to finish the question logic demanded.

"I can see that he *was* here, but -" The receptionist tapped away at the keyboard, looking at the screen for answers. "Why don't you take a seat. I'll make a few calls."

Ayisha perched on an uninviting chair. Opposite her, unmistakably, leaning against the mint green wall of the corridor was the disinfecting equipment used to spray down the walls of the wards. She heard a toilet flush followed by an explosion of air from a hand dryer. A man emerged wiping his hands on the trouser pockets of his boiler suit, whistling softly. He slung the canister over his shoulder as if it was weightless. Feeling she might be sick, Ayisha put her head between her knees and stayed in that position until, apparently proud of her detective-work, the girl cheerfully announced she had tracked Jim down. He had been moved.

"Moved?" Ayisha heard herself ask, laughing at this previously unentertained possibility.

"Yes. He's in B3."

She stood, undergoing the swiftest of transitions from euphoria to anger. "In future, you might want to choose your words more carefully!"

After losing herself in the maze of corridors, all of which led straight back to the main entrance, on the brink of frustrated tears, Ayisha asked a porter for directions. Now, another uniformed receptionist continued angrily tapping away behind her computer. Despite the technology, the workstation was in disarray with a surprising quantity of yellow Post-It notes and a rainforest of paperwork.

"When you've finished," Ayisha said, trying to convey an impression of patience she didn't feel. Having been convinced, however briefly, that Jim was dead, she would not trust that there hadn't been a mistake until she saw the evidence.

"I never finish. Go right ahead."

"I'm looking for Jim Stevens." Ayisha expected to undergo a repeat quiz about her medical history and receive a sternly-worded reminder about infection control.

The nurse angled her head towards a whiteboard. "You've found him." Jim's name and bed number was there, scrawled crookedly in black marker by someone less accustomed to writing upright than Ayisha. *I've found him.* The nurse's hands finally paused, but it was only so that she could waltz her wheeled chair towards the whirring printer and grab another wad of paper. She seemed surprised to find Ayisha still standing there. "That way." The nurse dismissed her, not remotely concerned that she might be a journalist.

In stark contrast to H.D.U., B Ward was a bustling place.

Still disorientated, Ayisha passed through a corridor crowded with abandoned equipment, feeling her tension increase at the sound of an inhuman groan, which a group of gossiping nurses (most of them overweight) seemed capable of ignoring. She passed a shuffling patient pushing his own IV drip on its wheeled stand. No one enquired what she was doing there or thought to offer assistance. She located room 3 and, at the sight of Jim lying asleep on an elevated cot, gripped the doorframe, breathing properly for what felt like the first time in half an hour. She paused to survey Jim's surroundings, her senses assaulted by the gaudy curtains; the smells of disinfectant and decay that went hand in hand with sickness. It was difficult to imagine a more depressing or a less restful environment. She reminded herself to get round to looking into the cost of BUPA.

Approaching the narrow metal-framed bed, at the sight of the simple sheet and woven blanket tucked tightly round his chest, *hospital corners* was the phrase that came to mind. *But of course it would*, she mocked herself. The tubes had gone from Jim's nose. Ayisha removed the newspaper from the visitor's chair and perched awkwardly. The ward heated to the point of oppressiveness, she loosened her linen jacket, knocking an elbow against the bed-frame.

Jim opened his eyes, focused and clear. "You're back," he said.

"And you're awake," she replied, laughing with relief. Today she would get her life back!

"I am now."

"Perhaps 'conscious' is what I should have said." Light-headed, unable to stop smiling, she observed, "You look so much better. I can hardly believe it!"

"I feel as if someone's been rummaging round in my insides," Jim grumbled, the effort of speaking making him breathless; to be expected for someone with a lung injury, Ayisha knew.

"They wouldn't have moved you unless they were happy with your progress."

"Have wheels, will travel: that's my new motto. So, how do you like my new home?"

Ayisha looked around her, trying to give the impression that she hadn't already completed a damning mental appraisal. She took in more detail this time: signs that patients had set up camp with a few smuggled possessions; newspapers and paperbacks; the ubiquitous bunches of grapes; bottles of lemon barley water, energy drinks. There was nothing on Jim's bedside cabinet or on his wheeled table, save for a covered water jug and a plastic tumbler. She could hardly say that, in Jim's position, she would be climbing the walls. "It's a step in the right direction," she said. "And it won't be for long."

Jim's smile was accompanied by a doubtful snort.

Conversation meant competing with an unending drone of news and sport and constant comings and goings.

"Huh?" His head jolted slightly as if she had woken him.

Ayisha had been warned that Jim might have difficulty concentrating. "I was asking whether the police have been back to see you?" She was tempted to pull the curtains around the bed so that his view of the television, bracketed at ceiling height, would be interrupted.

"Have they!" He lowered his voice and nodded. "The nurses here put up quite a fight. That one -"

Twisting her neck, Ayisha saw two uniformed backs.

"The one on your right? She can be quite fierce."

As wide as a house, she looked it. Ayisha made a mental note not to get on the wrong side of her. "So, what did they have to say?"

"They think it was a brother protecting his sister's honour."

Whether she wanted him to or not, Ayisha imagined! "Don't

tell me. The boy was the wrong colour."

"Or something."

Ayisha grasped the issue, nodding. "Wrong religion." Brought up a Muslim, she had since found her own way, free from the constraints of family. But her parents had long-since adopted Britain as their home and, as time marched on, it seemed (although she had yet to put her theory to the test) any boyfriend would be welcomed into their home. "From the number of knives recovered, it looks as if it was planned."

Jim shook his head. "Coincidence. The brother wasn't one of ours."

Ayisha recoiled. "Surely the percentage of kids carrying knives can't be as high as one in five?"

"Twenty per cent's not bad. According to the kids I speak to, it's nearer fifty."

"What good will Mr Peel's wand do if that's what we're up against?" She winced at her turn of phrase, embarrassed as Jim snorted in lieu of a laugh. "His detector wand!"

How to deal with teachers' increased powers of search had been another cause of staffroom contention.

"The cost is prohibitive," Mr Peel had cautioned the majority who favoured the installation of a detection arch, something every student would pass through. "And I would need volunteers…" His eyes traced a semicircle and Ayisha was one of those who had averted hers.

A shout came: "I didn't apply for a job as a bouncer!"

After several abortive attempts on Mr Peel's part to broker any semblance of order, Mr Baker had taken it on himself to roar: "SHUT IT, ALL OF YOU!"

Aside from a single piqued, "Well!" the room's occupants were stupefied into silence. The Head appeared momentarily dazed. "Quite unnecessary, Mr Baker, but thank you nonetheless. Right, the decision is this: a wand." For a moment, relief was palpable. Optimists shrugged their coats on, fumbled for handsets, checked text messages. "Not so fast! We still need to agree a system of checking."

A collective groan had subsided into resignation.

"How about every twentieth pupil through the door?"

"What? And let the ones we suspect traipse straight past?"

"I can see it now!" Mr Baker threw up his hands. "Accusations of violations of human rights, racism, sexism - and homophobia, no doubt."

Although every suggestion was met with derision, this new crescendo lacked the same energy as before. Mr Peel raised his voice and was heard. "I'm not asking anyone here to conduct searches. For that we'd need suspicion."

This was the new regime Ayisha would be returning to in the autumn. "What about their target?" she asked Jim. "I assume *he* was a pupil."

"His was the one name I could give them. Christian Knoll, would you believe?"

She recalled a quietly spoken boy, blond, unexceptional. "How appropriate!"

"They haven't found him. Yet."

Jim's meaning clear, goose-bumps prickled Ayisha's scalp. Being found would mean the police were too late.

He shook his head, an expression of hopelessness. "A press conference is going to be shown tonight on BBC London, I'm told."

The scary thing, Ayisha reflected, was that the disappearance of a teenage boy wouldn't normally receive television coverage. It was only the McCann's ongoing battle with the Portuguese authorities that had kept the disappearance of four-year-old Madeleine newsworthy for three years. Sixteen-year-olds, boys especially, had a tendency to slip between the cracks. For Christian, it was only his association with Jim - hailed a hero - that had elevated his importance. "And not *one* of the other kids saw anything?"

"To be honest, I'm not sure I'd speak up if I were in their shoes."

"Why does no one trust the police?" Ayisha aired her frustration.

"Because once they've caught the guy with the knife, you're left to fend for yourself."

She acknowledged she was out of her depth. "Am I the only one who doesn't understand how this works?"

"Gangs are like family. You hurt one of them, it's personal."

Ayisha balked at this reference. Her knowledge of gangs started and ended with those Gary Glitter lyrics and, let's face it, no one played him at their parties any more. The view that, provided you don't go looking for trouble it won't find you, had served her in good stead. She avoided eye contact with people she didn't know and booked her cab home before going out for the evening. Of course, there was that unfortunate young woman who, caught in cross-fire at the Urban Music Awards, was only saved by her under-wired bra, but she was an exception. Aside from the underwear angle, that was why the story had made headlines. Ayisha wondered now if she'd been living on Planet Wiltshire. "And the girl?"

The corners of Jim's mouth stretched into a wry smile.

"No, don't tell me: no one's talking." She caught sight of a hanging coil of plastic tubing on the wall behind Jim's bed, the purpose of which she doubted she wanted to know. Remembering she mustn't tire him, her mind racing ahead to the questions still unasked, she decided on a breather. "Before I forget." Ayisha raised the carrier bag from her lap into Jim's eye line. "The hospital's website said not to bring fruit or flowers…"

Straining, Jim managed to lift his head half an inch. "Is that a bar of Green and Blacks? You're a saint."

She deposited the chocolate on the table, as if it were his compliment she wished to distance herself from. Jim might revise his opinion of saintliness if he knew she'd been masquerading as his wife. "Hardly!" Suddenly Ayisha was acutely embarrassed by the intimacies she had shared without Jim's knowledge. The facts she had accumulated: the length of his eyelashes; the patterns his stubble grew in. What had been intended as small kindnesses now seemed selfish and contrived, all leading up to the point when she could demand answers.

"To be honest, I can't tell you how glad I am to see you. The first time I woke up it was my dad. God knows how they tracked him down!"

This was the first cue Jim had handed her. It wasn't too far a stretch for Ayisha to say, "I can help you out there. It was your friend, Shamayal." Jim's eyebrows jumped inwards. They both knew she wasn't referring to the boy's role as assistant first aider. "He's very worried about you, by all accounts."

"Go ahead. Ask me."

Jim's expression was so open that Ayisha was confident he was about to allay her fears. "Ask you what?"

"I found him wandering around in the early hours, so I did what any reasonable person would do: I gave him a lift home. But when I saw what he had to face there -" Jim broke off and raised his eyebrows, indicating that he was singularly unimpressed. "His father - when he's there at all - is drunk. And violent at that."

An explosion of laughter from the nurses' station seemed particularly inappropriate at this juncture. Ayisha found herself glaring in the direction of the door. "Where's his mother?"

Anger twitched at the corners of Jim's mouth. "Gone."

"And the rest of his family?"

"He's never met any other family. His parents left everything behind when they came to the UK." His hand was at his throat. "Could you pour me some -?" Jim broke off coughing and pointed to the water jug.

"So," she prompted, settling back down. "You've been assigned as his mentor."

He responded to her suggestion by taking a sip.

"If you haven't, tell me you reported it, please!"

Very slowly, he shook his head.

"How could you *not?*" Aware that the scary nurse's neck had twisted towards her, Ayisha felt like the child carried mid-tantrum from the mosque. She offered an apologetic smile, assurance that she was aware of the Polite Notice asking visitors to keep noise levels to a minimum. But she could feel her own shaking as she leant closer, hissing, "I've put my neck on the line for you!"

Jim's response was one of confusion: "How have you done that?"

"*How?*" Ayisha checked her volume. "I'll tell you how! Shamayal made a disclosure to me and I - I didn't act on it because I thought..." She realised that her rage might appear unjustifiable to Jim, but something inside her wanted to scream, *Don't you understand? I thought you were going to die!* Even today, less than an hour ago, she had thought this. Sitting on a chair in a hospital corridor, Ayisha had begun to mourn, and then the light-headedness, the euphoria. What had she done? Each of the wasted moments when she might have acted! Her walk across the quad; Mr Peel's concerned eyes; hand-delivering her incomplete report. She would lose her job - they both would. But Jim had brought this on himself.

"How could I not?" Oblivious, Jim was repeating her original question, as if examining it from a different angle. "If he was a few years younger, I wouldn't have hesitated. Listen: this is a bright kid with a good school record, who's managed to keep his nose clean. I couldn't guarantee how kindly Shamayal's father would have taken to that sort of help. And, say Shamayal was taken into care? What then?"

Unacceptably, he was using his 'voice of reason' with her.

"If what you say is true, he'd be better off!"

"You know as well as I do, that's where sixty-five per cent of the prison population comes from."

This sobering statistic brought them to an impasse. Searching for the source of an irritating clicking, Ayisha's gaze fell on a slump-shouldered teenager wearing earphones, nodding her head miserably. It was only when she felt Jim's hand stilling hers that she realised she was making the noise with her fingernails. "So what is he to you?" she demanded, no longer caring if Jim thought she was unreasonable. "A project?"

After a moment, he spoke. "I'm sorry you feel as if I've let you down." No excuses, he didn't try to secure a promise of silence from her. "But, Ayisha, he has no one. Do you understand? No one."

Why this boy? What made Shamayal so special? She shot back: "That's exactly why there's a system -"

"One that demands I betray any kid who puts his trust in me! Look, I'm not saying it was a smart thing to do. But, really, what is the situation? I've offered him my sofa for the night. Cooked him a few meals -"

Ayisha was agape: "You took him *home* with you?"

"I could hardly leave him. It was the middle of the night. The boy was soaking wet. What would you have done?"

"I wouldn't have stopped to give him a lift in the first place!" As soon as she had spoken, it struck Ayisha that the truth made her sound uncaring. And it was the system she put so much store in that demanded this.

"No." Was the look he gave her pity or disappointment? "You're probably not daft enough to go driving round at two in the morning! But say you took him to his front door to find a man staggering out with a bloody lip, his father throwing bottles after him. Just for a minute, pretend you were in my position." Jim's eyes searched hers.

She ignored the hope she saw in them. "That would involve pretending I'm not a teacher! These aren't rules you can take or leave!" Heart pounding, Ayisha looked at the floor, shaking her head. The man lying next to her in the hospital bed clearly wasn't a bad person. The fact that he'd ended up in this mess suggested he was more caring than she was. If naivety was his only failing, then wasn't that something she too could be accused of? Relenting slightly, she offered, "It's not the way we had to grow up, thank God."

"Actually -" The television no longer a distraction, Jim was staring intently at the foot of the bed. "In my case, it's almost too close to home. Not only the same estate, would you believe, but I actually lived in the flat next door!" He paused for her to absorb this information. "When we went for a drink you asked me why I chose teaching as a career."

Ayisha recalled the conversation. Competing with the pounding of the jukebox, she had narrowed her eyes - a look designed to unnerve. "I'm interested in you, Jim Stevens," she had said. "You fight authority at every opportunity." It surprised her to recall she had recognised this in him then.

"Do I?" He had sought innocent refuge in his pint.

"Come off it, you know you do. So," Ayisha shivered as the pub door opened for a new arrival. "Why become part of it?"

He recited the stock answer - "The holidays" - but she hadn't let him off the hook.

"If you must know, it's the kick of knowing I've infiltrated the system."

"I'm not buying that - although I rather enjoyed Jeanette's expression when you suggested bringing a gangster in to give a talk about knife crime." Members of gangs, gangsters: Ayisha reflected she hadn't made the distinction. "Come on. Between you and me." She had leant forwards hoping to appear invitingly conspiratorial.

He shuffled, unsettling his stool. "Kids walk into my class

saying, (adopt bored tone), 'His-tor-y!' I challenge myself to change the way they say the word by the end of the autumn term."

Ayisha approved of personal challenges and this one seemed noble. "So what's your success rate?"

"Seventy-five per cent."

Her empty glass had thudded to the table. "You're delusional!"

"It might just be that I'm very good."

"The minute I switch to algebra, I lose the majority. That's my seventy-five per cent!"

Now, lying in a hospital bed, Jim added to his explanation. "It doesn't take many people to believe in you for you to believe in yourself, but it does take one person. Occasionally I'm asked to be that person. And, in case I forgot to mention it, I like Shamayal."

"You like him?" Ayisha found herself repeating stupidly.

"He makes me laugh - at myself mostly, I admit."

"Well!" She exhaled loudly. "Why didn't you say so? At least I haven't put my career on the line for a pupil you didn't like!" Sarcasm, the trait she most despised. Wisely, she acknowledged, Jim didn't rise to the bait. Opportunity for escape presented itself almost immediately. A nurse approached with a trolley-wheeling waddle. "I need time to think," she said in a low voice.

"You have to do whatever you think's right." Ayisha saw how Jim lifted his chin, smiled and checked the nurse's name badge before issuing a greeting. "Hello, Martha."

"How are we today, Mr Jim?"

"I've still got the pain in my shoulder and back."

She pushed herself to standing, hooking the strap of her bag onto her shoulder. "You know, I should be off."

"You alright, darlin'." The nurse expressed surprise. "Just step outside a few minutes for me."

"No. I've already tired him out."

"Suit yourself, but I won't be long doing Mr Jim's dressings."

Thinking there was something more she should say, Ayisha turned back. "Is there anything you need?"

"Actually, there *is* something you could do for me."

She bridled, feeling that she had already done enough. "OK."

"My keys are in the top drawer. Would you mind going to my flat to see if I've got any post?" Jim's eyes were pleading. "If I have, perhaps you could bring it in?"

Ayisha pulsed with resistance. Jim seemed to be assuming her silence, adding weight to her instinct that it was too late for anything else. Going through the motions, she jotted down the address he dictated and dropped the keys into the depths of her handbag among the crumpled receipts and the skeletons of Bic biros.

"And if you could bring me a couple of books. They're in the living room."

"You'll want your own jim-jams and a dressing gown," Martha pointed out. "For when you're back on your feet."

"I don't own any. Tracky bottoms and a t-shirt will have to do. My dressing gown's hanging on the back of the bedroom door."

Ayisha didn't particularly care if the nurse detected sarcasm of the What-did-your-last-slave-die-of variety. "Anything else?"

"No, that's it, I think."

"Well." Her smile was tight. "I'll see what I can find. No promises."

CHAPTER 14:

JIM - APRIL 2010 - THE BRIDGE

"You're not gonna bail on me, are you, Sir?" Shamayal asked.

Hesitating at the bridge, Jim had adopted the stance he used when stretching his hamstrings at the beginning of a run. Head down, his binoculars dangled from their strap. "It's not that easy, knowing where to start." But it wasn't just a case of where to start: he wanted to do the people in his story justice.

"Hey, you know what? People say you should start at the beginnin' for a reason."

Shamayal wasn't yet old enough to understand that memory doesn't work like that. The original memory is replaced by the *memory* of the memory. Fine-tuned as a result of later discoveries. Re-defined.

Bypassing the barrier, Jim began to run down the concrete steps to the side of the cuttings.

"Oi! What you doin'? You can't go down there! That's private property. Man!"

He looked over his shoulder to see the boy slashing through air with his forearms. "Coming or not?"

"If I get arrested, I'm holdin' you responsible!" Shamayal's feet were quick-fire, dancing on coals. He looked about him, unimpressed, with the expression of someone who has a bad taste in his mouth. "This is where the junkies hang out, you know."

"It is, at night." Jim tried to see their surroundings as the boy did: crushed beer cans; an empty Jack Daniels bottle; abandoned needles, foil squares, used condoms. But he also saw the dense shrubbery; berries; downtrodden routes that marked the regular passage of foxes. "It's also one of the best places to see migrating birds."

"Yeah?" The boy's darting eyes suggested he was dubious.

"Swallows, house martins, swifts: they all navigate to South Africa using landmarks. Their route used to follow rivers and hedges, but now it takes in railway lines and roads. Birds follow the flow of traffic. They even change direction at motorway junctions."

"No way, they never!"

"And," Jim focused on the top of a bush, "It's also where I met Aimee. That's why we're here, isn't it? She's the girl Bins told you about."

Shamayal shrugged dismissively. "He might of said something 'bout a girl, but Aimee weren't the name he used."

Ignoring this, Jim flicked through the first few chapters:

"Over there," he said. "Top of the bush. Small brown bird, lighter underneath, stripe across the eye." Having offered her the binoculars Jim allowed himself to focus on the bruising around her eye.

"Got it! What's that then?"

"It's a Chiff Chaff."

"How can you tell?"

"It goes 'Chiff Chaff'"

"They put a lot of thought into that, didn't they?" Laughing lightly, she passed the binoculars back. "What's the Latin for this one?"

"*Phylloscopus.*"

"*Sounds like a dinosaur.*"

"*It means the leaf explorer.*"

"*The Leaf Explorer. That would make a good title for a poem.*"

"*You and your bloody poems! It's all about lunch. It checks both sides for insects.*"

"*So,*" she said, tucking her hair behind her ears to display ruptured blood vessels under the surface of her delicate skin. "*Are you going to ask or aren't you?*"

Jim was glad that the binoculars were masking his eyes. "*None of my business.*"

Aimee's hair fell forwards. "*I wish my mum thought like you.*"

"*What did you tell her?*"

Aimee sighed, "*If you must know, I told her I asked for it.*" And something in her voice said she believed that.

"*Unusual tactic.*"

"*Yeah? What excuse would you have used?*"

Jim didn't hesitate. "*Ball in the eye playing cricket.*"

"*I don't play cricket.*"

"*Then, whatever it is you girls do. Rounders?*"

"*If you're so smart, what should I say about this?*" she asked, lifting up her top and twisting round.

Jim only caught the briefest glimpse of what appeared to be a stamp mark, but that was enough to wake in him a rage so intense he had nothing to compare it with, one he had no way of expressing. "*That'd have to be footie.*" His hands gripped the barrels of the binoculars. "*Bad tackle.*"

"*Do I look like I play football?*" she laughed bitterly. "*But wait, I forgot. We're only talking about pretend football.*"

"Was she your girlfriend or something?" Shamayal was asking.

It was still a question that troubled him. Jim winced as he

looked past the boy to the place they used to sit. "Or something," he blinked.

"I can't wait for Thursday." Aimee clutched her cardigan around her. "Dad goes back to days for two weeks."

Pleased with how his conversation was improving, Jim now thought of it like football. Someone passes you the ball and you can either run with it, pass it back or pass it to someone else. "What does he do?"

"He's a doctor. When he's on nights, he just hangs round the house all day. What about yours?"

"As little as possible!"

She elbowed him sharply in the ribs. "For a living, Doughnut."

A moment passed. "He's sort of in sales." Supply and demand: what was the difference? "But he's out of work at the moment."

"Something'll turn up."

"Always does." He needed a subject change, fast. "So, d'you live round here?"

She hugged her knees to her chest, all face and legs. "Durnsford. Do you know it?"

Everybody knew Durnsford. One of the best roads in what was already a very nice area. Dangerous when nice areas back onto the not-so-nice. Way too much temptation - even with a railway line in between. The irony of folks on the estate looking down on folks on the other side of the tracks was part of the local vernacular.

"My mum's got a mind to move your way when she wins the pools."

"If I won, I'd get as far away from here as possible," Aimee said bitterly.

At the time, Jim had felt insulted: did 'far away from here' mean far away from him?

"D'you know anyone else from up the hill?" he asked after a while.

Eyes glinting, she shook her head. "Nope."

Jim found that his chest was deflating: the tail of a heavy sigh. Shamayal was looking at him intently. "Aimee was the first friend I had who lived on the other side of the tracks."

"Your side, you mean?"

"Back then, it wasn't. I had this stupid idea that everyone who lived there was ultra-privileged."

Jim stumbled on some pages that he would prefer not to re-read.

She wrinkled up her face. "Sometimes, when I'm sitting here, the trains go by so fast it feels as if I could get sucked along behind. Or else I look at the track when they're coming and think -"Aimee broke off, her unfinished sentence hanging.

"How d'you mean?"

"What if I was on the tracks somehow?"

"Are you supposed to be some kind of damsel in distress?"

"No, that's not what I was thinking of..."

If she wasn't acting in a black and white film, tied to the tracks... He tried to back away from the conclusion he reached. "Is that *what you're thinking about while we're sitting here?" Jim had been furious with her. "I mean, why would you want to go wandering onto the tracks in the first place?"*

"I didn't say I was going to." *She sulked, in the way girls do.* "It's not like it's an obsession."

"Don't you dare try anything when I'm not looking!" *Jim shot back, as he imagined a big brother should.* "Anyway, you'd fry before you had to worry about a train hitting you." *And he did what he always did; turned it into a big joke with his best impression of a cartoon character frying: head jolting, everything else stiff, his hands clawed. And they laughed...*

Jim blew out his cheeks. You say these things, do these things, they're not supposed to mean anything. He began to speak, somewhere; anywhere to get him away from there.

"It was the summer holidays and things at home were going

from bad to worse. My dad was around, which was unusual in itself. My parents did their best to keep up a pretence in front of me, but they were at each others' throats as soon as I was out of the room."

"What about your bruvver?" Shamayal asked. "Where was he?"

Jim sighed. "Long gone - or so I thought."

"He'd already left home?"

"That was what I was supposed to tell everyone. My mum had thrown him out."

"How come?"

"He doesn't set foot in this place!" Cowering in the hall, he heard his mother yell.

"He's my son and this is still my home!" Frank bellowed, matching her for volume.

"You're out all day. What difference does it make to you if I bring him back here?"

"I want Nick kept away from Jim, do you understand?"

"What about me? Should I be kept away from Jim for his protection too?"

"As it happens, I never have to worry about that for too long!"

"Bad influence." Jim flinched as ancient loyalties tried to reassert themselves. "Part of me was scared I'd turn out like the two of them. But, the truth was, I didn't like the sound of hard work and long hours either."

"I don't want you hanging about the pub all day with your father."

"I haven't been to the pub, have I? I've been out bird-watching." Jim wanted an end to his mother's questions. He reached into his rucksack for his notebook and opened a page, jabbing the day's entry. "There's one of these for every day of the holidays. Check up on me if you want to."

Abandoning her washing up, Jean wiped her hands on

a checked tea towel as she joined him at the kitchen table. "I never knew you could draw!" She looked at him as if he were an imposter.

"It's copying, mostly." Remembering what else was in the sketchbook, Jim was suddenly shy.

"Give it time. I like this little fella." She pointed to a picture of a wagtail before continuing to flick through the pages, letting a small amount of pride in with the relief as she checked the date of each entry, missing nothing. When she asked, "Who's this?" Jim knew she had found his sketches of Aimee. "You didn't tell me you had a girlfriend."

"She's not my girlfriend!" He snatched the book, avoiding his mother's gaze while he bundled it into his rucksack. "A few of us go together, that's all."

"I already knew I could remember things if I was interested enough in them. I could reel off the Latin for birds and flowers. It was Aimee who opened my mind up to the idea of education."

"Is this part of the story, Sir? No disrespect, but you haven't even got to the owl part, and there's a limit to how long I wanna hang out here." Shamayal pointed to a discarded pair of jeans dangling limply from a reedy branch. "I mean, what the hell happened to that guy? Looks like he disappeared into thin air."

"I'm getting to it." But Jim shivered; somehow the Levis were not just washing-line empty, but ghost-like. "You're right about this place at night: when we got hungry it was our cue to head for home, but sometimes we'd doze off. One of those times we were both woken by a voice asking what we thought we were doing there. I opened my eyes to find a pair of eyes leaning in close. 'No need to rush off without saying hello,' he said. Or something like that. Aimee was hugging her duffel bag. Our way out was blocked by two other guys. Being robbed wasn't my greatest fear. These guys were drunk or high."

"Prob'ly both." Shamayal was standing with his hands tucked under his armpits.

"All I could do was watch while the first bloke turned my rucksack upside down. I hoped he just wanted to play tough. He had enough ammunition - if only I could keep my mouth shut. He threw my binoculars aside once he'd got a laugh out of them. I joined in, trying not to let Aimee see how scared I felt. Then he took Aimee's bag off her. She had a book of poems in there, something she'd been threatening to lend me. 'What you two need is a lesson on how to enjoy yourselves,' he said, then he called the other two over. I hadn't paid much attention to them, but Nick was one of the names he used. The man who responded was a clone of the first. The same shaven head, the same hollow eyes, but wearing a yellow t-shirt with a smiley face on it."

Shamayal shook his head. "Not your bruvver!"

"I was shocked by how much he'd changed."

"Right, right."

"I had hoped he might be our passport out, but there was no way Nick could admit knowing a puny guy with a book on bird-watching."

"How old did you say he was?" Shamayal asked.

"Sixteen. Too young to be living rough. 'They're not worth the hassle,' he said, but the others egged him on. That was when I thought things might turn really nasty. He started shouting, 'Didn't you hear me? I said, *forget* it!'" Even now, the memory of the voice sent shivers coursing down Jim's spine: it was his father speaking. "But they wouldn't leave it. So Nick took our wallets off us. Seeing how little money we had, he said that he'd told them we weren't worth it. Then he grabbed me by the neck. For a minute, I thought - I thought, *Not Aimee. Leave her alone.* But he just let go, saying that he didn't want to see us there again."

What Nick had actually said was, '*I don't want to see you*

or your dirty little girlfriend here again,' but Jim couldn't bring himself to repeat that.

"And then what?" Shamayal was asking.

"We legged it." For the first time in a long while, Jim wished he had a cigarette on him. He could still hear his brother's voice, ugly with laughter: *'The face on him! Thought he was going to cack himself!'* The same brother who'd taken punches for him.

Shamayal was interested now: "Did you rat on him?"

"Aimee was hysterical. She would have gone to the police if I hadn't told her the second guy was my 'no-good junkie brother'. That's how she referred to him after that."

"You looked up to Nick 'til then, din't you?" Shamayal asked.

Jim smiled at the boy's perception. "Come on. We should get out of here."

Welcoming the suggestion, Shamayal was generous. "You can finish up some other time. Bins din't mention no shaggy dog story. I thought it was somethink small I was aksin'."

"What next?" Jim asked as they emerged into the roar of traffic, bypassing the warning signs. Heads down, feet synchronised on see-sawing paving slabs: no longer a boy and his teacher.

"I'm starvin'. Cheese on toast, then *Medal of Honour?*"

"You're on."

Shamayal shoulder-barged him. "You wait. I'm gonna whip your arse, man!"

CHAPTER 15:

JIM - JULY 1992 - THE BUNNY RUN/ AUGUST 2010 - ST HELIER

Rain tumbled in fat drops, leaving domes on the surface of puddles. It was what Jim's grandfather would have called 'proper weather'. Anything less and the old man would shake a fist at the sky: "Is that the best you can manage? You've interrupted a perfectly good day's digging for *this?*" A sharp left between two houses led the way into a fenced labyrinth. Cartwheeling his arms, Jim experienced something close to joy: running through the rain on a warm summer's afternoon after a skinny girl.

"What do they call this?" he asked.

"The bunny run - although it only gets used by foxes now. I haven't been down here since I got my own front door key."

"'King ace!" He whooped loudly, throwing his voice as far as it would travel.

She laughed over her shoulder at him. "You're mental!"

He didn't know it then but, drawing a graph of his emotions, this would have been the highest peak. If Jim had possessed the vocabulary, he might have described the weather as glorious; the day magnificent; himself, elated.

Aimee came to a halt in front of a high wooden gate.

"Servants' entrance?" he enquired, his attempt at BBC English.

"Ha bloody ha!" Reaching her arm over the top, grinning back at Jim, Aimee fumbled and managed to lift the latch. "Stay here," she commanded, an individual raindrop suspended between two eyelashes. "I'll make sure the coast's clear."

"Hurry up!" He shook his head, letting his darkened hair release a scattering of its own, like a dog that has been hosed down. The tall white house shivered a long way off. Jim was used to a shared patch of grass out the back, which turned into a patch of shared mud when it rained. When Aimee reappeared minutes later, he commented, "You could have a half-decent football pitch here."

"Come on!" She beckoned, leading the way to an octagonal wooden building, its door facing away from the house. It was furnished expensively, something Jim mistook for sparsely: sun-loungers; wicker chairs; an ornamental watering can resting on an otherwise bare tabletop. Aimee dived straight onto one of the sun-loungers and stretched out luxuriously. There were garden accessories too, propped up against the walls: a large crate of garden candles, solar-powered lights, that sort of nonsense.

Retrieving his binoculars from inside his t-shirt, Jim tried to erase the half-moons of condensation from the lenses with the driest patch of material he could find along the hem. "What is this place, anyhow?"

"It's our summerhouse," Aimee said. "No one ever comes here but me. Da-da!" she fan-fared, sliding a packet of Benson and Hedges out from under the lounger.

"They're never yours!"

"I borrow them from my dad," Aimee shrugged. "It's not like he can say anything. He's supposed to have given up." Nudging one cigarette proud of the others, she waved the contraband under Jim's nose, a temptress.

Reaching out and taking it would have been easy. "Nah." He shook his head.

"Suit yourself."

His eyes longingly followed the cigarette's journey from packet to lips and, after Aimee had lit up, closed her eyes and taken a long draw, to its resting place between her fingers.

This was new territory. There should have been at least half a dozen yellow DO NOT ENTER signs at the gate. Penned in, there was nothing for Jim to do but perch on the second sun-lounger, frightening for its bed-shaped quality. Adopting an elbows-on-knees stance, intended to look casual, the effect Jim achieved was awkward as anything. There was no birdsong to transform silence into magic, no squirrels to provide a diversion. His emotional graph already dipping, Jim polished a porthole in the steam and pointed his binoculars in the direction of Aimee's house.

The garden was dissected by a path - a stepping-stone effect - leading from the patio to a shed. He mentally positioned goalposts in the wider section of lawn to the right. Beyond, a black cat, still but for the roll of his tail, was sheltering under a veranda that was dripping with lush vegetation.

"Is he yours, the cat?"

Aimee propped herself up on her elbows and swung her legs around. "Don't tell me that bastard's shut Tomsk out while it's chucking it down!"

Ambushed by her banshee transformation, Jim tried to pacify her: "Relax. He's in the dry." Perhaps she was as weirded out as he was.

Through his lenses, Jim followed the line of the cat's gaze. A flash of yellow, he back-tracked in time to see a small bird land in an apple tree, making the slender branch see-saw. White-faced, with a black stripe resembling a pair of wrap-around sunglasses, topped with a blue hat. A second flash of yellow and blue followed closely behind.

"See anything?" Aimee asked.

Jim felt himself redden all the way up to his armpits. There was no way he could mention blue tits to a girl whose top had plastered itself to her, highlighting every curve.

"Too wet," he said.

"Jim." Leaning down, Aimee positioned her cigarette on the rim of the ashtray and then folded her arms, drawing attention to the cross-section he was trying very hard to ignore.

"What?" Swallowing - too noisily, he felt - Jim fixed his eyes on hers, praying, *Don't look down.*

"Chill out. You're making me nervous."

When he glanced away too quickly, scurrying sounds suggested sudden movement. By the time Jim dared look again, Aimee had made a tent over her knees with her t-shirt, stretching the material as far down as it would go.

"This rain isn't going to let up," Jim said, glad of the excuse the monotonous drumming on the roof tiles gave him. "I may as well be off."

He detected relief even though she said, "You'll drown."

"The state of me!" he shrugged. "It's not going to make any difference."

Arriving home only half-drowned, Jim paired his trainers on the mat by the front door. Over the muffled blur of television commentary, he heard his mother's voice saying, "- not how I want things to be. It's just the way they are."

Checking his watch, Jim found himself frowning.

"No, no. He doesn't know yet. He's still out. Actually, hang on... that might be him now."

Loitering outside the living room, he saw his mother, one hand resting heavily on the telephone receiver she had now replaced, her back to him.

"You're home early." He pushed the door fully open, standing, dripping; noting that there was no unread newspaper littering the coffee table, no half-empty mugs, no crumbed plates and no crushed lager cans. A cleaning frenzy had erased every trace of his father.

People leave. He'd got used to it, pitying the small boy who had sobbed as he watched his father waving out of the back window of a police car. But that was a long time ago. When the end result is the same, does it matter if they go on good terms with hugs and kisses, or in anger, vowing never to set foot in this hell-hole again; at peace in the garden, digging the soil they love, or silently, slipping away? In his father's case, leaving had become a habit. Jim despised Frank when he was there and kicked himself for missing the bugger when he was gone.

His mother turned, her face fixed in a smile. "Jim, love, sit yourself down."

Oblivious, Linford Christie repeatedly ran to the finishing line in slow motion, arms outstretched.

"So he's gone then, has he?" Jim stayed where he was.

She looked at him intently and sighed. "They came for him earlier." Jean's voice took on a distant quality: regret and nostalgia. "I was going to make his favourite for tea tonight. It doesn't seem very long ago that I cooked it to welcome him home." A tremor at the corner of her mouth betrayed the fact that she was only just holding it together.

It was up to Jim to roll the dice, to kick-start the slow ascent up the ladders. "We'll be alright, won't we?" A role reversal took place. "You look tired. Why don't you go for a lie down?"

Jean navigated the woodchip wallpaper with her fingertips as if the route was inscribed in Braille. "You're not out this evening, are you?"

The fact his mother imagined he was in demand brought a smile of sorts to Jim's face. He had outgrown the kids who played outside after their teas, but was that bit too young to be anything other than an object to poke fun at for the older kids. Besides, that meant gangs; a reality Jim wasn't ready to face up to. "I'm staying put," he assured her. "I'll bring you a cuppa in a bit."

As he peeled off his sodden clothes and threw them in the bath, it struck Jim: the only person who had never left him was his mother. It was stupid to let Aimee get too close.

For two whole days after his father left, Jim was the adult; his mother, the child. Jean lay curled on top of the bedclothes, fully dressed, eyes staring. Sitting with her, drawn curtains propelling the room into unnatural dusk, Jim amused himself conjuring faces out of the textured wallpaper. He brewed endless cups of tea, taking them away when they were cold. He ate the sandwiches he had made when the bread had reached the consistency of cardboard. He even tried reading to Jean from her true-life magazines, but the love stories horrified and embarrassed him. What some people were willing to reveal about themselves for a measly twenty-five quid! It didn't matter that they changed the names, someone might recognise you. He ran a comb through Jean's hair and, although he tried to be gentle, the teeth caught on a knot. She barely winced. He only had one more card to play.

"*Eastenders* is starting, Mum," he announced, letting the theme music drift through her bedroom door. Working in empty houses, Jean's most frequent contact with other people was watching her favourite soap. Confused that Walford didn't appear on the Tube map, she spoke about the characters as if they were real people. With no time to invest in friendships, she had adopted this speeded up version of life. Witness to the births, the marriages, the funerals; the heady beginnings and the tumultuous ends of relationships, Jean was an authority on them all. "Up you get, Mum!" he encouraged.

When Jean simply blinked, Jim knew that his mother was ill. He got as far as imagining standing by the side of her coffin inhaling the sickly-sweet smell of lilies; his father and brother staring back at him from the front pew, a reminder that there was no choice: it would have to be the family business for him. In desperation, he found himself hopping from foot to foot outside Mrs O'Keefe's. Their next-door neighbour was nervous and middle aged (although, with her tight perm and spectacles, she appeared old to Jim). She lived alone with her short-haired tabby, whose only entertainment was throwing himself against the glass of the kitchen window when people passed by. Keeping her nose out of other people's business, Mrs O'Keefe thanked them for offering her the same courtesy, and most of the time they complied. A knock on her door in the evening would throw her completely off track, but Jim had had no choice. A crack opened up, the security chain straightening.

"Yes?" she spat, a Cyclops smeared with lipstick the wrong shade of coral for her skin-tone. The tabby forced its head into the gap, the feline equivalent of a face-lift.

"I'm Jim. Jean's Jim."

"I know who you are! What do you want?"

"I was wondering." He had hoped to address the whole of her face. "Could you come and take a look at my mum?"

"Your mum?" The eye narrowed to a slit.

"She's hasn't got up for over two days."

"Think I'm some kind of witch doctor? What does your father say?"

"Nothing: he's gone."

The door was unbolted and, seeing a rare opportunity for escape, the cat shot out. Its mistake was hesitating in front of Jim's legs, undecided whether to dart to the left or the right. Before Mrs O'Keefe could cry out, Jim had scooped her up and deposited her safely in his neighbour's arms, an initiative which created an impression. "Your brother fetched me the last time. It'll pass. We just need to give her time."

She disappeared, emerging with a headscarf tied over her

tight curls and a square green handbag, which she fished about in, withdrawing an impressive array of keys. "You can't be too careful. Mind you, those who are out to cause trouble tend to take it away from their front doors. No, I don't mean *you!* Not even your brother, although he turned out to be a loose cannon. It's the *changes* round here I'm not comfortable with." Jim had heard similar views before: it wasn't only birds that were migrating. She wasn't a racist. Credit where credit's due, Mrs O'Keefe followed any reference to her Indian doctor with the words, "But he's ever so thorough."

"Kitchen through here, is it? That's the good thing about living on an estate. The flats are all the same."

Whether 'good' was an accurate description was debatable. Someone decides to have curry, you may as well all have curry. Someone decides to listen to Metallica, you all headbang. Someone else has an argument, be grateful: it saves you the energy.

Choosing not to follow, Jim tracked his neighbour's movements by her persistent dry cough, which seemed to have no purpose other than to remind him of her presence.

"Has she eaten?" Mrs O'Keefe called through to him in the living room.

"No. I've tried everything."

He could hear her opening and closing cupboards, tutting. He thought he had better see what she was up to.

"Soup," she said, extracting a tin. "Where are your pans?"

Jim complied.

Mrs O'Keefe fussed as if she were entering Masterchef rather than heating a tin of Campbell's. With minute adjustments, the bowl and spoon were laid out on the tray just so; the soup tested for temperature, ladled rather than poured. Jim thought of the extra washing up.

"Door!" she commanded.

In the musty gloom, Jim could just make out his mother's

shadowy outline, prostrate on the bed.

"Jean, love, it's Deirdre." Mrs O'Keefe slid the tray onto the bedside table. "Why don't we sit you up? I've brought you some nice soup."

The shadow shrank.

"I know, I know," Mrs O'Keefe mewed, then in sharp contrast: "Jim, help me out!"

As Mrs O'Keefe hauled his mother into a sitting position and he wedged two pillows behind her, Jean's peering eyes accused him of betrayal. "I was worried, Mum," he mumbled.

"I expect those trains have got to you again," Mrs O'Keefe said with conviction, feeling Jean's forehead with the back of her hand. "One went off the top of the Richter Scale earlier. Honest to God, I'm amazed this place is still standing. Now let's put this tray on your lap, shall we?" Then, accustomed to dealing with cats, Mrs O'Keefe shooed Jim out.

Jim didn't know what miracle his neighbour performed, but half an hour later there was an empty bowl in the kitchen sink and she pronounced her verdict: "Leave her be this evening. She'll be up and about tomorrow."

The following day, Jim was woken by the sound of running water. He urgently needed to pee but, padding down the hall, found the bathroom door locked. His mother was singing along loudly to Take That. Crossing his ankles, he rattled the handle. "Are you going to be long?"

"I'm having a soak!" came the cheerful reply.

"I need the loo." Jim pressed the bones of his knees together. "Can't I come in?"

"Sorry, love! Can't hear you!"

Jim found himself torn between exasperation and marvelling that Mrs O'Keefe's unlikely-sounding prediction had been accurate. Brought back from the verge of despair by soup. As he pissed into the empty can (secreted away until he could dispose of its jaundiced contents), he considered that

Campbell's could add that to their slogans: 'Life-saving Soup'.

When Jean finally emerged, wrapped in her lilac towelling dressing gown, Jim elbowed past into the steam carrying the concealed can. He made a pretence of unzipping his flies and then poured his orange-tinted sample slowly in the bowl. The stained towels used by his mother for the monthly ritual of dying her hair were half-hidden behind the shower curtain: a sign she was preparing to face the world.

But not everything was back to normal. Competing draughts running through the hallway hit him from all angles.

"What are you doing, Mum? It's freezing." He climbed onto the sofa to close the living room window.

"I'm letting the church bells in. Listen!" As she stood, apparently transfixed by their off-key other-worldliness, Jim knew that Jean was thinking of village fetes and tea with cucumber sandwiches. Things that didn't concern them.

He made it his job to trail his mother around the flat, watching her every move. Was she drinking enough? Had she eaten? Had she lost the knack of cleaning?

"Give me some space, will you!" she snapped at him eventually.

Fine. The best test of whether she was herself was to do something wrong and see how quickly she jumped down his throat. He lay on the sofa, positioning his shoes on her favourite cushion, a revolting concoction of fake satin and embroidered roses.

"Right!" Her voice boomed from the kitchen doorway. "That's it! Get out from under my feet!"

When Jim grinned she grabbed the cushion, swiping at him playfully. "I show a moment's weakness and you think you can take advantage!"

"Leave it out, Mum!" He wrapped his arms around his head as the cushion rained down. "You had me scared."

The blows stopped and she sat down next to him. "I'm not

going anywhere." He grimaced, but allowed her to tousle his hair. "We've got to stick together, you and me."

"Why aren't you back at work?"

"I needed a couple of days, Jim." He could see the exhaustion in her eyes. "Time to myself. That's not too much to ask, is it? I've got to think of answers to all those awkward questions I'll be asked, for starters. You're the world's leading authority on excuses. What would you say?"

"Who am I talking to?" Jim asked.

"Oh, I don't know... Her at the Post Office asking when your dad's coming to pick up his benefit."

Jim didn't feel any obligation to protect his father, but his mum didn't like him repeating the truth: that, she labelled 'gossip'. Experience had taught him that an obvious lie can be good to make the point that it's nobody's business but your own.

"Where's your dad, Jimmy?" A lad would sneer, tackling him on the football pitch.

"On his annual vacation in the Bahamas," Jim would reply, kicking his tormentor's ankle. "Sorry, didn't see you there. I hope that didn't hurt."

On the other hand, the genius of a good lie could be completely wasted if no one ever found him out. The truth should be covered up for just long enough.

"Hey, Jimmy! Where's your old man?"

"Don't say anything, but my mum's kicked him out."

"What did he do this time?"

"The usual."

"Think she'll let him back?"

"She'd be mad to."

The idea of telling a lie - or a series of lies believable enough to fool everyone in the longer run - wasn't one of Jim's specialties. He shrugged and she sighed.

"Well, if you've got no advice, you can nip down to the shop for me."

The boy's thoughts turned to escape. Cooped up for three long days, Jim was in need of a friendly face.

"We've got nothing for our tea." As he opened the door, she shouted after him, "Get a Viennetta! We deserve a treat."

With pockets weighed down by pound coins, he by-passed the Happy Shopper and made his way to the tracks. She was there: a skinny girl staring blankly at the tracks, an open book lying cover up beside her, unread. As soon as she saw him, Aimee jumped up.

"Where have you been?" She ran at Jim, all hair, spit and angry fists.

"Whoa there!" He warded off her attack. "Give us a minute and I'll tell you."

To his embarrassment, Jim realised Aimee was sobbing. "Why didn't you come?"

"I'll tell you." He tried to look into her red-rimmed eyes through her nest of hair. "Could we just sit down first?" Jim steered her to a flat piece of grass and, since he was holding her wrists, they dropped to the ground as one.

"You can't just not turn up like that!" she started again, before he had the chance to speak. "We had an arrangement -"

Anger brewing, Jim replied, "D'you want me to tell you or don't you?"

"Five minutes!" she mouthed through a membrane of sticky saliva. "That's all it would have taken!"

"That's it, I can do without this!" Jim stood, furious at the realisation that, now Aimee had moved in on his turf, he would have to find somewhere else to watch his birds.

"You haven't even told me what happened!" Back on her feet, Aimee was running to keep pace with him.

"That's because you haven't shut up!" He kept moving, elbows pumping.

"So where were you, then?"

"I couldn't get out." Jim turned to face her. "It's my dad."

Something in his tone must have warned Aimee to stop her tirade. "Is he ill?"

"I wish!"

"What, then?"

Jim knew that his next sentence would spell the end of whatever it was between them. "He was arrested."

Her immediate reaction was to laugh.

"Accessory to armed robbery. Glad you think my life's a joke!"

"You're serious," she recoiled. They both sank to the bottom of the concrete steps, mirror images: chins in hands, elbows on knees.

Jim addressed Aimee's scratched feet, pointing inwards in their yellow flip-flops. "I tried telling you. It's what he does."

"But I went on," she said, "and on…"

"You weren't to know. My mum went into meltdown. I fetched a neighbour in the end."

"Is she alright?"

"She must be: she's got me running errands. First chance I had, I thought I'd sneak down here to see you." He allowed himself a small laugh. "Christ knows why!"

"I'm sorry." Aimee hung her head. "It's just that I waited and waited. I thought something really bad had happened."

"Something bad *did* happen!"

"You know what I mean. You could be lying in a ditch somewhere and I wouldn't have a clue. You're my best friend, but all I know is your first name, that you like bird-watching and that you live in a block of flats." She nodded in the vague direction of Ralegh Grove. "Somewhere up the hill."

Jim couldn't help feeling touched. He had never had a best friend. They were a girl thing. "That's all you need. You go to Ralegh Grove and ask for Jim."

"It's as simple as that." Aimee folded her arms.

He shrugged. "Don't see why not but, if you can't find me

there, you could always go to the park and ask about Jim who plays left back."

"Yeah, right." She scoffed. "Like I'm going to go down the park and ask a bunch of guys I don't know!"

"You forget: I've seen you handle yourself. So where would I go if you went missing?"

"Well, you know the back way to my house. And you've met my cat."

"Alright then," he said, levering himself up; matter closed.

She looked up at him in panicked surprise. "Where are you going?"

"I was only supposed to be gone a quarter of an hour. Mum'll have the tracker dogs out if I don't get back soon."

Girls! he thought as he trudged up the steps, shaking his head in disbelief. It took a while to digest what had just happened: Aimee liked him enough to worry. Plus, she knew all his bad stuff, and STILL wanted to know him. It was what his mum would have pronounced a *Singing in the Rain* moment. Jim was no Gene Kelly - fact was, he was tone deaf with two left feet - but he walked to the shops with a swagger, too pleased to ponder what had caused Aimee to promote him in the pecking order of her friends.

"A penny for them."

Jolted awake, Jim heard his own intake of breath, the slightest of snores.

"You alright? Want me to fetch someone?" a pale orderly with dyed red hair offered. She was standing between his hospital bed and the tea trolley, with its four unlabelled flasks, allegedly tea, coffee, hot chocolate and Bovril.

"I'm fine," he said, rubbing his eyes, trying to adjust.

"Drink?"

"Tea, please. Milk, no sugar." For all the difference it made.

"Coming right up." She poured extravagantly, lifting the flask away from the cup and then bringing it back down. "Got to keep your fluids up."

'Fluid' was a more accurate description of the couple of inches of uninviting luke-warm liquid that he lifted to his lips and smiled his appreciation of: Bovril with milk.

CHAPTER 16:

AYISHA - JULY 2010 - JIM'S FLAT

Ordinarily, Ayisha would have been pleasantly surprised by Jim's tree-lined neighbourhood - a conservation area - but annoyance at having had to pay for parking, to estimate how many quarter hours she might need, added weight to her put-upon feeling. Despite the confidence she tried to convey while walking up the path, she was consumed by the fear of the guilty, convinced something about her appearance would suggest she was up to no good. It was on attempt number three that she identified the correct front door key, only to find herself fumbling again in the lobby.

Tellingly, save for a Chinese takeaway leaflet, there was no scattering of post on the varnished pine. Her eyes didn't have to flit far before they settled on the neat stack of envelopes on top of the narrow cabinet in the hall. Someone had been here.

"Shamayal?" Her footsteps echoed.

Ayisha shuffled the post, unable to shake the feeling that she was prying. But no: she had been asked to come. Specifically for this purpose, in fact. The majority of envelopes were junk, but there was a white envelope she suspected was a bank statement and a square one with a handwritten address that had the appearance of a get-well-soon card.

"Shamayal?" she called out again, stowing them inside her handbag. Nothing. She hesitated, listening. "It's me, Miss Emmanuel." Idly pulling on one of the handles, Ayisha saw that the cabinet was designed for shoe storage. *Clever!* A glance over her shoulder to check she'd closed the door revealed two tidy shelves above, crammed with paperbacks. And then she saw precisely the same coat hooks she had been trying to source on the internet. Where had Jim managed to find them?

Hesitating in the doorway to the living room, drawn curtains filtering soft light, she gasped at the sight of the owl. Then she laughed at her own foolishness: what she was looking at wasn't a live bird, but a photograph. A very good one, but a photograph just the same. Even now, Ayisha found she was holding her breath: *it was literally breath-taking.* With no backdrop to detract from its outstretched wings, individual feathers splayed, the bird glowed in the half-dark as it would when hunting. Deciding to draw the curtains, she subconsciously gave the owl a wide berth. Its eyes appeared to follow her. Suspended, hovering, the position of the talons made its intention clear: Ayisha was its prey.

The recesses on either side of the fireplace were shelved: CDs and DVDs to her right, the books Jim had asked for to her left. A row of greeting cards had been placed in front of the paperbacks. In the process of moving them aside, a photograph slipped through her fingers. She gave chase as it drifted like a paper aeroplane. A blond-haired boy dressed for Halloween grinned up at her, gap-toothed. Kneeling on the leather armchair, she located the card it had fallen from and found herself smiling as she read the words: 'Dear Uncle Jim, I won first prize for best dressed ghoul. You can help me make costumes any day.' The card and these simple sentences, heading crookedly downhill from carefully ruled lines, were joyful things. A footnote was written in an adult hand: '*Uncle*

Jim! Callum has forgotten to thank you for his Build Your Own Volcano kit. It erupted quite spectacularly. How many times must I tell you? Nothing that needs more than four batteries and nothing that explodes. Next time you visit, you will be painting the kitchen ceiling.'

"What you doin'?"

One of Ayisha's hands leapt to her chest as she twisted round: "Shamayal!" She exhaled loudly, blood pounding in her ears. "You made me jump!"

He nodded at her, arms folded. His low-slung jeans were pushed down over his hip bones. Ayisha noticed that he was barefoot, accounting for his stealth-like approach.

"Why didn't you reply when I called you?" She bent down to retrieve the photograph, reuniting it with the card.

"I was busy, wasn't I?" Adopting a protective air, he took it from her. "I don't fink you should be goin' through Jim's private stuff."

"I was moving it out of the way -"

"Looked like you was readin' it to me."

"I was *trying* to get to the books. Jim - Mr Stevens - asked me to pick up a few things for him."

The boy's eyes widened greedily. "They let you in to see him? How's he doin'?"

"The surgery went well, but it's going to be a slow recovery."

"You fink they'll let me visit?"

The next leap was the big one as far as Ayisha was concerned. But Jim would want to thank Shamayal. Surely the boy deserved that much? And it wouldn't be so extraordinary for a boy to visit his teacher in hospital, the teacher whose life he had helped save. So she allowed herself one ordinary human reaction. "Why don't you come with me? But first we need to get a few things straight."

Shamayal raised his eyebrows, shrugged. Suddenly, it seemed, he could take it or leave it.

"Mr Stevens could get in trouble for having a relationship with a pupil outside school." *What am I saying?* she thought. *It's me who's here on my own with a pupil.* "You understand that, don't you?"

"A *relationship?*"

Not in the mood for attitude, Ayisha sighed impatiently. "You know exactly what I'm talking about! Anything that doesn't fall within the strict definition of teacher and pupil."

The boy folded his arms sulkily. "Whoever made them rules is stupid."

"You're entitled to your opinion, but unfortunately they're necessary. I need to know, did you say anything to the police about Jim being a friend?"

He made a face like a tortoise. "Why would I go tellin' the *police* anything?"

"You told the officer you knew about his family!" she snapped back.

"Yeah, an' I know the name of Mrs Small's budgie. That don't mean nuffin."

Ayisha put one hand to her temple. "OK." Pain was building up behind her eyes, an accumulation of sleeplessness and worry. By the time she looked at the boy again, something in his expression had changed. "What is it?" she asked, unnerved.

"I was wrong about you," he said, nodding, as if he knew something about her that she hadn't yet grasped. "You came lookin' for me, din't you?"

"Jim thought I might find you here."

"I bin keepin' an eye on the place, you know? These days, you only have to go off on a week's holiday and squatters move in. And you can't just kick 'em out. I saw it on the news."

The boy clearly had his own key. Ayisha dismissed the thought: didn't want to make it any more of her business than it already was. She made a decision to be as professional as was possible, given the circumstances. "Maybe you can help me find a bag to put some things in."

Shamayal headed straight for the under-stairs cupboard. He knew his way around.

"He wants his books, right?" Shamayal by-passed Ayisha and put the kitbag on the seat of the armchair. His fingers moved over the tops of the books as if he were practising a piano scale. Ignoring the novels, he tipped three spines forwards. She read the title of the one he slotted back into place: *RSPB Pocket Guide to British Birds*. "Nah, not that one. He keeps his favourite on the kitchen table. He's got the best view from there."

Following in the boy's footsteps, Ayisha waited for him to expand. Balking at a putrid smell, she located the fruit bowl: heavily freckled bananas, the brown threatening to dominate what was left of their yellow skins.

"These are the ones. These, and his notebooks. Everything in the other room, yeah? The novels and all that?" Ayisha recalled a few Stephen Kings, a Douglas Adams, John Peel's autobiography. Shamayal screwed up his nose. "Just for show, innit?"

Ayisha, who liked to fill her living room bookshelf with titles she thought said something about her, even though she hadn't actually read any Hanif Kureishi, found herself laughing. "So which one's his favourite?"

Shamayal reached across the fruit bowl and picked up a battered specimen with a photograph of a green woodpecker on the cover. "First one he ever owned."

She regarded him blankly. The first what?

"I know what you're finkin': bor-ing! But it's cool, man. He's showed me stuff I never would of noticed before. Mind you, you got to sit still for a *long* time."

Ayisha admired the way Shamayal elongated the word. She gave the image of the woodpecker another look. Was he saying that they went *bird-watching?*

"We tell each other all our stories. Well, I gotta be honest, it's mainly Jim who does the tellin'. Fact, he was halfway through somethink I wanted to hear the end of when all this happened. Then he sketches, of course. He starts off with a couple of lines and, before you know it -"

"A regular Rolf Harris!"

"Who's that, then?"

"I'm showing my age."

"Never! Not you, Miss." The boy looked Ayisha up and down in a way that might have been flattering in other circumstances. She was about to issue a stern reminder about acceptable boundaries when he continued, "Hey, you think Jim could do some drawin' in hospital?"

"You know, that's a really good idea."

He grinned. "That's me: full of 'em."

While Shamayal went in search of pencils, Ayisha peeled back the top corner of the cover of the notebook, revealing the edge of a line-drawing: a head. Opening the page, what she saw was not the simple outline of Shamayal's description, but a perfectly executed sketch of a bird, rich in detail. She would never have had Jim down as an accomplished artist.

Being in his home enabled Ayisha to flesh out his bones. She pictured him sitting at the kitchen table, a half-eaten croissant abandoned, a golden trail of flakes on the tabletop. He was looking out at the small courtyard - its iron table and chairs and its terracotta pots overflowing with lavender and rosemary. Pencil poised, he watched the birds - her knowledge of birds being limited, these were blackbirds - as they landed on the tired ivy-clad fence. She imagined walking into the scene, drawn by the smell of coffee and warm pastries, and hesitating in the doorway; not wanting to let him know she was there, observing the careful lines his pencil made on the page. She was wearing his dressing gown, its smell musky and earthy, towel-drying the ends of her hair; the whole day ahead. Later she would make a salad dressing using the expensive olive oil she had spied on the kitchen worktop and the lemon from the fruit bowl. They would eat lunch outside, perhaps drink prosecco...

"Course, we do other stuff as well." The boy's voice wafted through the door.

Ayisha checked herself, confused. Where had these thoughts sprung from? She saw that a few dandelions had sprouted between the crazy paving stones. *You need to get out more,* she mocked herself. Holding the bananas by their woody stalk, she took them from the fruit bowl and dropped them into the pedal bin.

"He kicks arse at *Medal of Honour.* He had me on my knees, beggin' for mercy." Shamayal appeared in the doorway, laughing, a deep and unexpected sound. Attempting to look busy, Ayisha began opening and closing kitchen drawers. His smile froze. "What you up to now, Miss?"

She deferred to him. "Looking for plastic bags. I thought we could take him the rest of the fruit before it goes off."

"Bottom left," he said, eyeing her suspiciously. "Hey, what d'you do with them bananas?"

"I binned them."

"You din't!" He stamped on the pedal, looked inside. "Man! They was just gettin' to how the recipe said they should be."

"They were making the place smell." *Move the conversation on,* she told herself as Shamayal set his face. "The nurse suggested pyjamas. Jim said he doesn't have any, but he thought tracksuit bottoms and t-shirts would do." She would have preferred not to go rummaging round in his bedroom, but this was something she definitely couldn't ask Shamayal to do. Walking past him, Ayisha found herself submerged in calming olive-green.

"Ahem! Should you even be goin' in there, Miss?"

There was a smell not dissimilar to her imagined scent of the dressing gown, except that it had lost its warmth. "Should *you?*"

"I guess we could both go - if you fink you can trus' yourself with me, that is."

"Please don't joke about it."

He groaned. "That's your rule book speakin', right?"

Couldn't Shamayal see how inflammatory the situation was? "No. This is me."

"Doubt it," he muttered, clearly intending to be heard. "No one's that uptight."

Choosing to ignore this - what was there to be gained? - she located Jim's dressing gown hanging on the back of the door, where he had said it would be. Shamayal gently eased folded t-shirts out of a drawer, laying them on top of the duvet to square the shoulders. Against the black of a t-shirt, his nails were perfectly white. Seeing underpants in the open drawer, Ayisha reflected how humiliated she would be, having a male colleague go through her underwear. Perhaps it was best to leave Shamayal to it. She tried to give the impression of disinterest in the bed - its leather headboard and good white linen - but opened the door of what she imagined to be a closet and flicked the light switch. Whatever the small room's history, it was now another example of Jim's ingenious use of space. The walls were lined with history books, one wide shelf at desk height. How perfect! A hidden office. There was an old-fashioned style desk lamp in shining chrome; his laptop; a discarded pair of rimless glasses. It was as if Jim had just left. Ayisha thought of her own poor attempts at balancing exercise books on knees, or sitting up in bed as she corrected formulae and equations, and graded tests with no one to tell her it was time to turn the light out. Before she could stop herself, she had conjured up an image of bringing Jim a cup of tea, finding him hunched over an essay; kissing the crown of his head.

"What you lookin' for, Miss?"

Feeling as if she had been caught red-handed, Ayisha flicked off the light, saying, "Nothing," but turned back to enquire of the office door. "You don't think he'd want his laptop, do you?"

"Might have some games on it. You fink they let them have electrical stuff?"

"Everybody else does. I don't see why not."

"I'll chuck his i-Pod in, then."

"He needs toiletries. We should do the bathroom next."

Ayisha wasn't disappointed with what she found: chrome, natural stone with a mosaic inset. Her hands idly brushed against a towel: hotel quality. Shamayal went straight to the bathroom cabinet.

"Get this!" He thrust a can of Lynx in Ayisha's direction. "This is the stuff girls go wild for, right?"

She turned up her nose. "Not me."

Shamayal hesitated, closing the mirrored doors carefully. "Can I aks you something, Miss?"

She sat and folded her arms. "Within reason."

He turned, leaning back on the sink. "Jim's an attractive man, right?"

Ayisha blinked, deliberately slowly.

"Them rules don't apply when you're sittin' on the side of a bath. 'Sides, I'm not asking if *you* fancy him."

"Alright," she relented. "He's not unattractive."

"And this is a nice place! Ignoring his taste and the fact that it's quite pokey - it's nice, right?"

"It's very nice," she agreed. And not pokey at all when compared with her own flat. Used to having everything handed to them on a plate, kids had no idea about the value of things. Or interior design, apparently.

"You're his friend -"

She opened her mouth to contradict him, but all that emerged was an *Ah!*

"Why do you think he's single?"

Shamayal was right: the intimate setting did demand honesty. He had sat down on the closed toilet seat. "Shamayal, what I said to you…" She shook her head. "I don't actually know Jim all that well. I like him very much, but as a colleague."

The boy's look was despondent rather than triumphant. "Man! I thought as much."

Realising she had extended a hand towards him, Ayisha swiftly retracted it. "What is it, Shamayal? Is there something you want to tell me?"

"I don't think he's got anyone. I mean, it's fine in term-time, isn't it? It's easy to keep busy. But once the holidays start…"

She smiled. Jim had voiced concern for the boy in similar terms. Who was feeling sorry for whom? Gripping the sides of the bath, Ayisha stared down at her painted toenails, visible through the peep-toes of her shoes. Anyone who has time to varnish toenails has too much time on their hands! Her smile slipped in stages at the thought of the long weeks ahead: the few days earmarked for tasks; the prospect of visiting her parents. She had fostered ideas of a week on the Amalfi coast; winding roads with sheer drops; walking through lemon groves; bathing in a turquoise sea. But the idea of asking for a table for one, wondering where to look while she ate a solitary meal, was too painful. Instead she had blown the money on a Mulberry handbag.

"You got a boyfriend, Miss? Stupid question. Someone as hot as you must have, right?" The boy was still seated, elbow resting on the toilet roll, but his expression was earnest and slightly embarrassed.

Her smile clicked into position; her voice, formal. "Not at the moment."

"For real, Miss? I mean - and I don't mean no disrespect - but you're proper buff. Still, you got lots of friends, right? You all out having your likkle girly lunches, drinking your cocktails..."

"Oh, yes." Never having been described as 'hot' or 'buff' before, she was thrown by the unexpected compliments. Girly lunches, rare occurrences taking a month of fraught email exchanges to arrange, were taken in family-friendly cafes with ample facilities for baby-changing and staff who didn't object to customers spoon-feeding their children home-pureed sweet potato. "My life's one long episode of *Sex in the City.*"

"Right, right!" He laughed easily, but his grin became suspended. "Hey, you're not the lesbo, are you?"

"That's none of your- !" If that's what other people thought, it was no wonder it had been a year since her last date.

"I'm not prejudiced," he coaxed.

"No, I'm not the lesbian!" God! "No more questions."

His Cheshire-cat grin was infuriating. "I ain't got no problem if you are. I'm jus' about the most open-minded person you'll ever meet."

CHAPTER 17:

JIM - AUGUST 1992 -
RALEGH GROVE

His mother called out the minute Jim's key was in the door. "Ben's here for you. I've just been saying that we haven't seen him for a while."

Not since Nick 'left home'. Thick-set and broad, Ben was the youngest lad from a large Irish family. His older brother - self-proclaimed leader of the local gang - had a reputation for being a nasty piece of work. Jim imagined the day had come when he was going to be asked, "So: you with us or against us?" and there would be no more stalling.

"Alright, mate."

They nodded without smiling, sizing each other up. Jim couldn't tell what Ben's blank expression was hiding but had himself down as the faster of the pair.

"Thought you might fancy a kick-about."

"Could do," Jim replied, his non-committal tone implying it was obvious he knew there was no game of football to be had. What was his mother thinking? There was no ball tucked under the older boy's arm. And she should have asked herself what a lad of Nick's age would want with him in the first place.

"I said you'd be dying to get out." Jean turned to Ben. "I've been laid up with that nasty bug that's been doing the rounds. Jim's been nursing me back to health."

"Is that right?" Ben nodded, pretence at being impressed proving an acting challenge.

"I'll take that, love." Jean reached for the Happy Shopper bag, leaving Jim exposed.

"Where are you off to, then?"

"Is the park alright with you, Jim?"

Jim, who never used names unless it was strictly necessary, could smell his own sweat. "Why not, Ben?"

"See you at tea-time." Jean smiled at Ben. "I don't know what we've got in but you'd be very welcome." A polite invitation, designed to be declined.

"My Nan's coming round tonight." A perfectly weighted reply to a fake invitation.

Jean's nod projected just the right level of disappointment. "Another time, then."

She stood waving as they ambled wordlessly towards the staircase, hands in pockets, matching each other pace for pace.

"Where *are* we off to, then?" Jim asked, once in the stairwell, out of earshot and out of view.

"I only go as far as the corner." Ben took his hands out of his pockets. They weren't clenched into fists. If Jim was in danger, it would come from elsewhere.

"So you're the messenger, are you?" Expecting to be jumped at the bottom of the stairs, he swung wide on the handrail. The space underneath was empty.

"You know me," Ben sneered. "Anything for an E or two."

Of course: Ben was expecting payment.

They passed the Wednesday-ripe bin sheds which had attracted the usual shimmer of pigeons. Jim winced at the sight of them picking through the overspill. "Filthy birds."

"And there was me thinking birds was your thing."

"Not pigeons. You can't respect anything that doesn't give a toss what it puts in its mouth. They only have thirty-seven taste buds - that's 9963 less than you and me -"

"Jesus!" Ben's hands made stop signs. "Did you hear me say I was interested, Freak-boy?"

Jim shrugged. He stepped over the puffed out males who were strutting in that ridiculous way of theirs. Others fought off stiff competition from black-headed gulls (a misleading name, given that they're only black-headed when they're in season). Although not officially vermin, Jim thought them just as bad. Attracted by leftovers; screeching loudly enough to drown out the B.F.P's persistent cooing; bullying anything smaller that had the bad judgement to get in their way. *Right at home*, he thought, glancing sidelong at Ben.

They passed a skinny kid lying in an estate road beside a speed bump. All of five, he was small enough to hide behind it. Football shorts displayed knees that stuck out like golf balls.

"Alright, Stef," Jim hovered over the boy, one foot either side. "What you doing?"

"Waiting for cars. Mark dared me."

"Leave 'im." Ben mustered all the authority a sulky teen-ager can carry.

There was an official five-mile-an-hour speed limit on the estate, but some joker had changed the signs to read fifty miles an hour, which was closer to the mark. "How much danger money is he paying you?"

The young boy sat up, scratching his head.

"Hadn't thought about it, had you?"

At the washing lines, one of the kids was spinning a rotary dryer hand over hand, while another hung from it. A few yards away, the official play area was occupied by a couple of heavy-set pigeon-heads baiting an American Pitbull. Ben chuckled as they forced the seat of a swing into the dog's jaws and let go, sending the animal reeling backwards and forwards, legs scrambling. Jim turned away from its whimpering.

Further into the centre of the estate, the roads ran out; high-rise replaced low; concrete replaced brick. The bright spark who had decided that the balconies should be decorated with blue panelling hadn't anticipated how his colour scheme would look thirty years on, tired and peeling.

Perched in his usual spot, Bins was fully galoshed, fishing rod at the ready. "Jim Stevens!" he announced the boy's arrival.

Self-conscious, Jim felt eyes flit to him, some with sympathy, others with respect. He'd never been so well known, that was for sure. "Bins." He nodded casually.

A rolled up piece of newspaper on the end of his hook, Bins winked. "I'm feeling lucky today. Like it, eh?"

"Alright, Jim."

He spun around at the sound of a voice to see two lads of Ben's age. *So this is it,* he thought, his pocketed hands squeezing into fists.

"Tony Maloney and Jake Stewart!" Bins raised one hand in cheerful greeting. The lad's real name was Tony Malone, and it wasn't just Bins who struggled. He had been given the nickname Bugsy at an early age, but was only just getting a proper feel for it. Rumour had it, the previous week he'd dangled a young lad who wouldn't willingly donate his lunch money from a balcony by the ankles. Sixth floor. What good fists would be, Jim had no idea.

"How you doing, Bins?" Tony returned the salute.

"Alright, Bugsy," Jim said flatly. Everyone was at their most civil when Bins was there to referee.

"Get your skinny arse over here!" Jake called out.

"Good news travels fast," Ben said when Jim joined them.

A hand was clapped on his shoulder. Swallowing - show your fear and you may as well lie down there and then - Jim turned to look whoever it was straight in the eye. His jaw dropped. "Nick!" A few weeks earlier he would have been relieved to see his brother. Now he wasn't sure.

"Good to see you too, bruv." Nick nodded in Ben's direction. "You can get lost now."

"I'm in no hurry," Ben said, leaning against the wall of the block, cupping a cigarette as he lit it.

"No sense of community round here anymore." Something cellophane-wrapped was extracted from an inside pocket, conveyed in a closed fist. "Brixton's finest."

Ben held his cigarette packet open. "That'll do nicely."

"I said I'd never set foot here again, didn't I?" Nick's appearance was ruffled, a nocturnal creature out of its comfort zone. His baseball cap was pulled low, his eyes just visible enough for Jim to note that the wild look had retreated.

"So, what *are* you doing back?" the younger boy asked.

"You cocky bastard! I wouldn't be here if it wasn't for the old man."

The cogs turned slowly. *The family business.* Jim backed off, the childhood myth that featured brother as hero trampled. "You were in it together!"

"Keep it down, will you!" Nick grabbed his elbow, steering him round the corner of the block. "What do they know?" he demanded, halting sharply.

Jim shook the hand off his arm. "No one's been around. I got home. Dad was gone. End of."

"You sure?"

"I haven't seen anyone. Unless you count Mrs O'Keefe."

"How come?" Nick's face was close. Several days' growth littered his chin.

"Mum was taken bad, wasn't she?" Jim then realised that his mother must have reached the same conclusion before him. Little wonder she'd spent two days on hunger strike.

"So, what will you say if you're asked when you last saw me?"

Jim squared up to his brother, keen to hear what Nick had

to say for himself. "I'll say I haven't seen you since that night down by the tracks."

A couple of girls' giggling faces appeared around the corner but, on seeing the pair of them lock-eyed, decided better of it.

His brother's eyebrows travelled down and up, then he reached inside his pocket. "I didn't think I'd have to pay *you* to keep your gob shut, you little shite." He peeled a tenner from a wad of limp notes.

"That's only what you already owe me." Wanting distance, Jim put two hands up at chest height. "To think I used to look up to you." Then he turned on his heels, his brother hurling a stream of abuse after him. Sticks and stones. He could play at that game. "Mum didn't have any choice when she chucked you out. You're bang out of order!"

Striding over a speed bump, Jim almost tripped over Stef.

"Jim!" the boy called out, sounding elated. "Got my danger money sorted."

"Yeah?" Jim said without stopping, trainers kicking up loose tarmac. "Who's going to give a shit when you're dead?"

Hearing bass vibrations, Jim glanced back in time to see a Ford Fiesta screech around the corner, the shadowy peaks of five baseball caps nodding.

"Stef!" he yelled over his shoulder. "Car!"

Music thumped closer. His eardrums vibrated *boom, boom boom-boom* to *Rhythm is a Dancer*, the summer's big hit spinning the air with positive messages. Two stiff armed girls bent at the waist, lifting their hands in a robotic dance. A third snaked her arms overhead, singing the melody.

The boy didn't react. "Get up, you eejit!" Using his foot as a brake, Jim changed direction and broke into a sprint. He threw himself into the path of the vehicle. Five heads fell forwards, arms flying to soften the blow, hands leaving fingerprints on glass. When Jim dared open his eyes, he was bent over the bonnet. The driver had stuck his head out of the open window and was yelling: "If you've dented my motor, you're fucking dead, Bird-boy!"

Backing off, Jim kept one hand raised. He hauled Stef up, speaking through gritted teeth. "Trying to get us both killed?"

Seeing this, the driver threw open the car door. "Christ's sake, man!" He thrust one foot out. "What d'you think you're playing at, bro'?"

Breaking free, Stef turned to jab the index fingers of both hands sharply upwards. "Fuck you both sideways!"

"Oi, wash your mouth out! Where's your bleeding manners?"

"And you, Stevens!" Stef ran backwards. "You owe me my danger money!"

"Little fucker!" The driver spat, acting shocked at the boy's nerve. "Should've left him where he was."

Jim wanted nothing more than to go home. He slammed the door of his flat on the world outside.

"That you already?" Jean called out from the living room, "I thought footie was forty-five minutes each way."

He flopped down next to her on the sofa. "Nothing much doing. What's on?"

She tapped his knee distractedly. "A film: *Beaches*."

"What's it about?"

"It's a weepy. This woman's dying of cancer, only her friend doesn't know it yet."

A groan escaped from Jim.

"Don't ruin it! If you don't want to watch you can go and make me a cuppa."

For some reason even Jim couldn't understand, that sent him storming out of the room, too stubborn to emerge from his bedroom even when the smell of bacon wafted through the keyhole.

CHAPTER 18:

JIM - AUGUST 2010 -
ST HELIER HOSPITAL

A West African orderly whose plastic nametag identified her as Imelda had Jim's bicep trapped in an
armband of pressurised air. A vein throbbed its protest as yet more air pushed it to capacity. Just when he thought
it would burst, the pillow began to deflate.

"How's it looking?" he asked as the air hissed slowly, forcing itself out.

"Hang on," Imelda said, dipping her head at the digital
numbers. "Hang on... there! Not so bad." She recorded the
result on a digital keypad. "If you didn't keep yourself fit,
you'd be feelin' a whole lot worse."

"We'll go running together once I'm out."

Her scornful look said *I don't know about that!* Jim wasn't
convinced he would be up to it either. For someone entered
in the Wimbledon half-marathon in just two weeks' time,
he should have been planning his final training runs. He
wasn't used to inactivity but already, muscles wasting away,
Jim could understand its appeal. He would have to dig deep
for the motivation to start from scratch again. Those painful
walk-jog-sprint-jog-walk-jog-sprint sessions.

Joyce from next door was yelping for help again. Imelda sighed knowingly. "Poor, lonely old soul just after a bit of attention. How you feelin' otherwise? Is there much pain?"

He attempted to shrug.

"Think you can handle it, Mister Have-a-go Hero? Look at that!" She mused, picking up his newspaper. "Nice picture of you on the front cover today."

It was a graduation photograph that had appeared in the local paper. *The Comet* must have kept it on file. "They captured my good side."

"And who have we here?" She raised her voice, addressing someone in the corridor. "You there! You lost?"

Shamayal's head appeared over Imelda's shoulder, twisting from side to side. "I'm lookin' for Jim Stevens."

"Congratulations. You just found him."

"Come to see you, din't I?" The boy's stance was awkward, his face saying *Barely recognised you*; his feet saying *Not sure I want to be here.* "It's thirsty work trackin' you down. All them corridors look the same. And man, the noise! Have they stuck you in a lunatic asylum or somethink?"

Jim identified the kitbag slung over Shamayal's shoulder as his own. There were two white envelopes in the boy's hand. "Imelda, this is Shamayal. He's the one who saved my life."

"I like to think it's been a team effort," Imelda said curtly, sniffing. "How's your bowel movements?"

Jim accepted he'd asked for that. Here, everything was reduced to basics. His roommates got considerable mileage out of discussing the side-effects of codeine - with each other, with visiting family members, in fact, with anyone who was prepared to listen. "Fine," he said.

"Those laxatives must be doing the trick." She dispensed meds in a small paper cup. "I'll leave you and your friend to it."

"Bit personal, innit?" Shamayal approached the bed after Imelda had moved on to her next victim.

Jim strained to look around the dividing curtain towards the door. "Are you here by yourself?"

"Ayisha's down in the shop, in't she?"

He was appreciative of his colleague's tact, the opportunity for a few moments alone with the boy.

"She said they don't give visitors no drinks here. Man, this place is like an oven! I need some air." Fingering his collar, Shamayal ambled towards the open window. Rather than address the relatively mild-mannered Imelda, he picked on Sophia. "Whoa! These radiators are on full blast. Haven't you lot heard of global warming?"

Thankfully, he appeared to have caught her in a docile mood. "We have." Clipboard in hand, Sophia sighed a bored sigh. "We just don't give two hoots."

Jim noticed that Shamayal's accent was more pronounced. "All them superbugs will be busy breedin' in the heat."

"Oh, they'll be up to no good alright - if you marched them in with you." She waddled past, her hip grazing Shamayal - deliberately, Jim suspected. Seeing the boy recoil, the nurse paused to inflict further torment. "Hey, why don't you take off your jacket and your hat, Mr Know-it-all? I wouldn't want you to pass out."

Shamayal abandoned the kitbag on the floor, peeled his jacket off and sat, the plastic cushion emitting the sound of escaping air. "Is she always such a bitch?"

"I can still hear you! Mr Stevens, if you don't ask your friends to be polite, I tell Cook to serve your chicken raw."

The boy shot up, staring into the empty soup-bowl left over from lunch, lips parted in disbelief.

"Take it easy. She's joking with you."

"Well she shouldn't, should she?" He rearranged his wounded shoulders, unaware that the nurse was only inches away.

"She's a pussycat."

"Yeah, but what kind of pussycat am I?" The question came from behind the curtain.

Jim raised his voice. "You're a lioness, Sophia."

Shamayal tightened his mouth as he acknowledged that a fast one had been pulled, then took advantage of his elevated position to examine his teacher's face. "So, you're... you know."

There was only one hero as far as Jim was concerned. "I'm alive - thanks to you."

"*Hah!*" Confusion darkened the boy's eyes as he realised that Jim was absolutely sincere. "I just did what you told me."

"And if you hadn't - or if you'd listened to Miss Emmanuel! - I wouldn't be here now."

"What's that?" Flushed and flustered, Ayisha appeared at the foot of the bed and Jim was struck by the sheen of her long silky hair. She was holding two red-capped water bottles and had a newspaper tucked under one arm. He wondered if she was there as a friend or a messenger - whether she had telephoned Mr Peel - but her deep brown eyes gave nothing away.

"I was just telling Shamayal that, if it wasn't for the two of you, I'd be down in the basement," he said.

Rather than react, Ayisha held one of the water bottles out to Shamayal. She used her free hand to remove the newspaper, looking angry to see that Jim already had a copy, as if he should have known she would bring him one.

"You look different, Jim." Shamayal's eyes darted towards Ayisha, as if he knew the Jim was a slip.

Glaring straight ahead towards the corridor, she leaned against the wall and folded her arms. Her hips were pushed forwards, her jeans tight all the way to her ankles where the denim gathered above towering heels. Of course she'd made the call. What choice would she have had? Jim's eyes drifted to the door expecting to see Mr Peel, but no one was there.

"I don't know about that. I managed to shave." He jutted out his chin for inspection but Ayisha was still preoccupied. Everything about her was petite and pert and disciplined. Completely unintentionally, he suspected, she had displayed her covered body to full advantage.

She must have felt his eyes on her. Ayisha started arranging fruit in a bowl on the bedside cabinet. Like most visitors, she seemed to have decided that the rule about not bringing food-parcels was there to be ignored. Strange that she was so confident about which rules to take and which to leave.

"What?" she asked, a tangerine suspended in her hand.

With sweet-smelling citrus invading his nostrils, Jim decided against embarrassing her by informing her of the purpose of the bowl. Plenty more where that one came from. "Nothing."

Clearly, Ayisha thought she had detected criticism. Silver bracelets jangled as she extended one arm. "Pass me the bag, Shamayal. There's room in the cabinet for Jim's clothes."

The boy bent down and unzipped the kitbag. He groped around inside and pulled out several books, piling them on the table. Jim recognised his notebook, a pencil case, but the lined pad wasn't his. "You brought my drawing things!"

"You're lucky." Ayisha's arm dipped as she received the bag. "Shamayal knew his way around."

Jim wondered how he should react - if at all - but the boy was speaking: "I've bin keepin' track for you."

"Oh?" Jim asked.

Embarrassed, the boy opened the lined pad at the first page to reveal several childlike drawings of a nondescript bird. Arrows pointed to various body parts, labelled: beak, yellow; head, black. The entry was dated and timed and the words *out the kitchen window* were underlined. "Hey, I tol' you I ain't no artist. I just worry that the RSPB's gonna fall apart without you. Miss, I bet you never knew Jim's a spy."

"He keeps a lot of things very quiet." She raised her eyebrows - sarcasm.

Jim's eyes fell away to the page that Shamayal was holding up for him. In the space of three attempts there was clear improvement. He found his throat constricted as he tried to say, "You did this for me?"

The boy's face reshaped itself with pleasure. "Here. You have it."

Jim felt a dip on the mattress next to him. "Well," Ayisha said, her voice suggesting she was impressed. He received the point of one elbow and said nothing. "Even I know what that is: it's a magpie."

The two of them chatting over him, Jim experienced cold foreboding. One for sorrow, the old saying went. He had been here before.

CHAPTER 19:

JIM - AUGUST 1992 - RALEGH GROVE

"**M**orning." Jim caught a yawn in his fist as he shuffled into the kitchen, bare feet slapping on cold lino.

"So we're talking again, are we?" His mother referred to the previous night's performance, but she hummed as she cascaded cornflakes into a bowl and thumped it down on the table.

He was ninety-nine per cent sure she knew Nick was in on it with his father. The one per cent's worth of doubt meant he couldn't say anything. He wondered if she was thinking the same, except that her version would be: *He worshipped his brother. It would kill him if he ever found out.*

Mumbling what was intended to be an apology, Jim slumped into a chair and poured milk through a hole punched in the foil cap. He turned his focus to what he had to do today. Only yesterday he'd convinced himself that Aimee liked him. But really, what was there to like? His life could have provided the plot for an episode of *Eastenders*. They'd been mugged by his own brother; his father - not an unemployed salesman as he'd let her believe - had been arrested for robbery. And now, the latest: "Get this: my dad and my brother were in on it together."

If Aimee hung around with him much longer, his luck would rub off on her. It didn't take a boffin to spell it out. A girl like her should be taking piano lessons, going horse riding, or memorising her favourite lines from one of those dead authors she obsessed about. He would have to lay down the law: "Today's the last day. After that, you've got to find yourself another hobby."

"Did Ben say something that upset you, love?" Jean probed as she filed cereal packets in a head-height cupboard.

"No." Spoon collided with front teeth as Jim shovelled. Why must parents ask these questions?

"Slow down! You haven't got a train to catch."

He crunched exaggeratedly, moving his head from side to side in demonstration. One of his legs began to swing in protest at this show of obedience. Even if Ben *had* said something - his foot skimmed the floor - he couldn't tell his mum because she would make things ten times worse by having it out with Ben's mother, trying to cover up for Frank. And he would have to go along with whatever unlikely story Jean had spun, or call her a liar.

"If he did, you're going to have to rise above it -"

"Nothing happened, Mum!" Jim insisted through a mouthful of masticated corn.

"So there's nothing for me to worry about." Her smile curt, Jean rinsed suds from the bowl she had been washing. "Off out today?"

"Bird-watching."

"Where does that take you?"

"Oh, you know." Deliberately vague, Jim glanced at his mother who appeared to be putting a lot of thought into drying the webbed skin between her fingers. Although Jean

approved of his hobby, she had no inkling it required trespassing on British Rail's property.

The seven fifteen rumbled past, rearranging the contents
of the cutlery drawer.

"That's me!" Jean retrieved her handbag, pausing to give
Jim one of those looks where smiling is accompanied by
quick-fire blinking. He was one step away from being smoth-
ered. "Back to normal. You won't mind only having your
mum for company, will you?"

Batting away the hand that was poised to ruffle his hair,
Jim growled, "Gerroff."

She sighed. "Lock up after yourself, won't you?"

Finding himself alone in the flat was strange rather than
liberating. All about him, the day was coming to life, sounds
travelling at volumes unrelated to proximity: an argument,
coming to its peak, was bouncing off the walls of the stairwell;
a washing machine clattered into the spin cycle; in the gaps
between a baby's screams the muted blah-blah-blah of the
news and weather seeped through the woodchip wallpaper;
someone was expelling an extended *Ahhhhh* as they released
a stream of piss, punctuated by several false endings. It was
hardly *Who will Buy?* from *Oliver* his mother had made him
watch for the millionth time last Christmas.

Jean had optimistically left the washing up water in
the sink. He watched the milky brew engulf his bowl, then
addressed the empty sofa from the doorway: "I'll get out your
way, Dad. You'll have no one to stop you having a few beers
before lunch, or lazing in front of the telly all day."

*"You off out? You don't see your old man for the best part of
three years and now you can't wait to escape."*

"Hey!" His index finger was braver than it would have
been had his dad actually been there. "You weren't around
when we needed you. I'm not hanging around and waiting
on you now."

"Come here and say that, tough guy!" The voice was Robert de Niro's, circa *Goodfellas*.

Jim slung his rucksack over one shoulder and greeted the bulging bin liner his mother had left blocking the door. "Aw! Not again!" Manhandling it over the threshold, he stooped to turn the key in the lock.

Standing at her kitchen window, Mrs O'Keefe rapped on the pane. Jim realised he had completely forgotten to call round and say thanks. Displacing her cat, she nudged the window open and spoke from above a display of cleaning products, arranged in height order. "I've just seen your mam. She seems to be doing well."

He shifted the bin liner from one shoulder to the other. "She's back at work. I was gonna tell you."

"She's up and about, that's the main thing." She frowned. "You alright, are you?"

He shrugged. "S'pose."

"Good lad. Keep me posted." The metal frame of the window closed. The stubborn cat reclaimed its rightful post. Mrs O'Keefe retreated behind locks and bolts, out of sight and out of mind.

Crouching near the bin sheds, Bins was happily rummaging through other people's leftovers. "Jim Stevens," he acknowledged, accepting the black sack as if it were an expensively wrapped present. "What have we here?"

"Nothing you'd be interested in," Jim shrugged. "My mum never chucks food out."

"Let me be the judge of that," Bins beamed, untying the careful knot. Tipping the bag upside down, the older man used a magician's hand to spread the haul over tarmac. "Oh, yes!" His eyes gleamed. Delicately, using only thumbs and index fingers, he extracted curves and shards of eggshell, picking them clean and laying them in a neat row on the edge of a raised kerb.

Jim hovered between fascination and disgust. "I'll be off then."

"Righto." One hand rippled and, as Jim turned away, he heard the opening lines of an old nursery rhyme: "You shall have a fishy, on a little dishy, you shall have a fishy, when the boat comes in."

Dawdling in the direction of the tracks, Jim's feet dragged under the weight of his thoughts. He knew what he had to do - wanted it over and done with - but who would sit still long enough to let him sketch her? Who would care if he knew the Latin for *house martin?* Who would say he was a good teacher? He kicked an empty Coke can and tripped after it ricocheted off a wall, back into his path.

"Watch where you're going, son," the postman said as he sailed through the concrete bollards, both feet on one pedal of his bike.

"Watch where you're going yourself!" the boy muttered, feeling brazen. Jean believed in him, Jim knew that, but that was what she saw him as, tops - a postie doing his rounds. He recognised where he'd come from and what that made him, and a new-found desire to break loose. One path meant getting dragged into the family business, the other meant leaving everything he knew behind. Both were terrifying.

Arriving at the main road, he waited for a break in the traffic. As a bus approached, its driver locked eyes with him, mouthing, "Just you dare," pointing repeatedly to the zebra crossing, not twenty feet away. Giving him the one-fingered salute Jim watched the bus roll by, empty but for pensioners and teenage mums whose snotty-nosed offspring were carted round shopping centres for entertainment.

Big ideas had no business taking up the attention of an eleven-year-old. He needed to get back to the important business of playing footie, plastering posters of Pamela Anderson on his bedroom wall and giving his mother cheek. As the traffic lights turned red, a Ford Fiesta slowed to let him limp across. Perhaps Aimee wouldn't show up. That would be best for both of them. Yesterday's tantrum had probably just been for show. But as he reached the top of the concrete steps his heart lifted and fell.

"Jim!" she yelled from where she was sitting on the grass bank. Nothing more.

Her hands were linked under her knees and she rocked a little. He forced a smile. Her lips were stained guiltily with blackberry juice. There was no hint of yesterday's madness, no questions, no demands. A white plastic bag caught in a branch above her head stirred. The snapping of a twig revealed something rat-like in the dense weave of brambles. Sniffing the air, Jim threw his rucksack down in the long grass and dived closely behind it.

"Been keeping my place warm?" Note: *my* place.

Aimee failed to heed the flatness of his tone. "Come and see." She handed over her notebook, opened at the latest entry. Tucking her hair behind one ear, she smiled, revealing the gap in her front teeth. "It was the best I could do without binoculars or your book."

She sat, leaning on one arm that was placed just behind him. The breath that brushed Jim's cheek was sweetened by fruit. He concentrated on her pencil sketch. "Looks like a wren."

"It was tiny." She formed a C with one hand. "Much smaller than the others."

Before Jim could protest, she posted two blackberries into his mouth. "Sounds about right." He gulped back the tart juice.

She sucked the ends of her fingers, one after the other, then used them to turn the page. "I wasn't so sure about him."

Her chin nearly touching his shoulder, Jim was relieved there were words demanding to be read. "Medium-sized, brown upperparts, white chest with brown arrowheads."

"He spent a good ten minutes pulling this worm out of the ground. It was stretched out like an elastic band."

"Must be some sort of thrush." Flicking through the book, Jim found the entry for the Mistle Thrush.

"No." Her nose wrinkled, her hands reaching for the page. "It wasn't as white as that."

He thumbed through to a picture of the Song Thrush. "What about him? They go for worms. Nestlings eat over ten foot a day."

"That's gross!" Hearing her protest, a scrawny old fox hesitated on the opposite side of the tracks. One ear rotated, radar-like.

The pretence at normality proved too much for Jim. He had to get what needed to be said over with. "I saw my brother yesterday."

"Where?" she asked, sitting upright.

The fox tensed, neck straining, muscles taut: watching.

"He came looking for me."

Jim saw the realignment of Aimee's mouth, heard saliva move to her throat. "Not at your place?"

"My mum would never let him in." Jim shook his head. "He was asking after my dad. And I just knew."

"What did you know?" She knelt up. The fox bolted.

Aimee was supposed to be the clever one. She shouldn't need him to spell it out: "They were in on it together."

She created a breeze, forcing breath out through her mouth. "Shit."

They both stared across the short scrubby grass at the tracks.

"I think you should find somewhere else to go," Jim blurted. Aimee's once pale feet were tanned save for the white arrows left by the thongs of her flip-flops.

"I can handle myself." She seemed determined to make this difficult for him.

"Sooner or later something bad's going to happen to you - and it will be because you know me."

"How d'you work that one out, Einstein?"

"Yesterday," he watched a bumble bee making its strenuous up-and-down journey through the grass, "someone was sent to find me. I thought I was in for a kicking. Turns out I was wrong, but anyone could follow me down here. I can't take that chance."

"You think you're the only one with problems!" She rammed her feet back into her plastic shoes, her softness becoming sharp angles.

Jim took refuge in brotherly concern. "Look, I just think you'd be safer -"

"Safer?" She made a small huffing noise. "You know: fine. Have it your way! We'll go somewhere else. Meet me on the bridge. Half eight." And, displacing a pair of nervous blackbirds, she took off before Jim had the chance to open his mouth to argue.

CHAPTER 20:

AYISHA - AUGUST 2010 - ST HELIER HOSPITAL

Ayisha returned her gaze from the view outside the hospital window to Jim. "The answer's no." She uncrossed her legs and pushed herself out of the visitor's chair. "I can't believe you're even asking!" Having told him that she had decided she couldn't report Shamayal's disclosure without implicating herself, Jim's response was immediately - unbelievably - to ask her to keep an eye on the boy!

Jim sighed. "I understand."

The fact that his tone was completely reasonable grated. She was used to her mother's accusations and complaints. Those, she could handle. Ayisha hooked the strap of her bag over her shoulder and supported its soft underbelly with one hand. "It's really unfair of you to try and involve me any more than I already am."

"I know. And, if I wasn't lying here, I wouldn't dream of it." Amid the bleeping equipment and the drips Jim was tucked in tightly with only his arms free.

Because raising her voice wasn't an option, Ayisha felt the need to state the obvious: "I can't tell you how angry I am with you!" There was a lot more she would like to have said, but part of her rage was directed inwards. She had misjudged the situation when she chose to give Jim the benefit of the doubt, and now Ayisha had seemingly set a chain of events in motion.

Somewhere on the other side of the corridor, a woman was crying out for help: *Why doesn't anyone answer? Why does no one come?* Jim had explained that the voice's owner was senile; that her cries often went unheeded, but the tone of voice suggested pain. If this was confusion, surely reassurance wouldn't go amiss? The hospital wasn't the quiet place of healing Ayisha had imagined. How Jim could stand it, she didn't know. After only an hour she was feeling desperate to extract herself.

"I don't blame you." His eyes appealed to her earnestly. "But I'm stuck in here and I have no one else to turn to."

A needle was lodged in Jim's hand, the entry-wound covered by sticking plaster. Ayisha followed the thin plastic tubing to a liquid-filled pouch. When he stood - which he was encouraged to do - he must wheel a drip with him. He certainly looked trapped. How had she managed to get into the situation where it all came down to her? "It still might not be too late," she back-tracked, thinking out loud.

"Ayisha, believe me, I'm not asking for myself. Don't call Social Services. Please."

A glance at her watch provided a much-needed excuse. "I said I'd meet Shamayal by the car ten minutes ago." It was a lie. The boy had insisted on getting the bus.

"Promise me you won't. He trusts me."

"Fine," she said impatiently. "Then I'll speak to his father."

"I wouldn't -"

"Then what? You know, I could -" A sound like fury erupted deep in her throat. Conscious of having attracted unwanted attention, Ayisha rounded the end of the bed and turned her back on the elderly man in the bed opposite. To her right, the door was beckoning. "Tell me! What exactly would you *have* me do?"

"Look out for Shamayal, that's all."

Ayisha gaped at him. "Keep an eye out for a fourteen-year-old boy, who may or may not be staying in your flat? How do you suggest I do that? Babysit? Or perhaps you want me to ask him to stay with me!"

Jim's pleading eyes suggested she had struck upon a solution.

"Oh, no!" She took a step back. "No way." Her feet appeared to be performing a small circular dance. "I have plans! There are things I should be doing right now."

"But -"

"You know something?" The hand that she had raised in protest delved into her handbag and extracted Jim's keys. She set them down onto the wheeled table. "I'm done with buts."

Waiting impatiently for the lift, watching the numbers stall - *come on, come on!* - a cold patch on her forehead alerted Ayisha to the fact that she had clasped a hand to it. *Why should I feel guilty?* she asked herself. *This isn't my problem.* A ringing sound signalled the arrival of the lift. She shook her hair out. Doors opened lazily to reveal a gum-chewing, boiler-suited cleaner and his floor-polishing machine crammed into the tight space. The man's face was unapologetic. Mid-turn towards the staircase, Ayisha's feet made a decision on her behalf. She found that she was storming - as effectively as heels permitted - back to the ward, sidling past the tea trolley, rounding a huddle of gossiping nurses. The elderly man opposite appeared delighted. She gripped the metal frame at the foot of Jim's bed. "I'll pay him to help me decorate. That way I can't be accused of taking advantage. *If* I can track him down."

Jim frowned up at her. "Isn't he waiting for you in the car park?"

Ayisha was surprised she had made such an obvious slip. "He's making his own way home," she admitted. "And I'm going to have to get better at lying!"

The keys were still there on the table. Understanding there was no option, Ayisha reached out and took them, furious that she had allowed herself to be blackmailed. She could already hear her mother's complaints: *But I was expecting you...* "If he says no, there's nothing more I can do."

"Thank you," Jim said with obvious relief. "You're a good person."

"Good?" Ayisha emitted a single syllable of frustrated laughter, then hissed, "I'm in breach of our professional code of conduct, that's what I am!"

"But it's the holidays."

This was too much; too much. "Don't you *dare* joke about it."

"Seriously, then." Lying there, Jim looked suitably chastened. "Will you let me know what he says?"

She shook her head, glaring at the lecherous old man in the bed opposite. "You know something? You are *really* pushing your luck."

CHAPTER 21:

JIM - AUGUST 1992 - CARSHALTON

Aimee had perched on the wall, her knees drawn up, feet flat against the brickwork. Jim noticed she was wearing his denim jacket. Colours blurred, his view of her obscured then revealed through glass and in the gaps between cars. It was impossible to avoid her, but he could make her wait.

"Thinking of doing a runner?" she asked when at last he ambled across.

"Fat chance."

"I thought as much!" A shake of her head revealed gold gypsy earrings. "I know you too well."

It seemed strange now that he'd mistaken her for a gypsy. "And I can't work you out."

"Does it matter?" She thrust her duffel bag at him then sprang, landing lightly. A series of complicated adjustments followed. She hoisted her leggings up from the waist, stretched them down over her knees, pulled the back of her baggy top down. The bag beginning to weigh heavily, he coughed impatiently. Aimee grabbed her hair at the nape of her neck and let it slip through her hand. Applied cherry lip gloss. This, it seemed, was revenge. Finally, she took the bag without a word of thanks and set a military pace, glancing back to demand, "Coming?"

After satisfying himself that no one was following, Jim set off at a sluggish trudge.

Down Pound Street, Aimee's eyes lit up, gleaming. She pressed her nose against the plate glass of an old-fashioned shop to admire a display of antique clocks. Despite the early morning sun that bounced off the pavement, standing on tiptoes, hands blinkering her eyes, she reminded Jim of Christmas. Not Christmas at Ralegh Grove, but the Christmas of *The Muppet Christmas Carol*.

"See the grandfather clock, third from the left?" She tapped on the glass, pointing to an ivory face decorated with a sun and a moon. The open door of the walnut case revealed a brass pendulum, swinging hypnotically. When Jim made no attempt to match her enthusiasm, she frowned. "I thought boys were supposed to be interested in the way things work."

"All I want a clock to do is tell me the time."

She made a playful grab for his arm. "Show me your wrist!"

"Get off!" Jim snatched it away. Too late: she had danced around his back and pulled up his sleeve.

"I thought as much!" she said judiciously. "It's digital."

Self-conscious, Jim covered his garage purchase protectively. "Does what it's supposed to."

"I thought your problem was that you had no poetry in your soul, but it turns out you've got no soul at all!"

The sum total of his body heat migrated to his ears. "Can't afford one."

Vehicles had achieved the usual rush-hour stalemate where the road narrowed to the width of a cart in front of the ponds. They picked their way between mud-splattered bumpers and purring engines. The trees and sky were reflected Monet-style in the water.

"What are we doing here?" Jim asked as they walked

under an overhanging canopy, stepping in and out of shade as if making their way over an elongated zebra crossing.

"A bit of local history for you."

He groaned, dragging his feet. "His-to-ry!"

Aimee's method of converting non-believers was low key. "You'll like it," she grinned, her confidence grating. "Money-back guarantee. So, where are we?"

"Duh! Beddington Park."

"And what can you see?"

It seemed there was to be a quiz. Looking about him, Jim saw a sausage-shaped bulge in a grounded plastic bag next to a receptacle for dog turds. "Nothing much."

"Try harder."

His view was restricted by horse chestnuts in full leaf. Heavy loads of conkers would be ripe for the taking in a couple of weeks' time. He blew at a cloud of midges. "Can't see a sodding thing!"

She grinned. "Can't see the wood for them?"

Two squirrels ran helter-skelter down a knotted trunk, a frantic cork-screw chase.

You want me to say trees. He resisted.

"They're hundreds of years old. This was once a royal deer park."

Jim snorted a stray gnat out of one nostril. "I still don't get why we're here."

"Come on, sulky boy. You're going to learn how Ralegh Grove got its name." She pointed beyond the foliage to a low flint wall. "There!"

"What?" Jim focused on the blue and yellow livery of the twin towers. *"Ikea?"*

"Why do you always have to be such a smart arse?" Jim followed the direction of her index finger to a squat flint tower and flinched. "St Mary's."

He had a healthy horror of churches born of the few

occasions he had actually set foot inside one, the last time being his grandfather's funeral.

Aimee did little to disguise her disappointment. "You've got absolutely no idea who Sir Walter Ralegh was, have you?"

Jim shrugged. "I've heard of him." He vaguely recalled an episode of *Blackadder*. He had only been six, but a six-year-old can find men wearing tights and a queen with a squeaky voice amusing.

Aimee shook her head and exaggerated a sigh, capable of ignoring the couple on the bench: the girl straddling her boyfriend, sucking on his face. "He was only one of the greatest explorers ever! He was the one who introduced potatoes and tobacco to Britain."

So that was the joke: someone had tried to smoke a potato.

"I know that! He was at the court of Queen Elizabeth I, wasn't he?"

"I take it back." Aimee turned, apparently stunned. "So you must have heard he's the only man in history to have been sentenced to death for treason twice."

"Twice?" Having been separated from her by a floppy-eared Labrador who had circled him playfully, Jim jogged a couple of paces to catch up.

"He bought his way out the first time. Come on. There's something I really want you to see."

She dragged him under the lych gate, past the most recently dug graves, topped with flowers and photographs that had yet to fade; up the overgrown path to the heavy oak door. Lifting the knocker using both hands and turning, Aimee produced a metal-on-metal grinding sound. "Help me out."

Jim strained, producing slight movement. "Our luck's in." She smiled, showing him the gap in her teeth. "This is one of my favourite places in the whole world." She held the door open for him. "Top five, anyway."

Inside, with the door closing on the world outside,

everything was gloomy, scented with centuries of damp, dust and decay.

"Don't tell me: it's haunted."

"It might be." She lowered her voice to a whisper. "Some people say that Sir Walter's body is buried in the vault underneath us. Others say it's only his head. After he was executed, his widow carried it around with her in a little velvet sack."

Despite his lack of soul, goose-bumps rose against Jim's collar. Perhaps it was the sudden drop in temperature, but the place had an undeniable presence. Claiming ownership of all she surveyed, Aimee strode up the aisle, leaving Jim shy of an imaginary threshold between stone porch and terracotta tile. As his eyes became accustomed to the half-light, they were drawn upwards: stars in gold leaf and coats of arms in greens and cobalt blue, all against a ceiling of ruby-red; gilded angels hovering horizontally, the tips of each pair of golden wings almost touching those of its opposite. He flinched at the clunk of a bench, its echo ricocheting off the walls.

"Over here!" Ahead - somehow always one step ahead - Aimee was walking backwards, then with a skip she disappeared somewhere to the right of the aisle. Her voice rang out: "The Carew family chapel!"

Jim skirted round a cleaning lady who was on her hands and knees, cringing an apology on behalf of his wet footprints.

Standing by a stone knight with stone arms folded across his chest, Aimee read respectfully, "Here resteth Sir Francis Carew, knight, sonne and heire of Sir Nicholas Carew, knight of the honourable Order of the Garter…"

The cramped space forced them close together. Jim stood, arms tight at his sides, knowing the electric fence to be something only she was allowed to breach. "What's that?"

"Basically," her coconut-scented hair brushed his cheek, "it was the gang you wanted to be in if you were anyone. The King and the Prince of Wales were both members." She traced each letter with a stubby index finger, its nail bitten painfully short. "...*Master of the Horse*... He was in charge of everything to do with the royal horses and hounds. The equivalent would be - I don't know." Her mouth was so close that he felt the warmth of her breath. "Minister for Transport, the Armed Forces and Sport... *and Private Councellor to King Henry VIII*. Sadly, being a friend of Henry VIII and a famous jousting star wasn't enough to stop the King having his head cut off." *Admit it*, the light in her eyes challenged, *you're excited*. "His whole history is right here in front of you."

Keen to prolong this whispered sharing of secrets, Jim asked, "What did he do to deserve that?"

She shrugged. "Being connected with the royals was dangerous."

"And then what?"

"After -" Aimee drew one hand across her throat and made a strangled sound - "Henry VIII confiscated Carew Manor. That was when he turned the grounds into a deer park."

"You haven't explained where Walter Ralegh comes into it."

"Patience, I'm getting to that. His wife, Bess, grew up here before she was called to court by Queen Elizabeth to be one of her ladies-in-waiting. Remember how Sir Walter was the Queen's favourite?" Jim recalled Rowan Atkinson making ridiculous promises. At that moment, without too much torture, Aimee might have been able to extract similar promises.

"Well, Bess and Walter started a secret affair." He was so close that he could hear her swallow. "Everything was fine until Bess fell pregnant." She put one hand against her stomach, to demonstrate, he presumed.

"I know what pregnant is!"

"They married, of course, and when Elizabeth found out..."

"All hell broke loose."

"Officially, it was more serious than jealousy. Bess should

have asked the Queen's permission to marry."

"They were related?"

"Nothing like that. She had a distant claim to the throne. Walter and Bess were thrown into the Tower."

Seeing that Aimee's lip was quivering, Jim thought she seemed rather too involved in the story. "Want to go?" he asked, embarrassed.

They walked outside, blinking back daylight as if they'd been to a matinée at the cinema and expected to find it dark. As his goose-bumps smoothed, Jim experienced a sense of betrayal. Something had changed - he wasn't sure what - but everything was just as it had been: the overgrown path; the tombstones; the lych gate. "How come you know all this?"

Aimee glanced back over her shoulder, wearing a wan smile. "This is where we go to church. It bugs me how no one else notices what's in front of them."

As she was talking, a flash of green and yellow dissected the sky. Jim raised his binoculars to see a pair of ring-necked parakeets land in a sweet chestnut tree. "I've heard about them!" he enthused. "That one's a good sixteen inches." Charitably, he handed Aimee the binoculars.

"The story goes," she panned in on a single bird, "that they escaped when *The African Queen* was being filmed."

"Never heard of it." The persistent squawk filled his ears.

A fat lady panted past on the pavement at walking pace, elbows pumping furiously, feet scraping the ground, her lycra-encased bottom rippling on the off-beat.

"One of the greatest films ever made and he's never heard of it! Doesn't matter. Turns out that they were breeding in the wild even before the 1900s."

"So," he said, scratching the side of his face. "Where to tomorrow?"

"Caught this history bug, have you?" She said smugly, her recovery complete.

In the days that followed, they went walking in the woods at Woodmansterne which were alive with life - midges mostly - and they caught the bus to Cheam to see the site of Nonsuch Palace. One day they took the train all the way to Box Hill. Serenaded by the roar of Harleys, lying in the long grass with sunburn on his face, Jim felt as if he were really on holiday. He rolled onto his belly and grinned. "Don't tell me: *this* is your favourite place."

"Top five." Aimee's eyes were closed as if she already knew what she would see if she looked. "People go halfway round the world, ignoring what's under their noses."

Each time Jim returned home, the estate looked greyer and greyer, and the people emptier and emptier. Heads down, hoods up, bodies disguised in baggy clothes, their problem appeared to be what Aimee would diagnose as a lack of soul. Avoiding bad influences to please his mother had meant cutting himself off. He no longer belonged. Perhaps he never had. Kneeling on the sofa, Jim turned his binoculars towards the houses he intended to live in, seeing nothing to erode his rose-tinted view that life on the other side of the tracks was sweeter.

Aimee only *thought* she had problems. Her battle wounds weren't real. Even she said she bruised easily, and it sounded true enough. The one with a doctor for a father, she should know.

Jim thought that Aimee was taking him on a tour of her world, showing him what he'd been missing out on. He didn't realise she was doing the rounds to say her goodbyes. Just as surely as you do the rounds before leaving a party.

CHAPTER 22:

AYISHA - 2010 - JIM'S FLAT

"Shamayal?" Ayisha called out as she closed Jim's front door. A muffled blur was coming from the living room. "Don't tell me you came straight here without going home!" She heard her momentary intake of breath as the owl confronted her, talons extended.

"Heard the news?" His voice was lifeless.

"No. I had a CD on in -" He was sitting on the sofa, trainers off, knees tucked tightly under his chin, eyes fixed on a 24-hour news channel. Something about his stance made a ripple of anxiety course through her even before she recognised the quad. "That's -" she stalled.

"They found Christian, din't they." The boy's meaning was plain.

"My God," Ayisha said in a whisper, goose-bumps prickling her scalp. She perched on the arm of the sofa, remembering Christian Knoll's mother, whose appeal had been aired on BBC London last week, moments after an interview with Mr Peel who had described how Jim Stevens was heroically fighting for his life. Broken, hunched under the weight of grief, Mrs Knoll had pleaded into the microphone, "I just need my son home. I need someone to tell me he's OK," before clutching a tissue to her mouth. And the District Commissioner had encouraged members of the public to check their sheds and outbuildings as if Christian were a stray cat. While stock footage of tracker dogs was played, the Missing Persons Helpline number rolled across the bottom of the screen and the District Commissioner's voice said gravely, "It's our belief that Christian is intent on not being found."

Little wonder!

"How?" she asked Shamayal, knowing at the same time that the details were irrelevant. A boy was dead.

"They're cleanin' up after themselves." His voice was matter-of-fact. "Wait up." He pointed the remote control at the television as an old school photo of Christian appeared on the screen. A child! Bars increased in number, and the volume edged up: "...*The Surrey teenager was pursued across a suburban park before he was stabbed through the heart and collapsed in the doorway of a house, where he was found by its owners. Victim, Christian Knoll, was thought to have been the intended target when schoolteacher Jim Stevens received a stab wound to the chest at Ashfield Comprehensive on the last day of the school term. As the gang fled, witnesses say they waved their knives in the air.*"

Ayisha felt numb. No. Beyond numb. Empty. Jim's prediction had been right. She had spent the past week selfishly thinking it could have been her lying on the tarmac, but she had underestimated whoever had carried the knife. Now she saw that Jim might easily have been killed. Arms empty, she hugged herself in an attempt to contain the void that had opened up inside her. Unthinkingly, she was mirroring the boy's stance.

Because the Knoll family had asked for time to come to terms with their loss, Sky was playing the reel of Mrs Knoll begging for the return of her son, her voice breaking under the strain, *Anyone, anyone.* It had torn Ayisha apart when she watched it the first time. Now its poignancy increased further. Hunted down. What a dreadful way for a young life to end!

Yet Ayisha felt strangely disconnected. Did Christian's murder - the fact of it - feel more or less real because she was seeing a news report? Sometimes, on waking, Ayisha succeeded in convincing herself that she'd dreamt up that horrific bloodied version of the last day of term, so she kept newspaper clippings as evidence that it had been true.

It was some time before either of them spoke, and then it was Ayisha who murmured, "Poor woman."

"What was he thinkin' of?"

She turned to Shamayal, surprised that anger was his reaction.

"Din't get far enough away, did he? Should of got himself out of town."

"Did you know Christian?" Saying his name out loud, Ayisha was struck by how quickly present could turn to past.

"He was two years above me, wasn't he?"

"I suppose he must have been."

"You goin' to get that, Miss?" Shamayal's voice was impatient.

"What?" It was only then that Ayisha realised her mobile was ringing.

"Might be Jim. They've always got the news on at the hospital."

"Yes, hello," she answered.

"Ayisha. I'm glad I've reached you. It's Mark."

It took her a moment to process this information: Realising it was her Head speaking, Ayisha's stomach gave a guilty lurch. "I'm just watching the news. I don't know what to…"

"It's terribly difficult to know what to do with oneself, I know. That's why I thought you might prefer to be doing something practical. I've already opened up the school. Some of the kids were turning up to lay flowers in the quad.

I wondered if we shouldn't put on a few refreshments in the hall. Make sure they have somewhere to come and talk. I think that's important, don't you?"

"Good idea."

"So, I can put you down for this afternoon and tomorrow?"

"Give me a couple of hours and I'll be there." Hanging up, she noticed that she had missed a call. Of course: her mother would have seen the news. "That was Mr Peel. They're opening up the school hall so that pupils have a place to go and talk." She was about to suggest that the boy might like to come with her.

"And *you* said you'd help? We should go back to the hospital, that's what we should do! Jim's there all on his own!"

"It isn't your job to worry about Jim. Your father might be watching, Shamayal. You really ought to ring home."

Shamayal didn't move. "He'll be watching *some*thing."

Deciding she could only lead by example, Ayisha got up. "Well, I'm going to call my mother."

After an exchange, which she kept as brief as possible with the excuse of having to rush off, Ayisha found Shamayal with his eyes still glued to the television. "Come on. Up you get."

"What?" Shamayal's heels slipped off the sofa, his feet landing heavily.

"I'm taking you home. I know *all* about difficult parents. Trust me, your dad may have a funny way of showing he cares, but he'll be worried. Before you go anywhere else, you need to let him know you're OK."

They stood in the doorway to the living room, witness to Shamayal's father's grunting form sprawled on top of a woman.

"Sandi." She went limp in his arms, her clouded look clearing when she saw the two of them. "You might want to -"

But his bare buttocks still clenched and unclenched as he pumped away. "Almost there, almost there..."

Unlike Ayisha, who allowed the discarded clothes strewn across the floor to be her focus, Shamayal made no attempt to look away. "Hello, Dad," he said, an everyday greeting, son to father.

Mr Thomas performed a double take, then jumped up, fumbling for his flies, roaring, "What are you doing home at this time of day, you little shit?" Barely bothering to cover herself, the woman lay passively, fleshy and double-chinned, like a Lucien Freud painting.

"I've come to show you I'm still alive, so you don't need to worry." Shamayal turned to Ayisha. "That's what you wanted me to tell him, right? So we can go now, and he can get back to whatever he was doin'." As the boy walked past her, a dignified exit, Ayisha was surprised to acknowledge pride lurking among her muddled emotions.

"Aren't you going to stop him?" Ayisha demanded of Mr Thomas, as appalled by his lack of embarrassment as she was at the sight of the loose-skinned paunch he seemed determined to flaunt.

"Who are you, giving the orders in my home?"

She breathed in a warm concoction of bodies and beer. "I'm a teacher from Shamayal's school," she said caught off guard.

"He's not been bunking off, has he?"

"No." She knew she had no business being here with Shamayal. "In fact, your son's attendance is good. You may have heard on the news that one of our pupils has been murdered. We're encouraging the children to talk to their parents."

"Shouldn't you be the ones giving the counselling?"

"It's August, Mr Thomas." Ayisha could see this information worming its way into his head. *He hasn't even realised that school has broken up for the holidays.* "With the best will in the world -"

"Then why are you sticking your nose in? Get out of my flat!"

"But don't…" Astonished, Ayisha had no idea what she was going to say other than make a protest of some sort.

"I won't ask you again. LEAVE!"

Jim had warned that this man threw bottles after invited guests who outstayed their welcome. She glared at the woman who was capable of lying there listening to their exchange without offering sisterly support. "Don't worry, I'm going."

Outside, a few feet from the front door, Shamayal was leaning on the railings, his back to her. She joined him, looking despondently at the car park below, the rotary driers, a single bench, not trusting herself to speak. She couldn't understand why the view struck her as so familiar until she heard the rumble of a train. All those times when she'd looked out of a carriage window as she neared Central London, the big wheel coming into view. Balconies and doors and windows; bicycles and washing lines and potted plants; but rarely faces.

"You're right, Miss." Shamayal said, not a hint of emotion. "My dad *has* got a funny way of showing he cares."

"Shamayal, I -" Humbled, she stalled. She'd never given a thought as to who might live on the estates she sped past on the way to the theatre or an art gallery, a secretive smile betraying the hope she had in store before her date turned out to be another disaster.

"Seen everything you wanted to?"

"Yes."

"Then we can go, right?"

Before reaching the main road, Ayisha pulled over to the kerb. This time she tried taking her father's advice and thought before she spoke.

"Whatever you're goin' to say, you'd better go ahead and say it," the boy said flatly, sitting low in the passenger seat, knees slumped sideways, touching the door.

She tried to keep it simple. "Shamayal, don't you think you

189

might be happier somewhere else?"

"You realise Christian's just been killed, Miss? You remember that, right? It was just on the news."

In her head it hadn't sounded so trite. Faced with his anger Ayisha felt foolish and naïve. "I know this isn't a very good time -"

"What you need is some perspective. I don't have this big expectation that everythin's goin' to be all hunky-dory or whatever you want to call it. 'Sides, I don't see that you're all that happy."

She felt her nostrils prickling at the shock of having the tables turned on her.

"So I don't get why you're aksin' me, like this is America or somethink."

Comparing his life to hers, Shamayal seemed to think it was *she* who had drawn the short straw. Bowing her head, Ayisha made a disclosure of her own: "You're right. I'm not very happy at the moment." The truth was, no matter where you grow up, however caring your parents might be, nothing guarantees happiness. How many times had she heard it said that teenagers think the world owes them a living? The main difference Ayisha detected between her and Shamayal was that he expected nothing.

The boy's voice had lost its edge. "Then I'm in the same category as you. That's all." Here he was, reassuring her in the way her job forbade, with an arm that pulled her to his chest. "Hey, you listen to me. We're going to be alright, Miss. Both of us. That's never in any doubt."

And how needy she was as she brushed away her tears and rested there for a moment, how she lapped it up! A lift, a sofa for the night, a few meals: what wouldn't she do for this boy? Ayisha's head throbbed, but she said, "I'm alright now."

"You sure? I'm in no rush."

She sat upright, smiling shyly, put her foot on the accelerator and the stop/start technology fired up the engine. "How would you like to earn some money over the holidays?" she asked.

"Depends what you got in mind," this open-minded boy sniffed, take it or leave it.

CHAPTER 23:

JIM - JULY 2010 -
ST HELIER HOSPITAL

"I hope you're behaving yourself for Ayisha," Jim said, looking at Shamayal, who was seated on the window-sill. He felt grateful that his colleague had made good her promise to offer him work. The boy needed to be kept busy.

"Yeah?" He counter-challenged, eyes trained on the hospital corridor. "And I hope you're behavin' yourself for that hot young nurse."

"I'm serious! She's paying you to do a proper job."

Jim preferred the straight-talking, honest-to-the-point-of-brutality version of the boy. This fake joviality was a cover. He had tried asking Shamayal how he felt about Christian's murder, but serious appeared to be a no-go area. Apparently, the boy saw it as his duty to cheer Jim up. And the effort was appreciated. Post-surgery, Jim had admitted to feeling depressed. The answer? Another prescription. Hardly a function took place in his softening body that wasn't chemically induced. Despite being labelled a hero (how he'd grown to hate that label), his feeling of worthlessness had multiplied. He couldn't say if he would do the same again, but he would have liked all this pain, the sheer boredom, the wasting of his muscles to have been for something. Not necessarily something noble, but *something*.

"What makes you think I'm not?" Shamayal toppled sideways with the effort of straining his neck. "Here she comes, here she comes... arse like Beyoncé's."

The man in the bed opposite perked up. "Where?"

"Show a little respect, Shamayal."

"I was only tryin' to cheer you up, innit!" The boy slapped his paint-splattered jeans. "You wanna talk about testpots, we talk about testpots. Shall I tell you how many shades of cream there are on the walls of Ayisha's living room? Nine! 'Just choose one,' I say. 'They're basically all the same.' But she wants to *live* with them. See how she *feels* about them. I go to her, 'If you want to get this finished before the holidays end, you'd better do that *Ip dip sky blue* thing.' And you know what she says?"

"What?" Inquisitive, the man in the bed opposite shuffled.

"She says," Shamayal adopted a ridiculous falsetto, his hands petals cupping his face, "'Actually, I've been thinking about changing my mind. I've seen a picture of a room I liked in sunflower yellow.'"

Jim swallowed, wincing.

"You got somethink 'gainst the colour yellow now? Lucky for you, she's changed her mind. Again. This time she's goin' for duck-egg blue."

Jim's laughter was relief. "Well, at least there can't be so many variations."

"You think? Then you don't know your Dulux from your Fired Earth. Why did I let her talk me into this? Women, they're very manipulative, f'you know what I mean. 'I've got a *likkle favour* to ask,' she goes, and she wrinkles up her nose, like she's all helpless. You're laughing! What you laughin' at? You fink it's *funny*?"

"Typical Ayisha!" Jim said, wondering what 'typical Ayisha' might be. The detached teacher of the staffroom; the vulnerable person he glimpsed sight of in the pub; the passionate individual she tries to rein in.

"Yeah, well." He repositioned himself on the sill, rocking from side to side. "Hey! You got somethink to do with this? I wouldn't put it past you."

Jim feigned shock. "Me?"

Passing the double doors, Sophia performed the mother of all double-takes. "You!" She entered the ward, hands on hips. "Wachoo you doin' up on the windowsill, boy?"

"Tryin' to locate some fresh air, aren't I? 'Cause there ain't none down there."

"Did I ask for back-chat? Get yo'self down"

"I ain't breakin' no law."

"Now!" An erect index finger traced a path straight to hell. "You get your tiny brain round something: here, I *am* the law!"

Shamayal swung out his legs and hopped down lightly, his impish grin implying, *It's a fair cop.* There was no fear in his eyes, Jim observed. The real danger lay elsewhere.

"If you so hot," Sophia continued, "why you still wearin' that stupid hat?"

"Sister, this ain't no hat! This here's what's called a beanie."

"Jim!" She redirected her full-sailed bluster. "Your visitors can't go treatin' this place like home."

"In the chair!" Jim shot the boy a warning look.

Resigning himself to the inevitable, Shamayal complied with an unhurried amble. Only when she was satisfied he was in position did the big nurse swat the air with one hand and go on her way.

"She wants to watch her blood pressure," Shamayal observed. "She gets vexed way too easy."

Jim wondered how best to ask *Have you been home to see*

your father? without opening another can of worms. Ayisha had reported that not all was well in that department. He had seen her truly angry for the first time. No, he censored himself: the boy would talk when he was ready. "She's got a point about the hat."

"This here's *style,* man. Somethink you in your PJs clearly got no idea about."

Jim tried another tack instead, his voice low: "It's all over now." A reference to Christian's death.

"Yeah, yeah. Everything's back to normal, innit. So," Shamayal demonstrated the art of the natural subject-change, "You gonna finish telling me the story of your owl, or what?"

According to his doctor, Jim needed to make more of an effort to 'anchor himself in the present' but it was the present Jim found disturbing. He'd believed what he said when he told Ayisha that Christian would never be left alone, but he hadn't allowed himself to imagine the brutal reality. A boy was dead. And for what? The sake of family honour! Jim was long enough in the tooth to have some understanding of how a loss could send out far-reaching ripples, ripples that would still have an impact in five, ten, twenty years' time.

"Now would be a good time." Shamayal leant back in the chair and elevated his legs. I haven't heard one of your shaggy dog stories for a while." For everyone who wanted him to park himself in the present someone was willing to lure him back to the past, and he would rather let time slip.

"Feet." Jim's eyes traced a path to the floor.

"Man, you're as bad as her!" The boy grumbled, letting his feet drop to the floor heavily.

"I want to stay on Sophia's good side. She's the one with the needles." But already Jim was searching for his mental bookmark.

CHAPTER 24:

JIM - 1992 - RALEGH GROVE

"Jim, love!" his mother called, the minute he had shut the front door behind him. "There's someone here to see you!"

Suspicious after his meeting with Nick, he considered the possibilities: Ben with another excuse to get him out of the flat; the police wanting to question him about his brother. A gang member recruiting seemed like his best option! "I'll just get changed out of my football gear," he shouted.

"Don't worry about that." His mother appeared at the kitchen doorway, eyes widening urgently. "Come and say hello!"

Thinking that perhaps it was one of his aunt's rare visits, Jim dumped his kitbag and followed.

The unbrushable hair was unmistakable.

"Well?" His mum pushed for a reaction but, after relief, his next was anger.

Aimee turned her head, apparently pleased with herself, the gap in her teeth on display. "Did you have a good game?"

"Not bad." He leant against the kitchen units, trying to look casual, self-conscious that his scrawny legs were on display.

"Cup of tea?" Jean extracted another mug from a cupboard

without waiting for his reply. "Sit yourself down, love! You're making the place look untidy. "

He scraped a chair out and sat, tucking his legs under the chair.

"Aimee and I have been talking." Jean spoke with her back facing them. "She's just been telling me how you've taught her ways to remember the Latin names for birds." A steaming mug was placed on the table in front of him. "Aimee *says* you're good with languages…"

Aimee says, Aimee says. Having charmed her way in, Aimee clearly had his mother under her spell.

"She's going to stay for tea so she's here when it gets dark."

What the -? He'd been ganged up on. This was no less of a trap than being jumped in the stairwell. While Jean reached into the fridge, Jim shot Aimee a thundery look and she had the decency to appear ruffled. "You said I could swap your owl for my heron, remember?"

If Jim remembered rightly, Aimee had asked *him*. No way would he have agreed to this!

A splash of milk clouded the contents of his mug. "I told her how you thought you'd seen a ghost the first time we saw the barn owl. Tell Jim what you told me, love."

Aimee leaned forwards: "In English folklore, it's bad luck to see an owl at night."

If she was hoping to win him over, she had another thing coming. "Oh, yeah?"

"It means someone's about to die."

"What do you think of that?" his mother prompted.

Jim shrugged, unimpressed. "We've been watching the owl for months."

"Maybe that's because it's not your owl," Aimee persevered.

"Not *my* owl?" he laughed dismissively. "What are you on about?"

She adopted a tone similar to the one his granddad had

used for ghost stories. "Indian tribes believe owls carry the souls of living people and that, if an owl is killed, the person whose soul they're carrying will also die."

"And there's me thinking they're just supposed to be wise." But Jim couldn't disguise the involuntary shiver that coursed through his bones.

"Jim." He winced as his mother ruffled his hair. "Why don't you show your guest the view from the living room while I make a start on the spuds? On a clear day you can see all the way up to the City."

She was being so obvious, trying to act as a matchmaker.

Kneeling on the sofa with his back to the kitchen, he hissed at Aimee, "How did you find me?"

"I saw you leaving this morning from across the road. Do you want me to go?"

"She's making your tea now!"

"Can you see the NatWest Tower?" Jean called through from the kitchen.

"Over there," Jim pointed Aimee in the direction of a skyscraper sitting head and shoulders above the others.

"It's really clear!" Aimee shouted, then, to Jim, she said simply, "I really like your mum." As if that excused everything!

"We'll have to go up to town one of these days," Jean replied from the doorway, one hip resting against the frame, potato peeler in hand. "I never seem to find the time. We saw the space rockets at the Science Museum once, didn't we, Jim?"

"Years ago!" he protested in case Aimee thought he still needed his hand held.

As they sat down to tea, Jim predicted disaster: egg and chips with tomato ketchup. He was willing to bet Aimee had never had a meal like it in her life.

"Use your hands," his mum invited, piercing the membrane of her egg with the pointed end of a chip, spilling its golden contents.

That broke the ice, somehow. Once she laid down her knife and fork, Aimee looked right at home. "These eggs are great. My mum never gets the middles to stay soft."

Evidently pleased, Jean popped another yolky chip into her mouth and raised her eyebrows. "Where d'you live, Aimee?"

"It's a ten-minute walk from here," she replied. "Just down the hill."

Adding more salt, Jim began to feel excluded.

"Oh, it's lovely there! There's a park I used to go to when I was a girl. That's where they do the big firework display. We don't need tickets: we've got the best view in town." Right on cue, the six thirty-three trundled past. Jim watched his mother grip the table top. "In fact, the only downside of living here is those blasted trains."

Aimee nodded in agreement. "They rattle the glasses."

"They rattle my brains, that's what they do!" Then her expression dropped as realisation struck her. "You hear them as well?"

"All the time! We're even closer than you are."

"Course you are." Jim's mother's expression suggested it had never crossed her mind that the escape route she'd been dreaming of all those years wouldn't solve her headaches. Richard Gere's white charger was going to have to work that little bit harder.

Jim watched the two of them wash up, passing dripping plates between them, and thought about how easily women made friends.

"You can come again!" Jean was laughing. Unlike him, she didn't feel as if her home had been invaded.

Kneeling on the sofa, the unlikely trio watched dusk descend in waves of violet. They were rewarded with sightings of bats flitting like shadows.

Then: "Over there. A flash of white." His mother pointed suddenly, handing the binoculars to Aimee. "Have you got him?"

"Got him," Aimee replied in a half-whisper. "They really do hover," she breathed, before passing the binoculars to Jim.

Remembering his first glimpse of an owl through those lenses, recognising the same wonder in Aimee's voice, he found it impossible to stay angry. "Keep them for a while."

"Look at that wingspan!"

Eventually, Aimee turned and sat down, grasping the binoculars in both hands as if she was holding on to the moment. "I've seen my owl," she said, her voice quiet.

Checking his digital watch, Jim was surprised to discover how late it was. "It's gone ten!" he announced. It struck him: what had been different about that evening - aside from Aimee's visit - was that the television hadn't been switched on all night. Even when there was nothing they wanted to watch, it was the background noise that blocked out the neighbours.

Aimee glanced out of the window into the darkness, worry shadowing her face. "I should get going."

"I'll walk you home," Jim offered, shy to be making the offer in front of his mother.

"I think he should, love," Jean said, seeing that Aimee was about to protest. "At least as far as the bridge."

"Binoculars?" Jim said just as he was opening the door.

"What about them?"

"Can I have them back?"

"I left them on the coffee table."

When Jim returned to the living room to retrieve them, his mother lowered her voice to a whisper. "I recognised her from your sketches straight away!"

"She came to see the owls," he hissed.

"I know," Jean said, too smugly for Jim's liking. "She said so." Then she spoke at normal volume. "Don't you want your denim jacket? You'll catch cold."

Jim looked at Aimee who was standing by the open door.

He noticed that she had worn something of her own tonight.
"Nah! Won't be gone long enough for that."

Outside, Jim adopted the anonymous look everyone on the estate did: head low, shoulders slumped, hands in pockets. Aimee, walking tall and on the off-beat, stuck out like a sore thumb and yet she owned the place. Her lightning laughter fractured the darkness. "Your face when you saw me!"

Jim kept one eye on the shadows between the buildings. "Do you make a habit of inviting yourself to tea?"

She barged him sideways. "I'm usually asked!"

Somehow, without feeling insulted, Jim couldn't imagine receiving a return invitation. People like Aimee can adapt, but sit Jim at a table with the best china and he'd have been too nervous to touch it. Expect small talk and he'd have developed a stutter. And he suspected Aimee's folks would have checked his pockets for the family silver before handing him his jacket at the end of the evening.

"I forgot to tell you," Aimee was saying, "I ran into this weird guy earlier."

"Yeah?" He dribbled an empty Red Stripe can with the inside of his foot.

"He was dressed head to toe in green waterproofs and was carrying a fishing rod. He asked *me* what I was doing here. When I said I was visiting a friend, he asked, 'What friend?' I told him I was here to see Jim who goes bird-watching, and he said, 'What he does is none of my business, but I'd like your name for future reference.'"

As steam trailed from a boiler vent and dispersed, Jim smiled. "So, you've met Bins."

"You know him?"

"Everyone knows Bins."

"I thought he was some nutcase."

"Nah."

"What does he do?"

Jim shrugged. "Fishing."

"Fishing?" Aimee repeated, bewildered. "There's no water round here."

"There's no fish either, but it doesn't bother him."

She laughed. "I feel bad about lying to him now."

"You lied to Bins?" Jim feigned shock. "What did you say?"

"I told him my name was -" Aimee broke off, giggling.

"What?"

"It's stupid." She covered her mouth with one hand.

"How bad can it be?"

"Bad: Verity Parsnip."

"You doughnut!" He exploded as they circumnavigated the bollards. "Where did you dream that up from?"

"I did exactly what you said. I made up something that was obviously a lie."

"Well, from now on, that's how you'll be known. And it's not a good name to have round here."

"Or anywhere else!"

They scampered across the main road at the first break in the traffic, heading towards the bridge.

"You know what next week is, don't you?" Aimee turned to Jim, still grinning.

He groaned, elongating the words. "Last week of the holidays."

Her eyebrows twitched. "New school."

Under the streetlights, the warnings on the signs were as pronounced as they would have been by daylight.

"Welcome back, Miss," Jim joked.

"We must have stayed away long enough. Let's come back here for the last couple of days." Leaning on the side of the bridge, she sprung lightly onto her tiptoes looking over the edge. Then she froze. "What's that?"

"Where?" Jim grabbed the barrels of his binoculars.

"I saw something move."

He trained his lenses. Two shadowy figures were just visible in the yellow light of a small fire. Smaller criss-cross beams suggested they had torches. "Junkies, probably."

"Maybe."

They heard a loud crack followed by a shriek, then, as they locked eyes, the unmistakable noise of a creature in distress cut through the night.

"Let me look!" Aimee grabbed the binoculars, the strap chafing the skin of Jim's neck as he was jerked towards her chest.

He hooked his thumbs under it, protesting, "Are you trying to strangle me?"

"They've made torches from the fire and they're taunting something." Her voice was becoming more and more frantic. Jim crouched low, his only view the brick wall. "I think they've got it trapped. Come on."

"You're never going down there!"

"That's exactly what I'm doing. We can't see properly from up here."

Released, there was no point lecturing Aimee about safety. Soothing his grazed skin Jim tried a different tactic. "What about your parents? Won't they be worried?"

"Anyone would think you're chicken." She wrenched his hand away from his neck. "Solidarity."

They crept down the concrete steps, Aimee hanging off Jim's arm, and crouched behind the metal barrier.

"See anything?" Aimee whispered.

"Nothing." Jim shook his head and let go of the rail. The liquid roar of the bonfire, its occasional crackles and bursts of ugly laughter were loud enough to mask the snapping of twigs accompanying their low-stalking approach. All the time, Jim chanted a silent mantra: *Don't let it be Nick, Don't let it be*

Nick. But seeing what lay on the ground he came to a halt.

A barn owl!

Not satisfied, the boys were poking it with glowing branches, particles of shrivelled leaf taking to the air like fire flies. Its lifeless body rocked and settled with each prod. Unable to remain silent, Jim bolted upright and yelled, "You fucking eejits!"

Half-illuminated orange-tinged faces twisted towards him, the corners of mouths that had been lifted with laughter dropping. One belonged to Ben, the boy who would do anything for an E; the other to Nick, the older brother who had taken punches for him. Their bodies stiffened.

"What the hell are you doing?" Jim moved forwards furiously into the circle of heat.

Ben recovered his voice first. "It's only your kid brother. Shit, Jim, you had us worried!" He sacrificed his burning branch to the flames, his head zig-zagging as he squinted over Jim's shoulder. "Who's that you've got with you?"

"What the fuck have you gone and done?" Jim spat, clench-fisted, shaking with adrenalin and rage.

"It was an accident," Nick offered feebly, hands raised, displaying a quarter of Thunderbird. "We were just checking to see if it was alive."

Above the acrid smouldering, Jim smelt the alcohol reek on his brother's breath. Searching for an explanation, his eyes wandered from the bottle to a dozen toppled Red Stripe cans strewn round the fire to an air rifle lying close by. The skin of one side of his face taut in the heat, his words were disbelieving: "You *shot* it?"

"It was only a bit of fun -"

"Fun?" Jim barked. "Torture's your idea of fun, is it?" High knees, careful feet, he approached the owl. One singed wing outstretched; hardly a stain on its white underbelly where the pellet had entered. Crouching down, one of Jim's hands found his mouth, reshaped it. The owl's dark unseeing eyes stared up from its heart-shaped face, a residue of last-moment surprise.

"It came at us out of the dark."

"It was a gut reaction," Ben said. "Simple as that."

Excuses.

Jim had seen roadkill before. Mice that cats had toyed with then abandoned when they got bored. Pigeons left half-eaten by foxes. Squirrels that had wandered onto the railway line. The results of real accidents, or nature taking its course. But never this personal. Bile rose in his throat: that someone he knew - someone he was related to - was capable of *this*.

"Listen, Jim -" Nick was saying.

"Fuck you!" No longer disappointment, this was hate. The boy didn't look at his brother. Not because he was embarrassed that Nick would see his tears - there was nothing unmanly about mourning the death of another creature. Jim's saliva, thick and sticky, cloyed his speech. "I don't care if I never see you again!"

"Let's go." Nick said quietly, his slow-rustling footsteps retreating.

"What the -?" Ben muttered. Jim heard him spit. "Are you going to let your kid brother give the orders?" Cans were displaced noisily as Ben kicked his way through out-lying embers to snatch the air rifle from the scrub. Then, as his footsteps receded, Jim heard Aimee's timid approach.

"Is it -?" she asked shakily, one hand on his shoulder for balance as she knelt beside him. Her amber eyes, burning orange, asked what she couldn't.

It was Jim's turn to spit: "Bastards!"

Trembling, Aimee gently reached for the tip of the owl's outstretched wing. Face edged in pale gold, half hidden by liquid shadow, her bottom lip stretched painfully between the grip of her teeth. "Do you think he's the one I saw earlier?"

"It's a female," Jim blurted, textbook facts the only

language he was capable of using. "See the black spots on her chest?" He began to examine the bird. It was the length of a standard ruler, each wing about half the length of the body again. Underneath, the wings were purest white. On top, silvery-grey feathers nestled among the tawny gold.

"Someone's in for some very bad luck." Aimee hugged herself, attempting to contain her shivering.

Jim saw genuine fear and wondered, "Do you actually believe that story?"

A shrug: "The Indians have been proved right about lots of things."

Again, his hate emerged. "Let's hope it's my brother, then."

The fire snapped as it burned itself out, noises reducing to the bursting of bubble-wrap.

The half of Aimee's face that was visible was wet and streaked. "What are we going to do with her? She deserves a proper funeral."

"The ground's too tough to bury her," he said. "Too many roots."

Aimee's attention moved to the embers. "We could give her a cremation."

"Not enough dry wood. We'd end up doing half a job."

"Then let's take her to the woods tomorrow. We'll put her in our summerhouse overnight. She'll be safe there."

It felt like the right thing to do. Jim peeled off his tracksuit top and spread it flat, lifted the owl by her wings - light, so much lighter than he expected - and placed her in the middle.

He folded the sleeves neatly, as if packing a suitcase. The first time he had come this close to an owl - felt the softness of her feathers he had read about - and she was dead. He gently picked the package up and hugged the owl to him, still warm, talons digging into his flesh through the thin cotton of his t-shirt.

"Let's go."

Approaching the summerhouse from the bunny run, to Jim, that glorious rainy day already seemed like a distant memory. He laid the owl in the centre of the hexagonal floor, amid the metal and canvas furniture. Meanwhile, Aimee had picked up a large crate and, having read the instructions, nodded decisively and ripped into the packaging. "We may as well do this properly," she said, handing two candles to Jim and quickly tucking the paper label and plastic into the back pocket of her jeans. "Let's surround her with them."

She made minute adjustments to each candle until the circle was to her satisfaction and then journeyed the full 360 degrees, crouching over each with the lighter she had stowed away with her contraband cigarettes. Hugging his knees, nose tucked into the angle of one arm, Jim watched each wick flicker to life. "What words do you say for an owl?" he asked.

Aimee sighed deeply. Jim hadn't really expected a response, but she began speaking. "The owl, night's herald, shrieks, 'tis very late; The sheep are gone to fold, birds to their nest, And coal black clouds that shadow heaven's light, Do summon us to part, and bid good night."

Of course, Jim had no idea it was Shakespeare. She planted quotes to catch him out in years to come, when he least expected it. "Good night," he found himself repeating, an Amen of sorts.

Aimee checked her watch, winced: "And now I really do have to go."

Jim nodded from his bird-like position. He felt her hand on his shoulder for just a moment; a nervous hand, unsure what business it had lingering there. His eyes followed as it was withdrawn. "That was good, what you said. You should say that again tomorrow."

"Tomorrow?"

"For the owl's funeral."

"Right. The funeral. I could if you like." She hesitated in

the doorway. "Aren't you coming?"

"Shouldn't we blow the candles out?"

"No, they last for twelve hours. I want to be able to see them burning when I look out of my bedroom window."

"Mind if I stay with her for five minutes?"

"OK." And then, before shutting him in, she smiled for him. As much as she was able to. "Five minutes, no more! Your mum will wonder where you are."

CHAPTER 25:

JIM - AUGUST 1992 - RAILWAY SIDINGS

The next morning, rising early, Jim dressed quickly, picking up yesterday's clothes from the bedroom floor. There was no point in taking a shower when everything smelt of smoke; besides, the clanking of the plumbing would have woken his mother. Creeping out, he clicked the front door shut and headed down to the railway tracks. All that remained of his brother's campfire was the acrid smell, bone-pale ash, a few sticks of charcoal and the scattering of beer cans, burnt to the colour of rust. Close by, caught in the scrub, was a single white feather. He ran it through his fingers, smoothing the vane. *The barbules on the ends of owl feathers are missing. It gives the feathers an incredibly soft and light quality, meaning they can fly more quietly than other birds.* Stowing it safely in a pocket of his rucksack, Jim contemplated that soon this single feather would be the only part of the owl that was left.

An hour passed, then another. Workmen's shouts volleyed up and down the track. Jim caught the occasional glimpse of an orange jacket, the sound of a spade colliding with something solid. Perhaps Aimee couldn't bring herself to pick up a dead bird. Maybe she was pacing up and down, cursing him. He set a mental deadline and, when ten o'clock arrived, set off to tackle the maze of back alleys.

Passing a post box, he identified graffiti at the base of a streetlight and saw the fence-bound track disappearing between two semis, only to see a policeman coming in the opposite direction. Jim stood aside, trying the confident approach. "I thought me and my mates were the only ones who used this shortcut."

The officer pointed to Jim's binoculars. "What are those for?"

"Bird-watching." *Breathe*, the boy told himself, as the policeman raised his eyebrows. "Want a look?"

"No, you're alright. One thing I've learned in this job is that it's the most unlikely-sounding things that turn out to be true. Careful how you go. There's been a fire in a garden shed."

Goose-bumps prickled the back of Jim's neck. He had imagined that the smell invading his nostrils was the residue of last night's bonfire. "Whereabouts?"

"Up on the right."

He swallowed. "Can I still get through to Durnsford?"

"You should be fine. But don't go getting in the way."

"Right."

Jim stopped beside charred fence panels, ripped down to stop the spread. Beyond, he saw scorched remains. The entire roof of the summerhouse was gone, burnt or hacked out by the fire brigade. Shattered glass. Coils of springs from the sun loungers. Blackened wood in what little remained of the hexagonal floor. *The owl had already had its funeral.* The candles, Aimee's prayer and a cremation; unplanned, but more spectacular than anything he could have dreamt up. As he was imagining the pyre, Jim heard a nearby voice: "…not your typical case of arson."

He held his breath. Three figures stood a short distance

away, their backs towards him: two firemen and a man with a denim shirt belted into his jeans. The rear portion of perfect striped lawn had been reduced to a mud bath.

One of the firemen was saying, "There seem to be some animal remains. Did you keep a pet in there?"

"We've got a cat, but she was safe in the house."

"Maybe a bird of some sort?"

"We've never kept birds." The denim man sounded disbelieving.

"Can I ask what the building was used for?"

"Storage, mainly. But my daughter sometimes came down here to get a bit of privacy."

"Likes candles, does she?"

"If I didn't know better, I'd say it looks like someone's been performing a pagan ritual."

The denim man looked at the others, uncertain whether this was his cue to laugh, experimenting cautiously.

As one of them turned towards the debris, with every sinew taut, Jim stepped back behind the fence panels. It was only when the voices moved away that he chanced another look. The man was standing, his lace-up shoes muddied, staring up at a window. Through his binoculars Jim could see the dark silhouette of a girl with long hair. Trapped. Who would believe she had brought a dead bird home overnight to keep it 'safe'? Damn it! Aimee's telephone number might have come in handy, but phoning might mean a grilling - and that was if her parents would even let him speak to her. Still, it didn't seem fair to let her take all of the blame.

He paced up and down her road looking at almost-identical pairs of houses, trying to work out which of the solid-looking fronts was attached to the back he had just seen. Was it the house with the black-and-white tiled path, or the one with the fleet of polished cars parked on the driveway? Then Jim remembered Aimee telling him that her neighbour's house was up for sale. That left a choice of two. His eyes were drawn to movement: a black cat had jumped up and was sitting on the windowsill.

He skulked on the pavement opposite, staring at the front door. He might just make things ten times worse by knocking. On the other hand... Each time he thought he had moved closer to a decision, doubt seeped in. Eventually, in a moment's clarity, he strode across the road. Unable to find a doorbell to ring, he lifted the letterbox to knock. Raised voices reached him, the words indistinct. Then he heard Aimee's voice, shouting, distressed: *"Alright, I'll tell you! Just get off me!"*

Images came to him: Aimee lifting up her top to check her bruises. Aimee telling him that she'd asked for it. Jim felt a fresh surge of anger. His desire to break down the door was interrupted by the sound of tyres displacing gravel. A silver jeep pulled onto the drive, and a long-haired lady threw open the driver's door. There was no doubt she was Aimee's mother. The resemblance was striking.

"Not more junk mail!"

Mistaken for a delivery boy, Jim stood open-mouthed. With towering heels and a large handbag at one elbow, she didn't look like the sort of mother who had time to make eggs with runny middles.

Making his excuses, Jim heard her voice join the shouting. "What's going on, David?"

He didn't look back. Aimee would be fine now. She might even find an excuse to escape. He returned to the tracks, but by four o'clock he had lost the heart for it. Returning home, he dropped down heavily on the sofa, asking, "What are you watching?"

Jean patted his leg. "It's an interview with Sally Gunnell. She's won gold in the 400-metre hurdles. Nothing doing?"

"Not much."

"Me neither. My three thirty cancelled. We could have an early tea if you fancy it?"

"Could do."

"Sure you're OK? You're usually starving." She laughed, not waiting for his reply before making her way to the kitchen. A cupboard door was opened, contents rearranged. "Is pasta alright?"

He loitered, slouching against the doorframe.

"What time did you creep in at last night?" Mum was filling the kettle. "I thought you were only going as far as the bridge."

"I got held up," Jim muttered.

"Oh?"

He hadn't planned to tell her. It sort of slipped out. "Some idiot had shot one of the owls."

"No!" A saucepan handle in one hand, she froze. "What did you do?"

"We decided to put it in a safe place until we could give it a proper funeral. That should have been today, but it all went wrong." There was no point stopping there. Jim censored the details, deciding what Jean needed to know: how the summerhouse had burned down; the firemen's suggestion that there might be more to it; the shouting. He couldn't tell her about Nick's role - not when things were just getting back to normal.

"But there's an innocent explanation. I'm sure Aimee's parents are reasonable people. We'll go round after tea, sort this whole mess out."

Jim felt far less certain than his mother. "And say what?"

"We'll explain that you and Aimee were trying to do right by the owl."

He winced. "I don't think her parents know about the bird-watching. Or about me."

"What about you?" Jean asked, crossing her arms in front of her.

Jim hung his head.

"And what's *that* supposed to mean?" His mother put her hands on her hips, indignant. "*You* don't judge people because of where they come from or who they're related to. I mean it! I clean up after those folks and I can tell you, they piss and they shit just the same as we do." That had his attention. "It's time you started believing in yourself." As if reading the thoughts that had been playing bagatelle in his head, she said, "You've got a good brain, Jim. If you've got any sense, you'll use it to get out of here."

CHAPTER 26:

JIM - AUGUST 1992 - DURNSFORD ROAD

The visit might have been his mother's idea but, as he watched the way she straightened her coat, Jim saw he wasn't the only nervous one. Jean knocked on the front door then stepped back, shielding herself with her handbag. A new notice had been attached to the inside of a small side window: *Please, No junk mail and door-to-door sales callers.* He reckoned they would be marginally less welcome than Mr Everest. As footsteps approached, his mother pressed her lips together, blotting her lipstick. This was some performance she was building up to.

"Good evening." Jean sprang to life as the door opened inwards, adapting her voice to her surroundings. She smiled as if auditioning for a toothpaste advert. "You must be Aimee's father."

The man was tall with what his mother usually referred to as 'a good head of hair'. Unlike Mrs White, Jim failed to find any resemblance to Aimee. Somehow that pleased him.

"And you are?" He looked blankly from Jim to his mother and back again.

"I'm Mrs Stevens, but do call me Jean." The man snatched

at the hand she offered before it infiltrated the threshold. "And this is my son, Jim." Jim found himself grimacing. "I don't suppose we could have a quick word? There's been a bit of a misunderstanding I'd like to clear up."

Folded arms barred their way. "Oh?"

"Perhaps *misunderstanding* is the wrong word." Jim admired his mother's patience but, if he'd been directing her, he would have recommended sounding slightly less apologetic. Mr White was being intentionally rude. "My son heard about the fire in your garden. He was worried people might've got the wrong end of the stick."

People? Jim thought, but it seemed to have done the trick.

"Perhaps you'd better come in," Aimee's father said.

The door closed, they stood in the hall rearranging their hands. Despite all the space, there was something claustrophobic about the house. Something that made him want to run in the opposite direction as fast as he could.

"So, young man." One hand on the banister, Aimee's father turned himself into a stair-guard. Aimee was upstairs, that much was obvious. It was equally plain that she wouldn't be making an appearance. Something told him there would be no offer of tea and Jammy Dodgers. Jim recognised his denim jacket underneath Mr White's hand. The jacket Aimee had claimed to have forgotten about. "I take it you know my daughter."

Standing on the mat between his mother and Mr White, Jim knew that he was being hemmed in. He resigned himself to saying his piece: The quicker you do it, the quicker you're out of here. "Aimee's a member of my bird-watching club."

"Forgive me." Mr White closed his eyes and pinched the bridge of his nose. "But I know nothing about a *bird-watching* club."

"I have to admit," Jean latched onto his sceptical tone, "That was my first reaction, but it's a wonderful thing for young people to be involved in. Jim's been almost every day during the holidays."

"I see." Mr White blinked at him.

Knowing his credentials were being questioned, Jim's only option was to speak his lines with conviction. "Last night, after watching the owls, I was walking Aimee home when we came across one of them, lying on the ground. Someone had shot it with an air rifle -"

"Where did you *come across* the owl?" Aimee's father interrupted.

Jim hesitated. He hadn't anticipated cross examination. "Sorry?" he asked.

"It's quite simple. I asked *where* you found the owl."

Bones showed through the knuckles of the hand that grasped his jacket on the end of the banister. It was obvious Aimee's father had already extracted the story from his daughter, but Jim felt in control of his facts. "We were on the bridge when we heard something crying out, so we went down to see if we could do anything to help."

"Do I take it you mean down by the side of the railway?"

Rather than say he thought he'd already made that clear, the boy decided to nod.

"But that's trespassing, isn't it?" Mr White's presence loomed all the larger because he was reflected in a mirror that hung over the telephone table.

"They could hardly ignore an animal in distress!" Jean intervened.

"Of course. And what exactly did you find -" Mr White's mouths, both real and reflected, were smile-shaped, but there was nothing pleasant about them. "*Down* by the side of the tracks?"

Jim found that he had backed up against the front door. "There were two lads with an air rifle."

"Stand up straight, love."

"They said it had been an accident, but they'd been drinking -"

"You took *my daughter* somewhere where there were two drunks with an air rifle?"

Realising they'd reached the part of the story he'd been economical with, Jim accepted there was no prospect of Mum coming to the rescue. The idea of taking Aimee anywhere she didn't want to go was beyond him. The alternative - saying that he'd tried to convince her to go home - would hardly help. He was angry with his mother: she shouldn't have made him come. He was angry with himself for having listened. When it emerged, his voice was uncertain. "We couldn't see them from the bridge. It was too dark."

Mr White appeared prepared to let that pass. "So you came across a couple of drunks who had killed an owl with an air rifle."

"That's right."

"Why on earth didn't you call the police?"

Unease was growing. "I didn't see any point."

This time his mother saw fit to volunteer. "I think what he means is the owl was already past help."

"What about this bird-watching club of yours?" Mr White asked. "Surely they have a procedure for reporting this sort of thing?"

His mother's expression said *It's a reasonable question - one a member of a bird-watching club should know the answer to.* "It was the first time I've ever found a dead bird. Let alone an owl."

Aimee's father changed tactics. "Then let me ask you this: did you know the lads with the air rifle?"

A tight ball blocking his throat, Jim wished he hadn't stepped away from the front door. He could have done with the support. "I recognised them."

"Are you sure you weren't with them before this so-called

accident happened?"

"Now, hang about." His mother's clipped vowels failed her. "Aimee and Jim had spent the evening at ours."

"Thank you for that, Mrs Stevens." Aimee's father's self-congratulatory smile suggested a scoring of points. "I have to say, I wasn't aware you were such close friends. Go on, Jim."

Now that Mr White had succeeded in tripping his mother up, Jim couldn't tell where the questions would land next. His delivery sounded stilted. "We decided to give the owl a proper funeral, but we didn't want to leave her out overnight where the foxes could get at her, so we put her in your summer-house."

"A *funeral?*" Mr White was incredulous, his distorted face huge and ugly. "For an *owl?*"

"The children were devastated. They were just trying to do the right thing -"

"And while they were *trying to do the right thing*" - Mr White's reflection reddened - "not only did they put them-selves in danger, but they burnt my summerhouse down! I've just spent the morning being interrogated by the police."

That explained it, Jim thought. He was being given a dose of the same medicine.

"What if the fire had spread?" Mr White was continuing. "What then?"

"Wait a minute!" Jean protested. "It was an accident."

"Jim, perhaps you can tell me, who *accidentally* left dozens of candles burning overnight in a wooden building?" Aimee's father sighed, pretending to pally up to him. "Was it your cigarette lighter you used, sonny?"

Beside him, his mother bristled. Jim noted how she held her breath, waiting for his reply. It was tempting to say, *No, Mr White, in fact it was yours.*

"If you can't answer that, tell me this: who lit the candles?"

Jim thought he saw movement in the periphery of his vision. He tried to disguise the fact that he was looking upstairs to the landing by rubbing his forehead. A small hand was withdrawn. No signal. Just a small hand. "I was the last to leave," he blurted.

Mr White raised his eyebrows, apparently impressed that he would risk pre-empting the next question. "And you didn't think it would be a good idea to blow them out?"

It wasn't as if he hadn't suggested it. Aimee was the one who had read the instructions and assured him they would be safe. "It said that they would burn for twelve hours."

"It *said* they weren't for indoor use!"

Jim felt his eyebrows jump inwards before he could control them. Aimee was as obsessed with detail as he was. No way would she have missed something as important as that. Was it possible? Had she started the fire *deliberately*?

"Well, it must have taken guts for you to come here and apologise, I'll give you that."

Jim felt his breath catch: he had only come to get Aimee off the hook.

"You're lucky. Our insurance will cover most of the damage," Mr White continued. "I told Aimee I would expect her to pay the excess from her allowance. Perhaps you'd like to go halves? We'll call it twenty-five pounds each." He turned to Jean. "I think that would be a good lesson about respect for property."

It was Jean's turn to sound shocked. "Jim doesn't have that sort of money!"

"A bright lad like him will have no trouble getting a Saturday job."

"He's not old enough..."

Mr White feigned oily regret: "I was hoping we could sort this out without involving the police again."

Jean's face paled.

"According to them it was arson, but I'm prepared to be persuaded that it was carelessness."

"You'll get your money." Jim's mother reached forwards and snatched his denim jacket from the end of the banister.

"Hang on! What do you think you're doing with my daughter's jacket?"

"It's my *son's* jacket. I should know. I bought it for him." She opened the front door and shepherded Jim out. "Does your daughter tell you the truth, Mr White? Because I can't see much in your reaction to encourage honesty."

"Jim!" Aimee's father called over the top of Jean's head. He turned, still absorbed by the confusing image of Aimee secreting the instructions for use of the candles in her pocket. "Did you tell your mother it was your brother who shot the owl?"

The words paralysed him. He should have known this self-satisfied man would insist on having the last word. He imagined walking back up the path, his fist crossing the threshold, knocking that smug expression right off the bastard's face.

Behind him, the door slammed. The display of solidarity over, Jim's mother elbowed her way past and marched ahead. "I can't believe you've been smoking behind my back!"

"Where would I get the money to smoke?" He fired back. If that was the only thing his mother could think of to blame him for, it might still have been worth it. Mr White had as good as promised to go easier on Aimee. Although whether she deserved it…

"What am I supposed to think?" She stopped and turned on him. "*Why* didn't you tell me about Nick?"

He shrugged, meaning that he hadn't wanted to upset her again after what she'd been through.

Jean had formed a triangle with her hands, fingertips together framing her nose, thumbs under her chin. Above, her eyes were scrunched closed. "I'm your mother. It's my job to protect you, not the other way around!"

The roots of a tree had broken through the tarmac in the place they were standing. When Jim looked up, his mother was watching him. "I don't want you doing anything stupid. I'll get you the money."

He knew what she meant: she didn't want him to steal it. Desperate that she knew she could trust him, Jim said, "I'll earn it," lips pressed together, hoping to disguise their wobble.

"No need. It's what I'd put aside for your birthday next week."

CHAPTER 27:

SHAMAYAL - AUGUST 2010 - ST HELIER HOSPITAL

"Man, you was well and truly screwed!" Shamayal sympathised, pacing the six feet of lino to the left of Jim's hospital bed. "That Mr White was bang outta line!"

"I thought so at the time, I admit, but now I've got a place of my own I'd be pretty pissed off if some kid burnt it down. Even if it *was* an accident."

Shamayal was surprised to hear Jim taking the man's side. Only a minute ago, he was the enemy. "Sounds to me like you was tricked into owning up. Anyway, like he said, he was insured."

"Does that mean I should have been let off?"

What the -? He'd thought they were on the same side. "The whole point was that it was Aimee's fault. Man, why you turnin' round and lecturin' me all of a sudden?" Shamayal leant on the metal frame at the foot of the bed. "I'm just trying to show a little... what was that word you called it?"

"Solidarity."

"Right, right: solidarity. You wanna throw it back in my face, that's up to you! You know somefink?" He straightened up and pointed. "I get what this is about: it's about you switchin' sides."

"Which side am I supposed to have switched to?"

One of Jim's neighbours pitched in. "Keep the volume down! Some of us are trying to sleep."

Perhaps it had got a bit out of hand. "You started out one of us." Shamayal, lowered his voice, nodding his head to the window side. "Now?"

Jim's raised eyebrows challenged him, *come on*.

The boy nodded in the direction of the corridor, where an alarm of some sort was going off. "You're Mr White."

"What? Because I dared to pass the warning signs?"

"You was stickin' up for him a minute ago!"

"I was playing devil's advocate! Incidentally, which side are you living on at the moment?"

Don't get all *incidentally* with me. "Unlike you, right, I haven't forgotten my roots!" Where was this going? He had already been told off by that fierce nurse for stressing Jim out, and he hadn't set out looking for an argument. "So." He navigated a 180 degree turn. "You never said. What happened to your friend, Aimee?"

Jim's sheet rose and fell. His voice came out sad. "The holidays came to an end. That's what happened."

They were back on track. "Sometimes, yeah, that's just the way it is. I don't s'pose Ayisha will be invitin' me round once I'm back at school. Fact, I don't s'pect she'd be caught dead speakin' to me. But you -" The boy clapped his hands together and rubbed them. "You're sorted!"

"I doubt it." Teacher-Jim appeared to shrink down under the covers. "I'm not in her good books."

"Why d'you say that?"

"Let's just say she's feeling put upon."

"Uh-uh. You got that back to front, man. Why d'you think she keeps on comin' back? She *likes* to feel everything will fall apart without her. You should hear her go '*Jim's going to need this when they let him out.*' '*I'm just recording a programme for Jim because he'll be missing it.*' I'm warnin' you, you got some majorly dull documentaries to watch. You'll be wishin' you was back in here. '*I've made extra dinner and frozen it because Jim won't be able to cook when he gets home.*'"

"Stop it!"

Shamayal collected his things. "'*Maybe I should re-decorate my bedroom. Do you think Jim would prefer pea-green or ultra-violet?*'"

Jim shook his head. As he closed his eyes and laughed, crow's feet appeared at the corners of his eyes. That was better. Shamayal inserted his earphones, raising his voice over the top of Usher: *Baby, let me.* "You better start usin' that wrinkle cream of yours again." *You make me wanna say,* "Oh, oh, oh-oh, oh; oh, oh, oh-oh, oh; oh my gosh."

Outside, the afternoon was bright, the paving slabs star-spangled with pigeon shit, dappled with shadows, the tarmac pock-marked. Shamayal couldn't put it off any longer. His sense of being followed escalated as he walked towards Ralegh Grove, causing him to glance over his right shoulder.

"How you gonna protect me when you 'fraida your own shadow?" his mamma used to ask, and, to prove her wrong - that he would always be her big brave man - he would stamp his foot as he came to a sudden halt and turn, threaten it with hands clasped into the gun of the Bond credits.

"You my hero," she'd swoon.

He tried a zillion ways to catch his shadow out, but there it was with its shape-shifting trickery. Today it was behind him at a right angle, shortened, flat as road kill. It wasn't his own shadow that frightened him now. What happened to Christian, being hunted down: that's what you've got to worry about.

Ayisha, he had been surprised to discover, liked to be

frightened for fun. They were working their way through her back-catalogue of horror films, although she'd taken a lot of convincing to let him watch any 18s. She knew all the lines - "Oh, yes… there will be blood" - and she did this Count von Count vampire laugh - "Ah hah hah hah hah!" - whenever a baddy was on his way. She didn't hide behind her fluffy cushions or bury her head in his shoulder, as he'd hoped. Matter a fact, she was well into her gore.

"Are you shocked?" she had asked, legs tucked up to one side. Posting popcorn into her mouth, her expression suggested she would have liked to shock him. And after one glass of wine, her face half-lit by the glow from the TV, she was hardly like a teacher at all. Definitely not like his mamma, nah-uh.

The image on the screen had made him nauseous. "Be-have! Trus' me," he lied. "Like I tol' you, I'm about the most open-minded person you'll ever meet." Say it often enough, it might even become true.

A woman, whose hips were as wide as the double buggy she was steering, refused to swerve from a straight line down the centre of the pavement. Either he's invisible or she must be one of those zombies. She was wearing what could be described kindly as a floaty top, unkindly as a tent. Her eyes were *Shaun of the Dead* dead. As she passed, she glanced a blow off his Adidas bag, packed with the clothes he wanted to exchange for fresh ones. Forced into the gutter, he couldn't let it pass.

"Man! Are you for real?" He dipped his head, raising his right elbow and staring back through the triangle between bag and arm. A guy who was walking twenty yards behind him stopped, didn't seem to know what to do with himself and then checked the sole of his shoe. That wasn't in the instruction manual for following people. You were supposed to light a cigarette; duck behind a parked car. The man scraped his shoe on the kerb, and checked again. Did Christian see them coming for him? What you needed was eyes in the back of your head. A couple of minutes later Shamayal checked again. No sign of the guy. Looks like he may have genuinely stood in something. *Don't relax, you're not there yet.*

Immediately after Londis, Shamayal swung wide on a concrete bollard and passed a sign dictating, No Ball Games. Heinous crime, he thought, liking the comic-strip way the words sounded. His hands practised fists, clenching and unclenching like Iron Man. Red-brick fortresses rose on all sides, a city within a city. He tensed at the sound of a foot scraping. A scooter whizzed past - too close for comfort - powered by a pint-sized chariot-rider, all frilly ankle socks and sparkling sandals. *Get me: scared witless of a five-year-old girlie!*

A defiant football skittered. Shamayal trapped it under his right foot, scanned the car park and located a boy with one hand in the air. No danger there. They exchanged friendly nods.

"Yo! Chuck it over!"

Shamayal scooped the ball up; grinning. "Can't you read, man?"

"Don't give me all that." The boy ambled across, extracting a spray can from the depths of a pocket and blasted it at the *No.* "Happy now?"

"Static." Shamayal launched the ball overarm, then consulted his watch. His father would be sitting at the kitchen table, a fat silver chain hanging over his vest, necking one final sober-me-up *Nescafe* before the evening shift. Ten minutes and he would be gone. With time to kill, Shamayal decided to pay Bins a visit. Got to keep your options open, in case you need to move fast. Besides, he could give him an update on Jim; maybe convince him to pay a visit. Christ knows, Shamayal's jaw was achin' from playin' the fool. He could do with some help. But he wasn't sure Bins ever left his manor. An outcast who has convinced himself he belongs so completely, he thinks there's no place for him on the outside. Perhaps he's right. The world would chuck him right back, overarm.

Safe side, he rounded the corner of the block, waited. Last thing he wanted was for anyone to know where the old man lived. Shoe-scraper guy hadn't followed. People with dogs really should clean up.

Bins opened the door inwards, eyes lighting up the way Shamayal knew his mamma's would. "Stands for no crap!" He held up one hand with the palm flat. "Gimme five."

"Yo, blood." The boy obliged with an improvised five-point handshake, ending in a clenched fist. "You bin lookin' after yourself?"

"Oh, yes." The old man shuffled down the hall, shoulders hunched, the soles of his shoes flapping. "I've been taking care of business."

The hall was lined with plastic bags full to overflowing, some tied with string.

Business! "If they don't come round and collect your recycling, we should have us a likkle car boot sale."

"I told you, it's all -"

"I know, I know!" Shamayal held his hands up. "Hee-hee-hee. This is the stuff we agreed you need to keep." He expelled air, then ran his tongue over his teeth. What *was* that taste?

Shamayal hesitated at the threshold of the first door he came to and, on instinct, opened it. It hit him: slap bang. *What the -?* No single smell was identifiable. It was all there: the baked-bean-digestive-biscuit-sour-milk-bile-piss-puke rotting stench. "Whoa!" He pulled the door to and breathed. "When was your living room claimed for landfill? I fought we cleaned up in there so you had space to sit down and watch telly."

"I watched telly," Bins blinked. "A pretty lady did the weather. She said it wouldn't rain and then it did."

Shamayal counted to three and pushed the door open again to assess the damage. The down-trodden brown carpet pile that had started life patterned with orange swirls was littered with crud: empty pizza boxes, polystyrene burger cartons, egg boxes, toilet roll innards, a chicken carcass, a half-eaten Pot Noodle and - *Jesus, no!* - was that a nappy bag? Here and there, items were grouped together as if mingling at a litter convention. Others were stashed on the floral cushions of the threadbare three-seater. The greater portion looked as if it had been tipped out of black bin-liners and left to lie. It was hard to take in. He couldn't hold his breath any longer. Circumferencing his neck, Shamayal said, "We could use a likkle air."

"Are you too hot?" Bins arrived behind him, eyes concerned, senses immune. He was layered for outdoors in his uniform Fair Aisle cardigan with toggles for buttons, a tweed sports jacket and his once-beige raincoat. Standing with his hands in the small of his back, stomach pressed forward like a child's, he gave no hint of self-consciousness.

"Swelterin'." Shamayal picked a crooked path through the detritus, careful where he planted his feet. "Mind if I open a window?"

"Be my guest. I don't want you to be uncomfortable."

The bellybutton-fluff lining the sill was studded with bluebottles reclining stiff-legged on their backs, like they had just keeled over. Shamayal had to force the yellowed glass with his palm, gulping down the fresh air before it could blend with the stale and putrid.

Those hours of careful negotiation and hard graft: wasted. Is this what it would always be like if he befriended the old guy? Where was the home help? Putting in her time-sheet and claiming the money, no doubt. It was all very well Teacher-Jim turnin' round and sayin' that Bins has decided how to live his life, but there should be a system to stop him choosing to live like *this*. Who says he wouldn't be better off in a home? Shamayal's mamma always said a bit of sewing was therapeutic. She was into her cross-stitch; used to make these little pictures. Teddy bears and old red telephone boxes - like a proper English lady. He would organise her different coloured threads when she got them tangled up, making a cardboard spool with notches cut into the ends.

Shamayal composed himself before facing Bins across the dishevelment. The old man was humming, his face serene. What might have emerged as anger came out as scorn: "You sure you got enough double-sided sticky tape for this lot? What are they makin' on *Blue Peter* at the moment, anyhow? I mean, it must be something you need to get planning permission for."

Seeing fear flash across the old man's face, Shamayal felt bad. "Chill, man! I's only foolin' with you." He loped over and clapped Bins on the arms as if to prove it. "See?"

Bin's recovery was swift and complete. "Oh, very funny." He double-punched Shamayal's chest affectionately. "Bo-boom."

"So seriously, man, what's all this you been doin'?"

Clearly expecting the boy to share his delight, Bins's expression told of enterprise and accomplishment. "Like it, eh? That's my stocktaking. I'm putting it all in order."

"Right, right," Shamayal nodded, detecting no evidence of order.

"Starting over there -"

"Uh-huh, uh-huh." His nostrils protested at the assault.

Bins pointed to a cardboard box, "- with Alpen."

"It's in *alphabetical?*" Bewildered, the boy blinked at the picture of the cereal bowl in front of the mountain.

"Course, I'm only up to 'O'."

"As in *Oh my gosh*." Scanning the room, Shamayal's eyes settled on an Oddbins carrier bag and the packaging from an Orange phone. He censored himself, using one hand as a gag.

Index finger and thumb clenched his nostrils, warm breath moistening his palm. Sucking in and then releasing flesh, he felt like he was breathing through mechanical apparatus.

Bins pursed his lips to one side and his dirt-encrusted fingernails scratched the side of his troubled face. "My dear old mum always told me, 'O is for Owl.'"

"True, true. Tell me, what you plannin' on doin' with this lot when you finished?"

"This here's my recycling plant."

Shamayal saw movement in one corner of the room. No doubt it was visitors of the furry variety.

Bins turned, as if suddenly remembering something that being a host demanded. He rubbed his hands together. "Tea? I've got a packet of pink wafers open…."

The thought of eating was repulsive. "To be completely honest with you," Shamayal concocted the whitest lie, "I'm just on my way home, aren't I? I fought I'd stop in and tell you how Jim's gettin' on." The boy made barrels out of his hands and raised them to his eyes, as he'd seen Bins do. It was sign language. He got the high five; Jim, binoculars.

"Bird-watcher Jim?"

"That's my man! You remember how he's in hospital, don't you?"

Bins appeared to be thinking. Behind one hand, his face took on a squashed appearance.

All the time, Shamayal was making his way towards the exit. "You're havin' me on now! I gotta watch out for you!"

Releasing his serious mask with an "Ah-ha!" Bins celebrated his triumph with a broad yellow-toothed grin.

"Well, he's feelin' much better now. Fact, now I come to think about it, we should go and see him together." But, come to think about it, looking at Bins's infantile-aged face, Shamayal wondered what Sophia would make of the string and safety pins that held his clothes together. Would a hygienic hand-wipe be any match for a walking germ-factory?

"Oh, I don't know," Bins mumbled nervously. "I'm very busy with my work."

"Tell you what." Walking backwards on his heels, a quick glance to his left and his right, Shamayal pointed to the old man who was standing in the doorway of his castle. "You get back to me."

CHAPTER 28:

JIM - AUGUST 1992 -
RAILWAY SIDINGS

After two more mornings of waiting for Aimee to appear, Jim was forced to face facts: her father hadn't bought the story about the bird-watching club. As an expert on excuses, he had to admit he wouldn't have done either. Even things with an element of truth can sound less believable than a good lie. Trying to cure himself of loneliness, Jim told himself it would be like the old days: "No one else to worry about; no need to make stupid conversation; no need to admit you don't know a whole lot about anything." But it wasn't the same. *Jim* was changed. He had thought he liked being on his own, but there was no joy being down by the railway line. No buzz at the thought of trespassing. The whole thing had been tainted by the killing of the owl - and the fear that Nick now knew where to find him.

On the third day, a Sunday, workmen claimed the track, springing into action the week before the start of the new school year. No doubt, they'd insist that engineering works had overrun, when they'd had a good five weeks to make a head start. At home, the restless feeling in the pit of Jim's stomach made it impossible to sit still.

"Ants in your pants?" his mother asked, slapping the leg that swung in a wide arc. She was reading an article on *How to Discover the Real You!* (which apparently involved several trips to the gym, a quick haircut and changing into a skirt) as she waited for the theme tune to the *Eastenders Omnibus*.

"Bored."

"Only boring people get bored." She licked the end of one finger and made two attempts at scooping up the corner of the page. "What about your other owl? Any sign of him?"

"Nothing since the night of the shooting."

His mother smiled weakly. "I expect he's been frightened off, poor thing."

With nothing to keep him indoors, he planted his feet and launched himself up from the sofa.

Jean raised her eyebrows. "Where are you off to?"

To find answers, he thought to himself. "Out," he told her, one hand already on the door handle.

"Not like that, you're not! The whole world doesn't want to see your underpants! Pull your jeans up."

"But -"

"Don't try telling me it's fashion! They're hardly Calvin Kleins. I can see the *BHS* logo from here."

"Fine," he sulked.

Jim held his face up to catch the early evening sun's lazy warmth. Give it a couple of weeks and it would be dusk by this time. The younger lads were still out playing: weaving figures of eights with the wheels of their bikes; riding the kerbs on skateboards, Bill and Ted haircuts and matching vocabulary.

"How's it going, Dude?"

Sounds of scraping gravel reached him.

"To me! To me!" one lad yelled at a couple with a ball.

A bounce. A ricochet.

"Unlucky!"

Girls sat in self-contained groups, treating little sisters like dolls with hair to be plaited. That sly look was already creeping into their expressions. Glances were thrown towards the boys, some practising how to flirt, others mocking.

"You alright, Jim?" one asked from under the pink plastic peak of a baseball cap. He removed it to identify the speaker. Instead of jumping up and chasing him as she would have done a year ago, Kylie shook out her blonde hair and leaned back on her arms. The word *babe* was emblazoned in glitter across her silver top.

"Sound, Kylie. You?" He replaced the cap on her head.

"You tell me," she said, pushing her tiny chest out even further, causing an eruption of giggles.

Jim found it unnerving. Why would she even think an eleven-year-old boy would be attracted to an eight-year-old? "Sorry 'bout your top." He threw her a casual glance over his shoulder as he ambled off. "You must be gutted it shrank."

She stood up to shout, "What do you know about fashion, Bird-boy?" but she tugged at the hem self-consciously. "Freak!"

"Kylie!" A gruff voice hollered from a second floor window. Jim looked up to see a beer gut in string-vest cladding lean over the balcony. "Get your arse inside, young lady! *NOW!*"

Jim sauntered on. Leaning on the bridge, the railway snaking in front of him, he watched the sun creeping towards the trees and rooftops, edging the clouds in pink. "Pink sky at night, gas works alight," his granddad would have said. Tomorrow was going to be another fine day. Shame he'd have no one to share it with.

His feet seemed to have decided on their route: down the bunny run to the back of Aimee's house. He slid aside plywood panels slotted into the charred fence and stalked a path among leafy shrubs and blackened ruins, crouching down in a place where he would be safely out of sight until it grew dark. Curtains not yet drawn, the downstairs lights were already switched on. The full-length windows provided a doll's house view. Through the binoculars, he observed the family. Seated around the dining room table, heads bowed, cutlery in motion. Since Jim's view of Aimee was partly blocked by her mother, he trained his vision on Mrs White, noticing that she didn't once lift her eyes to her husband's face.

After a while, Aimee's mother started to clear the table and Aimee left the room, disappearing into the hall. Jim watched Mrs White load the dishwasher. She moved as if programmed to perform designated tasks, deliberately but without enthusiasm. All this time, Aimee's father sat, staring at the table. Reading, Jim presumed. When Aimee's mother brought him a drink he barely acknowledged her, but as soon as she left the room he stood, ear to the door leading to the hallway. Then, he turned and opened the French windows.

Minutes passed before Jim dared breathe. Aimee's father had sat down on a garden chair. Raising the packet to his mouth, he took a cigarette between his lips and lit up, then closed his eyes. The cat approached him, mewing softly.

"Puss, puss." He leaned forwards and lowered one hand, rubbing his fingers together. The cat - Tomsk was the name Aimee had used - arched its back and pressed against his trouser leg. Aimee's father tapped his lap twice. Tomsk crouched on his haunches like a coiled spring and then leapt. He turned, tail brushing Aimee's father's chin, before settling like a mother hen, one paw either side of a knee for balance. Aimee's father winced, shuffling in his seat. In terms of luck, Jim assessed, things could go either way. A cat on his lap reduced the odds of Aimee's father venturing down the garden, but he wouldn't be going anywhere fast. With no option but to remain crouched on the balls of his feet, pins and needles that had merely prickled now shot up towards his knees. At the very moment his discomfort was becoming unbearable, rescue came in the form of a shout: "David! Your programme's starting!"

Mr White tensed, glancing over his shoulder. "Be with you in a minute, love," he shouted back, took one last luxurious drag, dropped the cigarette and ground it into the patio. The cat was squeezed sideways off his lap as Aimee's father bent down to retrieve the stub, removing the evidence. He extracted a mouth spray from an inside pocket, used the statutory three squirts and then breathed on his hand, smelling his reflected breath. One more for good measure, he stood. "Coming in, puss?"

Tomsk snubbed him.

"Suit yourself," he shrugged, closing the door behind him.

Aimee's bedroom was illuminated. Jim counted to twenty, and then stamped his feet until the pins and needles reduced to a slight tingling. Picking up a few stones, he weighed each one by hand, stowing them in his jacket pocket. Head up, knees bent, hands low, he edged towards the house, closing the gap in fits and starts; eyes trained all the time on the hallway.

He stopped just shy of the patio, where a shrub-filled border would provide cover if needed. Misjudging the distance, he launched the first stone. It clattered down the roof of the veranda. He froze and waited. Nothing. He selected a heavier stone. This time, it hit the edge of the glass, but there was no movement inside. He followed it in quick succession with a third and fourth. An outline appeared at the window. Aimee opened the window and, leaning out, looked about blindly.

"Is that you?" she hissed, her voice shaky.

Jim stood up. "Are you alright?" he spoke only as loudly as

he thought was safe.

She located him via his voice. "Jim? You didn't need to come!" Her mood seemed to change, her voice suggesting she was glad he had.

"Thought you'd seen the last of me, did you?"

She was grinning. "Bugger off before my dad catches you!"

"When are you coming out?"

"I'm grounded."

"For how long?"

"Forever, I think!"

"Your parents must leave you on your own sometimes. Try to get out! You know where to find me."

He turned to go.

"Jim!" she called out after him.

He turned back.

"I'm sorry," she called out.

There were two things she might have meant. Dropping him in it by telling her father about his brother, or lying about the candles. She'd had no business taking it on herself to decide about the owl's funeral. Jim had opened his mouth to tell her so when she said, "I know, I should have told you. But it was a spur of the moment thing."

Floored by her honesty, her tone of voice, any anger he felt dissipated. It had been a grand gesture, risky too. Better than anything he might have planned, in fact. He just would have liked to have seen it. "How did it look?"

"You got your twenty-five pounds worth."

"Did you do the words again like we agreed?"

"I did."

He dismissed thoughts of the Game Boy that he had intended to save up for, using his birthday money. "Next time, don't keep it to yourself!"

"What next time?"

"Next time you fancy setting fire to things." He looked around him. "The shed?" he suggested, grinning.

Before slipping between the plywood boards, Jim paused. Aimee was still standing at the window. Her silhouette had two raised hands. She was resting her forehead against the pane. Thinking she was waving, he waved back.

CHAPTER 29:

SHAMAYAL - AUGUST 2010 - RALEGH GROVE

"Oi! Schmail!"

Shamayal heard his name deliberately mispronounced. Rhymes with snail. An annoyance at primary school, now it made his legs go cold. Heart banging, he ambled slowly through 180 degrees, hands dug deep in pockets. He looked at the older boy - no one he knew - and threw his head back. "Bro," he said, standard issue greeting.

The boy standing there could have been a ghost-maker, someone who gets paid for doing dirty work, in which case he couldn't be there unless the Ralegh Boyz said it was OK. Shamayal thought of all the times they'd offered him protection - "You got to ask yourself, when the shit hits the fan, who's gonna cover your back?" - and he had turned the Ralegh Boyz down.

"You had us worryin' 'bout you." Shamayal didn't like the familiarity. He liked the plural even less. *Us* has implications. "You ain't bin around."

"Got myself a holiday job, haven't I?" He hoped his paint-streaked jeans would fill in the gaps, provide a distraction from his trembling voice.

"Yeah?" The boy shook his head dubiously. "Your old man din't say nuffin 'bout no job."

Oh, he means business. "My ol' man? You can't take him too serious, f'you know what I mean. Spends half his time off of his face." Now that he was talking, it seemed he couldn't stop.

Another boy jumped down from a wall. Shamayal's mouth dried up, as quick as that. Light on those feet, Shamayal assessed number two guy's build, light *and* fast. Maybe the first was only the messenger. That's it. Number one will probably be off now...

A single drop escaped from one armpit, trickled down his torso. Any minute.

The tip of a trainer arrived around the side of the block. Just a trainer, but aggressively yellow. Shamayal felt a dredging in his bowels. Number three boy only had to pivot into view. Taller, broader, he stood feet wide apart, arms crossed.

Three against one. Shamayal didn't fancy his odds. Evolution demanded he made a choice: fight or flight. Adrenalin encouraged, *Get the fuck outta here.* But running tends to give the unfortunate impression of guilt. Unlike Christian, who must have known exactly what rules he was breaking, Shamayal's sense of justice insisted, *You have nothing to feel guilty about, man.*

"What's up?" He hoped that the hammering of heart against ribcage was concealed inside his jacket. Looking at the American-footballer build of the geezer (those weren't no shoulder-pads) Shamayal had to ask himself if rules were going to apply. He tried to swallow but his mouth had issued a drought warning. Being in the wrong place at the wrong time could get you mashed up. *Looking* like the guilty guy could get you shot.

"We bin hearin' things we don't like the sound of."

"'Bout me? I don't know what you can of heard." Shamayal

focused every ounce of attention on keeping his voice even and low, forcing it out through this narrow tube that used to be his throat. "I bin keepin' myself to myself."

Boy two consulted his burly mate. "That's not wot we woz told, izzit?"

One of American footballer's eyebrows was razor cut. He scrolled up his top lip to show off gold incisors. "That ain't the story that reached me."

They all had their hands thrust forwards into the pockets of their hoodies. Pockets that could have had anything hiding in them.

"No?" It was the squeak of his voice breaking that Shamayal hoped he had left behind. The sweat he could smell was his own. Trying to calm himself, he visualised them breaking into some mean MTV dance move - Old School, like Jay Z. They would make one bad-ass boy band. Truth was, the best he could hope for was someone appearing at the end of the gap between the two buildings. Maybe a mother pushing a pram. Maybe Bins. Fuck knows, he could do with a guardian angel.

"Our people heard you've bin talkin' to the wrong kinda people."

If there was still any doubt about who they represented, that cleared it up. Course they were hired hands. You don't go showin' your own face. Enforcers have a reputation for enjoying their work. The fact that they get paid, that's a bonus.

"Our people *heard* you've been helpin' certain people with their enquiries."

This was the point where disagreeing wouldn't do. Teacher-Jim talked about choice of language, adapting to your surroundings. Here, nothing less than the right words would hit it. "I fink I see what your people *might* of heard." They came in a rush. He couldn't slow them down; he could only make them sound surly. "The pigs aksed me, same as they aksed everyone else who was there, but I din't say nuffin. There was nuffin *to* say because I din't *see* nuffin. And you can't *say* nuffin if you don't *see* nuffin." *Jesus! Think what you're saying, boy!*

"You expect us to believe that crock?"

They were still, too still, like a pack of lions before the kill. You didn't have to have seen too many wildlife documentaries to have a good idea how this was going to end.

"Like I told 'em, time I arrived, he was jus' lyin' there."

"That's wot you told 'em?" There was nodding, as if the possibility of him telling them just this, and only this, was plausible. Shamayal wondered for one glorious moment if he might actually convince them, but there was one problem: he knew Mr American Football didn't give a shit what he had or hadn't said. He'd get his money either way.

"If I *had* said something -"

"So you *did* see somefink." Fact.

Bo-boom. Shamayal had slipped up. "N-not if they aks me -"

"See, from what you're turnin' round and sayin', I'm not sure you can be relied on to get your story straight."

"I'm wonderin' if you need to be tutored, see?"

You can still turn it around. "I'm just tryin' to show you, man: I got your peoples' backs covered. All a them."

"Well, that's very reassurin'."

"But they'd be *more* reassured if you hadn't bin visitin' your teacher-friend in hospital. Because, word is, he's still talkin'."

Shamayal nodded, seriously. "Is he, is he? Now *that* I din't know." Could he be held responsible for what someone else said?

"And if you've been talkin' to him... well, it makes it very hard for us."

It seemed he could. "True, true. But I haven't -"

"I knew you'd understand." Wide-stance-boy turned to his

those-ain't-no-shoulder-pads friend. "I told you he'd understand, din't I?"

Shamayal understood. He understood only too well. He
should have ran while he had the chance.

CHAPTER 30:

JIM - AUGUST 1992 -
RALEGH GROVE

Jim's twelfth birthday arrived without fanfare. He padded into the kitchen scratching his neck, finding the table laid with an unwelcoming mug of cold tea and a plate of toast with a scraping of Marmite, an envelope tucked underneath the rim of the plate. The message was clear: brown for business. Ripping it open, Jim leafed through the three notes inside: twenty-five pounds. The lack of a card and other niceties reminded him he wasn't off the hook. Nothing appeared to have arrived in the mail. "Cheers, Dad."

He stirred the tea to break the wrinkled skin and slammed the mug in the microwave.

"No card! Birthday money I have to give away!" Waiting for the ping, he stared out of the window into the grey: the first rain for days. "Great! Not even the chance of a game of footie."

When Jim was little and it rained on a Saturday, his grand-dad would take him swimming, winking, "We can't get any wetter." Jim wasn't a good swimmer. You could spot him a mile off. Follow the trail of white foam and he'd be splashing away at the front. "You put the 'dog' into doggy paddle," was the old man's assessment. He let Jim put his arms around his neck and hang off his back. He'd been in good shape for a man in his sixties, a lifetime of labouring etched into his muscles. It was the closest Jim came to flying. If Granddad had still been alive there would have been a card and a present, and he would have made sure that a rainy birthday wasn't a complete write-off.

Jim imagined the inverted pyramid of kisses Aimee would have written under her name in a card. He decided to get the business of the day over and done with. Who knows? Once Mr White had his money, there was a slim chance he'd let Aimee off the hook. Because money *was* the issue, wasn't it? They might be able to go somewhere. Of course, Jim wouldn't actually tell Aimee it was his birthday. She'd think he was turning thirteen, when, really, he was a good two years younger than her. But who doesn't imagine being made a fuss of?

As soon as the rain eased, he headed out. In need of a friendly face, Jim scanned the part of the estate known as 'out the back'. Even Bins, who always dressed for bad weather, was nowhere to be seen. Puddle-filled craters reflected the small amount of sunlight that had managed to filter through the clouds. Imagining his granddad's, "It's trying," Jim said out loud, "Yeah? Not hard enough!"

The swish of wet tyres accompanied Jim across the bridge as he trudged, head down, towards Durnsford. He considered posting the envelope and making a quick getaway, but part of him saw the opportunity to show Aimee's father he was someone who could be trusted. Perhaps Aimee would answer the front door and he could at least say hello. Jim reached up to knock and then stepped back, straightening his shirt. He heard the quick approach of footsteps: chin up, sarcasm at the ready. But it was Cyborg woman who opened the door. She looked beyond his shoulder, as if expecting to see someone else.

"I've come to give this to your husband." Jim showed her the envelope, no intention of letting it out of his grip.

Her voice was impatient. "I'm sorry, do we know you?"

"I'm Jim," he announced as importantly as he could. "Friend of Aimee's."

"You'd better come in. David!" She shouted up the stairs. "Someone called Jim here to see you!" Loud enough for Aimee to hear, he expected her head to appear over the banisters. But, with Mrs White staring at him intently, Jim realised he'd been mistaken thinking of her as uncaring. Something was wrong. "Have you seen my daughter?" she softened.

"Isn't she grounded?" he asked.

Face crumpling, she raised the back of one hand to her mouth, dropping onto the bottom step. "She's gone."

"Gone?" He heard his own stupid-sounding question, as if there could be any other meaning.

She nodded, hand still in place. "We've phoned around all her friends. Most of them haven't heard from her for weeks. David says she's been out all day, every day. He thinks she's joined a -" A look of bewilderment clouded her face. "- a bird-watching club."

"That's how we met," Jim nodded, although he had little reassurance to offer. "But she hasn't been around these last few days."

A heavy hand slapped the banister, lifting and falling ahead of each laboured step. Jim was struck by the same claustrophobic feeling he had experienced at the time of his last visit. *Did you tell your mother it was your brother who shot the owl?* Brown leather brogues paused, then walked slowly down the remainder of the flight. With one hand squeezing her shoulder, Mr White edged around his wife. "I see you've told him," he said gently, and she responded with the briefest of nods.

Neither seemed prepared or able to volunteer more. "When did you say you found she was missing?" he asked, knowing full well Mrs White hadn't said.

Aimee's mother pushed herself to her feet, her hair falling forwards and covering her face in the same way that her daughter's did. "When I went to wake her this morning. Her bed hasn't been slept in."

"She's run away?" he asked.

Aimee's mother made a choking noise in her throat and leaned against her husband. "She hasn't taken anything with her."

As Jim tried to absorb this information, her father said firmly, "We're giving her time to calm down and come home. Chances are she just needs some space."

Mrs White bit down on her bottom lip.

"Did she leave a note?"

"Nothing." She shook her head. "Just a couple of books on top of her bed. Poems and a notebook of some sort."

Jim tensed. They were what Aimee always kept with her. He asked himself why she wouldn't have taken them with her if she'd run away. Maybe - just maybe - *it was a message.* Aimee was out there looking for him!

Reading his face, Aimee's mother clutched Jim's arm. "Do you know where she might be? If there's anything you can think of…" she wavered. "Anything!"

"This is for you." Jim pressed the envelope firmly into Mr White's hand. "It's the money I owe you." He watched it disappear, disappointed that, even with his daughter missing and wife distraught, the man wasn't prepared to forget his so-called principles. What was twenty-five pounds to someone like him?

"Let us know as soon as you hear from her," he said, and Jim felt guilty. Perhaps the money wasn't worthy of mention because it was so insignificant compared with his wife and daughter. "Let us know she's safe."

"He knows something." He heard the hope in Mrs White's voice as he walked away. "He'll find her."

She was almost as certain as Jim was.

CHAPTER 31:

SHAMAYAL - AUGUST 2010 - RALEGH GROVE

"I can disappear myself," Shamayal said, quick-fire, hands forcing his head back and to one side flat against the wall. "You won't ever have to hear from me again."

The point of worrying about hearing himself beg had passed. Already the hot taste of blood was in his mouth. It was just a question of degrees of humiliation versus degrees of pain. Wide-stance boy was doing the holding; American footballer guy, the hitting. This was how it was going to be: teamwork.

"No?" American-footballer guy clearly took pride in his work. No knuckle duster for him, he liked to feel his victim's soft flesh give. There was no lunatic gleam in his eye. He was professional about the job. A hint of a smile, he adjusted his shoulder and took aim. Shamayal couldn't help himself: he closed his eyes. Brickwork skinned his cheekbone like a cheese-grater. One eye was hammered deep into its socket and seemed to want to stay there, pulsing with a heartbeat of its own, pouring a river of water.

It seemed important to keep talking, even through the

shock of it. To be civil while convincing them of his sincerity. Last chance: "Course, man." Hauled back up by the collar, his other cheek was turned for him. At a time when he might have been tempted to cry out for her, it suited him to speak about his mamma; things he's never told no one. "My muvver did it four years back. No one's heard from her since."

"How d'you know she din't have no help?"

Another fist in his stomach, then a knee. His body wanted to slump to the ground, curl into a tight ball, but hands insisted on holding it up. "She din't need no help." Only the final shove his father gave her. Pushing her past her limits one time too many.

"Where have you been?"

"Where d'you think I've been, woman? Working!"

"You bin drivin' in that state? Watching you slowly kill your-self is one thing, but I am not *going to stay and wait for you to wipe someone else out with you."*

Slap!

Slowly, slowly it grinds you down. And there is the one thing - that little thing - that drives you over the edge. Some-thing so small that people think you're weak, when all along you know you've taken more than they could ever stand.

He asserted himself, like a marathon runner sprinting for the finish. "The only help my muvver had was from *me.*"

Another foot forced air out of him and his mouth hung open.

The word "You?" was aimed mockingly at him, like he was some kind of worm.

These boys were equipped. They could finish it at any moment. Looking into the snarling face brought to mind a pitbull who they say is only playing while it sinks its teeth into you. *This is nuffin,* Shamayal told himself: *they're toying with you.*

Another fist and he was dazed, his vision blurred. It was

his father leaning over him: *"You know where she is, son? You know where your mamma is?"*

"I knew where she was -"

A knee.

"- But I din't never tell."

They let him drop to the ground, hard onto his kneecaps; the different kind of pain a distraction. "Because I can keep my maaf shut, see?" Then he was kicked sideways. His elbows instinctively made a mask to protect his face, but wide-stance boy dropped down behind him, prising them away, exposing his head, his face, his chest. Now he was all pain, the time for words was over. What had he done but dragged the whole thing out? At least it had been fast for Christian. Shamayal felt the fight go out of him and it was such sweet relief that he wondered why he had been holding on. Out of one eye, he saw the yellow trainers trot backwards so that they could take a run-up. A yellow trainer, his father's shoe: it was all the same. He prayed he wouldn't lose control - you heard about that sort of thing; prayed the next kick would be the last.

CHAPTER 32:

JIM - AUGUST 2010 - ST HELIER HOSPITAL

With no visitors to rouse him, Jim had dozed fitfully through a day that blended into others, punctuated only by Joyce's tortured shouts, what passed for cups of tea and the painful changing of his catheter. There is time and there is NHS time. Elsewhere, the hands of clocks travel at the same speed; here they operate to the same set of rules as pots that will not boil. Jim found he had passed beyond boredom, beyond exhaustion; like a long-haul flight with no prospect of landing. A burst of startled laughter rose from the nurses' station, fracturing his semi-conscious state. He saw a rush of wings as panicked birds broke free from the foliage that would have camouflaged them. Opening his eyes, he was caught in another Groundhog Day, except this was not the same day being replayed. The date on his newspaper told him it was a different day. Exactly the same as all of the others.

This time Jim remembered what he had been dreaming of. He could still smell the smoke-infused yarn of his granddad's jumper as he listened to the legend of the phoenix, a fine story for an autumn bonfire. Many countries had laid claim to the mythical bird: the most beautiful creature that ever lived, a bird with red and gold tail feathers. "They say the phoenix was the only bird not to be banished from the Garden of Eden after Adam and Eve disgraced themselves." But what impressed Jim most was this: "Only one phoenix can exist at any time."

"Isn't it lonely?" he'd asked.

"I would imagine it is. You see, lad, it can regenerate when it's injured, so it can live for hundreds, if not thousands, of years."

Wolverine was Jim's reference point, the superhero equivalent. "So what kills it in the end?"

"When the time's right, it builds a nest and sets fire to it. Both nest and bird are reduced to ashes, but a new phoenix egg comes from the embers and the cycle begins all over again."

"How does it know when the time's right?"

"Instinct, lad, instinct. It just knows."

When Jim relayed the story to Aimee, she had nodded. "It's an art, knowing when it's time to leave." At the time he'd thought of his mother's warning never to outstay his welcome.

He blinked up at the air-conditioning vent in the white ceiling, his lashes wet: *I spent my life observing things, sketching things, making notes. So why couldn't I see what was coming?*

CHAPTER 33:

AYISHA - AUGUST 2010 - AT HOME

Two minutes had passed since Ayisha last checked her watch. She was cutting it fine - normally, she would leave fifteen minutes to walk to the station. When she had called her mother, after an animated, "Hello," and, "I'm so relieved to hear your voice," Ayisha heard the thin rasp of a colleague phoning in sick. Fake or not, having spent the promised time at school, she could hardly claim that visiting Jim in hospital was more important than visiting her own mother, and so she had volunteered: "I'll bring you chicken soup."

"Oh, I don't want to be a -"

"There's no point arguing. I'm coming."

"But the roads -"

"I'll catch a train. It's only an hour from the centre of town." There: she had admitted it. Details of the journey would be filed away for future reference and used against her.

Opening her handbag for the umpteenth time, Ayisha assured herself that her tickets were stowed inside, but where was Shamayal? So far, she had been impressed by his punctuality, his cheerfulness, the quality of his work. To be honest, she has paid so-called professionals to do half the job he has done. She'd been even more impressed that he seemed instinctively to know when she wanted company and when she wanted to be alone. The past few weeks have been fun. She'd laughed out loud when, normally, she wouldn't call herself a laugh-out-loud kind of girl. Even the small accident with paint being trodden into the hall carpet - from the soles of her own trainers! - hadn't ended in disaster because Shamayal had been ready with the turps. He owed her nothing. If he chose to spend the last few days of the holidays elsewhere then, really, what could she say but 'thank you'? If half of what he boasted was true, there would be a girl somewhere - and a lucky one at that.

Shamayal was just like any number of boys Ayisha would have dismissed as having that bit too much attitude, demanding respect and giving none in return. It had been Jim who detected the boy's vulnerability hiding behind big words with missing 't's, the hard 'k's. And it was because of Shamayal that she had re-written her internal rulebook, justifying this to herself as temporary. Things would be different once they were back at school - they would have to be. And yet she couldn't help wondering how many other vulnerable kids she might find lurking in her class. If only she wasn't obliged to pass the problem on to someone else as soon as one of them reached out to her for help.

Not concerned that Shamayal had her spare key, Ayisha was only sad that she wouldn't get the chance to thank him in person. She began to scribble what she hoped had the appearance of a rushed note: *To my number one helper, Got to run - off on a mission to take chicken soup to my sick mother! Help yourself to anything in the fridge*. Her pen stalled. What was she *doing*? Five weeks of holiday and she was forgetting herself. *Imagine this in the wrong hands!* She balled the note and dropped it inside her handbag. As she did so, Ayisha caught her reflection in the hall mirror. The face that stared back was Miss Emmanuel's. So far, despite her constant and crippling fears, their blatant breaches of the child protection policy seemed to have gone undetected, but a moment's stupidity and everything could change. She pulled a plain envelope from the drawer, put the exact amount she owed inside, wrote Shamayal's name, then added, *Post keys through letterbox.* Just as she would for any other workman. There could be no more lapses. But, as Ayisha, she reflected that no one would tell her she looked hot in decorating overalls. No one would add matching spots of paint to the manicure she had ruined with drips of duck egg blue before she went out for the evening.

Thrown together under *those* circumstances, she had convinced herself it would be a catastrophe.

"Is it time for a coffee break?" Shamayal had asked less than five minutes after arriving on her doorstep, just after she'd climbed back up the creaking stepladder.

"I thought I might get some work out of you first." But she had climbed down.

"Proper stuff!" he insisted when she reached for the jar of instant.

"You've got expensive taste." She tightened the lid, imagining it was the boy's neck she was wringing. Or perhaps Jim's.

"You're gettin' cheap labour. Everythin' evens out. It's Karma, innit?"

As soon as she had poured the boiling water, Shamayal reached for the cafetiere: "Let me, let me!"

But when she deposited a mug in front of him, he had said, "You don't fink I *akchully* drink that stuff?" and opened a can of Red Bull.

"Then why have I -?"

"Rots your stomach, dunnit? I fought Jim would of told you I like to do the plunger. I *know* you been talkin' 'bout me behind my back."

Ayisha had been about to protest but the wrinkling of her brow must have betrayed her.

"Blatant. I *knew* it!" He took a triumphant swig from the narrow can and wiped his mouth on the back of his hand. "If the two of you are plannin' on adoptin' me, I'm gonna have to put my foot down. I had enough of being the victim of a broken home. The two of you get it together first, *then* I consider it."

Locking the front door behind her, Ayisha smiled to herself at the memory - the cheek of the boy - acknowledging she needed time away to think. A fresh coat of paint hadn't quelled her desire for change. Not adoption - God, no! Added to her experience of dealing with other people's children, the memory of poor Mrs Knoll's face was enough to make her question whether she would ever be ready for responsibility of that magnitude.

Once on the train to St Pancras, she fished about in the depths of her bag for her phone, and dialled Jim's private number at the hospital. Every other day, she had visited him, an hour at a time, always just on her way to or returning from somewhere. The gym, the supermarket; once with her skin still smarting from a bikini wax. He would expect her that afternoon.

No, she clicked the red button, the first feeling of control she had experienced for weeks: *Let him miss me.*

CHAPTER 34:

JIM - AUGUST 1992 - CARSHALTON

Jim knew where Aimee escaped to when she was in pain. It was the same place she'd accused him of hiding. Only as he broke into a sprint did it strike him: she'd recognised he was in hiding because *she'd been doing exactly the same thing.* He could have kicked himself. Dammit, how could he have been so slow?

As he approached the bridge, Jim's pace dropped to a jog and then faltered when he saw workmen dressed in yellow jackets. His mind turned to where else Aimee might wait for him if she hadn't been able to get down to the side of the tracks. Jim was so focused that he didn't see the policeman, but he heard an unmistakably uniformed voice:

"Not this way, son. You'll have to take the long way round."

It was then that Jim noticed the vans and cars parked on the far side, the cordons blocking his way. "Any chance you can let me through?" he gambled. "I need to get home. It's an emergency."

"Where d'you live?"

"The flats over there." As with all his dealings with officials, the boy tried to be vague. For all he knew, they might well be looking for Nick. If Jim was honest, after his brother's visit, he

259

was surprised *he* hadn't been hauled in for questioning.

"Sorry, the boss said no exceptions."

Lingering, still hoping for an opportunity to duck under the cordons, the bleeding text of a sign that was taped to a lamppost caught Jim's eye. *Missing, much loved family pet cat. Max is wearing a blue collar with a bell. He was last seen in the garden at 11pm on 30th July.* Over a month ago. No chance, mate! A nagging thought gnawed as he examined the photocopied photograph of a startled-looking tabby at close quarters.

"S'cuse me," he called out to the officer who was standing guard while a frustrated motorist made a meal of a three-point turn. Other cars were grinding to a halt behind, hesitating, as if they too thought exceptions might be made.

The policeman narrowed his eyes at Jim. "Still here?"

"I'm looking for a friend who's run away. How soon should her parents report her as missing?"

The policeman drew a circle in the air, intended to mean either, 'All of you!' or possibly, 'Turn around,' and then ambled over, looking as though a juicy morsel might tempt him into discussion. "Young girl, is she?"

"Thirteen."

"Depends on the history, but most would ring as soon as they find she's gone."

Jim had thought as much! Aimee could handle herself by day - he'd seen it for himself - but roaming the streets at night was a different matter.

Flipping open a notebook, the policeman consulted his watch. "What's her name, son?"

"Aimee." Jim was happy to supply the details. "Aimee White."

"Boyfriend?" he asked without taking his eyes off his notes.

Jim shook his head. "Just a friend."

"Not you, lad! I meant, does she *have* a boyfriend?"

Ego bruised, Jim said, "No."

"No. Known. Boyfriend." The policeman annunciated slowly as he wrote the words.

"Where does she live?"

"Durnsford. Number thirteen."

"Very nice, very nice." He raised his eyebrows, surprised, no doubt, that someone like Jim might claim to know someone from such a good address. "Can you describe her for me?"

"Quite skinny, long hair, frizzy-like, middle parting, amber eyes - like a cat's, gap in the front of her teeth." Jim reeled details off like a shopping list.

"Height?"

Placing one hand on his head, the boy lifted it by a couple of inches.

"I'll tell you what. I'll drop in on her parents as soon as I'm done here. Check she's turned up. Probably nothing to worry about. You know what girls that age are like."

Jim attempted a worldly laugh. He wondered if he deserved a sympathy-vote now the officer knew he had serious business involving law-abiding folk to attend to. "Sure you can't let me through?"

"Sorry, lad. Not my shout." His uniformed arm pointed. "Your quickest way is back the way you came, right at the end and right again at the roundabout."

"That'll take me half an hour!" Jim danced impatiently.

"Then you'd best get going!"

The route took Jim back past Aimee's house. He saw a figure leaning on the garden gate, her face hidden by long hair, clutching her cardigan tightly around her torso. All that worry for nothing! Laughing out loud with relief, he was ready to call out, "Forget something?" when Mrs White turned her pale and anxious face towards him.

"No luck?"

"Not yet." Jim swallowed. "The bridge is blocked off." He

indicated with his thumb. "Road works or something. I've been sent the long way around."

Hurrying on with a new sense of urgency, Jim forgot to mention the policemen. *No matter,* he thought. Mrs White would be glad of a visit. He'd already sussed it was her husband who was against involving the police. Mr White had said they would give Aimee time to calm down, when it was him who looked as if he needed calming.

The remainder of Jim's birthday was spent retracing the steps he and Aimee had taken together, returning home after each foray to make sure she wasn't there waiting: sitting on the wall by the road opposite Jim's block, calling, "Where have you been?" Shouting out his name and looking pleased to see him. Perched on a chair at the kitchen table, turning her gap-toothed smile towards him.

In his local park, Jim bypassed the courts where two boys were sitting astride the shoulders of two poor sods, gripping with their knees and shouting orders to charge at the park's single hoop, applying the logic that two puny twelve-year-olds equal one six-footer.

"And Magic Johnson shoots…"

"Oi! I thought we was Magic Johnson!"

"No, you're Michael Jordan."

"That's it!" The bottom half of Michael Jordon spun round. "If I can't be Magic Johnson, I'm not playing!"

Jim scanned the children's playground where he had once spied Aimee. But that would have been too easy. A child's buggy was parked in her hiding place under the slide.

In the afternoon, Jim retraced the route through Beddington Park, trying to remember everything Aimee had told him. Crows mocked him: from the tops of trees, walking boldly on the grass. "Kraa, Kraa, Kraa." "Look at you, acting like you belong." The air was humid, shimmering with ghosts; Sir Walter Ralegh's and Queen Elizabeth's mingling with their own. Jim's sense of Aimee became stronger as the church came into view, framed by the arc of trees. Sanctuary. Where else would she go? But the heavy handle failed to respond. There was no grinding noise, no give.

"It's locked."

Jim turned to see an elderly woman hunched over a grave, placing a single rose stem in a jam jar.

"Why's that?"

"Blame it on the vandals, spoiling it for the rest of us."

He located the tomb of the Carew who had forfeited his place in the family vault by gambling away the family fortune. Perching on the corner, the boy traced what little was left of the carved name with a stem of grass. "Looks like we're both locked out, mate."

"Alright, Jim Stevens?" Bins asked when Jim slumped down beside him on his low kerb.

"Would you mind?" Bins indicated to Jim's feet, which were tapping out an impatient Morse code message. "You'll disturb the fish."

"Sorry." The boy hugged his knees to his chest. Bins smelt strongly of potato peelings. "You see everyone, don't you?"

"You might say that." The man's brow furrowed as he carefully threaded a prawn onto a hook. "I keep an eye on things."

"I'm looking for a girl you met the other evening. Her name's Aimee."

Bins pressed his lips together as if in serious thought. "I don't know any Aimee."

Then Jim remembered: "That's only her nickname. She's got this really embarrassing name." He snapped his fingers, trying to summons whatever it was she'd called herself.

"Nervous girl? Not from round here?" Bins asked. "Fuzzy hair?"

"That's her!"

He threw the line, holding the hook just above the tarmac. "That's young Verity you're talking about. She hasn't been back to see me. The nearest she's got is the wall over the other side of the road."

Jim sat up sharply. "When was that?"

"A couple of days ago, at least. I don't go as far as there. All that traffic."

Sighing, Jim felt the first spits of the rain returning.

"I'll keep an eye out; tell her Jim Stevens is looking for her."

It was hopeless: she obviously didn't want to be found.

"Thanks, Bins." He stood up and turned around, feeling the need to tell someone. "It's my birthday today."

"My birthday's the twenty-fourth of October. Is that soon?"

"Almost two months to go."

Walking away, Jim heard singing: "*Happy Birthday to you, happy birthday to you.*" Bins, in a waterproof world of his own.

By the time his mother arrived home, Jim needed someone to talk to.

"Sorry, I'm late, love," she shouted out. "Blasted trains are up the spout! I got us a Chinese. Thought it'd make a nice birthday treat for you." She walked into the living room and, seeing him, pulled down the corners of her own mouth. "Why the long face?" It was the punchline to his granddad's favourite joke, designed to raise a smile: A horse walks into a bar and the barman asks… "That bad?" Jean perched on the arm of the sofa, bending to kiss the top of his head. "I take it you went to see Mr White."

He could see prawn crackers bursting free from the top of the plastic bag she held. "She's gone missing."

"Missing?" His mother looked troubled.

"I've been out looking for her most of the day."

"Have you been back to ask if she's shown up?"

"Not since this morning."

"Well, then. She's probably at home eating her tea right

now." The plastic bag rustled as Jean stood and walked into the kitchen. She stared out of the window as she said, "Your brother ran away once. He must have been about eight." Jim was dumbstruck to hear his mother speak about Nick. His name was almost unmentionable. "I can still remember my panic when I discovered he was missing. Camped out in one of the bin sheds, he was. If it hadn't been emptied the day before, he'd have been home a lot sooner. He said he'd forgotten his football. No apology: just that he'd forgotten his football." The smile on her face looked unnatural when she turned back to Jim, plain plastic bag in hand. "Enough nonsense. The food is getting cold," she said, setting takeaway boxes out on the table, removing lids, filling the room with the smell of sweet and sour. "It's not been much of a birthday, has it? Looks like the postman's late with your dad's card."

Fed up of the pretence that Dad cared enough to remember, Jim shot back, "I'm not bothered about my birthday!" Instantly, he regretted it.

"Course you're not," his mother responded quietly. "You'll want to head straight round to Aimee's after your tea."

They ate in silence. Jim looked up from the shovelling of glutinous rice and battered pork from time to time. If he had caught her eye, he would have said, "Thanks for the takeaway, Mum," and everything would have been alright. But her thoughts were still facing out of the window.

CHAPTER 35:

JIM - AUGUST 1992 -
THE BRIDGE/2000 - ST HELIER

Without thinking, Jim set out on his usual route via the bridge. The cordons cleared away, the road had been reopened, temporary traffic lights installed. He paused at the top of the concrete steps, looked both ways and ambled down: not too quickly, not too slowly. No barrier could have kept him out, not even the prospect of coming face to face with his no-good junkie brother.

Crouching low, Jim gripped his knees, attempting to divine answers out of the approaching dusk. *Where are you, Aimee?* They had never tried to walk further along the side of the track than was necessary to get out of sight. Even if it were possible, the going would be difficult, especially in her chosen footwear. The vegetation was machine-cut, leaving behind sharp woody stalks.

Unmistakable, the sound of an old-fashioned football rattle had him training his binoculars, searching for a flash of black and white. There it was: a magpie, sitting alone.

The bird shuffled round displaying tail feathers; not black but iridescent blue-green. It looked from left to right and then dropped to the ground below, where it began to nibble delicately at something, pushing its black tongue forward. Jim heard his own sharp intake of breath before he was conscious of what he was looking at: yellow plastic attached to a yellow base.

He could hear his own words nagging, "Why d'you insist on wearing your flip-flops down here? Your feet will get ripped to shreds."

Find a way to balance and Jim estimated the bird could carry the weight of the flip-flop. It was just a piece of foam, after all. A magpie won't give up a trophy easily, but Jim knew its one weakness: greed. A distraction was needed, something sufficiently shiny. He cast his eyes around. It didn't take long to gather enough squares of abandoned foil to roll into a ball the size of a walnut. Jim flashed his binoculars, letting the setting sun bounce off the lenses.

Once he was sure the magpie's watchful black eyes were on him, he rolled the ball between thumb and index finger, moving it from side to side, muttering, "Right, let's see what you make of this." Then he launched the ball. It landed a few metres away from the flip-flop where, among rusted leaves and dead twigs, it looked tantalising. Reluctant to tear himself away from the shoe, holding it down for fear it might try to escape, the bird walked the length of the foam sole for a better view. Still the nibbling, still the protruding black tongue, he succeeded in breaking the toe piece. Urgency gnawed at Jim's stomach-lining. He needed to do something more - before the bird took flight. Exaggerating the sweep of his arm, Jim faked a move in the direction of the foil ball. The threat of competition proved irresistible. With a sideways hop, the magpie swooped, carrying the foil ball off in its claws.

But victory was bitter-sweet. Jim retrieved the foam and plastic remains, having no doubt what he was holding. She had been - and gone.

"Aimee! Aimee!" Using his hands as a loudhailer, Jim spun

and spun as he called her name repeatedly. The silence was overwhelming. His breathing hard and fast, he struggled to pull in enough air. No one would deliberately take off a shoe by the side of the tracks, his mind raced. If the twigs didn't get you - cold sweat broke out on his forehead - the stinging nettles would. If there weren't enough stinging nettles to do you any serious damage, there were always the barbed-wire brambles. And that was without the list of things you would have preferred to avoid stepping in or on: what the foxes and the junkies left behind.

"If the Indians are right, someone's in for some very bad luck."

Then, out of the silence, came the electric buzz that precedes the approach of a train.

"Nurse, Jim's at it again. NURSE!"

Sophia padded into room 3, armed with her characteristic sigh, and gripped the iron rail at the foot of the bed. "What is it, Martin?" She placed her other hand on an ample hip. "You know what time it is? You'll have everyone awake if you carry on like that."

"I should have known! I should have known!" Glancing at Martin's neighbour, she saw Jim tossing from side to side. He seemed to be increasingly agitated. The doctor had been treating him for depression, but, of all the medical team, she had spent the most time with him. There was more to it than that.

"What about me?" Martin propped himself up on one elbow. "I've had to put up with his shouting these last two nights."

"That's the thing about hospitals. They're full of people in pain."

"Can't you give him something to knock him out?"

"We'll see." She whooshed the thin curtain between the two beds across: it caught midway on a join.

Whoosh! Jim stood back automatically, the thunderous ten-tonne wall of power slapping him smack in the face, jolting him backwards as a ghost passed clean through him.

Sitting in Jim's visitor's chair, Sophia took one of his hands in hers and stroked it with her thumbs. "What should you have known? Hmmmn, Jim?"

"No good." He stirred, his head writhing this way and that.

His skin was hot to the touch. He was burning up. Sophia hadn't been too happy with the appearance of Jim's wound when she last changed his dressing. Now she checked for tell-tale red spots, crooning, "You wanna cross the road, is that it? I got you. We do it together. Look right, look left -"

Her brow furrowed as she examined his chart: fluid intake good; output low.

"Spend-your-life-watching-still-does-you. Does-you-no-good."

"No, it most certainly don't," she said, keeping her voice calm while sighing in frustration.

Someone on the last shift had missed a trick - and she thought she knew who. Jim had all of the signs of septicaemia.

He wanted someone to tell him he was wrong; that Aimee had made her way home hours ago; that she was at home eating her dinner.

Durnsford Road in the early evening was a quiet place. Cars with ticking engines were parked in gravel driveways. The clink of cutlery and the laboured sound of piano scales wafted out of open windows. But Jim, normally so attuned to detail, was aware of little of this. Unable to suck in enough air to run all of the way, he had alternated with a furious march. Aimee's house sat in the shade, a few degrees cooler than the opposite side of the street. A police car was blocking the drive, but this didn't stop him. Now he could see his goal, his feet tripped into a final sprint. As the sinking sun blinked through the leaves, his eyes seemed more sensitive to light than usual. His elbows pumped the final few yards.

After pounding on the door Jim stood back, stepping down from the porch to the path. The pain in his chest made him wonder, Is this what a heart attack feels like? *Come on, come on, come on!* He was back hammering on the door again, when it opened inwards.

A policewoman with a flushed face demanded, "Yes?"

"Is she here?" Jim rasped, hands on knees.

The policewoman stepped outside, pulling on the letter-box. "Mrs White can't come to the door at the moment."

"Not her!" he said impatiently, head still hanging. "It's Aimee I've been looking for all day!"

"Calm down a minute. Breathe." Jim felt her hand on his back and, in the absence of alternatives, did as he was told. "Are you the friend who called round this morning?"

It was obvious that they hadn't tracked her down. The policewoman would have said so. "I'm Jim." He nodded, trying to haul himself upright. "I spoke to one of your lot on the bridge."

The sound of exhausted voices coming from inside gave the impression that the house itself was murmuring. Jim pulled the flip-flop from inside his jacket. "I found this." He pressed it into her hand. "It's one of Aimee's, I know it is. She always wore them."

The policewoman turned the sole over slowly, examining the bite marks and tears, smoothing the pad of her thumb over the raised number of the shoe size, as if she might be able to erase it.

Frustrated by her lack of urgency, Jim explained, "A magpie had hold of it, but foxes must have got to it first."

She nodded. "Where was it?"

It would have to come out, all of it. He would be forced to admit to his mother that he'd lied. There was no point pretending that Aimee and he belonged to a club, spending their days with bird-watchers of all ages. No point pretending they didn't use the railway cuttings. But none of that was important. The only thing Jim needed was for the policewoman to tell him his imagination was running wild. "Down by the side of the railway," he said.

"Wait here," she said, disappearing down the hallway again, leaving an astonished Jim searching for comfort in the carved scroll at the end of the banister, the polished table in the hall, the fresh flowers in the cut-crystal vase. He heard muffled voices, a cry, a door slamming. Those were his answers.

The boy was halfway down the path when the policewoman called his name. "Jim! Mrs White is fairly sure it's Aimee's shoe you found."

"I told *you* that! She's dead, isn't she?"

The calm on her set face was infuriating. "I'd like to ask you a few questions, if that's alright. How old are you, Jim?"

It was obvious from the way she shepherded him to the car that the policewoman wanted to get him as far away from the house as possible. Back to the side of the bridge he belonged. "Twelve," he said, his voice becoming louder as he forced it out.

"Will your parents be home?"

"She is dead, isn't she? *Isn't she?*"

"Now, we don't know that."

She was treating him like a kid who couldn't understand anything, but he knew. *He knew!*

CHAPTER 36:

SHAMAYAL - AUGUST 2010 - RALEGH GROVE

Shamayal came to, heels scrambling, blood pounding in his ears; feeling as if elbows and knees were digging into him from all angles. The shouts he heard were his own. It was only when it dawned on him that blows were no longer raining down - that he was alive - that he acknowledged the shooting pain in his ribs was his fight for oxygen, then his equally furious battle to expel the fetid reality of what surrounded him: a fug of slow-composting baked-bean-digestive-biscuit-sour-milk-bile-piss-puke. *Breathe or suffocate*, he told himself, nostrils flaring. He choked on stagnant air that tasted the same way it smelled, and this was a new problem, the coughing, tearing him apart from inside. People told you to breathe through pain, but what if it's the breathing that hurts? He felt he might weep: *I can't do this, don't ask me to*, as he curled in on himself like a woodlouse. Fine, his sterner side scoffed, then you die here - wherever 'here' is. *At least then the pain would stop, and I wouldn't have to look over my shoulder anymore.* A moment of weakness, he gave in to tears. *Your choice, innit?* He sniffed, focused, forcing himself to inhale. Breathing was an unnatural, torturous process. You would never think he'd been doing it for fourteen years. That's better, Pussy. Now think! Where the hell have they dumped you?

Like a water mattress, the surface Shamayal found himself lying on alternately gave and held. The crotch of his jeans felt damp. He opened his eyes to blackness (one eye was more reluctant than the other; he wondered if he still owned a matching pair and, if not, what he looked like). He strained his neck as if this alone might cause something to reveal itself, but the night was like no other he had known. Countryside black, there was no neon strobe-stuttering streetlight. Shamayal tentatively held a hand to either side of a thigh, unbending a leg one inch at a time. His calf muscle spasmed. Easy, easy! If I could just find myself a part that isn't agony, just one likkle part, then concentrate on that. He hummed with the effort, a strange and tuneless borrowed sound. Perhaps someone giving birth. *Man, when did I get to feeling so old?*

Whatever the toe of his trainer collided with only a few inches away had no give. He reached one hand above his head - the other had decided it was best off resting across his chest, like the tiny gnarled claw of a T-Rex, there to contain his gag reflex, while the braver one trailed through some kind of heavy-duty wallpaper-paste-cold-porridge-gloop. *Can't stop now*. His fingers splayed into the curve of a cold, ridged surface: metal. *What kinda cell is this?* His fast-and-shallow breathing sucked the flesh of his hand into his open mouth. Listen, he tried to talk some sense into himself. What can you hear? That noise, yeah, urgent and irritating? That's a dozen crazy pigeons cooing. That rumble there, that ain't your stomach, man. That's the early-morning freight train. There it goes, city-bound. Right, right, not so far from home, after all. Maybe not so long to wait until the sun comes up. I'll just close my eyes until there's enough light to see what I'm up against. OK, OK. That's what I'll do.

Shamayal woke again to the sound of rain pelting the

asphalt roof close above his head. He soon wished he hadn't. An uneven rhythm was being played out on some kind of percussion instrument. *Plink-plink, plinkity-plink.* It took a while for the boy to work out - I see, I see: the sound of fat raindrops bouncing off an empty can, trapped some place in the gutter.

The scrape of wood on concrete was Shamayal's next alarm call - or call for alarm, depending which way you looked at it. Chances were, it was someone come back to see if he'd stuck to his side of the bargain and disappeared himself, or to offer a likkle more encouragement. His greatest fear wasn't blades - although he'd seen the damage they can do. Flames are slower. You've got time to reflect exactly what's going on. The broken door was propped open. A crescent of morning light revealed to him what his senses had hinted at. He was seven feet from the rusted rim of the drum, lying on a bed of all kinds of miserable trash his weight had squished out of tie-handled bin bags. A flurry of wings, a new level of fear grabbed hold of his guts and twisted. He blinked away the last scene from *The Wicker Man:* Sergeant Howie's face full of horror - his cries, the silence and the single drumbeat - before you see the thing itself, there, on the hillside. He wished he hadn't watched some of those things with Ayisha, even though it was him who had insisted.

The rustle of plastic baggage and a happy-old-man whis- tle. Relief, sweet relief, urine warmed Shamayal's pants. He pushed his back into the curve of the barrel: incoming. A plain plastic carrier bag landed close to his face. It was so tempting to cry out *Please! Someone! Get me out of here!* But this was a test. Some do-gooder would have half the Met blue-lighting it round here within five minutes, and next time he found himself in a blind alley there would be no negotiatin' his way out. They would finish what they'd started. A half-hearted attempt was made at closing the door - his bright crescent was snuffed out - but the broken hinge protested and it swung outwards. As footsteps receded, Shamayal wanted to shout *Hey! Come back!* Instead he stared miserably into the carrier bag. The smell of cold tikka massala made him want to puke, but at least it was something identifiable.

He was lying in his woodlouse position with his T-Rex hands, listening to throaty cooing, when the next pair of shuffling feet arrived. *This is it*, Shamayal thought, speeding heart. *You don't get lucky twice.* The feet halted. That'd be the doorway. He prepared to beg: 'See? I din't tell. I could of, but I din't. I got your backs, all of yous.' He heard a cough; the sound of dry palms being rubbed together, then: *"You shall have a fishy on a little dishy. You shall have a fishy when the boat comes in."*

Was it? He needed to be 110 per cent sure. Shamayal redistributed his weight onto the elbow of the arm that would move, the contents of the bin redistributing themselves beneath him, as a new pain ripped through his torso, dissecting his chest. It was so far removed from anything he had felt before that he was sure there must be a stronger word for it.

The singing stopped. A pause. "Is anyone there?" a timid voice enquired.

"Bins!" Pushing himself to his knees was going to take a monumental effort. He had heard that only two things make pain easier to swallow: smiling and swearing. His face wasn't willing to co-operate - either that, or his brain had forgotten how to send signals. Swearing it was, then.

"Who's that?"

He blew a tunnel of air, hugged his poor ribs. "S'me."

"Who?"

"Shamayal." The boy heard shuffling, feet about-turning through 360 degrees.

"Who?"

Resting his forehead against the side of the barrel, the boy told himself *Disconnect from the pain. You'll be aware of it, of course, but it'll be far enough away from your brain that you won't experience its full force.* Pressing his palms into the metal wall, he went through his fuck-wank-bollocks repertoire several times over inside his head. Up shot his right foot, his other knee sinking into he-didn't-want-to-know-what. "Shamayal Stands For No Crap. I'm in here." Amazed his voice could come out so normal, he knocked his head against the inside of the barrel.

The sound of cardboard scraping, Shamayal imagined Bins pulling aside overspill from the bins, continuing his low-level search. "I can't find you."

Perhaps he would have to embrace it, after all. No pain no gain, that's what they say.

Here we go, here we go. *Fuck, fuck, fuck*: he brought his left trainer up to meet its partner. This was what they invented the word 'excruciating' for. Both feet sank. He was knee-deep in trash. "I'm in one of the bins."

"Are you hiding?"

"Right, right." The boy tried to get some purchase in order to straighten his legs. They were shaking as they had never shaken before. The last time he remembered feeling so off-balance was in the school gym, trying to stand on the blue crash mat after landing on the bar of the high-jump. "I'm playin' hide-and-seek."

"I won't tell anyone where you are. You can trust me."

Shamayal clamped his eyes shut in frustration. "I got stuck, innit? Think you could help get me out?"

"Got to find you first."

Shamayal reached towards the rim, his hand clutching air, his jaw locked in a silent scream.

He heard the sound of a steel drum. "Hello, hello." He imagined the likkle old guy with his ear to the first of the drums.

"You're cold, Bins! Try again!"

"Hello, hello," Bins tapped.

"Gettin' warmer." A boom! next to his ear caused Shamayal to throw his head aside. "Whoa! You win! Can you find anything to stand on?"

"Something for me to climb up on?"

"Yeah, yeah." Shamayal realised he needed to be specific. "And bring it back here!"

"Like a step ladder?"

"Anything you can get your hands on, man. Just be quick."

Five minutes passed, ten, and - hands tucked tight under his armpits - Shamayal wondered if his request had proved too big a challenge. Then, just as he was convinced he'd been abandoned, came the magnificent sound of something being dragged across the tarmac.

"Oh, yeah! Oh, yeah!" he sang, his spirit lifting with a hope he hadn't allowed himself to imagine.

"Stupid birdies! Out of my way!" Bins snapped at the pigeons Shamayal imagined clustering at his feet. "I've got nothing for you, you hear?"

The scraping grew louder and then stopped. "Shamayal Stands For No Crap?" Bins knocked on the side of the bin, as if, like the ball under the cup in a magic trick, he might have mysteriously changed barrels.

"Still here, Bins! Still here."

"I got the ladder."

"You done good, man!" So near and yet so far, Shamayal suddenly felt weighed down with responsibility. "Open it out properly," he supervised blindly from inside his industrial baked bean tin. "Make sure all four feet are on the flat."

"Don't worry. I'm good at ladders. I used to do window cleaning."

"You never told me that! Man, you're one dark horse."

"Coming to get you! Ready or not!"

"Believe me, I been ready for hours."

The sound of cautious climbing; the creak of the ladder as one foot was placed next to the other. Bin's bent-down head inched into view, then the old man rested his chin on the rim of the barrel and lifted one hand. "High five!"

Shamayal had never been so pleased to see someone as he was to see goggle-eyed straggle-haired Bins. "High five yourself! You won!"

"Do I get to hide next? I know an excellent place. Once you're there, no one will find you."

He looked for signs in the old man's face of how bad he looked. Nothing. The old guy's eyesight couldn't be up to much. "That might come in useful," Shamayal conceded.

"Mm-mm. Is that curry I smell?"

"You got it."

Bending down to retrieve the carrier bag then holding it up took a supreme effort, but it wasn't enough. With his arm extended as far as it would go, propped up under the elbow by his other hand, Shamayal was inches short of target. Hope sank inside him: "This ain't gonna work. We got us a serious shortfall."

Even if he could have reached Bins's hand, the old man wouldn't have the strength to haul him out, and Shamayal wasn't sure his acrobatics would be up to scratch. Chances were they'd both end up inside. Waiting for the arrival of a lit match.

Bins puff-balled his cheeks. "Where's Jim Stevens when we need him?"

"Man, you can say that again!" Cradling his ribs, Shamayal leant his backside into the curve of the barrel and stared despondently at a Domino Pizza logo. "Wait up…"

The stepladder rattled as Bins stood to attention.

One of Jim's shaggy-dog stories might just come in useful. "Are the other bins full?"

Bins's face disappeared. "Fuller than your hidey-hole." He

returned with renewed enthusiasm. "And there's more bags on the ground."

"Then we might be back in business. Chuck us a few in here."

"Won't you get buried?"

"I do the worryin' about that. See, Jim told me this likkle story about a crow who found a jug half full of water. He needed a drink but his beak couldn't reach, see? Instead of giving up, he collected a pile of stones and dropped them into the jug one by one. With each stone, the water rose up and up until, before long..."

Bins's eyes blazed. "I get to be the crow!" His dirt-ingrained hands disappeared and then his straggle-haired head inched down. The ladder creaked and strained. "Kaw, kaw," Bins called, throwing the first of the sacks over the top.

Shamayal rustled the bag into position and, with cautious knees, braced himself. "Bring it on, Mr Crow, bring it on."

CHAPTER 37:

JIM - AUGUST 1992 -
RALEGH GROVE

Pulling up outside the red-brick block, the policewoman cranked the handbrake into position.

"What's your surname, Jim?" she asked.

"Stevens," he replied, preoccupied. People always left him in the end. Part of him argued that it was selfish to be thinking of himself: part of him knew they left *because* of him. He was the exact opposite of a lucky mascot.

The policewoman glanced sideways at him. Her pencilled-in eyebrows dipped below the line of her uniform hat. *Rings a bell*, her expression said.

Eyes followed their progress as they walked the hundred or so metres from the panda car. Jim could almost hear people thinking, "Told you it wouldn't be long." "Both those boys were bound to go the same way as their father."

As he turned his key in the lock, his mother shouted out, "How d'you get on, love?" Jean appeared in the kitchen doorway. "Any n -" Hands she'd been drying on her pinny froze. The sight of police uniform wasn't welcome in her home. It brought shame and it brought gossip. And she looked to Jim for an explanation.

"Mrs Stevens." The policewoman took off her hat and smoothed her tied-back hair. Slightly more human - but for those drawn-on eyebrows of hers - she apologised, "I'm Police Officer Cowley." *Cow: cow eyes, cow bells, how now brown cow?* "Sorry for the intrusion. I need to ask Jim a few questions. Is there somewhere we can talk?"

"Come through to the kitchen," Jean said stiffly, circling Jim's shoulder and steering him ahead. "I'll put the kettle on." She moved a cake that had been in the centre of the table to the work surface.

"Somebody's birthday?" Police Officer Cowley asked brightly.

"It was supposed to be a surprise." Jean gave a wary smile. Instinctively she stood beside Jim: two against one.

He eyed the untouchable shop-bought cake: chocolate sponge with chocolate icing studded with broken Flake. A lonely second-hand candle leaned crookedly near the centre. Jim blinked away the memory of flickering wicks as Aimee completed the circle.

"Am I supposed to guess what's going on?" His mother's patience had been tested.

"Let's all sit down," Cowley insisted.

His mother complied, her expression steel. Jim followed.

"I don't know how much you know, Mrs Stevens."

"I know my son's spent his birthday looking for a friend who's gone missing."

"Well, he's made a small find."

Cold spreading to every cell in his body, Jim's feet hooked the chair legs. *Hold on, mate, hold on.* He detected relief in his mother's expression, but she had no idea what the police-woman was building up to, eking out the bad news like a game-show host.

"- What appears to be one of Aimee's flip-flops."

His feet gripped tighter.

"What I want to ask you, Jim, is why you're so sure this means Aimee is dead."

Jean gasped, "Dead?" One hand flew up to her mouth. The other clamped it in place.

"I'm sorry, I should have warned you. There's nothing to suggest Aimee is anything other than missing."

Jim couldn't accept this. No one in their right mind would take a shoe off down by the side of the track. "It must have been her owl, Mum. It's obvious, isn't it?"

"Oh, love, that's just superstitious folklore." Jean turned her pitying look to the policewoman. "Aimee was here watching owls only last week. There's a pair who nest down by the railway. She told Jim an Indian legend. How owls carry the souls of the living; and when one is killed, that person dies too. It was that same evening the children found a dead owl."

"*Her* owl!" Jim pointed out. He was only half aware of the scraping of chair legs, the touch of one of his mother's hands on each of his shoulders.

"They wanted to give it a proper funeral, but there was an accident. The Whites' shed was burnt down."

Jim's head jolted backwards with the ten-tonne slap, his ears filling with the rush of the train. Perhaps Aimee chose to give the owl her funeral, somehow staking her claim in a ritual of candles and words, making sure none of the bad luck floated in Jim's direction!

"Jim?" The boy started at the sound of his name. Jean's hands had dropped from his shoulders but their weight remained. "I'd like you to show me where you watch the owls, if you wouldn't mind. Would you do that for me?"

On automatic pilot, he led the policewoman to the living room where she mirrored his sofa-kneeling stance. Never properly dark, orange streetlights and moving car headlights provided a clear view of the tracks.

Cowley nodded to the binoculars that were still dangling

from Jim's neck. "Can I?"

"You may as well keep them." He hauled the strap over his head, catching one ear, and thrust them at her. "I don't want them anymore." Then Jim turned and sat down heavily, staring at the carpet.

From the kitchen doorway, his mother said wearily, "You don't mean that, love."

"I do!" Jim kicked out his legs, one at a time. "If I hadn't found them, none of this would have happened."

Cowley skirted the binoculars from side to side, always returning her focus to the railway tracks.

"You probably won't see anything," Jean explained. "There's been nothing since the night the owl was shot."

"Didn't I read somewhere that barn owls mate for life, Jim?"

Chin on chest, he looked down the full length of his body.

Suddenly, his mother's torso straightened. "There!" She pointed.

Jim knelt back up on the sofa.

"Where?" Cowley turned towards her, taking her eyes away from the binoculars.

"To the right! Far side of the bridge!"

Jim heard Cowley's intake of breath, slower than a gasp. Something of wonder and awe in it. It had been the same for him; for his mother; it was just the same for Aimee. If he'd had the vocabulary, he might have described her experience as spiritual.

Suddenly, he was back by the side of the railway that day early in the holidays when he'd seen Aimee for the first time: her wildness, her anger, but what he hadn't recognised then - despair. And there was no doubt in his mind, she'd been ready to do it. He had stopped her with a loan of his jacket, a cheese and pickle roll - but she'd been thinking about it ever since. All those 'what ifs'. Aimee's owl hadn't changed anything. It had only reminded her of what she meant to do in the first place. *The phoenix always knows when it's time to leave.*

"Aimee walked onto the tracks." The shaking of his head was involuntary as realisation hit home, another punch in the guts. The reason must have already been there! Jim had been wrong to think Aimee had left *him*. He just hadn't done enough to make a difference.

The policewoman glanced at his mother and nodded, and Jim recognised a pass when he saw one.

"How can you be so certain, Jim?" Jean asked, accepting the cue.

"Because she told me she was going to, that's why!"

CHAPTER 38:

SHAMAYAL - AUGUST 2010 -
BINS'S FLAT

Holding onto the handles, Shamayal eased himself - *gently, gently!* - into the pink tub. A brown tide-mark stood proud of the water level. The taps were crusted with scale; not just white, but green. Mould had blackened the sealant and decorated the grouting. Lying back - the position that seemed to suit him best - Shamayal saw that a leak from the flat above had gone unheeded. A strip of wallpaper hung limply from the ceiling. Elsewhere, paint had bubbled and blistered. This was a place where silverfish made no attempt to hide. It wasn't one Shamayal would choose to linger in. On any other day, he would have got to work with serious quantities of Domestos before he even considered taking a bath, but priorities had changed. Shamayal could only face dealing with one thing at a time (for now, he refused to contemplate what germs might be lurking in the shag-pile toilet surround). Bins's flat was probably the one place it wasn't necessary to fret about personal hygiene, but number one on Shamayal's list was to rid his body of the bin-shed stench. Number two was Bins's speciality: stocktakin'.

One glance in the dappled mirror at his half-closed eye - *oh man!* - had persuaded him to save that particular pleasure for later. His skin tone did a fair job of masking bruises, so he commenced a fingertip exploration. Shamayal already knew his chest hurt when he breathed in, when he breathed out, when he coughed and twisted - fact, whenever he moved, full stop. Now he applied pressure to individual ribs, arriving at the conclusion that three were busted, at least.

"A & E won't do nuffin for you," he was telling them when Bins shuffled in and, facing the toilet bowl, started fumbling with the knot of his string belt. "Do me a favour!" Forgetting it was going to hurt, Shamayal sat up and used both hands to cover himself. He cried out in pain.

Bins twisted his oblivious head. "Go ahead. Just help your-self. *I'm a little teapot short and stout. Here's my handle, here's my spout -*"

No way, man.

"*- When I get all steamed up hear me shout, tip me up and pour me out.*" Bins angled his chin upwards and released a stream of piss. "Aaahhh."

"Are you for real?" Shamayal asked after the wave of agony had subsided and the flush had reduced to a gurgle.

"What?" The old man looked about him, confused. "What?"

"The singin' and all that!"

Bins blinked. "That's the Toilet Song. I can't go without it."

Shamayal could only stare. "I guess you don't have too many visitors."

"Kitty used to come on Mondays and Thursdays, but I think I must have upset her." Bins scrunched up his face.

Pushing his heels out and shelving his arms on the sides of the bath, Shamayal carefully slipped back into the water - OK, OK, OK - the bath groaning in sympathy. "She was your home help, right?"

"I don't know about help! She moved things. I had to

put them all back where they belonged after she'd gone." Unexpectedly, Bins crouched down and dangled his hands in the bathwater, as if it was a perfectly natural thing to do. As Shamayal was fighting to control his eyebrows, the old man pointed, apparently delighted. "Yours floats too! I thought only mine did that."

The boy thought he might actually have squeaked. Crafty old devil noticed things just fine. Must have chosen not to ask how his face got so mashed up.

Bins shot up. "Where are my manners? We've got special visitors' towels." He shuffled out into the chaos of the hall, with its plastic-bag-and-string skyscrapers towering against a sky of geometric wallpaper. "Now, where are you?"

Moments later he was back, carrying a carefully folded pair as if presenting a cushion to a king: they were lilac and scented like old ladies. Shamayal wondered what drawer they'd been stowed away in that they had avoided contamination. Bins appeared to examine the various options before deciding on a patch of lino. He strained, sweeping at the flooring with one hand, before positioning his precious cargo and squaring the corners. "Special visitors' towels," he announced, stomach out, hands in the small of his back.

The end of the finger Shamayal pointed was rippled with map-like contours. "I bet those belonged to your mamma, am I right?"

A response was nodded. "My dear old mum."

"I'll take good care of them."

Bins showed no sign of allowing Shamayal a little privacy. "You can get dry, then we can continue playing the game," he enthused.

"The game? Right, right: the *game.*" Shamayal braced himself, scooped water into his cupped hands and, dipping his face, winced. "Thing is, I need somewhere more or less permanent to hide, if you know what I mean." His thoughts turned to his mamma. How they decided on a place by closing their eyes and sticking a pin in the road map: the Middle of Nowhere. Same sort of place Christian would have gone if he'd had any sense. "Yeah, I need to find me somewhere... somewhere safe."

Bins perched on the toilet seat. A slow furrowed nod suggested he was dissecting words to fathom some sort of meaning. His heavily grooved tongue conducted a sortie, taking in the full circumference of his mouth.

"Basically, I got to make me disappear."

Bins appeared to have grasped the situation. His tongue reversed its direction, then he pointed: "I know, I know! *Invisible Man*. David McCallum plays the scientist, Daniel Westin. The reels go round, the red light comes on, then he disappears!"

"Right, right." Shamayal felt as if he had entered some kind of a parallel universe.

"But it goes wrong. The machine malfunctions and *boom!* Then the reversal serum won't work."

"He stays invisible?"

"Stuck," Bins agreed.

This was hopeless. "Yeah, that's what I'm looking for, basically."

"I've got just the thing!"

Shamayal raised his eyebrows. "I'd better have me some of that."

"If I can remember where I put it..."

While Bins was searching for his vial of magic serum, Shamayal took the opportunity to haul himself dripping from the bath. That way he could swear away at leisure without upsetting the old guy. The lino felt gritty underfoot. Fleetingly, a shadowy puffed face passed in front of the mirror. He ignored it. A memory: his mamma crouched down, waiting to lasso him with a big towel, hugging him to her so that she could rub his back dry. One of the towels, he made into a lilac sarong; the other, he draped around his shoulders. The towelling, however soft and scented, weighed heavy. As he patted his tender skin - gently, gently - he remembered his mamma teaching him the twist so that he could dry his own back. He wanted to see her smile at him that way again. He wanted it so bad it pained him almost more than his ribs.

The sound of boxes being cast aside, a scraping and banging of cupboard doors reached him. "Ah-ha!"

He shook his head. It was his mamma he was speaking to when he said, "This, I can't wait to see! Bins will have me dressed up in a sheet with likkle eye holes, and I got to look impressed. But first..." Shamayal steeled himself for what he knew would appear in the mirror. Putting one hand on the edge of the sink, he leaned closer. "OK, OK." He parted the lids of his swollen eye carefully. Where the white should have been, there was only red. At least he could see. "So, you haven't given up on me. *Jesus!*" Shamayal almost leaped out of his skin.

Over his left shoulder was a frog-man, dressed head to toe in shiny green. On his head, a peaked balaclava, Bins was trussed into a jacket, trousers, a bib and braces and thigh-length galoshes. He flapped his arms. "Da-da!"

Shamayal recovered his breathing first, but his heart was still pounding. "You know, you're not 'zactly what I call invisible."

"No, no, no!" The old man raised one hand as if he had earache. "That's not how it works."

"No?"

"No," Bins insisted. "I put my fishing gear on and, from then on, everybody ignores me."

"I see, I see."

"You try!" The old man began to peel the jacket off.

"Now?" Shamayal saw that Bins was shrugging off the sleeves.

"Well." Freed, Bins looked him up and down. "Your clothes are all ruined, and you can't go out looking like that!"

"Don't mock me, man." The boy looked down at his lilac sarong. "I thought I look like Tutankhamen."

After more enthusiastic shedding, Bins was naked. His little loose-skinned pot-belly stood proud. His old-man willy hung innocently. Wearing only the balaclava, Bins borrowed Shamayal's shoulder for balance - the boy winced in disbelief as arrows shot through his ribs - splashing as he stepped into the tepid bathwater. "Waste not, want not."

Shamayal grabbed the top of the balaclava and pulled.

"Oh, oh, oh!" cried Bins, ears catching, hands jumping to protect his steamed-up glasses.

"Sorry. I'll go gently."

"Gently!"

The boy rolled the edge of the material up and then pulled it down over his own face. The reflected beak turned from side to side in the mirror. Only his eyes were on display, the fully-open white one and the mainly-closed red one. Hardly invisible - but not so different from half a dozen other boys.

"See!" Bins approved, his hands making whirlpools and splashing water liberally between his legs. "Next, we're going to disappear you."

Mirror images, Shamayal and Bins sat, backs against the wall, knees raised, hands on knees.

"Who's coming to find us?" Bins asked.

In the darkness of the boiler room, they were invisible even to each other. Shamayal wondered if he was imagining things, or if the old man's voice wasn't slightly different.

"Dunno," he answered truthfully.

"I like to know people's names. It's important when you're no good with faces."

Every time Shamayal moved, he rustled. Each rustle

reminded him that something was about to hurt. "Are you sayin' you're one of those people who can't tell black people apart?"

"No, I'm one of those people who can't tell *anyone* apart."

"Not anyone?"

"With a bit of luck I might recognise the shape of their hair, or the sound of their voice maybe."

"Shit! So, how d'you know it's me?"

"Your hat."

This news was slow to sink in. "And if I wasn't wearing it?"

"Not so much. Perhaps not at all. These people: are they bad?"

"'Pends whose side you're on. They're frightened people. Basically, they're tryin' to protect someone. One of their own."

Bins snorted. "Like me."

Shamayal could feel trickles of sweat running down his body inside the waterproofs. "You're never frightened!"

"I am. A bit."

"Coulda fooled me." The air was moist and muggy, like the air inside the palm house his mamma took him to at Kew. She said dinosaurs lived somewhere like that. He accused her of getting him there under false pretences after he found out from a poster on the station platform that they lived at the Natural History Museum. He sulked all the way to the ice-cream kiosk, even though secretly he was impressed by the Venus Fly Traps. "You the man with the plan."

"The people who are coming to find us." It was 'us' now. For a moment Shamayal was relieved he wasn't on his own, then he thought, No, it couldn't be that way. The old man was a protected species. "They're the people who hurt you, aren't they?"

So, he noticed more than he let on. "Yup."

"Why did they do that?"

"Wanted to know if I can keep my maaf shut, didn't they?"

"Like a test?" Questions now sounded like logic.

Shamayal rustled as his head turned blindly. "Yeah, yeah. That's what it was. They was measurin' my integrity."

The voice that said, "You're in trouble," was as normal as normal gets.

"Shed loads. The people who came after me tol' me they'll hold *me* personally responsible." As Shamayal began his story, he knew that the trickle running down his cheek was not the sweat from his forehead.

"Maybe we should call the police -"

Shamayal rustled. "All the police are interested in is findin' the guys who knifed Jim Stevens and Christian Knoll. Ain't no way they're goin' to show their faces. These are diff'rent guys."

"Then we've got to go and see Jim Stevens."

"He don't know nuffin. Tell the truth, it's best it stays that way."

"He'd *want* to know."

"I can't go near him, not with them all peely-eyed."

"I can." The voice was small, measured.

"You? You've never bin off the estate in your whole life!"

"I go to the Post Office once a week," Bins protested.

"Strictly speakin', that still qualifies as the estate."

In the pause, there was breathing. Shamayal's chest felt like that instrument his mamma used to call a squeeze box, the one that has to be pushed in and out.

"I know a man from *Dial-a-Ride*. I think he owes me a favour or two."

"Man, you don't need to wait 'til he owes you a favour. That's a free service."

"Are you sure?"

"Sure I'm sure. Question is, are you sure 'bout this?"

Bins's hand squeezed and then pressed down on Shamayal's knee as his feet scraped the concrete in an effort to stand.

He has no idea, he thought to himself. That way, it was easier to forgive the old guy. "You'll be safe if I lock you in." The retreating paces reversed. "No, I won't do that. Just in case."

Shamayal didn't need to ask why. If Bins didn't come back, chances were he'd starve before anyone found him.

"Go safe, yeah?"

He saw the fluorescent yellow hands of a child's watch arc towards him. Mickey Mouse: just like the one his mamma gave him; proper retro. In the days when he was scared of his own shadow, he was also scared of the dark. In fact, looking at it, this might even be his.

"Take it. I always thought this might come in useful, so I keep it in my pocket."

"It's your watch, man."

"You can give it back to me later." Bins squeezed his hand around it. "But if the big hand gets to here," he pointed, "You should think about making your own way."

They'd always said they'd be together again, him and his mamma. He had no idea how to get there, but the old man was waiting for an answer. "Yeah. Yeah. I could go to my mamma's. That's my best option anyhow. Fact, if you could help with that."

"Good idea."

Then, for what seemed like an eternity, Shamayal was very alone.

CHAPTER 39:

JIM - AUGUST 1992 -
RALEGH GROVE, AT HOME

Jim knew he would tell his story to the policewoman who understood a thing or two about owls. He was prepared to let her have the facts. Those that affected him. But there were huge gaps in what he knew about Aimee. The black eye, the footprint-shaped bruise - previously capable of being brushed aside - took on new significance in this restructuring of events. Jim had more and more questions but instead he was expected to provide answers. Where were the answers *he* wanted going to come from?

And then there were the questions his mother would ask. Why had he lied to her? What else was he keeping from her? Could she still trust him? Because, if not, she had no idea how she could go to work, day in, day out. To Jim, it wasn't a case of being able to trust him or not. It was all very well an adult telling you that you can talk to them when there were so many things inside Jim's head that couldn't be put into words. Plus, he was at an age where he felt entitled to a few secrets. It wasn't as if he expected his mother to give him a running commentary on her thoughts.

He hadn't told her where he went every day because it was trespassing and she would have had to say she didn't approve.

That was her job, even if she would have said, "Leave him alone: he's not doing any harm," of any other lad he knew.

He didn't tell her about meeting Aimee because he'd had no idea they were going to be friends. She just turned up. It wasn't as if they had made arrangements - not at first. And if he'd said that he had met a girl, Mum wouldn't have been able to help herself. It would have been, "Where did you meet her?" "What's her name?" And that's before his mother moved on to the embarrassing stuff. "Is she pretty?" "Why don't you bring her home for tea?"

Plus, parents have this habit of clinging onto throwaway comments. Mention he liked something and it would be brought up a couple of years later under the most humiliating circumstances. Like the time she'd bought him a present a couple of years ago, and was beside herself, hands clasped underneath her chin, fit to burst, while he unwrapped it.

"I had to search everywhere."

And when he didn't react with quite the level of enthusiasm she expected, her expression melted away to disappointment. Controlling the urge to say, "Yes, I really wanted models of the Teenage Mutant Hero Turtles when I was eight, but now I'm *ten!*" he managed, "I can't believe you remembered." Because at least she *had* remembered, and maybe she'd been saving up all that time.

Girls, well, they were another matter. He didn't speak the language and the natives were hostile. He hadn't had any sisters or cousins. Nothing to explain why, when he hadn't found Aimee particularly attractive, it made him hot under the collar if her hand strayed too close; why he backed off when her hair brushed against his cheek; why he'd wanted to protect her from Nick and his junkie friends; why he'd been jealous when Andy Naylor looked at her that way in the park; why he got an erection when she blew in his ear, or teased him with a blade of grass. How he had been so aware of the rise and fall of her chest; the contrast between her long, lazy limbs and her busy hands with their chipped nail varnish; the intensity of her cat's eyes; the way her finger pulled her lips apart as she applied gloss - far too often, in his opinion. Even the sight of her tongue pushed into the gap in her front teeth.

To an adult, the question, "What's your relationship with Aimee?" might have seemed easy, something to get him nice and relaxed. To Jim, it was quicksand. He wanted to pass, but he knew it was the one question the policewoman would keep returning to: "Your final score is fourteen. You passed on two questions. The green woodpecker is found in all parts of the UK except Northern Scotland and Ireland -"

"Of course!"

"- and Aimee White is your *friend*."

Why was it so difficult to say? If Aimee had been a boy, he would have called her a mate and nobody would have blinked. It wasn't just the relationship: it was the tense that was proving difficult. Already, he was thinking of her in his past. Another person who'd left.

"In your own time," Cowley smiled.

A train rumbled past. Jim felt its vibrations enter his body through the soles of his feet.

"Can't you see he's upset?" his mother replied for him.

That was it: he was upset. Tomorrow he would be able to find the right words. He breathed for what seemed like the first time in minutes.

"Let's leave it for today," Cowley said. "Would you be able to come down to the station tomorrow? Or I can come here if it's easier -"

The thought wasn't left to brew for long. "It's best if we come to you." Fewer neighbours and prying eyes. "But it'll have to be after I've finished work."

"Jim, do you mind if I have a private word with your mother?" Cowley asked.

He was relieved to be able to escape to his room and close

the door. Taking out his sketch book, he flicked through to the entries Aimee had made, the place where she had signed her name. He compared her carefully joined-up writing - its round letters and curly tails - with his own miniscule scrawl. However confidently the policewoman spoke about how big a help he could be tracking Aimee down, Jim knew she was gone, and this was all she'd left him: these few words; some of them written only a week earlier.

Jean brought the policewoman another mug of tea and perched warily on the far end of the sofa, knees glued together.

"So," Cowley raised her hand to decline the offer of sugar, "What do you do work-wise?"

"Just a bit of cleaning." Jean held her mug in both hands, trying to steady them. She longed for a cigarette. Her eyes strayed to a copy of *Women's Weekly* on the coffee table. "You know."

"And who looks after Jim while you're out?"

"That would be his father. Until a few weeks ago." Jean glanced up at the sound of the upstairs neighbours thundering overhead. "You have him at your disposal at the moment." Try as she might, she couldn't keep the note of blame from her voice.

It was then that Jim remembered the white feather stowed away in the pocket of his rucksack, the only part of the owl that remained. Extracting it, his fingers became a loom as he wove it backwards and forwards, smoothing the barbs then ruffling them again.

He thought of Aimee pushing her tongue into the gap in her teeth as she drew in her notebook.

He thought about her silhouette against her bedroom window. Pressed against the glass with her hands raised. No longer waving, but an animal in captivity.

He thought about her staring at the tracks. Just staring.

He closed his eyes as he remembered the violence of the vacuum of air.

"I'm sorry," she had said. Well, sorry wasn't good enough!

"I see," Cowley nodded, no surprise in her voice. "Is there no one else?"

The corners of Jean's mouth twitched. "My father passed on over a year ago." Was it really only a year? It felt like an eternity.

"Sorry to hear that. No aunts or uncles?"

"I was an only child. I dare say there might have been more, but my mother died when I was three."

"That must have been hard."

"It wasn't actually. It worked just fine, me and my dad. That's all I can remember."

Jim felt the heat of his fury rise from his stomach to his head. Aimee had pummelled him with her fists after he hadn't shown up for three days. She had clawed at his clothes. "I thought that something bad had happened to you," she'd said.

"What about me? Did you think about that?" he said out loud, his face crumbling.

"I can't work you out."

"Does it matter?"

It mattered. Of course it bloody well mattered!

"Is Jim an only child?"

"His brother's long gone. Listen -" Jean leaned towards the policewoman "- Jim's as good as gold. I've never had an ounce of trouble from him."

"At the moment, Mrs Stevens, it's you we're concerned about."

"Me?" Jean's laughter signified disbelief.

Cowley nodded, deadly serious.

She sat back, one hand on the rise of her chest. What had she ever done but try to set a good example? "If I don't work we don't eat, simple as that..."

"You'd be entitled to benefits..."

"No!" Jean barked, then she softened. "Look, I'm sorry. Maybe I'm expecting you to know too much. My husband went wrong a long time ago. It broke my heart when my older boy -" She struggled to control her voice. "There's only Jim now. I have to show him there's another way. He's all I've got."

"I understand." Jean felt Cowley's hand on her arm.

"I'm doing the very best that I can."

"I know you are."

She appealed to the policewoman through blurred eyes. "Then why is it never good enough?"

Jim's head cleared. It was as if a familiar song had been playing in the wrong key. He realised he had interrupted Aimee a second time, and the weight of this knowledge - the absence of doubt - made something inside him sever. Looking down, he found that he had snapped the vane of the owl's feather. Jim hurled his notebook, with his sketches of Aimee in it, across his bedroom.

Cowley's tone altered and she asked softly, "Is there anyone who can be with Jim while you're at work?"

"He'll be back at school next week. I'm just glad he's got his birds. They're what he lives for."

Jim turned and kicked the door. Not satisfied, he punched it, yelled in protest at the pain, checked that all of his fingers were still operational and went at it again.

Jean frowned at the ceiling, then realised that the pounding was coming from the other side of her own hallway. "Is that...?" She put one hand on the arm of the sofa as if to push herself up. "Jim!"

"It might do him good to let off steam." The woman's eyes were knowing. They both stood. "Does he have many other friends?"

"Not that I know of." Jean hung her head. What mother wants to admit that? "There's some lads he plays football with, but he never brings anyone home." It was fairly obvious that Aimee invited herself - and he wasn't at all pleased about it. Jean followed the policewoman out into the narrow hall with its woodchip wallpaper. The lad from number 29 loped past, trainers scraping concrete, eying Jean accusingly at the sight of navy uniform.

"What about his brother?"

The four fifteen rumbled past. Jean gripped the wood of the door. "We don't see Nick."

"That's a shame. It might be just what Jim needs."

"I know you mean well, but you don't know us. To be honest, I thought you were here to talk about his brother. It wouldn't be the first time." Jean reflected that, if anything happened to Aimee, Jim would blame Nick. "Do you really think Aimee has just run off?"

"I don't think of it as *just*. We can only hope we find her before she lands herself in trouble."

Humbled, Jean blinked. "Of course." Sixteen. And she'd sent him out to fend for himself.

Jim heard his mother's voice on the other side of the door. "Feeling better now?"

"No!" He nursed his knuckles back into shape for another onslaught.

"Then I'll sit here and wait until you do."

CHAPTER 40:

AYISHA - AUGUST 2010 - ST HELIER HOSPITAL

"You haven't seen Shamayal?" Ayisha asked Jim, incredulous.

"I thought he was at yours." The impatience in his voice barely disguised, he clawed both sides of his face as if trying to rid himself of the growth.

"I told you: I've been at my parents'." There was no concern for the fact that she had gone AWOL for almost a week, but the boy... then she checked herself, acknowledging the jittery feeling in her stomach: where could he *be?*

Ayisha thought of all the time she had wasted. She hadn't worried when she arrived home to find the envelope still on the table in the hall, where she'd left it. After five days of being cooped up in a mock-Tudor semi and being dragged around National Trust properties (members, her parents liked to get their money's worth), her priority had been exercise. Because it was such a beautiful day, she had decided to walk to the hospital via the farmers' market. For her last few days' freedom, she chose uncomplicated clothes: a long sleeved t-shirt the colour of the spring sky when it is the backdrop to cherry blossom, a white ankle-length skirt, over-sized sunglasses.

She had dipped in and out of the shade of striped awnings, the soles of her Fitflops gently slapping the soles of her feet, enticed by punnets of yellow-skinned cherries. Apricots and plum tomatoes still on the vine were also rustled into brown-paper bags by a man with a pencil behind his ear, the corners delightfully twisted; a ten-pound note parted with, loose change tipped into her palm. After sampling a plump queen variety of olive, with oil dribbling down her chin, Ayisha had felt obliged to purchase a small tub. Fresh bread, too, made its way into her hessian bag, ridiculously priced for what she reflected was only a mixed grain loaf.

"He's left it two days between visits before - on the days he knew you were coming - but never longer than that."

Ayisha's anger, both with herself and with Jim, spilled into the question, "Why on earth didn't you call me?"

"This is my first day back on the ward."

"What do you mean?" she found herself snapping. His explanation had better be good.

"I had what was described as a bit of setback."

Looking at him properly for the first time that day, Ayisha was forced to admit to herself that Jim looked awful, his eyes hollowed out, his skin puffy. She was almost nervous to ask. "What kind of setback?"

"I've been back in H.D.U. They've been pumping me full of someone else's blood and yet more antibiotics."

"For what?"

"Septicaemia."

Her breath made an *Ah!* sound in protest: hardly just a setback. Seeing him struggle to find a comfortable position - "Here, let me" - she stalled for time, fluffing his pillows, holding the corners, shaking, then patting them into place. "Well, I'm here now. First thing's first, I'll go and check at your flat." Her priority was finding Shamayal - before some-one else did.

"He won't be there."

"Then *his* flat." Feeling it was her job to reassure Jim, Ayisha risked a laugh. "If half of what that boy spouts on about is true, he's probably seeing a girl!"

She felt her arm being gripped, the skin twisted. "There is no girlfriend. There *are* no friends."

"Don't you be so sure!" She sat back down and lowered her voice. "He's a fourteen-year-old boy. Do you think he tells us everything?"

Jim smiled wryly. "What teenager with mates - let alone a girlfriend - chooses to spend time with his his-tor-y" - Ayisha noted how Jim had reverted to bored-student pronunciation - "teacher?"

"You're not such bad company."

"Huh." Self-deprecating, he raised his eyebrows. "I take him *bird-watching*, for God's sake!"

"Still." She hoped the wincing of the corners of her mouth wouldn't betray her. "Five weeks is a long time in the life of a teenager."

"Is that how long I've been lying here?" With an expression more desolate than Ayisha could recall, Jim appeared to be in serious consultation with one corner of the ceiling.

She was keen to be on her way but, although his grasp had loosened, Jim's hand still circled her wrist. Had he forgotten it was there, she asked herself, or was he just distracted?

"There's something I ought to tell you." He blinked, his eyes looking down at the bedclothes, as if they might hold the answer. Ayisha didn't like the sound of this. She must have looked hesitant. "Something I *need* to tell you," he said with emphasis. "You see, I've not been completely honest with you."

He *had* been holding back on her! About to demand answers, she saw that he was in torment. She relented and prepared to listen. Anything that might help her track the boy down. "Alright."

He was slow to begin, so slow that she became concerned he was about to reveal something awful; something that would have her questioning her own judgement. "There was a time I was so caught up in problems of my own, I didn't notice someone close to me was in serious trouble. She -" There was such sorrow distilled in the voice that now faltered. "Well, the truth is, no one knows what really happened to her."

So, this wasn't about Shamayal. But what else could be so important that he must tell her now? Looking at the hand, Ayisha saw dark hairs standing out against the pale skin between the second joints and the knuckles. It showed no sign of letting go. "Do you want to talk about it?" Ayisha ventured, reluctant but curious.

"Out loud?" Jim laughed.

Lowering her head, Ayisha's hair fell forwards. She was deeply unsettled by her wildly see-sawing emotions. A decision of whether to place her hand on top of another person's hadn't seemed so monumentally life-altering since she was twelve years old. But, before she could move, Jim's hand was withdrawn, leaving her feeling deflated.

"That's better." He was tucking her hair behind her ear, a gesture so startling in its intimacy that she could barely breathe. "Now I can see you properly."

Now! she commanded her hand, but it seemed to be super-glued to the bed sheet.

"It was the summer holidays of the year I turned twelve." He picked the disobedient hand up in both of his as if examining it. *Do you mind?* his expression seemed to ask.

She listened, absorbed: *so this is who you are.*

This is why you teach.

Why I find you perched on the corner of desks talking to pupils.

The hospital, together with all of its smells and noises - the senile shouts, the arrival of the tea trolley, the constant to-ing and fro-ing of feet, the irregular *thop, thop* from the tennis courts next door - faded. There was nothing but the rise and fall of his voice, the movement of his mouth, the occasional intrusion of the hand that scratched at its corner.

Ayisha decided she liked the beard.

And this is why you have a picture of a white owl - a barn owl, you say - in your living room.

Why you hate the holidays.

As he closed his eyes, as he spoke about the press conferences he had memorised word for word, she felt her skin shrinking. "Aimee, if you're listening, please know how much we miss you. You're in our thoughts and prayers every minute of every day. There's nothing we can't work out between us. Come home. Whenever you're ready, come home."

Jim had been here before! Even before the news of Christian's death was broadcast, he thought he knew how it would end. But now his story was at an end. Had she missed something?

"So they just gave up looking? Aimee was never found?"

"I would have liked someone to prove me wrong, but no." He shook his head, berating himself.

No body meant there was hope. Not much, but hope all the same. Ayisha imagined a girl. A young girl; alone, on the streets. She had seen plastered-haired girls like this, under railway arches, on pedestrian bridges, holding out take-away coffee containers, asking, "*Got any spare change?*" And she had clutched her expensive handbag tighter as she walked past.

"You can't possibly blame yourself!" she said but, as Jim hung his head, she realised: he had spent his adult life trying to compensate for whatever wrong he thought he had committed as a boy. "You were twelve!" she said, incredulous, her eyes falling on his notebook, lying on the table, a pencil employed as a bookmark. She picked it up, opened it. "Have you spent all these years telling yourself that bird-watching should have made you an expert on *people?*"

His eyes flitted to hers, blue, questioning. Ayisha doubted that anything she could say would undo the damage.

"I tried to provide Shamayal with a distraction, but what if it's knowing *me* that's the problem? If they've been watching him - who am I kidding? They'll have seen him coming to visit me. They can't get to me but -"

A smiling nurse wheeling a trolley of goodies arrived at the foot of the bed. "Any painkillers for you, Jim?"

As their exchange passed, Ayisha had time to reflect. If they had been watching Shamayal, they would know where she lived; know she lived alone. An uncomfortable thought. One that would make her nervous if she dwelt on it. If not for herself, they might use her as a means to get to the boy. Ayisha waited until the nurse had passed on before picking up where Jim had left off: "You've been talking to the police."

"Anyone watching might assume that Shamayal's been feeding me information. He threatened to disappear himself once before and I didn't ask him what he meant because I thought I knew."

"We'll find him," Ayisha tried to assure Jim, squeezing his hand.

"You sound far more confident than I feel."

"It's something he said to me. He as good as told me we were both survivors."

All of a sudden, they became aware of something taking place in the corridor outside, close to the nurse's station; a re-grouping of resources. It was extraordinary in that voices were lowered.

The man from the bed opposite, who had decamped to his visitor's chair to read a newspaper also sensed it. "Why's it all gone quiet?" He sat forwards in his seat. "I can't see a sodding thing from here. Someone must have died."

"Who's died?" an unseen voice piped up from behind a curtain.

"I thought it might be you, Stan! You've been very quiet."

"It was a close call after last night's Chicken Kiev. Good God!"

It amazed Ayisha, the patients' capacity for complaining about hospital food. The man opposite addressed her as if he was suggesting she should stick around for a scheduled entertainment: "They'll be in to hose the walls down in a minute. You wait."

Sophia padded into the ward, detecting the sudden change in atmosphere. "What are you boys up to? Honestly! Soon as my back's turned, you're plottin' something!"

"We thought you might tell us."

"What you talkin' 'bout?" she said dismissively, approaching the corner bed. "Now if you'll 'scuse me, I need a quiet word with Jim here." As she trailed the curtain behind her, the colour and quality of the light became a tent-like glow.

Ayisha made as if to stand. "I'll wait outside -"

"Stay." Jim squeezed her hand urgently.

Eyes sweeping across their conjoined hands, Sophia lifted her eyebrows and sighed that she had expected as much all along. "Security have removed a man from reception. Thought he was causin' a disturbance, but it turned out he was having a panic attack! A man from *Dial-a-Ride* has brought him back in. Furious he is - says he's here to see you."

Jim frowned. "It can't be my father."

"Not your brother?" Ayisha suggested.

"Uh-uh. This guy's old and," Sophia sighed loudly, "How am I gonna put this politely? We couldn't let him in without puttin' him in quarantine first."

"Bins?"

"That's how they say he smells. He's refusing to go anywhere else without seein' you." The nurse threw up her hands.

"I'm not sure *what* we should do!"

"Is there any chance I could go down?"

"I don't know about that." Sophia's eyes flared. "I've seen you breaking out in a sweat getting back from the bathroom." Tight-mouthed, Sophia consulted the chart on the end of Jim's bed then sighed heavily. "I s'pose your friend here could smuggle you down in a wheelchair. But not for long. Don't make me come looking for you!"

"Sophia, you're a gem."

The nurse turned to Ayisha: "You're in charge, you hear?"

Ayisha stood aghast, but Jim was holding one hand out to her enthusiastically. "Pass me my binoculars, will you? They're on the table."

Ayisha picked them up, then brought them to her chest. "Have we got time for this?"

"Bins must be here because of Shamayal. Ordinarily, he never goes anywhere."

"They know each other?"

"Bins knows everybody."

"If it's not a stupid question, what do you need your binoculars for?"

"Because he won't recognise me unless I'm wearing them."

CHAPTER 41:

JIM - AUGUST 1992 - 407 BUS

Every detail of Jim's journey to the police station has been consigned to memory. Catching the bus; the hands that steered him past the inviting staircase into the first available seat; shuffling sideways across coarse tartan; hemmed into a window seat; grime-encrusted glass blotting out his view of the bridge.

The heater under the seat spewed ankle-scalding air, but Jim felt little. Save for the knot that tightened his stomach, all his pain was condensed into the door-punched knuckles of his right hand, the sight of which caused his mother to sigh so. Pretending to nurse them, he squeezed extra mileage out of his hand when it stopped throbbing quite so violently. The foot closest to his mother was idly tapping, poised for the first opportunity to escape.

Jean cupped the offending knee. "Just tell the truth. That's all you have to do."

Sinking down, Jim stared at the graffiti on the back of the seat in front: names of people who had marked their territory like dogs leaving scent on a tree. Where did that instinct comes from? Was it a way of warning other people off, or was it just the need to leave something behind? He thought again of the curves and loops of Aimee's handwriting. If his mother hadn't been seated beside him - if he'd had a pen or a Swiss army knife - he would have left a mark for her. An RIP.

Jim's chin rested on the knot of the tie Mum had made him wear. It was his uniform tie: the only one he owned. He was conscious of the way his mother held her handbag, elbows tucked in by her waist, making herself as narrow as possible. He knew how difficult any contact with the police was for her - particularly helping them with their enquiries. They'd taken away her husband. Despite the domino effect Frank had on their lives, she couldn't help feeling a certain loyalty. Still, she wanted Jim to 'do right'.

"All you can do is tell them the truth."

In the past, as far as Jim was concerned, truth was a dangerous thing. You tell the other guy where your weak spots are, it's like taking the stabilizers off your bike; going into battle minus your armour. The only person who had managed to extract anything resembling the truth from him was Aimee. It wasn't that he'd trusted her. It was just he didn't think she could harm him with it. The summer had taught Jim a very powerful thing: when you tell the truth you can be yourself. "This is me: like it or lump it." He had told Aimee the worst about himself, and she had shrugged, "You think you're the only one with problems?"

But what if it's not just your story you're telling? It wasn't as though Aimee was there to ask, "Is it OK if I tell them what you were doing when I first saw you?"

If Jim answered the policewoman's questions, would he be helping Aimee? Or should he leave the lid safely on that can of worms? Stare as he might, the letters on the back of the seat in front refused to spell out any answers, and then - too soon - his mother was saying, "This must be our stop," grabbing the pole to haul herself up and ringing the flat-sounding bell.

CHAPTER 42:

JIM - AUGUST 2010 - ST HELIER HOSPITAL

Ayisha wheeled Jim out of the lift. The first set of automatic doors whooshed apart as they approached, and a rumble of traffic accosted them. It felt strange to be venturing outside.

"Do you know?" he attempted light-heartedness, "This will be the first time in almost six weeks that I haven't had to look at the sky through a pane of glass."

A porter approached, addressing Ayisha: "Need a hand, love?"

"Thanks, but we'll only be a few minutes."

The second set of doors parted. Even greeted by the trill of a blackbird Jim felt apprehensive. Shading his eyes, he looked back at the entrance to read the raised letters of the plaque informing visitors that Conservative MP John Major was born here. He had always relied on his memory, but he could not remember arriving at the hospital or the two days that followed.

Ayisha rounded the front of the chair and pulled a pair of folded sunglasses from the v of her t-shirt. The sky's blue was the colour of her top and its wispy clouds were a mirror of her skirt. "Here. Borrow these."

They were the over-sized type that female film stars use to disguise themselves from prying photographers. He would look like a fool in them. "Bins won't recognise me if I wear them." As with all good excuses, this one had the benefit of being true.

"So you keep saying." She dangled the sunglasses in front of his face. "I don't remember being consulted, but apparently I'm responsible for you."

"It's true! He doesn't recognise faces, so he relies on the shape of your hair, what you're wearing, how you move -"

Ayisha seemed to find this amusing. It took Jim a moment to catch up. It wasn't Bins's disability she was laughing at: it was him. He hadn't had a haircut for six weeks, the shape of his face was altered by drugs and several days' growth and, here he was, in a wheelchair! The thought of how altered he was depressed Jim. Not the lack of a haircut: that could be fixed. It was his wasted muscles; his new pot-belly; the fact that his body had aged, to say nothing of his mind.

"Like Chuck Close?" she was asking.

"Who?"

"You know. The American artist."

Jim didn't.

"I saw a documentary about him. One of those unpromising-looking things that turns out to be really interesting. He was treated like an idiot when he was growing up, all because he didn't seem to be able to remember people's names, while the real issue was that he couldn't tell them apart."

Jim chuckled at this revelation. Suddenly it was very clear why he needed to wear binoculars.

"There's a name for his condition. Prospognose, prospagnose - something beginning with 'P'. Anyway, it means 'face blindness.'"

Was it possible that face blindness was all that had ever

been wrong with Bins, but they'd managed to convince him otherwise? With a new wave of nostalgia at the thought of seeing the old man, Jim looked about. Where could he have got to?

Colours seemed more vivid than their memory. Everywhere, there were contrasts: the red of a *Dial-a-ride* bus; the yellow of an ambulance; the brown of a dog studiously sniffing the base of the wall at the entrance while his owner - oblivious - tugged at the lead. The dog, who only then decided to cock his leg, was dragged, hopping and yelping, leaving a dark trail. Behind the low wall a congregation of loyal smokers - most of them nurses - watched the queue for the car park lengthen. Beyond that, the green of a playing field. As Jim filled his lungs with the diesel-perfumed air, he remembered its borders filled with daffodils when he last came to visit his mother. She always said it was the trains that gave her headaches. All those years... she should have realised something else was wrong.

"Can you see him anywhere?" Ayisha was asking as she pushed him past the *Dial-a-ride* bus.

Jim checked himself: he had become unanchored again. "No." He looked to his left; through the gap between two parked vehicles he saw a man wearing a fluorescent tabard, crouched down. "Wait! Back up a bit." The first man was speaking to an old man in a tatty raincoat, who was sitting on the kerb, shaking his low-bent head in a continuous flow of worry. "That's him."

"Poor thing looks lost." The chair jerked as Ayisha struggled to manoeuvre it.

On hearing their approach, the *Dial-a-ride* man glanced over his shoulder and raised the hand that was on Bins's shoulder in a gesture that was neither a wave nor a warning. "We don't want you blacking out again," he was cautioning gently. To Jim's frown, the man mouthed in an exaggerated manner that displayed his teeth, *'He's fine.'*

313

"That's it," Jim said. "I'm getting out of this chair."

"I'm the one in charge and I don't think you should," Ayisha warned.

But he was already pushing upwards. "Three steps, that's all. Then I'm going to sit back down."

She let out a frustrated sigh. "At least let me help you."

Once on his feet, Jim moved cautiously, a slow-sliding motion more suited to polished corridors. He was grateful for the arm Ayisha offered, but it was a far stretch of the imagination to think she could support the weight of a hefty six-footer. Pulling his dressing gown tightly over his backside, he levered himself down to the kerbstone. As he dropped the final few inches and rocked backwards, as his binoculars gently nudged his chest, something seemed to give - perhaps an internal stitch. "Blimey!" He laughed to reassure Ayisha. "That was further down than I thought."

Bins opened one eye and saw the binoculars. He curled his hands into barrels and squinted through them: "Jim Stevens! You've grown a beard."

The *Dial-a-ride* man reached one hand around Bins and said amicably, "Let me shake you by the hand, Jim. Good on you."

"Tony Maloney," Bins concurred, addressing Jim's binoculars. "He drove me here today."

"Tony." Stiffly, Jim twisted his body to reciprocate, although this was a stretch too far for him - both the physical reach and the matching of images in his head. "Good to see you." The man clasping his hand was balding, jolly and middle-aged, and the other... a bully who dangled small boys from balconies. "So this is your bus?" he said stupidly.

"That's me. We've had a right old song and dance, haven't we, mate? Never mind." Tony slapped Bins's knee before heaving himself up. "You're here now, Jim. I don't suppose there's anywhere I can get a cuppa?" He winked. "Leave the two of you to catch up."

Jim opened his mouth, but Ayisha was already pointing the way. "There's a café, just inside and to the left."

Bins appeared distracted. Following the old man's sight line, Jim noticed that, in the sunlight, Ayisha's linen skirt was see-through, revealing the smooth outline of her thighs and the t-bar of an insubstantial g-string. Ayisha would be mortified if she knew this. Thank God it wasn't something she'd wear to work: the boys would have a field day, posting photographs by the dozen on Facebook.

Only Tony appeared capable of ignoring the vision. "Keep an eye on him, won't you, Jim?"

"Bins, this is my friend -"

"Hello Princess Jasmine." The old man slowly inclined his head. "I'm sorry I can't stand up, but my head is dizzy."

You sly old charmer! Jim thought, turning to see Ayisha's unblinking reaction.

"Then I'll join you - if that's alright." She crouched, holding her see-through skirt modestly in place under her knees with one hand and putting the other on the kerb to take her weight.

"Actually, Princess," Bins winced. "I need to talk to Jim Stevens. In private." He copied her etiquette. "If *that's* alright."

Jumping back up, she employed her schoolteacher voice: "Five minutes and that's your lot! I'll go and keep Tony company."

They both watched her walk towards the entrance, pushing the empty wheelchair. A few yards away, she turned back to ask, "Does anyone want anything? Latte? Water?"

"No," they replied in unison, eyes lifting to her face.

Her eyebrows twitched slightly. "OK," she said and went on her way.

"She's lovely." Bins was toying with the frayed ends of the

string that hung from the belt-loops of his raincoat. "Is she your girlfriend?"

Jim thought of Ayisha's bedside vigil over the past five weeks, the softening of her large anxious eyes. He had no idea how to describe what had passed between them, except that he had never before trusted anyone enough to tell them what he had just told her. What had made him take the risk? "I don't know how to answer that," he spoke honestly.

"Does she know...?" He nodded after Ayisha. The further away she got, the more pronounced the outline of her thighs became.

Jim stopped Bins with a firm, "No." Then, seeing fear shadow the old man's face, he softened his voice. "Princess Jasmine! How did you dream that up?"

Bins grinned sheepishly. The plaque of his teeth was stained orange-brown. "She's the Disney character with the lovely brown skin and the dark hair."

"Her name's Ayisha," he said.

"Ayisha Stevens."

"Ayisha Emmanuel!" Even as he snorted air through his nostrils defiantly, Jim was aware of feeling light-headed. "Why is *everyone* ganging up on me?"

"No, no." Bins wagged a finger. "Everyone's ganging up on Shamayal."

Instantly, the small talk was over. As suspected, this was no social call. Jim's recent history with the old man would hardly justify the effort it must have taken for him to leave the estate. "You know where he is?" Jim asked.

Bins picked up what looked like a small button from the ground. "I know where I left him." He licked it tentatively. "Orange Smartie."

Jim refused to be side-tracked. He felt like demanding facts, but Bins had to be coaxed. "And where's that?"

"They dumped him in one of the bins, but I've moved him to the boiler room. It's warmer there."

Bins used to make it his business to know everyone. Jim doubted that had changed. He needed specifics. "*Who* dumped him?"

"It doesn't seem like a normal game of hide-and-seek to me. He says they're trying to protect someone."

Struggling to piece together drip-fed information, Jim's head pounded. The midday sun, directly overhead, threatened to burn his scalp. Perhaps he should have accepted Ayisha's offer of sunglasses.

A mute ambulance pulled up behind another ambulance outside the entrance. Its driver disembarked and eyed the empty vehicle disdainfully, as if it might be bullied into moving.

"What kind of a state is he in?"

Bins waggled his head, sighed. "He can walk. But we need to get him away from there."

Yes. Get him away from there. Jim wiped one hand from his mouth to his chin. "He's in this mess because of me." *Think!* "If I tell the police - even if they catch them - more will come. They'll keep coming."

"No police." The old man's voice was insistent. "That's what Shamayal said. He wants to disappear himself."

Feet traipsed past them: fat and squashed into court shoes; small and sandaled. A little-girl voice whined, "Why are *they* allowed to sit on the ground?" and was shushed. "Here! Have this!"

Watching the scrunched sweet-wrapper drop from a sticky hand, Jim's mind turned to the empty jeans dangling from a branch. "That's what I was afraid of."

"No, he has a plan." Jim found Bins's hand on his shoulder, its fine lines highlighted with dirt. "It won't be like Aimee White."

Hearing her name from his lips came as a shock. To think, Bins knew it all along. He must have somehow connected the Verity who introduced herself to him with the picture of the girl whose photograph was splashed all over the news - perhaps by her frizzy hair, perhaps by her gap-toothed smile - figured out there was a reason she didn't want to be known by her real name. Jim realised he had no idea what Bins's given name was, but it wasn't the time to ask. "I've got to get Shamayal away from here." He stood and the sky turned black. Blinking stars, he staggered backwards finding a woozy kind of balance.

"You alright, Jim Stevens? You've gone a funny colour."

"I'm fine." Instinct warned Jim to lean forwards. Letting his head hang, his view was of hands that looked peculiarly unlike his own.

The old man was now bending over him. "Are you feeling dizzy as well?"

The tarmac appeared to be at the wrong angle. At least as blood delivered oxygen to his head he began to think straight: "I can't go anywhere in this state." Defeat forced him to be logical. "Anyway, I'm no good to Shamayal. If I go near him, I'll put him in more danger. The same probably goes for Ayisha."

Angling his head, Jim saw anxiety in Bins's expression, but the old man's voice was decisive: "Your brother. Nick Stevens."

As his throat constricted, Jim fought the suggestion. His legs hurt under the pressure from his hands. The tarmac beneath his feet was fluid. Jim racked his brains: there must be an alternative. "What about Tony? He's got transport." Even with this small adjustment in gravity, his face felt misshapen. "Are the nurses still behind the wall?"

"Yes."

Speaking, even breathlessly, was an effort. "I'm going to need them."

"Over here!" Briefly, one of the old man's hands passed through Jim's line of vision. "A red bus stands out. It's got to be Nick. No one questions a locksmith."

Weight over the balls of his feet, Jim couldn't remember the mechanics of rocking backwards. Feathers exploded behind his eyes, like the aftermath of a pillow fight. He wasn't fit for one conversation, let alone two. "No idea where. He. Is." His voice came in rushes between gasps. "The nurses? Are. They?"

"They're waving back." Bins offered a commentary. "Now they're on their way." His head appeared, upside-down. *I do. Tony Maloney, your brother - I know where they all are.*

Let go of your knees. Get down before you fall down. "He won't help."

The old man blinked. "I - I think he will."

The light was so very bright. The old man was standing over him, peering down. Jim was fading. Before closing his eyes, he thought he said, "OK."

He was aware of a jerking movement as he was hauled onto a trolley, an oxygen mask being placed over his mouth. Speeding footsteps accompanied his journey. People were speaking very fast, their words indistinct but, rising above the orders, he recognised Ayisha's voice. Suddenly, it was imperative that he spoke to her. He tried unsuccessfully to raise his head but someone shouted, "Stop a moment!"

A face loomed close, a face that from its skin colour and the sheen of hair could only be Princess Jasmine's. His oxygen mask was moved to one side. With supreme effort, Jim managed, "Landed on a snake." There. He had said it.

She looked confused, disappointed even. Had she misunderstood?

"I thought he'd be alright with you for a few moments." Sophia was beside him too. He was in capable hands.

"You couldn't have stopped him," Ayisha was saying.

Jim willed his mouth to move: there was more. "Back to the beginning."

The mask replaced, the trolley was moving again. She was nodding now, keeping pace. "Alright." She smiled, eyes bright with tears.

"Alright."

Satisfied, once more he surrendered his body to the nicotine-scented staff of St Helier.

CHAPTER 43:

JIM - AUGUST 1992 -
SUTTON POLICE STATION

"Jim," Cowley said in the cramped interview room. "How are you feeling today?"

"Sit up straight, love," his mother encouraged, elbows tight.

He shuffled in the uncomfortable plastic seat, ending up back in his original position.

"- and answer when you're asked a question!"

The boy shrugged. "Alright, I s'pose."

The policewoman nodded as if expecting more. He picked the raised edge of the table top (Formica, white, with wavy black lines running through it), the flayed skin of his knuckles on display.

"Jim, there are no right or wrong answers here. If I ask you something and you don't know the answer, it's alright to say so. We just need to understand how Aimee had been feeling recently, OK?"

It was not remotely *OK*, not when she said one thing and meant another, but he nodded. What else could he do?

"Good. How long had you known each other?"

It stung him like a slap, Cowley's use of the past tense.

After all her insistence that Aimee was only missing! "'Bout six weeks."

"Only six weeks?"

Jim felt that Cowley was implying he didn't really know her that well at all. "We met right at the start of the holidays." He succeeded in prising up a good section of Formica before his mother's hand slapped his away.

"How did that happen?"

"I was out bird-watching, like I usually am, when she just showed up."

"And where was this?"

"Down by the side of the railway." From the corner of his eye, Jim saw his mother uncross and cross her legs. "Same place I found her shoe."

"Had she been there before?" Cowley continued. Jim saw that the hand holding the pen was the one that was wearing an engagement ring, a plain gold ring with a square-cut diamond: she was left-handed, like him.

"No." His right foot - the one further away from his mother - began to tap against a chair leg. "I would've seen her." The nails of the hand that held the pen were filed square across the top and the tips were very white.

"Why there?" It seemed like a genuine question. Aimee had asked him the same thing.

He might have talked about the migration paths of birds. "It's private," he shrugged. "No one to bother you."

"So, you were there on your own before Aimee came along?"

"Yes." He heard his mother's slight sigh. (Her nails were filed short: she didn't like getting 'gunk' stuck underneath them while she was working.)

"We found a lot of empty bottles and cans." Cowley smiled and lowered her head, trying to make eye contact. "It looked as if there'd been quite a party."

Raising his eyes, Jim found them locked on the curve of Cowley's chest - *Whether you're ooo, or whether you're shub-bub-do-wah* - and wondered what kind of bra she would be hiding under her tightly-buttoned uniform.

"Jim," his mother prompted with an elbow.

He blinked. Looking higher he located her mouth. "That's the people who go there at night. It's quiet in the daytime."

"He's always home in time for tea," Jean added.

Satisfied, or simply trying a different tack, Cowley asked, "So you met the once" - here, the mouth appeared to stretch into an involuntary smile - "And then what?"

"Aimee was interested in the birds. She started to come every day... almost."

"You mentioned a bird-watching club to her parents?"

"I made that up," he admitted.

"Can I ask why?"

Again, Jim didn't feel threatened. He thought Cowley might understand, and that she would help his mother to understand. He turned up the edges of his mouth. "I thought they'd be happier that way."

Cowley didn't ask who. She asked, "What way was that?"

"Saved explaining."

"Go on." Cowley's fingers walked the pen in windmills.

"S'embarrassing when people ask questions." He shuffled in his seat, avoiding his mum's gaze.

"What sort of questions?"

"You know." Jim felt himself redden. "About whether anything was going on."

"You were friends. That's right, isn't it?"

She got it. He'd hoped she might. "Yes."

"Did Aimee have a boyfriend that you know of?"

Jim needed to pee. He hadn't thought to ask before they were shown into the interview room. "No."

"And you thought her parents would have minded that you were friends?"

He pressed his thighs together, but he would need more of a distraction than that. "They wouldn't have liked it."

"Why do *you* think that is?"

His eyes moved to the single window. Its pane was frosted. There was a dead wasp on the sill. "They wouldn't have understood why she wanted to hang out with me."

"And why do you think she did?"

"How should I know?" Jim accidentally met Cowley's eyes: blue, concerned. He looked down and her chest came back into view. *Triumph's got the bra for the way you are.* Down again, until his eyes rested on the pen. A Bic. Plug missing from the end. The plastic slightly chewed.

She had moved on. "Apart from the evening when you found the owl, can you think of anything that upset her?"

There were lots of times, Jim now saw, that Aimee had been upset. What he was missing was reasons. "There was this one time it was getting late. These blokes turned up. I thought that they were going to rough us up, but they just swiped our money."

One of his mother's hands made an appearance on the table top. "You didn't tell me about that!"

"You would've told me not to go back there. We decided that for ourselves."

"When was this?" Cowley refereed, biro stilled and at the ready.

"Two, maybe three weeks ago."

"Did you report it?" Cowley asked.

"No point."

"There's always a point."

"I knew them." He thought that, if he used these words, his mother might understand that Nick had been involved.

"I see," Cowley said. "Did they hurt either of you?"

"One of them had me round the neck." His hand decided to loosen his tie, which suddenly appeared to be stifling him.

"They didn't lay a finger on Aimee - but she was upset. Like I said, we decided not to go back there."

"Where did you go instead?"

"The local parks. To the woods. We went all the way to Box Hill once. On the train."

"What did you do?"

It seemed like an unnecessary question. "What we always did. Bird-watching."

"Tell her about the pictures, Jim," his mother prompted.

"I sketch everything. It's like a record of what I see."

"There's an entry for every day," his mother said. "They're very good."

Cowley smiled. "I don't suppose you brought them with you?"

"No!" He was horrified at the thought of someone looking at his private stuff.

"Another time. Did Aimee seem worried about anything to you?"

She was going to have to give Jim more than that to work on. "Like what?"

"Jim!"

"No, that's alright. Had she argued with any of her friends?"

"I don't know anything about her other friends."

"She hadn't seen any of them for the best part of six weeks. Do you have any idea why that might be?"

"She never talked about them."

"Did she say anything about her family?"

"She told me what her parents did work-wise, stuff like that."

"Do you think she was happy at home?"

This was where he wasn't sure it was his business to say. What was *happy* supposed to mean, anyway? A brief moment - like lying in the grass with sunburn on your face - that you were too scared to acknowledge because that might chase it away.

Cowley's pencilled-in eyebrows, perfect semicircles, lifted. "Jim, Mrs White said that Aimee had a black eye at the beginning of the holidays. Do you know how she might have got it?"

"She didn't say."

"But you saw the black eye?"

He rubbed the inside corner of one of his eyes.

"Jim?" she persisted.

"Alright! Yes, I saw it."

"Did she tell you anything about it?"

The small room appeared to be running short of oxygen. "She said she asked for it." Jim felt as if the words had been squeezed out of him, but it wasn't enough. There were more questions. More and more.

"What did you think she meant by that?"

"Like she said."

Cowley appeared to be waiting for him to expand. "Didn't you ask her what she had done?" she asked at length.

"Where I come from, we don't ask questions."

Jim's mother sat straight-backed, tight-lipped, almost approving.

"How do you think she got it?"

"Looked to me like she'd been beaten up."

"Why do you say that?"

"Her clothes were ripped and she had a bruise on her back." *Damn!*

Cowley held the pen by both ends and rolled it between her fingers. "On her back?"

Too late to back-track, Jim nodded.

The policewoman's expression suggested this was something a mother should have known about. "You *saw* Aimee's back?"

Jim would have liked the comfort of a pen to hold on to. "She showed me," he stammered, looking from one of them to the other.

"What did it look like?"

He shuffled in his seat. "Like a stamp mark."

"It was shaped like someone's shoe?"

"It was more the size of it." Fingers wouldn't do the job: he needed hands to demonstrate.

While Cowley sighed, Jean's hand leapt to her mouth.

"Jim," the policewoman said. "You told me last night that you thought Aimee had walked onto the tracks. What made you say that?"

He sunk further down into the seat and folded his arms.

"Jim?" his mother prompted.

"Jim?" Cowley asked, her voice concerned. "This is important. It sounds as if the two of you were very close."

"Look!" He sat up and raised his voice. "People say stuff all the time! How was I supposed to know she was serious?"

Cowley glanced from his face to his mother's and back again. "You're right, Jim. People do say things like that and it doesn't mean they're going to do anything about it. If Aimee had been serious, we'd have found the evidence by now. Do you understand what I'm saying?"

Jim's lip twitched.

"It's a horrible thing to think about, I know, but, as it is, all we have is the sole of a flip-flop, and it's a common enough type of shoe. And you pointed out yourself that a fox had already had hold of it. Even if it *was* hers, it might have been carried there from somewhere else."

Oh, yes, what a bloody marvellous coincidence that would have been: carried all the way from Beddington Park to the precise place the pair of them went bird-watching!

"Do you hear that, Jim?" His mother put a hand on one of his shoulders. "It might not be Aimee's."

"Stop treating me like an idiot!" Disappointed in his mother, he turned sideways and sat with his head in his hands. "Of course it was hers!"

"He's still very upset," he heard Jean excusing his outburst, as if *he* was being unreasonable and not them.

"Jim, we believe we have a good chance of bringing Aimee home, but the next forty-eight hours will be crucial. We're throwing all of our resources at this. I know it's hard, but you're one of the very few people who -"

"I don't know why you're wasting your time," he mumbled.

"Can you remember exactly what Aimee said?" Cowley urged. "Her precise words."

Jim spoke into his hands. "She said how she'd imagined doing it."

"I'm sorry. I'm going to have to ask you to speak up."

Jim cast his hands aside. "I *said*, she said how when she sat looking at the tracks she imagined doing it."

His mother shook her head. "Poor girl."

"And how did you reply?"

"I told her not to be so stupid. I said she'd be electrocuted before a train got her."

"And then?" Cowley's voice was gentle.

They were both waiting. Looking at him and waiting. There was an electric buzzing in his ears. "Then we laughed." His voice sounded too loud to him. He pushed back his chair and stood. It tipped over, clattering to the floor. "We laughed about it, alright?"

CHAPTER 44:

AYISHA - AUGUST 2010 - AT HOME

Ayisha reached under the shade of the lamp on her bedside table and clicked the switch, releasing a bright halo. Her eyes protested. It was three thirty: half an hour since she last checked the hands of her alarm clock. Sleep had evaded her. Her mind seemed intent on providing a rolling newsreel for the scenes Jim had described.

Like a home-movie projected onto her bedroom wall, she saw a boy and his mother buying flowers from a van. White, like the underfeathers of the owl; white, like the missing girl's surname. A boy approaching the front garden of a large house with a bay window. Aided by recent events at the school, she had no trouble appreciating his shock at the sheer number of handwritten cards, candles and teddy bears. She pictured him running from this place that resembled a shrine, his mother calling after him, "Jim! Slow down, Jim!" He laid the bouquet by the dusty grey remains of the campfire where they had found the owl: their place. The only *respectful* thing to do. He looked up at the bridge and saw his mother beckoning, mouthing a silent *Come on!*

Throwing her duvet aside, Ayisha launched her legs over the side of the bed and edged her toes into her slippers. She sat very still, the cooling heels of her hands pressed against her closed eyelids.

She saw the boy and his mother arriving home to the sight of a police car, its engine running; doors flung open on either side, two policemen throwing their large shiny shoes out, the severe crease of their uniform trousers standing proud.

She saw the mother clutch her handbag and identify herself.

"We need to take the lad in for a few questions."

"Again?" Her voice was weary. "I suppose we may as well get it over with, then," she sighed impatiently, then turned to Jim and whispered, "When they say that Aimee's missing, agree with them. Understand?"

"In the car, please." Ayisha saw a policemen grip the boy's arm, marching him to the car. "Duck," he said, pushing the boy's head free of the door frame.

Ayisha padded into the kitchen and, distracted by moving images that wouldn't be stilled, warmed a pan of milk. After spooning honey into a white mug she sat at the rectangular kitchen table, cradling the mug in both hands. There were three empty seats: room enough for two policemen and a mother.

The room she saw wasn't her kitchen. It was the interview room Jim had described. The peeling tabletop - even the dead wasp - was the same. The questions were similar. It was the intent that was different. Asked about the nature of his relationship with Aimee White, she heard the boy respond, thinking he was giving the response that would send him home.

"She was my friend."

"*Was?*"

"She's gone missing, hasn't she?"

But that wasn't the right answer. They wanted to know if the relationship was physical. Whatever that meant.

"We went bird-watching. Down by the railway tracks."

And they said, "We've been down by the railway tracks and we couldn't find any evidence of bird-watching, but -" A sealed plastic bag full of beer cans and vodka bottles and tea-spoons and foil squares and foil wrappers and used condoms was dumped, unceremoniously, on the table top. "- we found all of this."

Ayisha heard the mother ask, "Is this really necessary?"

Ignoring her protest, one demanded, "Recognise this lot?"

"Even if I did," the boy stammered. "It doesn't make it mine."

The mother said Jim doesn't even smoke, suggested they do a drugs test.

"Tell the truth, we're not interested in the drugs. We're more interested in condoms."

"For crying out loud! He's only just turned twelve!"

"Then he's old enough. Mrs White found a pregnancy-testing kit in the waste. Do you want to know what the result was? Or do you already know?"

Ayisha pictured the boy reeling in shock, looking from one face to another. "No!"

"Because you used one of these?" Sensing doubt, one of the policemen sneered, pointing to something in the bag, something pale, balloon-like.

"Now hang on!" His mother protested. "Jim! Don't say another word."

"You're making it up!" She heard the boy raise his voice. "Aimee wasn't like that."

"Calm down, love." The mother used a restraining hand. "We can clear this up. I expect there are tests you can run on those as well these days."

"We will, don't you worry. It just looks better if the boy volunteers the information."

"Better?" The mother's expression suggested disgust. "This

is a missing girl we're talking about! Rather than pulling young boys in for interview, shouldn't you be out looking for her?"

"It's Jim here who insists we're wasting our time. We've put our heads together and the question we keep coming back to is how can he be so sure?" They turned to look at him. "Well, Jim?"

Why could no one see the obvious? "It was *her* owl, wasn't it?"

The mother stood, her head held high. "We've given you all the help we can. You think I don't know my own son? I've lived with a husband and a son who were bad. You think I can't tell the difference?" And she herded the boy out of the room.

Ayisha released her grip on the mug, finding she needed to wipe away the tears that were streaming down her face. The kitchen table was the kitchen table once more. The silver S-and-P-shaped salt and pepper pots were there in the centre. No longer a uniform jacket, her blazer was just a navy blazer, hanging on the back of a chair.

Jim was a very different man to the teacher she thought she knew. Or perhaps it was that she had led such a sheltered life. At twelve, Ayisha's big rebellion was joining the Girl Guides, a Christian organisation. She was the girl Jim imagined Aimee to be: privileged, her only worries imagined. But, as Shamayal had already recognised, a little money doesn't make you immune. It doesn't make you happy.

Maybe it was good that everything was out in the open. Usually, you gleaned little pieces of information dropped into conversation, as light as feathers: "I saw my little girl at the weekend." "Cheers! Here's to being a divorcée." "Would you mind driving? My ban doesn't expire until next month."

She understood why a boy would love a mother like this, why Jim cherished her memory. She thought of her own mother; of how little she appreciated her. But then she was *so* infuriating!

Abandoning the kitchen table, thinking she should at least rest her eyes, Ayisha climbed back into bed. But the reel refused to stop rolling. Knowing that she wouldn't be able to sleep, she rotated a pillow, plumped it into a shape intended to resemble Jim's shoulder.

"Go on," she encouraged, nestling against it. "I'm listening." And the reel began to roll again.

CHAPTER 45:

AUGUST 1992/ AUGUST 2000

What Jim told Ayisha that he didn't know - wouldn't know for many years - was that, while he curled up on his bed feeling sorry for himself, his mother took his notebook and presented herself a second time at the Whites' imposing front door. It wasn't easy for her. A woman who had thrown her teenage son out onto the streets going to see a mother distraught because her daughter was missing.

What she hadn't told Jim, he explained, was that his sketches of Aimee had troubled her. So much so that she'd studied his notebook after he had gone to bed. In the early hours, sitting at the kitchen table, she had learned that Jim had drawn the sketches before he even spoke to Aimee; before she had told him her name. And when Aimee had arrived at the front door announcing that she'd come to see the owls, recognising her from Jim's sketches, Jean had seen a child in need of poached eggs, the kind of comfort food you might cook for an invalid.

The two mothers sat at the breakfast bar in the Whites' pristine kitchen, Jim's notebook lying in front of them. Jean knew that what she had to do was necessary, but it gave her no pleasure. It clearly pained Aimee's mother to have a stranger show her the sketches, knowing someone else had seen what she had been too busy to. The words he had written couldn't be ignored: *curled in on herself like a wounded animal.* Jean didn't consider herself to be a perfect mother: she empathised with a woman who couldn't keep watch all day, who'd had no option but to trust.

When Mrs Stevens asked if Aimee had a boyfriend, her eyes still fixed on those words, Mrs White simply said, "I suppose she must have done," not entirely believing her latest discovery about her daughter, the same daughter she'd described on national television as outgoing, but with a serious and studious side. "We thought she was too young for that sort of thing."

"But you knew she'd been interested," Jean prompted.

"Whatever do you mean?"

She'd taken the poor woman's arm. "Aimee told me. She said you'd changed your mind about which high school to send her to." She didn't go as far as spelling it out: they'd chosen an out-of-borough, all-girls private school.

"That was my husband's idea."

From this, Mrs Stevens understood that Mrs White really didn't have much idea about what had been going on in her daughter's life. She knew only too well it was possible to miss what was going on under your own roof!

At the sound of the front door being opened there was that terrible fleeting hope that took the form of suspended breath - both of theirs - and then a deep voice called out, "It's me."

Even then, something in Jean's chest lifted and for the briefest of moments, she thought... she thought, *Is it you?* But then she saw the disappointment that Aimee's mother so valiantly tried to hide. One more person, at least, was accounted for. Small mercy, that was something to be grateful for. How many times a day did the poor woman go through this? Jean wondered, exhaling. Every time a floorboard creaked? Every time the cat rattled the cat flap? Every time the phone rang? How many more times *could* she go through this?

Mr White appeared in the doorway, and Jean shared in his obvious fluster to find her sitting with a cup of tea in front of her.

"Mrs Stevens has been kind enough to bring her son's sketches to show us before she takes them to the police."

His wife's explanation didn't appear to calm him. As he perched on the edge of a high stool next to her, Jean said, "I thought it was only fair." It was as much as she could do not to move away. The man's presence made her deeply uncomfortable.

Visibly paling, he used one hand first as a blindfold, then moved it slowly down over the bags under his eyes and the dark stubble until it became a gag. Eventually he spoke: "Your son's talented."

"Thank you."

"But I wonder if he's -" Mr White replaced the gag.

"You wonder if he's what?" his wife coaxed.

"Don't you see?" Mr White said harshly. "Jim has superimposed his knowledge of wildlife on the drawings!"

"I don't think that's in any doubt." Mrs White reached for her husband's arm, only to be shrugged aside.

"You wait: the police will take this completely out of context!"

"But if it helps them find Aimee..." Mrs White was left talking to herself: her husband had walked out onto the patio, his shoulders hunched as he lit a cigarette. "He's under a great deal of stress." She turned to Jean with a wan smile.

It had been Mr White's moment of realisation that it would all come out, all of it. And the newspapers had a field day:

'Family of Aimee White wasted crucial time after disappearance, say police.'

'Mr White's Shame.'

'Father of missing teen swears: It was the first time I ever hit our daughter.'

'Father of missing Aimee tells of "uncontrollable anger".'

Mrs Stevens could turn the news off but, knowing she wouldn't be able to protect Jim once he left the house, she had sat him down and tried to explain. "The poor girl needed understanding, but what she got was violence."

But, although Jim shook, his voice had hardened: "She said she asked for it."

"What she was asking for was *help!*"

'Aimee was found in Bed with Mystery Boy.'

'Boy in Aimee White Scandal Identified.'

'Aimee: Secret Affair with Cousin.'

'Husband's Agony: I Couldn't Even Tell my Wife.'

But they didn't stop there: there were headlines everywhere Jim looked. Not only in the papers but on billboards; on the front page of the local *Guardian* that was shoved through the letterbox.

'Missing Teen May Have Been Pregnant.'

'My Pregnancy Scare Almost Drove me to Suicide, claims Soap Star.'

'Parents of Missing Teen Separate.'

'Exclusive: Cousin in Missing Aimee Tragedy Speaks Out.'

From his hospital bed, Jim recounted for Ayisha how, when he was an adult, Jean had told him what had struck her the most was how Mr White hit out at Aimee rather than the boy. Of how he could understand the cousin's behaviour better than he could his own daughter's. She assumed he felt betrayed to find his little girl had grown up - without his even noticing - and so he had punished her. Jim told Ayisha that it had only been then that he understood: his mother had always trusted him.

Ayisha's eyes were full. "It's no wonder Aimee enjoyed

your company. You gave her something to take her mind off her troubles," she said.

"For a while!" Jim had been dismissive as, lying in the hospital bed, he recounted to Ayisha what his mother had told him.

"Don't you see?" Ayisha persevered. "It was only when Aimee was prevented from seeing you that she couldn't cope at home anymore."

"I don't know about that. Anyway," he sighed. "The press had their villains and a new victim in Mrs White, while Aimee - well, she was virtually forgotten."

"And you went on believing she was dead?"

He nodded slowly. "I still do. At least I could mourn. Mrs White held a press conference on the first anniversary of Aimee's disappearance and the four that followed. 'It's the uncertainty,' she said. 'I can't help thinking the worst, but I have to go on hoping. Somewhere, there's a grandchild I would very much like to meet.' How can you live like that?"

"What about the cousin?" Ayisha asked.

"Who knows? He wasn't my focus. It's possible that he may have really loved her."

Jim looked drained. It was clear that his efforts had exhausted him. But he also looked relieved. "I'm glad you trusted me enough to tell me."

In bed, nestling against the shoulder-shaped pillow, Ayisha's thoughts turned to Shamayal. His plan for disappearing himself seemed so ideal that she couldn't understand why he hadn't taken the option earlier. The boy needed his mother. This was something she could agree to help with in good conscience. And she wanted to help.

She thumbed through the dog-eared book of British birds, lingering at the section on owls. Jim wasn't allowed personal possessions in H.D.U. and so he had entrusted them to her.

"For Shamayal... tell him -"

"I'll tell him to make good use of them," she'd forced her-self to say, the thought that Jim was giving away the things that were most precious to him leaving her cold. Critical but stable, he was far from being out of danger. "Back to the beginning," was what he had said.

If there was one thing she could do for Jim, it was to play her part in delivering the boy to a place of safety. And to secure Shamayal's safety - and Jim's peace of mind - she was prepared to lie. The boy would insist on turning back if he knew Jim was in danger. This time there was no moral dilemma: Ayisha couldn't tell him.

CHAPTER 46:

SHAMAYAL - AUGUST 2010 -
THE BOILER ROOM

S hamayal had been sitting in the humid darkness for too long. Sweat trickled down the hollow of his spine in rivulets. He stripped off some of the layers Bins insisted he had worn but, without them, there was little protection against the roughness of the brick wall. The only sounds were the rumbling of his stomach and the purring of the boiler. Mickey Mouse, wearing red shorts and braces, was cheerfully pointing out higher and higher numbers with his yellow boxing gloves, some combinations requiring a greater degree of contortion, his legs cowboyed to fit the confined space.

"What are you so happy about? You're stuck, ain't you? In the same predicament as me."

Mickey grinned back.

"Yeah, yeah. Ain't no one ever told you how annoyin' you are? Listen to me! Am I for real? Talkin' to a stupid watch!"

He heard knocking, the sound of the padlock - *shit!* - and, pushing with his heels, scuffled back behind the boiler. The effort had used up all of his concentration: he had forgotten to drag the discarded waterproofs. Nuffin he could do about it now. His heart a drum kit, he applied childhood logic: if his eyes were clamped shut, he couldn't be seen. The insides of his lids were orange. He willed himself not to breathe.

"Kaw, kaw," came a familiar voice.

Shamayal's ribs cracked as his chest deflated, his bad eye pained him as it unscrunched. "Thought you'd forgotten about me, Mr Crow."

"Is that you, Invisible Man?" The beam from Bins's flashlight tunnelled through the dark.

"Ain't no one else stupid enough to hang out in here!" Shamayal held one hand up to shield his eyes. "I don't suppose you got any food?"

Bins put the torch in his mouth, reached in one pocket, extracted something, then rummaged in the other and pulled out a Mars Bar.

"Proper genius!" Relieved to find its wrapper intact, Shamayal ripped through the paper with his teeth and spat it aside.

"There's more."

"Yeah?" The boy took a hungry bite, his mamma's voice reminding him to chew.

Bins opened the door and leaned out to speak to someone. Shamayal couldn't hear the words but it sounded as if negotiations were taking place. Surely Bins wouldn't have sold him out?

The door opened wider. Accustomed to the dark by now, Shamayal could just make out the old man's grinning face. "I got you transport for the first leg. This is Nick Stevens."

The owl killer! The caramel coating his mouth turned sickly.

"Hello, Shamayal." A crouching man deposited something heavy on the floor and extended a hand. His balding head loomed large. "I'm Jim's big brother."

"What kinda shit is this?" Shamayal protested, agape.

"It's alright, Invisible Man," Bins said. "Jim said it was A-OK."

"He won't have nuffin to do with him! Why should I trust him?"

"You're low on options," the man replied. "And no one else was available on short notice. Your stuff's already in my van -"

"You been in my flat?" Words flew at the thought of this violation. "You tol' my dad where I am?"

"He wasn't at home. But I did leave a note."

"You wh- are you mental?" Before he thought what he was doing, Shamayal's arms cut through the air and the pain was fresh agony. "Fuck! Man!"

"Calm down -"

"You want me to calm down? I'm up to my neck in ten kinds of shit and you go wadin' in, makin' it worse!" If Shamayal could have moved, he would have been right in the man's face, pointing.

"Do you want to hear what the note said?"

"You're crazy, you know that?"

"The note said, 'Your son is in trouble. He's done nothing wrong. We are taking him somewhere safe.' Don't you think he deserves that much?"

"How d'you get into my flat, anyhow?" he demanded.

"I'm a locksmith."

Shamayal remembered Jim telling him that his brother had always been an authority on locks. Now, it seemed, he had made a profession out of it. Sniffing, he felt as if he might actually break down. Control of the situation running away from him, he was reduced to basics. "You got my good kecks, right?"

"I brought as much as would fit in a kitbag."

"Did anyone see you?"

"Like I said, I'm a locksmith. People look right through me."

He sniffed again. "Right, right."

"All set?"

"Don't look like I got a fat lotta choice, does it?"

"The van's backed up to the door. There are blankets in the back. I'll just finish up on the door here, then we'll be off."

Nick ducked out, leaving the boy and the old man alone in the semi-dark. Shamayal wanted to be angry, but it wasn't the old guy's fault. Like the man said, his options were zilch. "I should get changed so I can give you your fishin' gear back."

"Do you think there'll be a river where you're going?"

"S'pose there might be."

"Keep it," Bin offered.

"Thanks, thanks." Shamayal tried to sound appreciative, although fishing was low on his agenda. "Hey, you fink Nick's OK?"

"He's an excellent driver."

"But is he cool, man? Would you go with him?"

"No -"

"See!" Shamayal's arms were pinned to his sides. Panic set in before common sense. It had been a long time since anyone had hugged him.

"I'm staying. I've got a business to run. Would I go with him if I were you? That's the question you should have asked."

"And?" He let himself go limp in the old man's arms, feeling his body heat.

"Of course I would!"

"Right, right." Shamayal had to believe it. What else could he do? He closed his eyes and breathed. "Then I guess this is it for you and me."

"High five!"

But the boy rested his chin on a shoulder. "Man, this sucks! I was only just gettin' to know you, you know?" Too late for reservations, he laughed despite himself. "You sure you don't wanna come with me? My mamma won't mind. I never had no granddaddy."

"Aw." Bins extracted himself. The torch back in his mouth,

343

he raised his hand, insistent on the high five. Fighting the pain, Shamayal went through the whole made-up handshake routine. The old guy had earned it.

Nick tucked his head inside the door. "All clear. It's time to go."

Shamayal rearranged his nose. "Keep an eye on my dad for me. You don't have to talk to him or nuffink."

The dark outside wasn't as dark as the dark inside the boiler room.

"Sun'll be up soon," Nick said as Shamayal took one last sideways glance at the silhouettes of the Lego-brick towers, all of those people piled on top of each other. Somewhere, music was playing, the *boom-boom* of a drum. Lady Gaga had gone and left her head on the dance floor again.

Bins was right behind him. "Don't stand for any crap."

The boy sat carefully - "You're family, man!" - then twisted his legs so that he was in the back of the van. Nick put his toolbox inside, whistling. "Lock me in, yeah?"

The door was slammed - the force hitting him like a slap - but he heard the jangle of keys. Muted conversation, just an old man passing the time of day with a locksmith. The cold floor below Shamayal's knees was ridged. There were no windows to let the light in - more importantly, no windows to let prying eyes in. He groped around and located his kitbag, felt for the zip, identified a hoodie by touch and shape. Raising his arms over his head to put it on sent pain ripping through his torso. "I fought I told you guys to mend!" he scolded his ribs, but the fleecy lining soothed his skin. A nest of blankets, a pillow of clothes, he lay down and curled himself up with his T-Rex arms folded over his sore ribs. His head jolted. Only a speed bump. Still, this wasn't going to be no comfortable ride. Corners sent the toolbox sliding. Shamayal rotated by moving his feet until he thought his head was safely out of the way. He would only relax when he arrived at the service station.

To calm himself, he imagined being in his father's minicab, driving through night-time streets. Open his good eye and he would see the domes of the big Tesco not doing a very good imitation of Brighton Pavilion. Next stop, Heathrow. Then the corners stopped. The stop-start ceased: open road. He was on his way. For better or for worse.

CHAPTER 47:

AYISHA - AUGUST 2010 -
MOTORWAY SERVICE STATION

Seated by the window, Ayisha nursed a cup of coffee, keeping one eye on the service station car park and the other on the sliding doors. She had been surprised by how many people were up and about at this time of the morning, how she had been unable to escape the statutory RAC salesman, how frequently she'd needed to defend the chairs slotted under her three-person table. Tired-looking businessmen stared at sports pages while devouring full English breakfasts en route to appointments. Their female colleagues rotated compact mirrors to check their make-up, portion by portion: smoothing eyebrows; widening eyes. Quick-marching mothers hauled toddlers in the direction of the toilets, scolding, "If you'd have gone before we set off..." Toes just touching, a young couple sat exchanging shy smiles. Ayisha felt envy: *Oh, for something so uncomplicated.*

Items were snatched up from the tabletop adjacent to hers and a none-too-clean looking dish cloth swiped briefly. She hooked her knees to the side so that the floor could be mopped.

As she was tearing off a morsel of blueberry muffin, she

heard a familiar voice, "Yo, Miss!"

Swivelling round, she wondered how she could have missed Shamayal's arrival, then her smile froze. "My God, your face!" The words were out before she could help herself. The boy winced away from her.

"I'm Nick," the man accompanying him said, extending one hand.

"Ayisha," she responded automatically. There was an awkward moment's silence. "Breakfast!" Picking up her bag, she slung its strap over one shoulder. "Who's having what? My shout."

She was glad for the queue at the counter; time to gather her thoughts - what she must and must not say - while sandwiches were toasted and pastries crushed by stainless steel tongs; as she inserted her card into the machine to pay, side-stepped other customers with a tray held high, identified sandwich fillings and sidled back into position.

"So, you work with my brother?" Nick asked.

"That's right." Her hands sought refuge on the side of her second cup of coffee. In dire need of a caffeine hit, her eyes felt tight and heavy, her skin pinched.

Nick wrapped his B-L-T panini in a paper serviette and picked it up with both hands. "Is he any good?"

"I've never seen him in action. What's your verdict, Shamayal?"

"He shows you stuff. He don't just say, 'Open a book and read,' like most teachers."

As stinted attempts at polite conversation continued, Ayisha studied Nick. So unlike his brother and yet the odd mannerism, the odd facial expression, suggested shared DNA. She felt more comfortable looking at him than trying to ignore the swelling on Shamayal's face. This was the man Jim might have become, had he not met Aimee White in the summer of his twelfth year.

As if reading her thoughts, Nick extracted a small square photograph from his wallet. "The four of us." Flat-palmed, he pushed it across the table towards her. "There aren't many pictures of us as a family. In fact, this might be the only one. There was usually someone missing."

Your father, no doubt, Ayisha thought.

He deferred to Shamayal. "It wasn't like today when everyone has cameras on their phones and snaps away all the time."

Ayisha couldn't help but feel touched. This man who didn't see his family carried a photograph of them in his wallet. The father, handsome and with sideburns, had one hand on each of his sons' shoulders. The mother's head was turned to kiss her husband's cheek. "Has Jim seen this?" She smoothed a crease out of one corner of the white frame.

"I doubt he remembers it."

Ayisha suspected the sight of his father posing as the family man might anger Jim. But the boys were jostling with each other, sharing a joke, and the mother appeared to be happy - not as Ayisha had imagined her, but somehow beautiful.

"Let's have a look!" Acknowledging that Shamayal was in no fit state to gallop his chair round the table, she handed him the photograph. "Man, who's that short arse? No way that's Jim."

Nick nodded: "Weedy little sod."

"For real? He's, like, six foot three."

"That's how I remember my brother. It was a shock seeing him lying in hospital, I can tell you."

It seemed strange that Nick expressed his shock in terms of his brother's height. Ayisha held her breath, expecting that at any moment one of them would ask *By the way, how is he?*

"He'd tower above me now. I stopped growing at sixteen. I hope you don't smoke, Shamayal."

At least this was a conversation she could contribute to. "That was the age you left home at, wasn't it?" Suddenly Ayisha worried that she had asked something terribly personal, but Nick didn't seem to take offence.

"Sixteen." He shook his head. "God, I was a mess! You name it, I was doing it. I'm not proud of myself. It took me years to get my act together." He addressed Shamayal. "The old man back there?"

"Bins?" Shamayal asked, a burger suspended halfway to his mouth.

"He put me up while I got myself clean."

"No kiddin'? Man, p'rhaps he *is* some kind of guardian angel!"

"He certainly was mine. Anyway," he checked his watch nervously. "I should get going. I'm on call. Thanks for breakfast, Ayisha. You tell that brother of mine... tell that brother of mine..." Faltering, he studied the photograph again before slotting it back into place. "Tell him Mum did the right thing. He'll know what I mean."

Knowing what he meant, Ayisha wondered what effort it took him to say this. "I'll tell him."

"Good luck, mate." He squeezed rather than shook the boy's hand. "Hope it all works out."

"You too, man." Ayisha observed that the boy looked sheepish. "Hey, thanks. I'm sorry 'bout what I said before. I never been kidnapped before -"

"Smuggled."

"Right, right. You did a good job. If you ever need a reference..."

Ayisha observed Shamayal watching Nick leave. He lifted one hand gingerly as Nick saluted from the door. She had time for a good inspection of his swollen eye, the red that should have been white, before the boy turned back to her. "He din't seem as bad as I thought. You think people can change?"

She tried to disguise her spark of anger. "We all make mistakes."

"What you goin' to tell Jim?"

There was a moment - just a moment - when she thought that Shamayal deserved the truth. The boy had put himself in danger, not only in running to Jim's rescue but in continuing their relationship, knowing all that time what it might lead to. He had taken more risks than Ayisha - and possibly even Jim - had. It had only ever been her job that was on the line, but this loyalty, this friendship, was real. Just as the boy had said it was. "I'll tell him about the photograph." It would be nice if Nick had the chance to tell Jim the rest.

Shamayal frowned. "Don't go stickin' your nose in, Miss."

"As always, that's extremely good advice."

"The situation... as I see it, it's complicated."

Yawning, Ayisha programmed the postcode Shamayal gave her into the satnav of her Mini. Caffeine wasn't compensation for lack of sleep. She distrusted the wired feeling it gave her. "Don't you think you should call your mother?"

"I want to see the look on her face when she turns around and sees it's me."

Looking at Shamayal's swollen face, Ayisha couldn't help flinching at the image this conjured up.

"What? You don't like surprises?"

Leaning across the handbrake, she pulled down the sun visor and lifted the cover of the mirror in front of him.

"Man, they mashed me up good and proper!" He pulled his beanie a shade lower and sunk back into the seat. It was as much as he was going to tell her. "Miss, you used to live somewhere else, din't you? What was that like?"

"It was very different." She buckled up. "Small. Quiet."

"Why d'you leave?"

"After I did my teacher training it felt - I don't know - claustrophobic when I went back home. Too much pressure." She refrained from saying that if he ever met her mother he would understand.

An unnecessarily complicated series of white arrows led back to the slip road, by-passing the queues at the petrol pumps. Ayisha waited for an articulated lorry to pass and then accelerated into the flow of the motorway.

"Get me, runnin' away."

"We're nearly halfway. You're not running anymore: you're moving towards your new home." Gripping the steering wheel, Ayisha risked taking her eyes off the road for a second, looked in the mirror and saw doubt she hadn't anticipated.

"Miss, does the smell of cut grass really stop you breathin'?"

"Where did you hear that?" She laughed.

He shrugged defensively. "Only aksin'."

"It's the smell of silage you want to worry about!" She pressed a button and Shamayal's window slid down, allowing the sickly-sweet smell into the car.

"Whoa! Are you for real?"

She laughed at the sight of his appalled expression in the rear-view mirror; the window sliding back up.

"You could have warned me, Miss!"

Seeing how coughing pained him, she relented and pointed to the dashboard. "Look in the glove box."

Shamayal leant forwards carefully and took out the carrier bag, its spare plastic doubled around the package. He weighed it in one hand and said, "I know what this is," before looking inside. "Jim's binoculars. And his book!"

"He wanted you to have them."

"Man, he din't hafta do that. They're, like, his history." The word was said with respect. "There's a whole load of stories to go with these."

It was a sobering thought. Maybe, if Jim pulled through, it would be possible for him to let go of the more painful of them. It might even be possible for him to forgive the person who once took punches for him. History meant something in Jim's world.

"When I first went to his place, yeah? I picked them up and he was like, 'Get your hands off my stuff.'" Shamayal slid the binoculars out of their case reverentially and hung them round his neck, even though the effort clearly pained him. "I don't want him goin' and thinkin' I was just another person who left."

"He won't."

From the corner of her eye, Ayisha saw Shamayal rearrange his nose. "You know, Bins will never recognise him now."

Bins, who had stood guard outside the hospital, refusing to leave until he heard that Jim's condition was stable.

"There was some reason - I never got to the bottom of it - but Jim stopped bird-watching for a few years."

Saying nothing, Ayisha thought she knew why.

"That's when he got fixated on his history books."

Aimee's gift.

"Then one day he saw Bins and the old man didn't know who he was. Jim called out to say hello, but Bins blanked him like he was a stranger, you know? He had to tell him his name and everything. 'Jim Stevens?' he asked, like he was some distant memory or somethink. 'You haven't got your binoculars on. That's like me not having my fishing rod.' Those were their things, yeah? Jim had his binoculars, see, and Bins had his fishing rod. And Jim goes, 'You'd still be you without your fishing rod.' 'Ah, but would I, Jim Stevens? Would I?' Next day, Jim finds hisself talkin' to a robin. That's when he started up again."

Ayisha discovered she was smiling. "What do you think you wouldn't be yourself without?"

"Dunno. Might be handy not bein' recognised, you know?"

She indicated left. "This next junction's ours."

"Thank Christ!" He sniffed. "No disrespect, Miss, but you're not that great a driver."

"You ungrateful little -" She went to swat his knee and

deliberately missed. *Eyes on the road.* "I got up at the crack of dawn for you!"

"Hee-hee-hee. Let Jim do the drivin'. But keep this car. A Mini trumps a Corsa any day."

Before long, they were no longer driving on A-roads by the side of fields: they were driving on single-track roads that dissected fields, hedged with hawthorn and hazel. While Ayisha worried what she would do if she met a tractor coming in the opposite direction, Shamayal said excitedly, "Hey, you know what? This is actual hedgerow!"

She had been trying to keep the wheels in between crenulated mud-tracks deposited by farm vehicles, but swerved to avoid roadkill. "I suppose it is."

"Proper owl country." He had dropped the almost compulsory questions tagged onto the end of sentences. "I never seen one of those. Not yet. I'd like to tick one of them off of my list."

Be careful what you wish for, she thought. But his enthusiasm was contagious, and she began to enjoy herself. "From the state of the roads, it looks as if it's badger country."

"Is that what they are?"

"Were," she said with emphasis.

"True, true." Shamayal turned his head for a better look at the entrails. "How far is it now?"

"Only another five miles or so." As she said it, Ayisha felt a dip of disappointment. Five more miles; perhaps ten minutes, and then...

"This won't be far from where I live. I could walk here if I wanted."

They approached a five-way junction with a painted road sign. Ayisha consulted the dashboard, backed up a few feet and turned left alongside a river. There was a church with a spire, a pub, a primary school, a signpost pointing down an unmarked road that said *Village Store*. Ayisha wondered how

Shamayal would cope here, but it wasn't her choice to make. She was simply the chauffeur.

She pulled over opposite the store, cranked on the hand-brake, killed the engine. "How did you manage to hide it from your father that you stayed in touch with your mother all these years?"

Grinning, he showed her a mobile phone, not a shiny slim-line model, but the kind of plastic-looking phone you might give a child. "No Ralegh Boy would be seen dead with this. I got your number in here too. Emergencies and all that. Hey! You're going to like my mamma, cast-iron guarantee."

Now that they had arrived, and faced with the prospect of saying goodbye, Ayisha acknowledged that she didn't feel predisposed towards the woman who had abandoned her ten-year-old son. "Let's get your bag out of the boot."

Their hands collided as they both reached for the handle. Shamayal pulled back, cradling his torso. There was no way he would be capable of lifting. He grinned, a hint of his usual self. "You tryin' to make a move on me, Miss? Go ahead. Might be your last chance."

"I'll risk that." Ayisha hoisted the bag over one shoulder and staggered. "This weighs a tonne!"

"Careful. That's everything I own."

"First thing you need to do is register for school, you hear me?"

She followed Shamayal up the two steps to the shop. There were sweet jars in the window: proper old-fashioned jars filled with sherbet pips and aniseed twists and fruit salads, over-sized lollies and boxes of toffees whose picture-postcard packaging had been bleached by the sun. A bell over the door jangled as they stepped inside. Ayisha put the bag down at the first opportunity. Behind the counter a short woman was rearranging tins of baked beans. She was wearing traditional African dress, as if her role was to provide novelty value. She turned to them, ready with her *Can I help you?* but before the words were out her face was transformed by a range of emotions. "Son?"

Shamayal nodded to one of the sweet jars, his voice serious. "A quarter of chocolate limes, please."

Astonishment moved to excitement. "Tell me it's you!" She struggled to move a display of newspapers aside so that she could lift a hatch in the counter, her hands dancing impatiently as if she couldn't go fast enough. Briefly, Ayisha set aside her earlier reservation and allowed herself to feel happy for Shamayal - this is how it should feel to be greeted. Here he was in front of her, clearly delighted: "It's me, Mamma!"

The woman tried to cradle him, but at barely five foot she settled for clamping his arms to his sides, insisting, "Tell me again." As she pressed her face sideways against his chest, her eyes closed in pleasure. "I've waited four years to see my boy and look at you: grown into a man!"

He shouldn't have to be a man at fourteen, Ayisha reflected, but he was. He might even turn out to be a good one - if he could drop the talk. No thanks to his mother.

"How did you get here?"

"I hitch-hiked. This lady gave me a lift." He was sticking to the story they had agreed on. Ayisha was to remain anonymous. Guard lowered, Shamayal sounded childlike as he asked, "Can I stay with you, Mamma?"

"Course you can, baby," she cooed. "Whatever happened to your face? Your father do this to you?"

Despite relief that her part was over, Ayisha found she was frowning. However concerned she sounded, if Shamayal's mother thought - even for a moment - that her husband was capable of *this,* how could she have left him behind? Was it Shamayal's choice (if 'choice' was the right word for a ten-year-old who has been the referee in his parents' relationship)? Did he stay because his father would never give up looking if both of them went? Or was it possible that the father was the better option? Perhaps, over the past four years, Shamayal had granted his mother saint-like status. Ayisha didn't care how bad things were, a mother who abandons her ten-year-old son didn't deserve to be raised up on a pedestal.

"No, Mamma, I was jumped. You got to stop squeezing. They broke some of my ribs."

"Let me feast my eyes." Her hands reached up to his face and, although Shamayal flinched, he didn't pull away.

A private moment. Ayisha felt the need to extract herself, and quickly. She wanted to get back to Jim's bedside. She cleared her throat. "I'll be off, then. Take care, Shamayal."

He was standing behind his mother, his hands on her shoulders. "Miss…" he ventured, then stopped as he realised his slip-up.

"Don't worry," she said, words heavy with meaning. "I was glad to."

But he followed her out of the shop door, closing it behind him and stood on the top step.

"Don't. Don't you dare." She swiped at the corners of her eyes. "Too many goodbyes."

"I wasn't gonna. My mamma sent me out with a bottle of water for you. She said you must be parched." He lowered his voice. "Did you know your skirt goes see-through in the light? I mean, I ain't got no problem with it. Fact, I'm all for that sort of thing."

"It does not!" But, looking down, she thought, *Oh God, it does! I hope Jim didn't notice.*

"F'you say so." Grinning. "Then you won't mind if I watch you walk to the car."

"Go back inside!" She batted the air behind her, running across the road.

Raising the binoculars to his eyes, he studied her and then angled his head sharply upwards. "You're not going to believe this!" he said in awe.

With one hand on the driver's door, Ayisha shielded her eyes and followed the line of his gaze to a black speck. "What is it?"

"That crazy pigeon followed me here!"

Perhaps this had been the right thing to do. Let's face it, if the boy could get excited about vermin, he was going to be fine. Her three-point turn, on the other hand, was a disaster. She blamed her lack of sleep. There was a ditch on either side of the road and she worried about ending up in it. By point three, she saw in the rear view mirror that Shamayal had gone back inside the shop. By point five he was back outside, his bag lying by his feet, the mother nowhere to be seen.

She pushed a button in the recess of the door and the window slid down. "Forgotten something?" she asked as casually as possible.

"Need another lift, Miss, don't I?"

"Get in," she said, wondering, *What the hell do I do now?* No nearer to a decision after loading the boot, Ayisha found Shamayal slumped in the passenger seat, knees nudging the door, arms folded.

"Fought I was only stayin' the weekend, din't she?"

"She asked you to leave?"

"Not exactly. There's only one room comes with the job. 'Parrently, there aren't too many buses. She said I was best off tryin' to catch up with you."

Ayisha bet she did! Making a meal of buckling herself in, she hated the fact that her instincts had been proven right. She felt it was up to her to make sense of the situation, but no words came to mind.

"Can we at least drive off down the road? She might be lookin' out the window."

Glancing in the rear-view mirror, Ayisha nudged the car into gear. Done with feasting her eyes, there was still no sign of the woman. Ayisha drove slowly, wondering if, having changed her mind, she would come running. But no.

"Just drop me some place. I don't care where."

"I'm *not* just dropping you!"

The boy sat up as they reached the junction, preparing to get out. "You haff to."

Ayisha stole a glance at the boy in the seat beside her as she took a left turn. She felt devastated on his behalf. There was no need to ask how he was feeling. Her thoughts turned to her own parents: self-sacrificing; solid; predictable. She may never have seen that look of joy on her mother's face, but she would never have to hear words of rejection.

Obeying a sudden impulse, Ayisha disobeyed the satnav and turned left at a signpost down an unfamiliar road towards a familiar name. In reverse, the fields were left behind, narrow lanes were buttressed by pavements; white lines marked the centre of roads; speed limits and requests to drive carefully through villages came into view. Shamayal turned to stare unhappily at a young black boy walking a dog. Eventually, she arrived at a roundabout she recognised. From here, the Mini knew the way.

"Where are we?" Shamayal asked as she cranked on the handbrake.

A face appeared at the bay window, then the front door opened inwards, the same face aglow, the crunch of gravel. "Ayisha, darling!" Her mother bent into view, her smile beaming. "How lovely. I wasn't expecting you!"

And Ayisha understood something she had never realised before. This was how it would always be if she surprised her mother.

CHAPTER 48:

NINA - AUGUST 2010 - WILTSHIRE

Gravel redistributed itself under Nina's sandals. It was immediately apparent that something was very wrong. The boy in the passenger seat was leaning against the door: his forehead; the elbow of a folded arm; his knees. He had the stance of someone who had been utterly let down. She selected an expression fit for a goddess as her daughter emerged from the car. "You're not on your own, I see."

"No."

It wasn't very much to go on. The reflection in the windscreen shifted, allowing a view of the boy's swollen face. Breath catching in her throat, Nina was glad she had already settled on her expression. Ayisha crunched around to the passenger door and helped the boy to his feet. His elbows were tight against his sides, hands high over his chest.

"Mum, this is Shamayal."

For a moment the car door was a shield between them, then she saw the corners of his mouth move: an attempt at a smile, as much as he could offer. He could barely bring himself to look at her. It must have taken all of his effort to say, "You must be Mrs Emmanuel."

Her daughter's expression was anxious, as if she was just holding on. She didn't gush, *Call me Nina*. "I don't know what my daughter's told you about me, but I don't bite."

Shamayal appeared to hesitate. "She ain't... she hasn't told me nothin'" He closed his eyes and corrected himself. "Anything."

Nina broadened her smile, masking disappointment: the truth didn't surprise her terribly much. "Go inside. Make yourself at home." She shepherded them into the house, through the hallway.

Her daughter's head twisted towards her. "Is that lamb I can smell?"

If Ayisha wanted to pretend this was an ordinary visit, that was fine. "Ah, you're in luck. You'll both be staying for lunch, I hope?"

"If that's alright. You'll love my mother's roast lamb," Ayisha told the boy. "She marinades it in yoghurt with chilli, ginger and garlic."

"Listen to you, giving away my secret recipe!" Nina scolded, with a certain amount of pride.

"Shamayal's quite a cook."

He paused again at the threshold of the large bright room that spanned the width of the house, and looked out to the garden beyond. Looking for somewhere to hide, Nina thought.

"My husband keeps koi," she explained, walking towards the open French windows and, as she did so, she saw the heron; a silent shadow, biding his time. "I don't believe it! This is his second visit today. I've already been out to chase him off. I don't suppose you'd...?" She deferred to Shamayal, who understood this as his invitation to go outside. "Tea?" she asked her daughter.

Ten minutes later, sitting at the kitchen table, a story was unfolding, her daughter unravelling. After what she had seen of the news, little of it came as a surprise, except in terms of the extent of Ayisha's involvement. How she could have kept all this to herself at her last visit, Nina didn't know. Probably, she had wanted to spare her father. He did fuss so.

"I don't understand it, Mum. I don't understand how she could leave him behind in the first place. He was only ten! And how she could reject him now, when he obviously needs her. The really sad thing is that Shamayal idolised his mother."

Nina sighed: one snip and the thread is broken. "And how did Shamayal end up in that mess?"

"Loyalty," Ayisha replied. A single word. A good word. Not a bad boy then. One worth going to an awful lot of effort for, apparently. Nina observed Ayisha's face, her daughter's dark eyes, rimmed in red. "You look exhausted, darling."

"Jim's back in intensive care. I didn't sleep properly last night."

Nina refrained from commenting about the mysterious Jim. Piece by piece, she must compile a picture of him, as clues are dropped into the conversation as lightly as feathers.

"And you drove all this way?"

"I didn't know what else to do. I was so sure that *this* would be the answer, but…"

Ayisha nodded towards Shamayal and Nina shifted her gaze to the boy. A mother has to train herself not to offer opinions to her adult daughter. She must wait until she is asked. There was no sign of the heron and the boy was sitting, his back to them, his head low.

"What do you think he's doing out there?" Ayisha asked at length.

"I expect he's talking to the fish. They're very good at keeping secrets."

Her daughter laughed. "What kind of secrets do you have?"

She didn't intend to be cruel, Nina conceded. It was simply

that Ayisha couldn't imagine the kind a mother harboured. Nina recalled the last time she confided in the fish after ending up in tears on the phone to her daughter. She restricted herself to what she hoped would be interpreted as a knowing sigh. She may have been a little selfish. Of course, she'd had no idea what was going on in the background. Ayisha had opened up to her today in a way she hadn't for years. Nina felt her daughter taking one of her hands.

"I'm glad I've never had to know how Shamayal feels." Ayisha stopped short of saying *Thank you, you were a wonderful mother*, but, with Nina's heart skipping a beat, it was enough. The fact that she had come to her when she had run out of options spoke volumes.

As if reading her mind, Ayisha leant her head against Nina's shoulder. "Thank you for worrying about me, Mum. I do appreciate it."

She felt a second lurch in her chest and tried to make her voice ordinary. "It's what I signed up for, isn't it?"

"But not this! I've messed up, haven't I?"

Her instinct was to protect her daughter, but Ayisha had made it clear that her concern was for the boy. And with her daughter's head still resting on her shoulder, Nina said, "For all the right reasons. You've made me very proud."

"I've been so scared that I would lose my job. So - so worried about letting you and Dad down."

"Nonsense. You've acted selflessly, just as I would expect."

"I've broken every rule in the book!"

"If the rules are unworkable, what choice do you have, hmm?"

Ayisha's hair curtained her face as she sat back, looking floored. "What do you think I should do?"

Nina weighed what she knew of the situation, aware that she had only been given the edited highlights - barely enough to counter her husband's inquisition. "Let's think this through. This mother of Shamayal's will have to phone her husband and tell him what's happened."

"I don't know. It's a strange set up."

"We have to assume she'll feel *some* guilt!"

Raising her eyebrows, Ayisha appeared to concede this.

"And as far as she's concerned, he will have hitch-hiked after you dropped him off."

A reasonable starting point. Nina needed time to think, to concoct a story. "I want you to go and have a lie down. I'll call you when lunch is ready."

"No," her daughter groaned, just as she used to as a little girl when told it was bedtime. "I need to stay awake."

"Do as your mother tells you, Ayisha. The best thing you can do is get yourself back to London, but you're not driving anywhere without a rest and a good meal."

"I can't leave Shamayal…"

"You may have to. Ah!" She looked up to see Shamayal conscientiously wiping his feet on the outside mat. "Here he is! Let me pour you some tea."

Beyond the swelling Nina observed a good-looking boy. The day had been tough on him, and Nina admired his lack of self-pity. Important to keep pity out of her own expression.

"My daughter and I have just been talking. Don't stand on ceremony. Have a seat, have a seat." Only once the boy was seated uncomfortably did she ask, "What is it you want, Shamayal?"

His answer was a shrug. It seemed to matter little to him.

"I can only work out how to help you if you talk to me."

He looked into his teacup. "None of this is what I wanted, is it?"

Nina was put in her place. "No." She paused. "Let me put it another way. One of us is going to have to pick up the phone and call someone. We need to decide who makes the call and who to ring."

Unimpressed, Shamayal turned to Ayisha, "Miss -"

"No," Nina said firmly. "Ayisha isn't here. She can't be here."

"Then what am I doin' here?"

This question forced Nina to think out loud. "I picked you up at the service station on the way home from visiting my daughter in London, just intending to drive you a few miles and drop you off, but we got talking and I discovered that you attend the school my daughter teaches at. And, naturally, I've been following the news. So when you told me you were the boy who helped Mr Stevens, and why you needed to leave, I volunteered to drive you to your mother's."

Ayisha picked up the thread. "And you could hardly leave him there, so you brought him back here and -"

"Not knowing who else to ring, I called my daughter. What then?"

"I gave you Mr Peel's phone number. He's the school's Designated Person."

"Who?"

"He's the person who deals with child protection issues."

"Hang about, Miss. He'll just ring Social Services, won't he?" Shamayal cut in sharply. "They'll make me go back, even though it's not safe."

"Look at him, Mum! He can't go back."

Oh, but you can! Nina thought. But countering this attitude was the beginning of acceptance that Ayisha had important work to do in London.

"What happens if you ring both my parents? See if either of them actually wants me."

It struck Nina then: "The reason you couldn't stay with your mother was lack of space, wasn't it?"

"That's what she said."

"If you want to live with your mother, the council would be under an obligation to house you both."

Nodding her agreement, Ayisha turned to Shamayal,

asking silently if he would be prepared to give her another chance.

It was too much to expect of the boy when he was so fragile. What he needed was time. Nina thought she might be able to buy it for him. "Would Social Services get involved in a private arrangement?" she asked her daughter.

"I don't see how they'd know. Unless the child had been identified as being at risk."

"So if I were to offer temporary accommodation and your parents consented - just for you, I mean - while you think about your next step."

"You'd do that?" the boy asked, looking at her as if he was seeing her for the first time.

As a Muslim, Nina saw hospitality as her duty. Remembering her daughter saying *I don't think Shamayal's had a lot of discipline in his life. Jim found him wandering the streets at two in the morning*, she added hurriedly, "You must understand, we live very quietly here. This isn't London. The door is bolted at 11.00pm."

"Quiet is good, believe me."

She was satisfied.

Two tense and heartbreaking phone calls later and Nina's faith in human nature dipped to a new low. At some point, while she was pacing, while she resisted saying, *And you're not embarrassed - you're not at all concerned - that a stranger is offering to take your son in, except knowing how much it will cost you!* She looked pointedly at her daughter: *Get him out of here. Get him out of here, because I don't want him to see me weep when I put down the phone a second time.*

"I don't want your money," she spoke into the receiver.

More than ever, what Nina wanted was for her daughter - her beautiful grown-up daughter - to come home, so that she would know she was safe. But, accepting that wouldn't happen, she made a decision to transfer her concern to a stranger. A boy who would provide a link.

Suddenly it seemed very important that Shamayal knew he was welcome. "My daughter tells me you're handy with a paintbrush. If lilac isn't your colour you could do something about that. When you're feeling up to it, of course."

Shamayal looked from Nina to her daughter - whose mouth was open - and back again. "I'm -"

"Well, darling! You did say that you don't need your room any more. Why don't you show Shamayal upstairs? Use the bathroom if you'd like. There's plenty of hot water. And Ayisha, I was serious when I said I wanted you to have a good rest. You can use the guest room."

Ayisha was blinking at her. "What will Dad say?"

What indeed? "Oh, I'll just tell him how Shamayal saved Abalendu from the heron's beak," Nina said lightly. Not just any fish. It would have to be his prize one.

She watched as, hand on his shoulder, Ayisha ushered an uncertain Shamayal into the hall and up the stairs. Her daughter looked down over the banisters and smiled. And, for now, her look of gratitude was reward enough.

CHAPTER 49:

JIM - JUNE 2011 - THE STRAND

L ooking over the heads of thirty or so pupils, Jim saw Ayisha standing on the pavement. She had volunteered for this trip: "An opportunity to see you in action," although he suspected she was keeping an eye on him, perhaps rightly so. No marathon running for him, he tired easily. He wondered if she regretted her decision. As soon as she had chosen where to sit on the train, a game of musical chairs had commenced; girls diving into position, ending up piled on each others' laps. Hemmed into her seat by teens with pony tails and hooped earrings, she was quizzed mercilessly about her relationship with 'Sir'. He heard her reply, "Mr Stevens is my colleague," hard 'k'. A small Shamayalism. They got no more out of her, despite attempted bribery with Pringles and compliments about her knee-high boots that seemed to please her - something Jim had never dreamed of commenting on, taking her excellent taste for granted. She had sat back, self-contained and smiling to herself, apparently eavesdropping on snatches of conversation taking place behind her.

"I went, like, shut up. Shut *up!*"

"I was, like, don't *talk* about that!"

Girls from the other side of the tracks spoke another language these days.

"If someone else goes, 'don't like them,' then, like, you're going to be, 'I don't like them either.' I know it's awful…"

So many words, so little meaning. Jim was standing, holding onto a handrail above his head, being given similar treatment by a cluster of boys.

"Haribo, Sir?"

"Thanks." He dug deep into a bag, examined what he held in his hand - a snake, shiny and rippled - and then bit its head off.

"Straight in there. I *told* you he'd be a head-first person, din't I? I win!"

He feigned shock. "I hope you're not gambling."

"I don't get why we have to walk to The Globe, Sir. What if it rains?"

"I want us to approach it from north of the river. And it's not going to rain. The forecast is good."

"But what if it does?"

"If it does we'll get wet, I suppose."

"Listen up!" Jim was speaking over the hiss of a bus as it let off steam. He was distracted by a loud, "Oi, wachoo -" Ayisha had removed a set of headphones from one of his class. Eyes darted furiously at her before they softened. "Aw, Miss."

It was not that her presence made him nervous, but he wanted to impress her. This was what he did. It was important. A chance to engage those who didn't respond in the class-room. "This road linked the world of politics to the world of finance and commerce. It was lined with grand houses and, in Tudor England, it was the only place to live if you were anyone."

One girl's hand shot up. "Sir, Sir!"

A question, already. They were taking the bait. "Yes, Jeanette?"

"Can we go to Covent Garden, Sir?"

He already had her down on his 'difficult' list. Disappointingly, this confirmed it. "No, Jeanette -"

"But I just saw a sign, Sir. It's that way."

"This is a history field trip, not a shopping expedition."

"His-tor-y." She stuffed her hands into the pockets of her puffa jacket and kicked the pavement with the toes of her shoes.

"Ignore the traffic, ignore the shop windows and ignore McDonalds. Instead, I want you to imagine that the church you can see standing in Trafalgar Square - St Martin in the Fields - is in open countryside."

"In the fields, Sir?"

Halleluiah, someone was listening! "Thank you, Dean. There are cattle grazing and women are laying their washing out to dry on the site of Leicester Square. Yes, Fiona?"

"About the washing, Sir. That's sexist."

"Not in the sixteenth century, it isn't. I'll tell you what, I'll swap you your laundry for my job."

"What's that, Sir?"

"I'm a gong farmer. I do my daily rounds of the private houses to empty their privies. Does everyone know what a privy is?"

Sour-faced expressions suggested they did.

"Then I dump their contents outside the city walls. Except that no one wants to see me do my job so I work at night. And I smell so bad, no one will live anywhere near me except other gong farmers. And as for my chances of getting married…"

"No, you're alright, Sir."

"I thought so. Now, does anyone know what the word *Strand* means?"

Curtis danced. "It's like a piece of string."

"No it's not!" jeered his neighbour.

"What do you know? It's like a strand of hair, innit?"

"That's one meaning," Jim intervened, trying to prevent

a full-blown argument. "But Strand also means 'the shore'. The Thames used to be far wider than it is now. Everything between here and the edge of the river is man-made. OK, everyone. We're going to walk towards Fleet Street and look at where some of those great houses stood. Try and keep together and let's not block the pavement so that no one else can get past."

One of the girls from the train was cozying up to Ayisha. "You like all this history stuff, Miss?" No doubt trying to encourage her to form a breakaway shopping party.

Between protests, insults - *Oi, gong-farmer!* - shoulder-barging and stragglers, the group managed to amble the short distance to the top of John Adam Street and down towards the Embankment.

"Over here -" Jim pointed "- was where the Catholic bishops had their great palace called Durham House. Its private apartments looked out over the river with views of what was then called Surrey. The palace passed to the Crown during the Reformation. We talked about the Reformation last week, if you remember -"

"I remember Jonathon Rhys Meyers in *The Tudors*. He's proper buff."

"Did you see the bit when they burned the bishops? Man, that was harsh!"

Another echo of the boy. Ayisha complained that her mother didn't seem to be able to praise Shamayal enough. Succeeding where she failed, he has introduced her to the internet. Apparently, ordering her weekly shop on-line was a revelation. From texts received, Ayisha said she knew the old Shamayal isn't buried too deep: he has just added her mother's so-called secret recipes to his repertoire. It was as if she envied him the easy relationship they have struck up. Ayisha's image of her mother as a difficult woman had been shredded, and she was struggling to adjust.

"I seen the scene with the red hot poker."

"Thank you, Sunta; thank you, Trevor! Queen Elizabeth I made a gift of the palace to the men of her court who were rumoured to be her lovers. A story goes that Sir Walter Ralegh" - Jim risked glancing over at Ayisha - "was smoking the latest drug called tobacco when a servant threw a bucket of water over him, thinking he was on fire."

"Tobacco's not a drug, Sir."

"Course it is, bonehead. It's, like, addictive."

"Who you calling bonehead? It's not illegal or nuffin."

"Then can I have a fag, Sir? I'm gasping."

"No, and you shouldn't have them on you -"

"But we're outside…"

"Yeah, and it's rainin'."

"It's raining, Sir. Literally."

They were right. The few drops he had tried to ignore were rapidly turning into a downpour. Jim let out a frustrated sigh. "Alright, alright. Let's head back to the tube. Wait just inside the entrance!" He skirted the group and bent his head towards Ayisha's ear. "I was hoping to show off," he whispered.

"It might clear up." Her hair was damp. "We could come back this way after the tour."

In front of him, Ayisha hesitated at the top of the escalator, then she took an unbalanced step forwards. After the cold blast of air, the slight feeling of fairground elation, they joined the noisy descent, adverts for theatre productions and abortion clinics passing them by. Faces with chewing-gum eyes. Looking at the backs and occasional fronts of heads, Jim tried to keep track of his class, issuing reminders to stand on the right. Then the lonely sound of a saxophone reached him, an old track that took a moment to identify. Something by Supertramp. *Breakfast in America*, perhaps? Sour faces sailing upwards eyeballed his rowdy teenagers, whose conversation was punctuated with bass shouts and descant shrieks. Jim responded with a look he hoped said, *Yes? I'm in charge.* When the tune reached the point where the chorus kicked in, he got it: *The Logical Song.* Congratulating himself, Jim was smiling as he neared the bottom of the escalator, and a woman travelling in the opposite direction seemed to single him out, her eyes lingering, her expression turning into a question mark. He experienced the same nauseous and suffocated feeling he did when a tube was stuck down his throat: amber eyes; a frame of unruly curls. He would know her anywhere.

Fighting to get the words out, he reminded himself to breathe: "Mrs White! Mrs White!"

Shuffling round, Jim was in time to see her mouth fall open before her face twisted away from view. He started back up the escalator with exaggerated movements of knees and elbows, offering apologies, ignoring protests: *"Mrs White!"* Past and present were washed away. Jim was consumed by one simple need: to reach her. It didn't matter that he had no idea what he would do or say when he did.

Pain now gripping his chest and twisting, breath ragged, he remembered wondering if this was what a heart attack felt like as he ran towards a shiny front door, pounded on it with his fists. Tapping the reserve of energy he saved for the final sprint, Jim pressed on. But upwards she continued, having swapped from the standing lane to the walking lane, one elbow gripping a small neat handbag tightly. Even her determination not to engage couldn't put him off.

"Jim!" A frantic voice broke through the pounding blood in his ears and he realised he had been hearing it for a while: Ayisha. "EVERYONE! WAIT AT THE BOTTOM!"

He remembered his class, the risk assessment he had written for the trip, himself. Pursuit was hopeless, he could see that. But to give up… Chest heaving, he glided back down, at first facing upwards, refusing to let the woman out of his sight, just in case… just in case… And then turning to see

Ayisha walking up a couple of steps to meet him, her dark eyes anxious, her voice school-teacher stern. "Bloody hell, Mr Stevens. I hope you're not thinking of doing a runner." She overlaid one of her hands on his. "Whatever this is about, it had better be good."

"Aimee's mother," was all he could manage, pointing over his shoulder. It took all of his remaining strength to hold himself upright and suck in breath.

"Where?" Frowning, Ayisha leaned out, squinting.

"Blonde, curly hair." His voice came in fits and starts as he turned his head. "Green coat... just stepping off... top of the escalator..."

Ayisha was frowning. "Your maths isn't up to much. That woman's no older than us. Christ, Jim. Look at you."

"I'd know her anyw-" As Ayisha's eyes widened, it dawned on him: when the woman opened her mouth, he had seen her tongue. Pushed into the gap in her front teeth.

"What? It helps me to concentrate."

Whoosh! The thunderous ten-tonne wall of power slapped Jim smack in the face, jolting him backwards, as if a ghost were passing clean through him.

MISSING TEENS:

THE FACTS

One in ten children run away from home before they reach the age of sixteen, a massive 100,000 every year. Shockingly, a quarter of those young people are forced out of their homes by parents or carers. Two-thirds of children who run away are not reported to the police. These children are highly vulnerable and at risk of substance abuse, sexual exploitation and homelessness. The use of mobile phones and social networking sites has made it easier to target vulnerable children.

Help for teens is available from:

Runaway Helpline - free, confidential and 24/7:

Call 0808 800 7070

Text 80234 (even if you have no credit left on your mobile phone.)

Email runaway@missingpeople.org.uk This e-mail address is being protected from spambots. You need JavaScript enabled to view it.

They will talk to you in confidence to explain your options and try to get you the help you want. They won't tell anybody you have called unless you want them to.

Help for parents is available from:

Parents and Abducted Children Together (PACT)

And for those who wish to help:

The Children's Society campaign to provide a safety net for runaways www.makerunawayssafe.org.uk

ACKNOWLEDGMENTS

I visited several wonderful websites when looking for inspiration: www.barnowltrust.org.uk not only provided me with descriptions of barn owls but also beautiful and moving photographs that left me with a very clear image of what I wanted to try to convey. For local history, I used www.british.history.ac.uk, but nothing prepared me for the wonder of discovering St Mary's Parish Church at Beddington on my doorstep. I turned to Anna Beer's account of the life of Lady Ralegh, *Bess*. Although many of the places described are real, the fictional Ralegh Grove is based on my experience of living on a South London council estate. *Kes* is an adaptation of Barry Hines's wonderfully gritty novel, *A Kestrel for a Knave*, published by Penguin Modern Classics. Thanks are due to Spike Milligan Productions Ltd for their kind permission to quote from the poem RAIN by Spike Milligan from *Silly Verses for Kids*. Aimee quotes from Thomas Hardy's *Tess of the D'Urbervilles*. Writers' Workshops provided inspiration and Debi Alper, editorial advice. Credit is due to the fabulous Gillian Davis for coming to my rescue with medical details and to Jack Naisbett for coming to the rescue with IT support. As always, many thanks to all of my beta readers and proofreaders, especially Matt, Cleo Bannister, Helen Enefer, Sue Darnell, Joe Thorp, Karen Begg, Sarah Marshall, Mary Fuller, Harry Matthews, Anne Clinton, Daniel Davis, Tina Edwards, Amanda Osborne, Delia Porter, and, last but by no means least, Louise Davis, who provided much of the finer detail from the 1990s that completely passed me by.

ABOUT THE AUTHOR

Jane Davis is the author of six novels. Her debut, Half-truths and White Lies, won the Daily Mail First Novel Award and was described by Joanne Harris as 'A story of secrets, lies, grief and, ultimately, redemption, charmingly handled by this very promising new writer.' She was hailed by The Bookseller as 'One to Watch'. Jane's favourite description of fiction is that it is 'made-up truth'.

She lives in Carshalton, Surrey, with her Formula 1 obsessed, star-gazing, beer-brewing partner, surrounded by growing piles of paperbacks, CDs and general chaos.

For further information, to sign up for pre-launch specials and notifications about future projects, or for suggested questions for book clubs visit www.jane-davis.co.uk.

A personal request from Jane: "Your opinion really matters to authors and to readers who are wondering which book to pick next. If you love a book, please tell your friends and post a review."